CALICO AND SILK

The Lancashire Cotton Saga
Book Three

Christine Evans

Also in the Lancashire Cotton Saga:
Song of the Shuttle
Twist of the Thread

CALICO AND SILK

Jessie had only ever had two dresses when she was younger, one for best and one for work. That was before she married Robert. Disturbed once again, she was exasperated with her daughter.

"Go down to the River Road," she said quietly. "There are girls there who haven't one decent dress to their name. Just be grateful you don't have to go in rags to Dora's. Really, Helen, I have more things to do than mither about your clothes."

"You don't understand!" wailed Helen again. She stormed upstairs, each stomp of her feet echoing around the house. Jessie was sure she heard a distant, "I'll ask grandmamma."

"What's up with milady?" asked Matt as he came into the parlour.

He was followed into the room by Jack, who looked very grubby and was carrying a ball.

"Don't ask!" said his mother, shaking her head. "I'm trying to finish my accounts, and she's in a tizzy about some dress."

Her son's voice was soft and sometimes hesitant. Jessie hadn't always understood what he said. She'd learnt to listen intently when he spoke. Jack always understood his big brother and often repeated it for his grandparents, who were growing hard of hearing. That didn't endear Matt to his grandfather. Matthias was always complaining that the boy mumbled.

"Oh, Helen's going to Dora's for tea," said Matt. "That's always a trauma. Dora is the queen bee of their little set at school and must be impressed."

Jessie knew precisely what he meant. Helen had invited Dora to tea at Overdale House, and her mother found the girl very inquisitive about the family's affairs. Jessie couldn't warm to her daughter's friend but treated her very politely for Helen's sake.

"Let's have a look at your accounts?" said Matt, scrutinising the ledger over his mother's shoulder. He sat down beside Jessie at the dining table and tapped through the figures with the pencil. Then he painstakingly wrote some figures at the end of the two columns. "I think you'll find it's five shillings and fourpence wrong," he said.

Jessie thought for a moment. "That will be the haberdasher's bill I paid for your grandmama," she decided. "She had no money with her when we went to buy her some gloves and stockings. I won't ask her for the money just yet. I'll wait 'til she remembers to pay me."

"That's *if* she remembers," said Matt with a grin. "She's getting very forgetful of late. She keeps calling me Jack."

"She's getting old," Jessie told him with a sigh. "We're all getting old."

She smiled at her eldest son. Now that his teenage acne was clearing, he was growing into a handsome lad, like his father. It was such a pity about his disability. Born as an unanticipated twin, he hadn't been expected to live and had struggled since birth.

"Thank you for sorting out the accounts," she said. "I'd added it up a few times and come to a different answer every time. You're very good at reckoning up. When are you due back with Reverend Tyldesley?"

The clergyman taught Matt and Jack at the vicarage. Jessie and Robert had decided that Matt might struggle at a school. Children were not always kind to those who were different. Reverend Tyldesley was a patient young man who gave her son plenty of time to complete his lessons. According to his grandfather, Jack was destined for the grammar school in Manchester when the time arrived. His older brother would continue his learning in Gorbydale, near the support of his family.

"Mr Tyldesley will be back from his sister's wedding in time for the Sunday service," Matt told his mother. "We start again on Monday."

"Good, then you'll be out from under my feet," Jessie teased him.

Yet the house felt empty when the children were away at their various lessons and Robert and his father were at the mill. Jessie decided there must be something useful she could do to fill her time.

CHAPTER 2: OLD HOME

Some days later, Jessie slipped on her second-best shawl and tapped gently on Melissa's parlour door. Hearing no call to come in, she nevertheless opened the door. Her mother-in-law was dozing, open-mouthed on the sofa. Jessie was about to ask Melissa if she would like to join her on a visit to her old home on Weavers Row. The weather had turned fine after a couple of days of grey, dispiriting drizzle. The lilac bush in the garden was in full bloom, scenting the soft breeze with its delicate perfume, and Jessie longed to be outdoors. The children were away from home, the boys at the rectory and Helen at her dame school. Melissa often complained that she never left the house. It had been a couple of weeks since Jessie had visited her father and stepmother, Alice. She was feeling unoccupied and restless, and a walk to Weavers Row was just what she needed.

Seeing Melissa so comfortable, she quietly closed the door and slipped to the kitchen to tell the cook and the maid of all work, Maggie, where she was going. She was sure that Melissa would have called for the gig instead of walking. The last part of the walk was a steep climb up the Row that usually left Melissa puffing for breath, and lately even Jessie had had to pause halfway.

"I'm getting old," she told herself again, though she was not yet forty.

There were signs that the town of Gorbydale was slowly regenerating. Ten years after the slump in trade caused by the American Civil War and the dearth of cotton, abandoned shops were reopening. Repainted doors and windows gave the main street a livelier look. As Jessie reached the steep rise to Weavers Row, she spotted Alice chatting to one of the neighbours and stopped to exchange a few words herself. They naturally asked about each other's families.

"And how's thy crippled lad?" asked the neighbour tactlessly.

"Matthew is fine, thank you, Mrs Stott," said Jessie stiffly. "He's studying with Reverend Tyldesley and doing well. My youngest, Jack, is being taught by the Reverend too. Both the boys are doing well."

"That's good to hear the poor creature's thriving," said her old neighbour, oblivious to the offence she'd caused. "I've seen your lass coming out of Miss Frodsham's Academy with her friends. She's a bonny one. You'll have to watch her when she gets interested in the lads."

Jessie smiled wanly, and Alice took control of the situation.

"Well, you must be parched after your walk from Overdale House. Come and have a cup of tea. I'll get the kettle on," she said, linking Jessie's arm and leading her towards her old home. "Your Dad's at the mill, of course, but he'll be pleased you called."

Jacob worked at the old Endurance Mill at the bottom of the valley.

They were out of earshot when Alice muttered, "Take no notice of that old biddy. She was so strict with her girl that the lass ran off with the first lad that smiled at her. The poor thing's got five kids now, and he knocks her about."

"Oh dear. Poor Violet. I remember the night she ran away," Jessie told her. "Her mother came knocking on our door, expecting Father and the boys to go and sort the lad out and fetch Violet back home."

"She never did!" exclaimed Alice, outraged at the woman's impertinence. "What did your Dad do?"

"He went and talked to the girl on his own, but she was adamant that she wouldn't go home. So Violet's made her bed and has to lie in it," sighed Jessie. "I suppose I should feel sorry for her."

"You can't help people that don't want help," said Alice reasonably. "Come on, let's get some tea. I think old Ma Stott was hoping to be invited, but she'll just have to hope."

Jessie automatically glanced round her old home as she went in. It had subtly changed, newly painted and with a bright and colourful rag rug by the fire. Her late mother Nellie had shunned bright colours as impracticable with three sons in the house. The furniture had been changed or moved too. But the hospitality was just as warm as Alice brewed the tea and cut a thick slice from a large fruitcake.

"Oh, just half of that for me," protested Jessie. "I'm getting stout from lack of exercise. This awful weather has kept me in the house for days."

As they shared the slice between them and chatted amicably, the latch on the front door clicked and a familiar voice echoed round the room.

"Anybody in?" came the call, and Mary, Jessie's best friend, struggled in carrying a chubby infant on her hip. "I saw you chatting outside, and I was just about to join you when me laddo filled his nappy," she said with a laugh. "Anyway, we're nice and clean now, aren't we, Con?" She parked him on the rag rug, and he beamed up at his grandmother. "What did old Ma Stott have to say for herself?" she enquired. "I noticed Violet sneaking round after dark the other night. Con was awake with his teeth, and I happened to look through the window."

"She never said anything about Violet," said Mary. "She upset Jessie by calling Matt 'a poor creature' though."

"If she knew him, she wouldn't say that," Mary defended her godson. "He's as bright as a button, despite his problems."

Jessie smiled her thanks. Both Mary and her mother had been very supportive of her son and never treated him any differently from the robust Helen. Thinking of Helen, Jessie voiced her fears. "The old dear wasn't wrong to say that I'd have to keep an eye on Helen, though," she said with a sigh.

"Why, she hasn't any admirers yet, has she?" asked Mary. "She's a very pretty girl."

"Not that I know of," said Jessie. "I'm hoping she's too young to take an interest in young men just yet. But she has such an attitude. She's been very spoilt by her grandparents and if I try and chastise her, she goes off in a sulk or appeals to them. I caught Melissa offering to take her to Manchester 'because the poor dear says she has no new clothes to visit her friends in'. I took her up to see all Helen's dresses, and she went very quiet. That minx had been whining to her grandmamma about her lack of clothes. I know the mill is working now, but there's still a large mortgage debt to pay off."

She felt perhaps that she had said too much about the family business. But Alice and Mary were family too, now that her father had remarried.

"It's her friend Dora Lightfoot I blame. She's that lawyer's daughter. He has an office on Market Street. Her mother lets her wear a bustle, and Helen's all fired up because I've told her she's too young to wear one."

"It's a daft idea anyway," said Alice, chuckling. "My backside's big enough without a bustle. How do they sit down?"

"I think you're supposed to perch, Mam!" Mary told her, joining in the laughter. "Like a canary."

"I'd make a funny canary! I'm no spring chicken either," laughed Alice.

"More like an old boiler," teased her daughter.

Alice laughed and condemned her for a 'cheeky young madam'.

Con was laughing too, though he couldn't understand the jokes. He lifted up his arms to be picked up, and Jessie lifted him onto her lap and tickled him under his chin.

"You're not getting broody, are you?" asked Mary with a wink. "You can have him if you want. Bring him back when he's finished teething."

"His daddy would have something to say about that," said Alice. "Your chick is the apple of his eye."

Mary and her husband had waited a long time before their baby had arrived.

"Dilwyn can get up and see to him when he's teething in the middle of the night, then," Mary joked.

Jessie missed all the teasing and the banter of her friends in the quiet rooms of Overdale House. Melissa's polite tea parties with select members of Gorbydale society consisted of nothing but gossip and a large dose of condemnation for the townspeople who had offended morality. Alice mixed her humour with a good dose of common sense.

"You mustn't worry about your Helen," she said. "You two girls were young and daft once. I was meself in my day. I remember your mother Nellie coming to me upset because you wanted to work at the mill and your Dad wanted you to be a pupil teacher, and the pair of you were hardly talking."

"Yes, that was an upsetting time," admitted Jessie, "and I had to leave the mill in the end, when Mother became ill."

"I remember Honora Darwen coming to help your mother with that Australian stuff," said Alice. "Nellie was dead chuffed with it. Said it helped her breathe."

"Eucalyptus," said Jessie. "Yes, Mother said it helped. Though of course it couldn't cure her cotton lung."

"Have you heard from Honora recently?" asked Mary. "How's she doing in America?"

"I don't hear from her as much as I used to, not since she broke her understanding with our Arden. I suppose she feels guilty about letting him down," said Jessie sadly. "He was heartbroken. But you can't help these things. If you're not suited, you're not suited."

"Aye, you had a lucky escape from Taylor Walmsley," said Mary. "Though we all thought he was a good catch at the time."

Jessie shuddered as she remembered the controlling overseer at the Invincible Mill who had taken a fancy to her. She changed the subject. "In Honora's last letter, she said how frustrating it is trying to find work as a doctor, even though she's fully qualified," Jessie told them.

"Will she be coming home?" asked Alice. "We could do with a lady doctor round here. You feel embarrassed to talk about woman's things to a man."

"Not yet, at any rate," said Jessie. "She can't get a licence in England yet. But we're all hoping that one day…"

"It can't come quick enough for me," said Alice. "That Doctor Braddock is an old fool. He should have retired long ago."

"His nephew Doctor Andrew is very nice, though. He was very helpful when Cornelius was born," Mary reminded her.

Little Con beamed on hearing his Sunday name.

"I'd feel very odd talking to a younger man about women's problems," decided Alice. "No, the sooner we can have a woman doctor, the better for all us women."

They chatted as they sipped their tea, until the chimes from the clock in the parlour reminded them of the time.

"I'd better go," said Jessie, rising from her chair. "The boys will be home from their lessons soon."

"And Helen too?" asked Mary.

Jessie chuckled. "Oh, she'll arrive half an hour later, after she's been gossiping with her friends. The boys just come straight home looking for something to eat."

"You mean gossiping like we've been gossiping all afternoon?" said Mary with a sly smile.

"Gossiping? Us? No, we've been putting the world to rights," Alice insisted with a chuckle.

Jessie strolled back thinking about her old house. Although it had changed, she felt at home there. Despite her years of marriage, she still felt like a cuckoo in the Overdales' nest. She would have liked to cook for her own family, but Matthias had vetoed the installation of a small range in her parlour, saying it would ruin the room. Melissa hadn't pleaded her case either, and Jessie knew her mother-in-law preferred the family eating all together so she wouldn't be left alone with her tetchy husband.

She had almost reached the drive to Overdale House when Jack came charging up behind her.

"Hello, Mama," he called. "Has Cook been baking?"

"I expect so," she said, laughing.

With that, he charged past her up to the house. She turned to find Matt labouring up the slope but at a fair speed.

"Hello, son," she greeted him. "Had a good day?"

"I'll say," said Matt, beaming. "We've been learning geography. It was all about America today. Reverend Tyldesley was very interested when I told him about Aunt Honora training to be a doctor there. I said you and Pa had been there too in the Civil War. And of course I mentioned our visit from Mr and Mrs Jacques and their boy Albert from Louisiana. He said I know more about America than he does. I wonder if I'll ever travel there?"

"You never know. I can't say I ever expected to go there myself when I was your age," said Jessie.

She had often told the children how she had travelled to America with Honora in the middle of the Civil War to find the missing Robert. Many times they asked her to tell the story of how, while nursing the wounded, she and Honora had discovered Robert in a Washington hospital, his leg with a terrible wound. They had saved his leg from amputation, but he stilled limped and the scar was awful. Like his son, he wore a leather brace to aid his walking.

Jessie was proud of the way her husband and son coped with their problems, bravely carrying on, oblivious to how others pitied them and with barely a complaint.

CHAPTER 3: HONORA

Honora sat nervously in a corridor, awaiting an interview at the New York Hospital for Indigent Women and Children. She knew she was well-qualified but also knew that first impressions counted for so much. Living in New York was expensive, and her savings had long since run out. She'd been working shifts as a nurse at a local hospital. Though she was qualified as a doctor, the hospital where she worked would not employ her as one, but she still needed the money she earned as a nurse. Her face in the mirror looked tired. She needed this job.

In her bag was an envelope holding her testimonials, one from her friend Susannah Daly, a nurse in Washington, another from Doctor Jacob, who had witnessed her sterling work at the Harewood Army Hospital in Washington. There was a briefer note from her tutor Doctor Walgrave at the Geneva Medical College in New York, where she trained as a doctor. He had only grudgingly given her a reference, despite her experience and her good examination results, as he disapproved of women doctors.

A woman called her in to be interviewed and introduced herself as Emily Blackwell. To Honora's surprise, she had an English accent.

"I am the director here," she explained as she asked Honora to take a seat. "You do understand that this hospital treats the poorest women in society and their children? The work is hard and there is plenty of it."

"I'm not afraid of hard work," said Honora. "I worked as a nurse alongside my doctoral studies to help pay my expenses."

Honora took the envelope carefully from her bag and offered it to Doctor Blackwell. The doctor opened the yellowing sheets and read them thoughtfully.

"Very impressive," she said. "Many of our doctors have trained here at our medical school, but my sister trained at the Geneva. She's gone to continue her studies in England at the moment. I'm sure you'll fit in nicely with our staff."

"You mean I've got the position?" asked Honora in surprise. She had expected a more formal interview.

"Oh yes. You mentioned in your letter to us that you helped your father as a child. You are familiar with all that being a doctor entails. With the amount of work we have here, we are crying out for doctors," said Doctor Blackwell. "With your experience, you should be an invaluable member of our staff."

"Thank you, thank you," said Honora with delight.

"When can you join us?" asked the doctor.

"As soon as possible," said Honora. "I shall have to inform the hospital that I'll be leaving them. I may have to move lodgings to be nearer this hospital."

"We may be able to help there," said the woman. "Some of our doctors and nurses can give you recommendations."

Doctor Blackwell gave her a tour of the wards and introduced her to some of the staff. Despite the poverty of the patients, Honora mentioned how impressed she was by the levels of hygiene in the hospital.

"My sister Elizabeth has written books on the subject. She's very keen to see her theories put into practice. It was she who helped found this hospital. We're very proud that she was the first woman doctor to be registered in the United States. I was the third," Emily added with a modest smile. "Elizabeth hopes to help found a medical school for women in the old country. But you know what Englishmen are like; they cling to their power like leeches. Even in America we lady doctors are shunned and denigrated. So we must struggle for the recognition of our skills. It's such a pity when there is so much work to be done."

Remembering Doctor Braddock and his summary rejection of her when she had offered to help in Gorbydale, Honora wholeheartedly agreed. She eagerly accepted the position at the hospital.

At a stroke Honora hoped her financial problems and her workload would be lightened, but she would later find the workload was endless as New York's poorest women and their ailing children continually trailed to the doors of the hospital.

Now that Honora was to work as a doctor at the hospital, she needed to change her lodgings and prevent the long journey to work. Doctor Blackwell introduced her to one of her colleagues. Arlene Stewart, a nurse in the maternity ward, was a tall, gaunt young woman who lived with her widowed mother. She had mentioned they were looking for a lodger to help with expenses.

"Perhaps you'd like to come and meet Mother," she suggested to Honora.

"I should be happy to," said Honora. "I'm tired of the hours I spend travelling to the hospital."

Eager to arrange her housing needs, she met Arlene after the nurse had finished her shift and walked home with her. The house was in a shady avenue in a quiet neighbourhood not far from the hospital.

Mrs Stewart, equally tall and as gaunt as her daughter, stood with her arms folded, brazenly scrutinising Honora. Honora hesitated when confronted with such a harridan. But the room she was shown was bright and airy and so much better than her old lodgings. She readily agreed to move in.

"I must make it clear that you are to have no young men calling," said Mrs Stewart sourly. "I will not have my house turned into a bawdy house."

Honora smothered a smile. "You need have no fear of that, Mrs Stewart," she said briskly.

She arranged to move in the following Saturday, and a rent was agreed that was similar to her old one. Honora was not offered a cup of tea.

"Betty Lacy, our previous lodger, had a beau," murmured Arlene as they left the house. "Mamma was outraged when she came home and caught them kissing on the doorstep."

Arlene looked wistful for a moment, as if she'd like to be found kissing on a doorstep, but with such a mother the consequences would surely be severe.

Honora went back to her old lodgings and began to pack her belongings. Her old friend Martha O'Brian arrived back from her shift at the local hospital and offered to help.

"There's not much," said Honora, surveying the meagre possessions she was arranging in her old trunk. "There seems so little after all the places this trunk has been."

"I'll be sorry to see you go," said Martha. "We've been good friends in the time we've lived together."

"Yes, despite our ever-clashing shifts at the hospital. I hope you'll come and see me in my new home," Honora told her. "There's more space there, and it's nearer to my new hospital. But I'll have to warn you about Mrs Stewart. She'll be keeping a beady eye on me — and you too if you visit." She laughed as she told her friend about the doorstep incident.

She wasn't surprised to find Mrs Stewart there to scrutinise her arrival.

"Watch that paintwork!" she screeched as the man delivering Honora's trunk struggled upstairs with the aid of a young boy.

He tipped his hat and winked as Honora tipped him handsomely. The trunk had been heavy with her books.

Honora arranged and surveyed her possessions, then sat at a small table and wrote a short letter to her aunt, first enquiring after the health of the family, then giving the details of her new address. She wondered if Melissa would write back. Since her defiance in staying in America to train as a doctor instead of going home, Melissa had hardly written. She'd given up pleading with Honora to return to Gorbydale and minister to Matthias after his stroke. Honora knew that was a waste of her time, as Matthias never listened to her advice anyway. Though her aunt always sent her best wishes at the end of Jessie's frequent letters.

Honora was fulfilling her dream of becoming a doctor, though sometimes her life felt very empty. She reviewed her sparse possessions and her sparser circle of friends. Her friend Verity had been murdered at the Geneva Medical school. Her great friend Jessie was far away in Gorbydale, getting on with her own life in the midst of her growing family. Honora was sorry she hadn't been there to help Jessie with her first pregnancy, or with young Matt. She was sorrier that she'd spurned the devotion of Jessie's brother Arden. She'd rejected him in the fever of a doomed infatuation with a fellow student. Arden had been a constant source of support in her life and studies, despite the fact that he was away fighting in the war during most of their relationship.

With a sigh she took a new sheet of paper and wondered how to begin her letter to Jessie. So much had happened in such short a time. At long last she was beginning her work as a doctor. Though once she'd started to practise, the tide of suffering women and children arriving at the New York

Hospital for Indigent Women and Children nearly overwhelmed her.

Jessie at least understood her burning ambition to be a doctor and had defended her to Robert. She often wrote to tell Honora if there was any news of the women's struggle to be recognised as doctors in England.

In her letters she'd also mentioned the curious case of a woman disguised as a man who had served in the army with distinction. The rumours were that Doctor James Barry's deception had only been discovered after her death in 1865. The doctor was said to have been born in Cork as a woman called Margaret, but the army had denied any such thing and Jessie could find no more evidence.

The rumours are very strong, wrote Jessie in her last letter, *and it would be typical of the authorities to cover it up and deny that a woman could actually be a doctor. Doctor Barry is said to be the first woman in the Empire to perform a caesarean operation successfully, and the mother and her child lived. I look forward to the time when you can come home and practise among us.*

Taking up her pen again, Honora began to write her own news, first giving details of her new address. She began to tire with the efforts of the day and put the letter aside to finish in the morning.

Though Honora was weary, she could not sleep. In the dark reaches of the night her mind seemed clearer, her thoughts more ordered. She thought about Verity and the awful shock of her death. The police had found nothing, despite a large reward offered by Verity's father. Honora had discovered that an odd dark hair found on her friend's body had come from someone who dyed their hair. The one person she had known with dyed hair had been Clement Duplege, the Civil War spy who had visited Gorbydale. She had betrayed him to the authorities, and his grudge had not been against Verity but Honora herself. She was convinced that Verity had been murdered by mistake. From then on she'd lived in fear, forever aware of those around her. It was with enormous relief that she'd heard from Duplege's widow Dolly that he'd been drowned in a riverboat accident. A tired Honora's last thought before she slipped into sleep was that she must tell Jessie to ignore the letter she'd sent as insurance in the event of her unexplained death.

She hoped one day she could go home to Lancashire. Doctor Elizabeth Blackwell's clinic was in London, but it was a stepping stone in the right direction. Maybe one day she could work in the slums of Manchester and complete her dear father's work.

CHAPTER 4: MELISSA

Jessie tapped on the door of Melissa's sitting room and found her mother-in-law asleep on the sofa once again. She had wanted to encourage Melissa to come for a walk in the gardens of Overdale House, perhaps even to venture as far as Matthias's folly, a little white temple high on the rise overlooking the town and the mill. Melissa had been dozing like this many times in recent days, and it didn't seem natural that she should sleep so much during the daytime.

As she gently shook her mother-in-law, Jessie noticed a small bottle on the tea table beside her. "Rayburns Patent Tincture," she read.

So that was the cause of her drowsiness and the apothecary's bills. Melissa was taking laudanum. She had once recommended the tincture to Jessie when Matt was having sleepless nights as a baby. After working in the wartime hospitals in Washington, Jessie knew its effect and refused to use it on a baby. She'd heard that many childminders used it to subdue the children in their care, with dire results. There was even a rumour that President Lincoln's wife was a laudanum addict. Jessie was concerned and dismayed that Melissa seemed to be regularly using the drug too.

"Mother-in-law," she called gently as she shook her arm.

Melissa opened one bleary eye and blinked against the light. She looked disorientated for a moment.

"Oh, hello dear," she said with a wan smile. "I was just having a little nap. Disturbed night, you know. Matthias does snore so."

Jessie could well imagine her portly father-in-law snoring like a warthog. He'd been liberal with the port decanter at their evening meal. Though he'd mostly recovered from his stroke, brought on by overwork and overindulgence, he'd slipped back into his old habits.

"I wondered if you'd like to come for a little walk. It's a beautiful day outside. The exercise and fresh air would do you good. I can go and fetch your bonnet."

Melissa looked doubtful. "I'm rather tired, dear. Perhaps another day," she said.

"I can ring for tea. That will revive you," Jessie encouraged.

"My rheumatism..." began Melissa, and then she glanced up at Jessie's determined face. "Perhaps a nice cup of tea would be good," she conceded. "It'll wake me up a bit." She noticed Jessie take up the small bottle and read the label. "It's for my rheumatism," she explained. "Doctor Braddock prescribed it."

"How much do you take?" asked Jessie.

"Only a couple of drops, dear," replied Melissa with a wary glance at the bottle that told Jessie she was prevaricating.

"You shouldn't take too much of this stuff, you know," Jessie warned her. "It has opium in it. You can become addicted and it will ruin your health. You don't want to become an opium addict, do you?" she teased Melissa with a light laugh.

"It's just for my rheumatism, dear," Melissa defended herself.

"Yes, I know," said Jessie gently. "But Honora and I saw a lot of problems with laudanum in Washington. It's very addictive. Some soldiers who couldn't forget the horrors of war took it whenever they could get their hands on it."

"Oh, I do only take a couple of drops, dear. Surely a little drop can't harm you. Doctor Braddock prescribed it."

Jessie was about to say that Melissa's good doctor was an old fool, but she refrained from commenting. Melissa's faith in the doctor was absolute, and it wouldn't make any difference what Jessie thought.

By the time they'd taken tea and made ready to go out, Melissa decided the walk to the temple would be too much for her. She and Jessie pottered around the flower garden and shrubbery. Though Jessie longed to stride up to the temple, she felt obliged to keep her mother-in-law company after she'd coaxed her into the sunshine.

Jarvis, the groom-cum-gardener, was being helped to trim some of the shrubs by his son, Michael. The boy had been apprenticed to a farrier and had sprung up into a handsome young man. Jarvis had been with the family for many years, but he was getting older and was grateful for the help. There were only two horses in the stable, Melissa's mare Lady for pulling her gig and Robert's sturdy cob Bob to carry him around the town, as he couldn't walk far with his damaged leg. He'd mentioned buying a pony and arranging riding lessons for his sons, and of course Helen had demanded that she too must learn to ride.

"You must ride side-saddle, like a lady," Melissa had told her. "We'll buy a special saddle for you."

"And who's going to shoulder the expense, then?" queried Matthias, though Helen was his favourite.

So the idea was shelved for the time being. Robert often led the children around the garden on his cob and tried to curb Helen's attempts to go faster. Matt loved the horses and often stopped at the stables on his way home from his lessons. They recognised him, and Bob stayed perfectly still when Robert helped his son into the saddle.

Gazing over the gardens, Jessie felt restless. She'd always been active and useful, but now with her children virtually off her hands, she lacked purpose. What was more galling was the fact she had no money of her own and had to approach Robert for every penny she spent. His own position was little better, as he didn't have a set salary and had to ask Matthias for expenses. Of course, his father was forever complaining about the money they spent and seemed to live in a world of his youth, when everything was much cheaper. Jessie had urged her husband to talk to Matthias about a fixed salary, but his father always prevaricated.

"When trade gets better," was his perpetual excuse.

Although the mill was back in production, the heavy mortgage payments incurred during the cotton crisis were still a burden. Jessie wished there was something she might do to feel useful once again. She'd recently received Honora's letter and knew her friend was working hard as a doctor. Jessie decided that in her next letter she would ask Honora about Melissa's laudanum problem. When she eventually received a reply, she was relieved when Honora suggested secretly diluting the tincture bottle with sherry to lessen the dose.

CHAPTER 5: HELEN

Helen skipped blithely down the drive until she remembered that young ladies were supposed to walk sedately. She was on her way to Dora's house. She had managed to convince her mother that her floral dress was becoming too tight because of her budding figure. Now she had the promise of a new dress, she was wondering how to connive in having one with a bustle. There was another reason why she had a spring in her step. Dora had casually mentioned that her brother Hadrian was arriving home from college.

From the moment that Helen had noticed his portrait on the Lightfoots' wall, she'd secretly admired Hadrian. She'd met him a couple of times and thought the portrait didn't do him justice. Though Hadrian Lightfoot was indeed handsome, to Helen's chagrin she found he was too lofty to condescend to notice or speak to his young sister's friends.

On Hadrian's last visit home, Sabina and Anna-Marie, two more of Dora's set, had openly vied for his attention at the Lightfoot house. He'd disdainfully answered their frivolous questions about his life at college and treated them as silly girls. Helen was glad she had had too much pride to join in with them. All the same, she was intensely anxious that he should notice her. A new dress in a more sophisticated style would surely do the trick. She entirely ignored the fact that Anna-Marie already wore the latest style, to little effect.

Her heart fluttered wildly as she knocked upon the Lightfoots' door. It almost ceased to beat when Hadrian answered.

"Oh, hello," he said casually and, turning his head away, called loudly into the house. "Dodo, it's one of your little friends." He scrutinised Helen disinterestedly. "I suppose you'd better come in," he drawled.

Helen followed him into the hallway, raising her chin despite feeling she'd been humiliatingly dismissed.

Dora appeared at the top of the stairs. "Oh Helen, how nice of you to come," she said. "Anna-Marie has just arrived. I've just borrowed Mama's *The Englishwoman's Domestic Magazine.* It's full of all the latest fashions. Some are so adorable."

Hadrian was about to disappear into the parlour when Dora stopped him.

"This is Helen from Overdale House, you know. Her grandpapa owns the Invincible Mill."

An illuminating smile lit his face. Helen stood like a rabbit in the light of a mesmerising lamp. Hadrian Lightfoot had smiled at her!

"We've met before, haven't we?" he said smoothly. "Yes, of course I remember you. You're the pretty little thing that didn't pester me with stupid questions. Well, have a nice delve into your magazine, girls."

Helen was transfixed as she watched him retreat into the parlour. At the last moment, he turned and winked at her. Her heart burst with joy, and she felt as if she were about to faint until Dora pinched her arm.

"Come along, before Mama wants her magazine back. We're up in my room."

Helen followed Dora in a daze. Hadrian had called her 'a pretty little thing'. All thoughts of her new dress vanished when she thought of that wink. She hardly glanced at the magazine. When Dora and Anna-Marie asked for her opinions on the lavish fashions portrayed, she automatically agreed with them. Helen Overdale was in love.

To her disappointment, she did not see Hadrian again that day. She wanted to rush to the bedroom window when she heard him call goodbye to his mother and the front door closed behind him. Instead, she preserved her decorum by taking an intense interest in the magazine. She didn't want the other two girls to suspect her infatuation and tease her.

As Helen walked home to Overdale House for high tea, she glanced slyly around her, hoping to catch a glimpse of Hadrian. She made a detour near to Mr Lightfoot's solicitors' office, hoping he might have been to visit his father at work. She knew he was studying law and was to join his father in the business. Her quest was in vain, but she waltzed up the drive to Overdale House, overjoyed that he'd called her pretty.

Her mother met her at the door. "Come along. You're late for tea. You know how your grandpapa gets tetchy when anyone's late. I was just about to send Jack looking for you," said Jessie. She gave a beaming smile. "And we've got a surprise for you."

Helen's eyes opened wide in anticipation. "What is it?" she asked.

"Tea first, surprise later," teased her mother.

Matthias glanced at his watch as they hurried into the dining room. Helen didn't hesitate. She ran up to her grandfather and kissed him prettily on the cheek.

"I'm so sorry I'm late, Grandpapa," she cooed.

Matthias patted her hand. "That's all right, dear," he said with an indulgent smile.

Hadrian Lightfoot was not the only one who knew how a smile could beguile.

Helen was restless with anticipation but also apprehensive. Surely her mother hadn't bought a dress for her without her own express wishes. She ate her food and drank her tea almost as rapidly as her brothers. The boys were always hungry, especially Jack. They were eager to leave the table and their grandfather's scrutiny. Her grandmother usually presided over the teapot, though lately she had left that to Jessie. Taking tea seemed maddeningly slow that afternoon, but finally Jessie allowed her sons to leave the table. Checking that the grandparents had eaten their fill, she beckoned to Helen. She held out her hand and they both went into Jessie's parlour.

There on the table was an unmistakeable box with a handle on top.

"A sewing machine!" gasped Helen in amazement. In all her imaginings she hadn't expected one of those.

"We'll be able to make our own clothes," said her mother simply as she pulled off the cover and revealed the gleaming black metal machine with its ornate gold decoration.

"I've bought some magazines containing patterns, and we can go to Manchester on the train to buy the material. It will be so much cheaper than buying clothes. I might even be able to alter some of my clothes to fit you."

Helen was horrified. What on earth would Dora and all her friends think of her when she wore homemade clothes? She chose to forget that most of the girls in her class wore clothes that their mothers had made.

"I'm sure we'll be able to master it," said Jessie, examining the machine and slowly turning the handle. She seemed oblivious to her daughter's lack of enthusiasm. "I made most of my own clothes before I got married, but by hand. There might be some patterns in your Grandad's attic. That was where I slept on Weavers Row. They might have been thrown out by now, though. I'll walk round tomorrow and ask."

"Surely they'll be too old-fashioned," murmured Helen.

"Oh, they'll be easy enough to adapt," said Jessie. She looked at her daughter thoughtfully. "We might even be able to fashion a bustle for you."

For the first time, Helen took an interest in the machine. It might just be the answer to her problems.

CHAPTER 6: MAGGIE

Helen's problems seemed insignificant beside Maggie's. Jessie and Robert had just settled in their parlour after the evening meal. The boys were at the table, working together on some homework. Matt was keeping an eye on Jack, whose mind continually strayed to the box of toy soldiers. They'd once belonged to his father, and he'd discovered them in the attic. Helen, seated by the wide French windows overlooking the town and her grandfather's mill, had a book on her lap. Her mind was anywhere but on the pages.

"Are you feeling tired, dear?" Jessie asked her husband.

He gave her a wan smile. "I am that. I must say, it's easier when Father leaves the mill early and I can get on with things without him mithering. But I was on my feet for a long time this afternoon when one of the machines broke down. We need new equipment really, but of course there's no money for that yet. My leg hurts abominably."

"Abominably," echoed Jack, taking a liking to the word.

"Don't be cheeky to your father," scolded Jessie. "I'll massage your leg with liniment later," she told Robert. "It seemed to help last time."

They were interrupted by a timid knock on the door.

"That'll be Maggie," said Jessie, recognising usual tap of the maid of all work. "Come in, Maggie," she called.

The older woman looked surprised that she had been recognised even before she'd entered. Then her habitual look of anxiety suffused her face.

"Please, Mrs Jessie, I need to go home. Our Tommo's been taken badly. A lad from River Road's just been and said I'm needed urgently."

"Then you must go," said Jessie, rising from her armchair to comfort the woman. "You could have asked Mrs Overdale, you know," she said quietly as she reached the door.

"She was asleep, ma'am, and you know the Master gets so tetchy, I didn't like to ask," whimpered Maggie.

"Do you know what's wrong?" asked Jessie. "Was he poorly this morning?"

"It'll be his liver," sighed Maggie, edging through the door, eager to be away. "The doctor said it'd be the death of him if he kept drinking, and he wouldn't listen. He's been bad all week with it."

"Would you like someone to go with you?"

"No. I'll be fine," Maggie reassured her. "I'd better go." With that, she scurried away.

Jessie felt sorry for the poor downtrodden woman. Her husband was a drinker and a bully.

Maggie would be on her own with her ailing husband. Both her children were away from home; Seth, her son, was in Strangeways prison and her daughter Dolly away in America.

"So it looks like the drink has finally got him," said Robert, who had been listening in on the conversation. "Let that be a lesson to you, boys. Don't overdo the demon drink, or you'll end up like Tommo Tate."

His sons sniggered at one another.

"Matt looks as if he's drunk already with his wobbly legs," teased Jack, earning a friendly cuff round the ear from his older brother.

"Really, how can you be so cruel, Jack?" scolded Jessie. She was very protective of Matt, though her sons were giggling together.

"Where the beer? I want beer, more beer," demanded Matt in a croaky voice.

He and his brother fell about laughing as their parents shook their heads at their sons' antics.

"I do hope Maggie's all right," said Jessie, turning her attention to the instruction book for the sewing machine. "She's never had much of a life with Tommo."

The news from River Road wasn't good. The cook served breakfast with Lizzie in the morning and told the family that Maggie had sent a message to say that Tommo had died in the night.

"Good riddance to bad rubbish," muttered Matthias. "That'll be one less drain on the rates."

"Matthias!" scolded his wife. "You shouldn't speak ill of the dead — and in front of the children too."

"I won't be the only one speaking ill of that scoundrel," snapped her husband. "I wonder if they'll let that son of hers out of Strangeways for the funeral."

"I expect Maggie will want us to write to Dolly in America with the news," said Robert. "I'll leave you to deal with that, dear," he told Jessie. "But send my regards to Nathan when you do."

Once she had commiserated with and consulted Maggie, Jessie wrote the letter to Dolly in Louisiana. They also sent a note to the prison authorities to break the news to Seth. Next day, Maggie arrived at Overdale House clutching a letter from Strangeways, and Jessie had to tell her that Seth wouldn't be allowed out for the funeral. The governor wrote that as Seth was likely to abscond, he wouldn't be released for the day.

"It's just as well," Jessie comforted Maggie. "When you think about it, Seth would have been in chains and guarded by a couple of warders, if they let him out."

Reluctantly, Maggie agreed. "Tommo would have been proper shown up," she said sadly.

Jessie couldn't point out to the grieving widow that the late Tommo was past being 'shown up'. He was beyond shame when he was alive.

In America, Dolly would receive her letter long after Tommo was under the ground. So Tommo Tate was buried in a pauper's grave with no one to mourn him but his wife, and she did that with more relief than sorrow.

Once Tommo was buried, Jessie suggested to Melissa that, now Maggie was alone, she might come to live in at Overdale House. Melissa thought about the idea for a few moments.

"Maggie wouldn't have to travel to and from River Road every morning and night. Then she'd be on hand if ever she was needed," coaxed Jessie.

"Yes, I suppose so, dear," murmured her mother-in-law. "I'd better ask Matthias."

Of course, he objected straight away when he was consulted. "What about the cost?" he demanded. "You're saddling me with another mouth to feed."

"Maggie arrives before breakfast," Jessie reminded him. "And she doesn't leave until late. So she has all her meals here anyway. There'd be no extra cost and Maggie would be on hand, say, if ever Cook was taken ill. She's getting on, you know."

She'd noticed that the cook was increasingly troubled by her arthritis, and Maggie and Lizzie were doing an increasing amount of her work.

Matthias was reluctantly persuaded, and Maggie readily agreed to move in. A small attic was prepared for the newly widowed woman. The house on River Road with its miserable memories was abandoned.

CHAPTER 7: DOLLY

Dolly Jacques, previously Duplege, was resting on her porch in Louisiana. The heat was stifling and in her advanced state of pregnancy, debilitating. She and her husband Nathan had hoped for a child for a long time. She had suffered two miscarriages, to their great disappointment. By some miracle, this longed-for baby was more tenacious of life, but she was nearing forty and feared complications after her previous experiences. Glancing up, she saw Albert, her son, strolling lazily over from his tutor's house. Through the wavering heat haze, he looked like any other worker in his wide-brimmed hat, but the moment his image cleared she noticed the pale white skin inherited from his red-haired father Clement Duplege.

Though she had been a widow when she married Nathan, Clement had been no great loss. Albert had been the only good thing that had emerged from that sham marriage, and he had been illegitimate. Clement had forced himself on her during a business trip to Gorbydale and only discovered he had a son years later. She had married him for Albert's sake and to escape the drudgery of her old home.

Marriage to Clement proved to be just as arduous, as she'd toiled to rescue the ruined Amiens plantation. Clement had been useless to her with his preoccupations of drinking and gambling. She'd also suspected him of murdering a young woman training to be a doctor called Verity Cain. Dolly had been very suspicious of times Clement went missing in New York when she had first arrived from England with her son.

Remembering hoofbeats one dark night at the Amiens plantation, she also suspected Clement had made an attempt to murder his niece in a hotel fire. Dolly had no proof of this, but she knew her husband was desperate to secure his claim to the plantation against two nieces with a prior entitlement. The eldest was living in Philadelphia with her husband, having escaped her fate at the hotel. Her lawyers had been unable to prove her entitlement to the land. Clemmie, the youngest, had been badly affected by the war and seen her parents die of starvation and disease in the siege of Vicksburg. She was now living with Dolly and Nathan, looked after by Dolly's old housekeeper Aunt Hattie.

Burning the hotel and murdering Verity Cain were not the only crimes Dolly suspected Clement of committing. Clucas, the old overseer from the Amiens plantation, had been found drowned not long after he had threatened to implicate Clement in the fire. It was a relief to Dolly when she was informed that a fight over a card game on a riverboat had led to her husband's subsequent drowning. There had been no love lost between them.

It frustrated Dolly that she had fallen pregnant after that one fateful moment with Clement in Gorbydale, yet now she was happily married to Nathan, she had struggled to have a child.

"Hello Ma," called Albert cheerfully. "How's the lump?"

"Cheeky," scolded Dolly with a smile.

Alerted by their voices, Aunt Hattie appeared at the front door. As usual, Clemmie trailed behind her.

There had been some awkwardness when Hattie came to live at the Jacques plantation. Julia, Nathan's housekeeper, had had charge of the house since his first wife had died. Hattie was used to being in charge at the Amiens place. But Hattie was getting old, and organising Clemmie was as much as she could manage. She still liked to fuss around the family, and Julia just let her get on with it, as she had plenty to do herself with a growing family in the house.

"You folks like a drink of somethin'?" asked Hattie.

"Oh Aunt Hattie, that would be lovely. You're a lifesaver," said Dolly. "I'd have got something for myself, but I'm weighed down by this lump. How long do you think it will be now?"

"Not long now, I reckon," said Hattie, surveying Dolly's prone figure.

"I hope everything will be all right this time," Dolly told her with a sigh.

"Folks havin' babies all the time, Mrs Dolly. You'll be fine. I'll be right here."

Albert sat down beside his mother.

"I've had enough now," she said wearily. "I don't remember being so large with you. It's just as well, because I had to hide my pregnancy or lose my job. But then I was just a skinny little thing. You could hide a lot under one of those big aprons. This time I was growing plumper even before I became pregnant."

"It must be contentment," said her son with a smile. "You are content now, aren't you, Ma?"

Dolly took his hand and squeezed it. "I am, very. Nathan's a good man. I never thought I'd deserve this."

"You worked hard enough for it," Albert told her, glancing over the fields burgeoning white with cotton. "There's no helping with the cotton harvest for you this year, though."

"No, this is bad timing," she said with a chuckle as she patted her expanding belly. She looked at her son as he gazed over the cotton, assessing it for the harvest. "Are you content?" she asked. She was taken by surprise that he did not answer straight away.

"Yes, I suppose so," he said eventually.

Her heart stopped for a cold moment. "You always seem happy enough on the plantation. You were always such a shy child. I didn't think you'd be happy away at school. Your father was always threatening to send you. Baton Rouge or New Orleans always seems so far away."

"Not as far as England," said Albert with a chuckle. "Do you ever think about going back there and seeing Mam?"

The 'Mam' he spoke of was Maggie, Dolly's mother. She'd brought him up as her own, as Dolly couldn't afford to lose her job as the only one of the family in work.

"I suppose you've been learning about England with Jeremiah today?" said Dolly.

Her son often came home full of ideas when he'd been talking to his tutor.

"I was learning about the cotton trade, yes," admitted Albert. "I remembered seeing Mam at Overdale House, and I just wondered how she was doing now that Tommo's gone."

"Hopefully Jessie will send us some news soon. Mam probably hasn't had time to ask her to reply since our last letter after Tommo died. I wonder how she's getting on myself."

It wasn't long before Dolly had her answer. To her surprise, she received two letters one dry and dusty afternoon. She struggled to leave her chair as the rider came up to the house, a familiar leather bag attached to his saddle.

Aunt Hattie came out almost immediately. "You stay where you are, lady," she ordered. Tentatively she approached the horse. "You like a drink, Mister?" she asked. "I reckon you could do with one in this heat."

"Thank you, ma'am. That would be fine," he answered, and Dolly smiled at his courtesy. Not everyone treated a black woman with respect.

"Mrs Jacques?" he enquired of Dolly, holding out a letter.

"That's right," she told him as she took it. It bore an English stamp.

He hesitated with a second letter. "This here letter says it's for a Mrs Duplege. I went to the Amiens plantation house like it says on the letter, but it looked abandoned."

"That's right. I was Mrs Clement Duplege, but my first husband is dead. I live here now with my husband Mr Nathan Jacques. The letter is for me."

He handed it to her with a look of relief. "The last man who rode out to your old house just brought it back with him. But I reckoned you'd know what happened to your neighbour when I came with this other letter. Turns out you were your own neighbour after all," he said with a chuckle.

"Well, thank you for your efforts," said Dolly, examining the letter.

It was an American stamp, and she wondered who would write to her. Though she was itching with curiosity, she waited until the man had left to open the envelopes. She had come late to literacy and still often struggled to read and write fluently.

Their visitor accepted a seat on the porch and slowly and gratefully drank the offered lemonade.

"What's happening in town?" asked Dolly.

She liked to keep up with the local news, though she didn't go to Picardy Creek, the local town, very often. Most of the news was brought in by the workers on the plantation or the O'Neill family, who were addicted to gossip. Nathan's son David had married Jassy O'Neill.

"Nothing much," said the man with a shrug. "With this heat, folks are too weary to do much but sit in the shade."

"Just like me," said Dolly, laughing. "At least I have an excuse."

"When is your child due, if I may ask, ma'am?" he asked.

"Any time now," she told him.

"Then reckon I'll be visitin' these parts more often with congratulations for the new arrival. Looks like letters from England too," said the postman, reluctantly getting to his feet. "I'd better get going. More news to deliver. And thank you kindly for the drink, ma'am," he told Aunt Hattie.

Hattie nodded politely.

The moment the rider mounted his horse, Dolly stared at the two letters. She decided to open the one from England first.

"Oh, Albert will be pleased," she said as she read down the lines. "Mam has gone to live at Overdale House. I'm glad she's left River Road. It's no place for a woman on her own. She hopes my confinement goes well. That'll be Jessie writing. I don't think Mam would ever say 'confinement'!"

Finishing the letter she read out scraps of news to Hattie, who nodded with approval. Hattie had met and liked Robert Overdale many years before when he had visited the plantation to buy cotton. She had met him again during the war when he had arrived at the slave village with his wounded leg. He had secretly left one night with the slaves Kezia and Abraham to travel to Washington along the Underground Railroad to freedom.

CHAPTER 8: AN ECHO OF THE PAST

Dolly stared at the second letter. It was addressed to the Amiens plantation. The stamp was of some American president, though she wasn't sure which. She knew what Lincoln had looked like, as Clement had cursed whenever he saw his image. Hesitantly she opened the letter. Her first instinct was to look at the signature. It took her a moment to realise that 'A. Kay' was Amelia Kay, an old friend of Clement's and, Dolly suspected, one of his former lovers. Dolly wondered why she was writing; she was no friend to Dolly, and Clement had been dead for nearly ten years.

Dear Mrs Duplege, Amelia wrote.

It was obvious that she had not heard that Dolly had remarried.

I hope you are well. I do not wish to alarm you, but I have received some information recently which disturbs me. I received a letter from Major Horace Corcoran from Baltimore, Maryland. His wife Alice was previously known as Mrs Domain, as you may know, when she was housekeeper to your husband in Baton Rouge. She was a great friend of mine, and her husband wrote that she has recently very sadly passed away. He is distraught as you can imagine, and because of this I do wonder if what he tells me is true. It seems that Alice was shopping in Baltimore when she befell a terrible accident. She tripped and fell under a team of horses and died of her injuries. Before she died, a witness swore that Alice whispered that she was pushed. It seems the town was crowded that day because of the races and that her death was indeed a terrible accident.

But I have been uneasy since I read the awful news and cannot help thinking of the grudge your late husband Clement had against poor Alice. In my house he swore revenge against her for selling his house without his knowledge and absconding with the money. He swore he would track her down. This may seem far-fetched, as he is now with his maker and his revenge could not be achieved from beyond the grave. My unease is because his body was never found. I write merely to warn you to be aware of the tragedy.

Yours obediently, Mrs A. Kay.

Dolly felt sick. An icy finger of fear stroked down her spine.

"You all right, Mrs Dolly?" asked Aunt Hattie, who had been hovering nearby, filled with curiosity. "You gone awful pale."

"I feel sick," said Dolly and promptly leant over the arm of her chair and retched.

"What is it, chile?" said Hattie, coming to her aid. "Shall I get you a drink of water? What in heaven's name did that letter say?"

"It says nothing in heaven's name," groaned Dolly. She heaved herself upright in her chair and picked up the letter from her lap. Slowly she read the letter to Aunt Hattie.

"Dear Jesus in heaven preserve us," gasped Hattie. "You surely don't think that that ole devil is alive. I don't believe it for a minute. Why, if he was alive, he'd be hangin' round his old home, trying to see his son."

"Not to see me, then," said Dolly with a hollow chuckle.

Hattie shook her head. "I know how you was fixed, Mrs Dolly. I saw things between you weren't natural as between a man and his wife. But young Albert now, he's another matter. He's Massa Clement's only livin' son. You don't forget that so easy. That ole Kay woman, she don't know what she's talkin' about. She just tryin' to frighten you."

Dolly took a deep breath and revived a little. "She's managed to do that all right. I expect you're right, Aunt Hattie. What you say makes sense. It's just … it's just … when I saw that letter I…" She suddenly clutched her stomach and swore under her breath.

"It started?" asked Hattie, with concern.

Dolly just nodded and tried to ride with the convulsing pain.

"Let's get you upstairs, then," said Hattie calmly, waiting a moment until the pain subsided. She took Dolly's arm and helped her from her chair. "We don't want no baby born on the porch with all the village gogglin' at you."

Slowly and carefully they made their way upstairs.

Nathan was sent for, and he hurried to his wife's bedside. "I thought you weren't due for another couple of weeks," he said, tenderly stroking Dolly's burning forehead.

"She had a bit of a shock," Aunt Hattie told him as she pulled some old sheets from a chest.

"What? Who?" he asked in surprise.

"I told her it ain't nothing to worry about. Let's get this chile into the world first and I'll explain it all later."

Nathan was about to be banished from the room as Dolly was convulsed by yet another contraction, but she held out a pleading hand.

"Don't leave me," she gasped.

Nathan looked confused.

"I never heard the like," exclaimed Aunt Hattie.

But Nathan was held firmly in a vice-like grip and could not leave his wife.

So he was there to witness the birth of his daughter. She was tiny but vocal.

"What will we call her?" he asked, smiling down at the swaddled infant in his arms. His eyes were moist with delight as he cradled his new daughter.

"I thought we could call her after my Mam," said Dolly quietly. "Not Maggie, obviously, but Marguerite, French like."

"Hey there, Marguerite," said Nathan with a chuckle.

"That's just beautiful," said Aunt Hattie, smiling with pride. "I told you everything would be all right. Babies bein' born all the time."

Dolly smiled with relief and exhaustion. It was obvious that the childless Hattie had never experienced being in labour.

Albert was pleased with his baby sister. He cradled her gently as he sat beside his mother on the porch.

"You'll have your hands full with this little one," he said thoughtfully.

"Don't worry. I won't neglect you," Dolly told him, patting his arm.

"I was wondering, though…" he began and then hesitated.

"What is it?" asked Dolly, a sudden foreboding seeping into her mind.

"I didn't want to mention it before the baby was born," he said, once again reluctant to continue. Albert took a deep breath and his request came out in one big rush. "I was wondering if I could go to college and perhaps travel a bit. Nathan and Barney and the men can cover the Amiens part of the plantation. They do most of the work anyway, and I wouldn't go until after the harvest. Jeremiah says I'd be fine."

"Is that what you want?" said Dolly slowly. "I thought you were content on the plantation."

"I was when I was a little boy," Albert told her, his eyes staring wistfully out over the land. "But I've been feeling restless for a bit now. I reckon I've studied enough to get by."

"Jeremiah says you've done really well," said his mother. "I expect you get your brains from your father. You didn't get them from me, that's for sure. Yes, you've got his brains and itchy feet."

The words came tripping out before she had time to think what she had said. Dolly suddenly remembered the letter and shivered. She had temporarily forgotten all about it in the turmoil of the birth.

"Do you remember your father?" she asked cautiously.

"You mean Clement? I can't really remember his face these days," admitted Albert. "We don't seem to have a photograph of him."

Dolly chuckled. "Oh, your father was always careful not to have his picture taken," she said with a dry laugh. "I suppose with his spying business it was understandable."

She had explained all about Clement to Albert as he grew older. He'd admitted that he'd often felt afraid when Clement was in one of his drunken rages. He'd confessed he'd sometimes hidden when his father was annoyed with him for his gentle ways.

"Has anyone approached you lately; some tall stranger perhaps?"

"No." Albert shook his head. "Just the usual people in Picardy Creek, and we haven't been to Baton Rouge for ages."

"Where were you thinking of studying?" she asked.

He had recently mentioned England, and the thought filled her with dread.

"Jeremiah knows a couple of people at the college in Baton Rouge. He's sure his sister would have a place for me at her home while I was studying there."

"So the pair of you have been hatching this up while I've been busy giving birth and settling the baby, have you?" Though in truth Marguerite was a placid baby and gave very little trouble.

"I didn't want to worry you. But I've been thinking about it for a long time," said Albert. "The world's a big place, and I'd like to see some of it at least."

Dolly thought for a moment. "If you go, promise me you won't get mixed up in gambling and drinking. It was the ruin of your father. He could have got a good living from the plantation like his family had in the past. In the end, his itchy feet got the better of him."

"I'll do my best, Mam," Albert promised. Then he gave a big grin. "But you know Clement taught me a few card tricks. He said it was so I wouldn't get cheated by some gambler and I'd know what to look out for." He saw the alarm on his mother's face. "But I know to stay away from cards."

"Good. I'll talk to your father," she decided.

Nathan had been a good father to her son. She desperately hoped that Albert hadn't another father lurking in the wings as Amelia Kay's letter had hinted.

Unsettled by her son's plans to go to Baton Rouge, Dolly began to worry about Amelia's letter. The more she thought about it, the more she realised what it might mean for her future if there was a shred of truth in it. What would Amelia's suspicions mean for her marriage? Could it really be possible that she was bigamously married to Nathan? Surely the letter was nothing but spiteful, written only to upset Dolly. She had only met Amelia Kay twice and felt the woman resented her unexpected appearance in Clement's life. Other people had witnessed Clement's fall into a river full of alligators. But, as Amelia mentioned, there was no body.

There were implications for others too if Clement was by some miracle still alive. She remembered Honora Darwen and her conviction that Clement had murdered her friend Verity Cain. If, as Honora suspected, the woman had been murdered after being mistaken for Honora herself, then she too was in danger.

Unable to quell her fears, Dolly consulted Nathan.

"My darlin', you know deep down that it's all nonsense. Aunt Hattie thinks so, and so do I. Clement's bones are at the bottom of the river. Hattie's right to say that he would have tried to get in touch with Albert if he were alive. You're just tired and anxious with caring for the baby. Put your feet up and take a rest," he advised.

It was true she was tired and, with her own ragged history, too anxious for her own happiness. She'd often wondered if she truly deserved it.

"Oh Nathan, I know you think it's just my silly fears, but what if that poor woman was pushed? And what if she was pushed by Clement? What if he survived the river and went underground because the law was after him? Honora Darwen could be in danger too. I really should write and warn her."

Nathan could not convince his wife. Finally he sighed and agreed with her to placate her. "If it would put your mind at ease and you'd feel better, write the letter," he told her. "Though I think you could be worrying this Honora unduly."

So Dolly wrote to Honora, carefully copying the letter from Amelia. She also repeated Nathan's arguments as to why the speculation must all be nonsense.

But I could not rest easy knowing that I had not warned you about the rumours, she added at the end of her letter.

With a sense of relief, she sealed her letter and arranged for it to be sent off at the first opportunity.

The letter to Honora took some time to find her. Dolly only knew the address of her lodgings near the Geneva hospital. She had written to Honora there to tell her that Clement was dead. Honora's friend Martha O'Brian who'd lived at the same lodgings had now moved away. However, the landlady knew that Honora had moved to work at the Hospital for Indigent Women and Children. Although she was a woman of means, she was anxious to consult a lady doctor about her problems and had met Honora working at the hospital. So finally the letter was delivered.

CHAPTER 9: HONORA'S LETTER

Honora reread Dolly's letter yet again, and a feeling of dread engulfed her whole body. She wanted to believe Nathan's sensible assurances that Clement was gone for good. But deep down, the niggling anxiety she had always felt until she had heard about his drowning seeped back into her consciousness. She began to scrutinise any man that came into the hospital. Now she became continually jumpy, as many men accompanied their wives for their treatment. There was also a stream of male visitors to wives and children who had to stay in the wards. Any tall man who arrived was made uncomfortable by her stare as she assessed them for disguises. Her anxiety spilled over into her homelife, such as it was with the long shifts at the hospital.

"I see you've locked your bedroom door," said Mrs Stewart, her eyes narrowed in suspicion. "And how am I supposed to clean your room if it is locked?"

"I'll clean the room myself," Honora told her calmly. "It will save you the effort of doing so."

Mrs Stewart's mouth pursed into a taut raspberry. She looked as if she would make some caustic remark. Normally Honora had left her room unlocked but knew her landlady had a key. To assuage her fears she'd persuaded a locksmith to change the lock whilst Mrs Stewart was out visiting friends. She also suspected the woman of rifling through her things.

"Very well," conceded Mrs Stewart. "It will of course save me some work. I suggest you put your dirty linen in the bathroom when you want your bedding changed. I can't be chasing after you all the time for a key. And do make sure you clean your room to the standard of the house."

"Yes, of course I will," Honora reassured her.

Yet her nerves could not settle and one morning as she walked to the hospital, she was approached by a man.

"Can you spare a little money, ma'am? My children have had no breakfast," he pleaded.

Honora glanced up into his eyes, shrouded by unusually shaggy eyebrows. She stepped back in fear. "Don't touch me," she squealed and began to run.

Some yards away she fearfully turned and saw a tall, shabby beggar staring after her in surprise and dismay. She felt so stupid. Because of her reaction, the passing crowd was avoiding him, and she immediately felt guilty that his children would go without their breakfast because of her fears. Before Dolly's letter had arrived, she would willingly have tipped something into his outstretched hand. She was tempted to go back and give him the price of their breakfast, but by now her anxiety had engulfed her and she was desperate to get to the hospital so she would feel safer.

Honora arrived breathless and almost tearful. Emily Blackwell, seeing her state, beckoned her into her office.

"Doctor Darwen, I have noticed that lately your manner seems very anxious. You work very hard for the woman and children of this city. I hope not too hard. There is much work to be done, but to heal others you must first be in good health yourself," said Doctor Blackwell.

"I wouldn't let my anxiety affect my work," protested Honora.

"So you do admit you are anxious about something?" said her superior. "It cannot be the state of your patients, because I know you worked in hospitals during the recent war and conditions there must have been so much worse than ours."

"Yes, yes, they were indeed," agreed Honora. "Appalling and overwhelming at times."

Emily Blackwell waited for an explanation of Honora's state of mind. Honora hesitated, unwilling to admit that the shadow of a living Clement had filled her with fear. How could she explain that she was afraid of a rumour, a suspicion, a phantom?

"Perhaps I have been overworking," she admitted, her face lowered to the desk, reluctant to reveal the true cause of her distress.

"Doctor Darwen, when did you last take a break from your work? I know you were working as a nurse during your studies to help pay for them. I know you went to the Geneva directly after your gruelling work during the war. Perhaps you should think about taking a rest."

"Oh, I couldn't," said Honora. "I've worked so hard to become a doctor. I just couldn't abandon my work."

Her superior looked thoughtful. "If you won't cease to work, how about a change of scene?" she suggested after a moment. "As you know, my sister Elizabeth is in London trying to establish a training school for lady doctors. The London School of Medicine for Women is in its infancy. I'm sure they would be glad of someone of your experience to help them in their work. My sister is helped by Doctor Sophia Jex-Blake, a lady who graduated from Edinburgh. Would you like me to write to them, suggesting your name? A sea voyage and a break before you continued your work would surely be advantageous to your health. An ailing doctor is no use to me."

Honora sat quietly digesting all the possibilities opening up before her. An escape to England might be just what she needed.

"Now go and see to your patients, but think about what I've suggested," said her mentor.

Honora thanked her and went to her work with a renewed will. In England she would surely be free of Clement, dead or alive. She remembered what her Mama had said, that she should sleep on a problem. Next day, she asked Emily Blackwell to write to her sister. She was going home, albeit to London, but there was much work to be done there too.

It took a little time to receive the letter approving Honora's appointment in London. Before she arranged her passage, she knew she had to speak to her landlady.

"You must remember that when you took the room you agreed that, if you should leave, you would pay your rent to the end of the month?" demanded Mrs Stewart.

Honora could remember no such arrangement. As she knew Arlene Stewart personally, she hadn't insisted on a written rent agreement, so was in no position to argue. Arlene was dismayed that Honora was leaving.

"It has been so nice having you here," she said. "But it must be good to know that you're going home." Then she began to whisper in confidence. "I know Mother can be difficult sometimes, but I have appreciated your stay with us."

Honora glanced up to catch the shadow of Mrs Stewart beside the door. "You must be brave, Arlene. You're a grown woman, and your life is your own. You're a fine nurse, compassionate and kind to your patients, despite their difficulties. Don't let anybody tell you different. You would be welcome in any hospital in the land."

"I don't have the courage that you've shown, coming to work in a strange land," said Arlene modestly.

"But you should have," insisted Honora. "Have confidence in your skill, because I've always relied on your competence to help me."

The shadow faded. It would not do Mrs Stewart any harm to know that her daughter could escape from under her thumb.

CHAPTER 10: SEWING

Jessie read Honora's letter with growing excitement.

"Honora's coming home," she said, waving her letter. She was surprised by Melissa's attitude.

"She's a bit too late," she complained. "There were lots of times in England she could have helped the family. There was Matthias's stroke for a start; and Robert's leg, and your confinement; and Mattie with all his problems."

Jessie stared at her and decided to proceed with caution. "When she arrives, she'll be based in London for the moment. It may be some time before she can practise hereabouts," Jessie told her. "But she'll surely come and visit."

"I'll have to ask Matthias if she can stay here," said Melissa with a sniff.

"But Honora's your only niece. She's family," protested Jessie, shocked at her mother-in-law's indifference.

"Matthias is master of this house," insisted Melissa. "I'm not sure he'll welcome her, what with her ingratitude after all we've done for her."

"But she wanted to become a doctor like her father," Jessie tried. "You know she couldn't have studied in Britain."

"Doctor Braddock and his nephew Doctor Andrew are quite adequate for our needs," said Melissa primly.

Jessie was about to argue that most women would rather be treated by a lady doctor but decided to leave that for another time. She was so excited and happy with the prospect of seeing her friend again that she didn't want to spoil the moment with Melissa's resentment.

Now she was faced with the dilemma that Honora might not be welcome at Overdale House. Jessie and Robert could of course let her stay in their rooms, but that might cause resentment with her in-laws. Although this was Robert's natural home, it was still his father's house. Jessie and her husband had been allocated a set of rooms in the house, yet she had always felt she was really just a lodger. Honora had written to say that she had booked her passage to sail in a month's time, so Jessie had some time to decide what to do. If her Aunt Melissa refused to receive her, Honora might stay with Mary, Jessie's friend, and her husband at their boarding house.

Mulling over her problem, she decided to head to her bedroom, where her sewing machine was set up in a corner. Sewing a long length of seam would need all her concentration, and so she could forget about her problem until she'd talked it over with Robert.

Helen had finally agreed on some fabric for her new dress and even helped to adapt and cut out the pattern.

"Just think, there will be no one wearing a dress like yours," said her mother, full of enthusiasm. "It will be unique."

Helen sniffed. Jessie had the feeling that her daughter would be quite happy to look the same as all her school friends. Now she had mastered the sewing machine, Jessie was eager to use it. She remembered all the nights she had handstitched her own clothes, with pricked fingers and eyes growing tired in the dim light of an oil lamp. The sewing machine made her work so much easier.

"You'll look lovely," Jessie reassured her daughter.

Helen picked up the sewn pieces of fabric that would form the skirt and turned and twisted it. "I wonder if we could just…" she said, assessing the work thoughtfully. "Could you show me how to use the machine, Mama?"

"I'd love to, my sweet," said her mother with a growing smile. "Come and sit here next to me."

It was a great pleasure for Jessie to see her daughter enthusiastic about something other than visiting her friends. Helen had somehow inherited her mother's natural talent for needlework. When Jessie decided she must go and supervise the evening meal, Helen took her place at the machine with a gleam in her eye.

Melissa's moods seemed more erratic since she had taken to relying on laudanum. Jessie had done as Honora had suggested and secretly added more wine to the tincture, but Melissa countered that by taking more of the stuff.

Jessie was slowly taking over the running of Overdale House. She began to hover in Melissa's parlour when her mother-in-law spoke to Cook about menus. The cook glanced over her mistress's head to Jessie when Melissa repeated some menu they'd already eaten the day before. Jessie just nodded and, slipping down to the kitchen later, privately agreed another option with the harassed woman.

Only once had Melissa spotted the subterfuge. "What are you looking at her for?" she'd demanded belligerently of the poor cook. "I'm the mistress round here."

"I've told Cook that pork doesn't always agree with Robert's delicate stomach," said Jessie hastily. "I was about to suggest a nice piece of fish," she added lamely.

Melissa grunted. Her only son Robert was her life's treasure, and she would do anything for him. All the same, she began to watch the cook like a hawk unless she had taken enough laudanum to dull her senses.

Melissa had been such a warm and welcoming woman when Jessie was first married and entered her home. She adored her grandchildren. Now they were growing, becoming more independent, and they spent less time with their parents and grandparents. Jessie felt her own importance in their lives was waning, and she was sure Melissa felt it too. She was anxious that her growing family might become unwelcome at Overdale House and urged her children not to neglect their grandparents. Matthias was frequently grumpy with the boys, especially when they had one of their boisterous moments. Although Matthias frequently left the mill early, he still interfered with Robert's decisions. Only Helen could charm him when she wished. Now Melissa was becoming irascible too, and she was often unsteady on her legs. She was continually tired and found sleeping in her parlour.

Jessie wished once again that she and Robert had a home of their own. With finances and the growing realisation that Matthias and Melissa were becoming frailer and beginning to rely on them more, she knew this was unlikely.

Now the evening meal was underway, Jessie returned to tidy her sewing away. She found Helen had somehow enhanced the projected bustle with a large protruding bow.

CHAPTER 11: ARDEN

Some days later, Jessie was thrilled when she glanced out of the French windows in her parlour to see her brother Arden strolling up the drive. He was wearing his uniform and looked as handsome as ever. She rushed to the door and waved to him as he strode over the grass towards her.

"Oh, I'm so glad you called," she said, linking him and pulling him into the house.

He was her favourite brother, the nearest in age. As the only girl among three brothers, she had been forever trying to copy the oldest two and join in their games. Arden was the only one who'd encourage her. Their eldest brother John wanted nothing to do with his little sister.

She scrutinised Arden's uniform. "Is that another stripe I see?" she asked.

Arden laughed. "You are now speaking to Second Engineer Arden Davenport of the SS Baltic of the White Star Line, madam. What do you think of that?"

"Oh Arden, I'm so proud of you," said Jessie. "Come and have some tea and tell me all about it. Robert will be pleased to see you."

Arden and her husband had struck up an unlikely friendship when Arden had worked as a junior engineer at the mill.

"My new ship's in Liverpool, being prepared for the next Atlantic crossing," he told her. "So I have a few days' leave."

"Are you staying with Father and Alice?" Jessie asked.

Arden nodded. "Yes," he said thoughtfully. "I find it very strange, though. It's the same old house but very different, if you know what I mean? Father and Alice make me very welcome, though it doesn't quite feel like home."

"I know just what you mean," said Jessie, smiling. "But they seem very happy together. Things don't always stay the same, do they? Otherwise you'd still be a greasy engineer at the mill, and I'd be an old maid at home."

"Instead of a grand matron at Overdale House with a family of growing children. How are your brood, by the way?"

"They'll be home soon. I think you'll be surprised by Matt," said Jessie.

"So now he's all grown up, he doesn't want to be called Mattie?" asked her brother with a chuckle.

"He's nearly sixteen now and he's doing well. He's learning with the local vicar, but he does struggle to write. Jack's being taught with him, but I think Jack will go away to school in a while. Robert wants him to go to the Manchester Grammar School," she told him.

"And what do you want?" her brother asked her, hearing the wistful note in her voice.

"I'd like to keep him with us, but he seems eager to go," said Jessie. "Robert fills his head with stories of what he did at boarding school."

"He told me once he hated it," said Arden. "How time glosses over the worst of our experiences. And what about Helen?"

"Her head is full of dresses and what her friends are doing. I suspect she has an admirer somewhere, because she spends that much time in front of the mirror." Jessie shook her head in exasperation and changed the subject. "And what about you? Do you have an admirer? Do you have a girl in every port like they say sailors do?"

Arden shook his head. "I don't need to find them in port," he said with a laugh. "The ladies in first class love to dance with us officers aboard ship. The captain expects us to entertain unaccompanied ladies in our leisure hours. To be honest, I'd rather spend time in the boiler room than with some of the old boilers who expect you to dance with them."

"I don't suppose you ever see Honora when you're in New York?" asked Jessie cautiously. She was unwilling to hurt her brother's feelings by reminding him of his old love, but she wanted to know if they were still friends.

Arden shook his head sadly. "No, I'm afraid that ship has long since sailed," he said.

Jessie felt sad that her brother and her friend had drifted apart.

They were drinking tea and chatting about old times when Helen bounced in from school.

"Uncle Arden!" she cried and flung herself into his arms.

Once Arden had extricated himself from her enthusiastic embrace, he took her hand and twirled her round. "And who is this fashionable young woman?" he asked with a chuckle. "This surely can't be my little niece Helen, all grown up and as elegant as any of the ladies in first class."

Helen was delighted with his compliments. She twirled again and paused to display her bustle. "My dress was a great success," she told her mother proudly. "Anna-Marie actually asked me where I had bought it! Oh Mama, it was just perfect."

"So you're going to thank your mother for all her work, then?" suggested Jessie with an amused smile.

"Oh, but I designed the bustle," declared Helen proudly. "She wasn't going to let me have a bustle, you know," she told a bemused Arden. "But it's just been a pure triumph."

"Don't grow up before you need to, my sweet," advised her uncle. "There are many, many ladies in our first class saloons trying to look younger, and all their wealth and privilege won't give them a bloom of youth like yours."

Helen was in no mood to listen to his advice. "A pure triumph!" she called as she skipped out of the room.

Jessie and Arden shook their heads at the folly of youth.

"Was I ever such a vain madam?" said Jessie, laughing.

"I'll only say that Jack and I had a hard time getting to our mirror," Arden chuckled.

"I do worry about her, though," said his sister. "She seems such an innocent compared to a couple of her friends. I'm not keen on the one our Matt calls the 'queen bee' of Helen's little gang. Dora Lightfoot seems a conniving madam to me. She's always asking questions about the business whenever she comes to tea. I can see her weighing up the room, the furnishings, the ornaments as she's sipping tea. I just can't take to the girl."

"I'm sure Helen will be fine," Arden told her. "How is Matt coping?"

He didn't need to wait for an answer, as Jessie's two boys arrived at the French windows.

"Is there anything to eat?" were the first words out of Jack's mouth, even before he greeted his uncle.

CHAPTER 12: LOVE'S YOUNG DREAM

Helen was carefully studying one of the dress patterns in her parents' bedroom when Jessie found her.

"Oh, there you are," said her mother. "I was looking for you."

"I was just wondering if I could make another dress in a slightly different style," asked Helen. "I'm sure I can master this sewing business. I didn't do too badly this time. If you'd give me a hand?" she pleaded, glancing up at Jessie.

"Material isn't cheap," said Jessie cautiously. "Though we've plenty of calico."

"Oh Mother! Only working girls wear cheap cotton."

"Oh, you mean like I used to be?" her mother said with a wry smile. "Money doesn't grow on trees, Helen, and you've just got a new dress. The mill still has a hefty mortgage on it. Though don't mention that to Dora Lightfoot, if you please. The mill's business is none of hers."

Helen looked surprised at the accusation that her friend was too nosy. Though when she thought of it, Dora did ask a lot of questions about her family's affairs.

"If you want to, we could look though my wardrobe and see if we could alter one of my old dresses," suggested Jessie. "There are one or two that I'll never be able to wear again, and there would be plenty of material in the full skirts to make a bustle."

Helen jumped at the chance and they rifled through a chest full of clothes, mostly that she and her brother had outgrown. Helen pulled out a dress in a deep rose colour and held it up to the light from the window.

"I wore that to your Uncle John's wedding," said Jessie. "Many years ago now. I made it myself."

Helen examined the dress carefully and saw the neat stitches her mother had sewn. Now with their wonderful new sewing machine, she was sure she could fashion something for herself. The dress had a full skirt, but it was faded in some of the folds.

"The material isn't worn," said Jessie. "We could unpick it and dye it. Or we can work around the faded parts. We'll turn it inside out and see what it looks like."

Faced with the prospect of a new dress, Helen readily agreed. There was lace round the neckline and the cuffs that she was sure she could reuse.

She had once turned up her nose at second-hand clothes, sometimes passed on from her cousin Eleanor. Now, with her new-found skill and the prospect of impressing Hadrian Lightfoot, her objections vanished.

Dora had mentioned that Hadrian was due home for the summer, and Helen couldn't wait to see him. She gazed in the mirror and pinched her cheeks to induce a glowing blush. Then she decided that her lips were too pale beside her rosy complexion. Slipping down to the kitchen, she headed for the larder.

"What are you doing in there, missy?" demanded the cook with her hands on her hips. "Don't you go pinching my sultanas again. Them's marked for a cake."

"It was ages ago when we took your sultanas," protested Helen. "When I was just a child."

When they were younger, with no sweetmeats in the house, Matt had suggested sultanas as an alternative.

"And what are you now, pray?" asked Cook with a disbelieving smirk. "An old woman at fifteen?"

Helen sidled out of the larder. She had been foiled in her plan to use some cochineal. Her mother had insisted that she learnt some basic cooking skills, and Helen had seen her use the pink colouring. She'd also noticed how it had stained her mother's fingers.

"You may not marry a rich man," Jessie had told Helen. "And if he's rich when you marry him, he may not always be so. You should learn to cook."

It had been useless to protest that the boys didn't have to learn to bake but, with their avid interest in food, the boys had wanted to join in the lessons anyway.

With all the confidence of youth, Helen had every intention of marrying a wealthy man and keeping him so. She was sure Hadrian Lightfoot's parents had money behind them. She'd often heard her grandfather say that lawyers were robbers and had plenty of money, all extracted from their clients. But she had no excuse to be in the larder, and when Lizzie arrived in the kitchen to fetch some tea for Melissa, she slipped away. Determined to get her hands on the cochineal, Helen decided to visit the kitchen again when Cook was out on one of her shopping trips.

"What on earth have you done to your mouth?" demanded Jessie.

Helen was just about to slip out to visit the Lightfoots when, to her frustration, her mother stopped her. Jessie caught her daughter's arm and turned her towards the light streaming from the skylight above the door.

"Helen, what is that stuff on your mouth? It looks just like cochineal to me."

Helen's stubborn silence gave the game away.

"Go and scrub it off, you silly madam. You look just like a loose wo… just like a clown. Honestly Helen, you're pretty enough without putting stuff on your face. I suppose this is another of Dora Lightfoot's silly ideas?"

"Dora has nothing to do with it," protested Helen. "I just thought I looked a little pale, that's all."

Jessie shook her head in exasperation. "Just go and wash it off," she told Helen with a sigh.

Helen went to do as she was told. No doubt Mama would be standing guard to make sure she'd carried out her orders. All the same, Helen looked surprised when she caught her reflection in the mirror. Her mouth did look startlingly pink. She scrubbed at her lips and slowly the colour faded, though with her vigorous rubbing, her lips were redder than usual.

She presented herself to her mother.

"That looks more natural," said Jessie with a chuckle. "You needn't join the circus today."

"Oh Mother!" protested Helen, pressing her lips to stifle a smile. Deep down, she knew her mother had saved her from looking ridiculous, but it wouldn't do to admit it. Then she had an alarming thought. "You won't tell Papa and the boys, will you?" she pleaded.

If they knew, they would tease her mercilessly.

"No, I won't," Jessie promised, and Helen knew she could trust her mother.

She hurried towards the Lightfoot house, eager to see Hadrian once again, her head full of the expected encounter. Would he notice that she looked much older and more stylish? Would he speak to her? She longed to speak with him but, if he spoke to her, she was sure she would stammer and look foolish. She meant to act demure and seem intelligent, remembering how he had praised her for not asking him silly questions and giggling, like her friends.

As she walked down the high street, alight with hope, a group of young men outside an alehouse on the other side of the road called out to her.

"Hello, my pretty. Would you like a glass of beer with us?"

There were more catcalls echoing across the road. Helen refused to acknowledge them, tossing her head and defiantly raising her chin, causing further comments and jokes. Flushed with righteous annoyance, she marched away to her friend's house.

A little maid opened the door, and moments later Dora arrived to greet her, followed by Sabina and Anna-Marie. Helen felt deflated. She cursed herself for having to stay and scrub her lips clean of the stupid cochineal. Now the other girls had arrived before her and had no doubt been trying hard to impress Hadrian. She expected the other girls to be giddy in the presence of Dora's brother as they usually were, but they had a distinct air of disappointment.

"Hadrian has gone for a drink of beer with his friends," murmured Sabina as they followed Dora into the parlour.

"Oh, really?" said Helen, feigning indifference.

Inside, her heart was sinking. She suspected that Hadrian had been one of the impudent boys outside the alehouse. Still, she had the satisfaction that she hadn't acted like a hoyden and acknowledged their raucous greetings. Helen felt proud that she had maintained her demure façade in the face of their effrontery. She hadn't noticed him, but no doubt her heart's desire would be annoyed that he had been snubbed. Now she almost dreaded to see him again. But fate stepped in to compound her confusion.

Sabina and Anna-Marie had reluctantly returned home without seeing their idol, but Dora had delayed Helen with some gossip about Sabina. Helen felt gratified to be the chosen one to receive this titbit from the leader of their little clique.

She was just about to leave when the front door swung open, and there before her was Hadrian. There was a distinct aroma of beer around him and a glitter in his eye.

"Well, if it isn't little miss hoity-toity," he said with a laugh. "Your friend here positively snubbed me and my friends at the Bridge Inn."

"I'm not surprised," Dora reprimanded her brother. "I expect you were in your cups and embarrassed the poor girl."

Helen was just about to say that she had indeed been embarrassed by their behaviour when Hadrian smiled at her.

"Well, when a pretty girl passes by, a chap has to say something," he said. "My friends were positively entranced by Miss Helen Overdale, and I was proud to say I had made her acquaintance, despite the fact that she ignored me."

Helen immediately wanted to apologise, but her tongue froze. Dora came to her rescue.

"Well, if I had been in Helen's position, I'm sure I would have ignored you too," she sniffed.

Helen was proud that she had behaved just as her friend expected, even though Hadrian had just called her pretty. What he said next surprised her.

"Miss Overdale, I do apologise for my raucous behaviour and that of my friends. I can assure you we did not mean to insult or embarrass you. We were just carried away with the joy of seeing a pretty face."

"Apology accepted," she murmured, her face burning.

"You are most gracious," he said with a smile. "Gracious and lovely."

Helen almost melted with pleasure.

"Would you like me to escort you home?" asked Hadrian. "Some of the fellows may still be at the Bridge, and I should hate for you to be embarrassed again."

"No, no," protested Helen quickly. She wanted to escape and savour her encounter with Hadrian on the way home. Besides, she was so overwhelmed that her tongue did not feel her own and she might well embarrass herself.

"Another time, perhaps?" asked Hadrian.

"Yes, yes, another time," murmured Helen, her heart beating loudly in her ears.

Dora escorted her to the door, looking very pleased with herself.

Helen walked home in a dream. She didn't even notice the half-hearted calls from the remaining drinkers. Hadrian Lightfoot had called her pretty. One day she would allow him to walk her home, when her thoughts and her beating heart were calmer. Then she would surely impress him.

CHAPTER 13: A CHANCE ENCOUNTER

Arden felt the boat pitch as it hit a wave and grabbed a nearby strut to steady himself.

"It's going to be a rough night tonight, lads," he told his crew. "Let's hope there won't be too much water pouring down into the bilges, or there'll be plenty of pumping to do before the morning."

The third engineer, Mr Braeburn, appeared in the engineer room. "Sorry I'm late, sir," he mumbled. "I had a bit of trouble climbing down here in this swell."

"Never mind. You're here now. I won't be off dancing now I've finished my watch," joked Arden.

"There'll be no entertaining the ladies tonight, sir," said Braeburn. "Most of them will be staying in their cabins turning green, from what I hear."

"God bless 'em," said Arden. "I might go on deck and get a breath of fresh air. It's really stuffy down here, what with the heat of the boiler and the smell of oil."

"Well, hang on tight," advised Braeburn.

Arden hauled himself up into the fresh air, struggling as the ship lurched from side to side.

"I wouldn't go out there, sir," a steward advised him as he clung to the handle of a door to the deck. "Captain's orders are no one on deck other than the relevant seamen."

Arden nodded, not wishing to countermand the captain's orders and get the steward in trouble. He was just about to return to his cabin when a light female voice assailed him.

"Oh Mr Davenport, how nice to see you here."

Arden turned to see one of his regular dance partners. Mrs Van Meyerson was a wealthy widow, forceful and prone to monopolising his company.

"Shouldn't you be safe in your cabin, Mrs Van Meyerson?" he advised. "We shouldn't like you to get hurt in this swell."

"Oh Mr Davenport, you mustn't worry about me," she simpered. "I've crossed the Atlantic in bigger seas than this. Now if you were to accompany me to my cabin…" She made an effort to link his arm, but at that moment the ship lurched and, despite his efforts to catch her, she crashed into the side of the corridor and slid to the ground with a cry.

The steward rushed forward to help as Arden bent over her.

"Perhaps I can help," said a cool female voice beside him. "I am a doctor."

Arden didn't know if he was more surprised to hear a woman claiming to be a doctor or the familiar voice. He glanced up to see Honora looking concerned. The moment she saw his face, she froze.

"Arden," she whispered in shock.

He immediately became professional to hide his confusion. "Thank you, Miss Darwen … er, Doctor Darwen. I would be glad of your help. Mrs Van Meyerson has had a fall, as you can see. I wonder if you would be so good as to check if there's anything broken and if she's safe to move?"

"Certainly," said Honora briskly and began checking the shocked woman. "Does this hurt?" she asked gently as she prodded her arm. "Can you move it?" She questioned and probed and finally pronounced that nothing was broken. "I'm afraid you will probably have some bruising to your arm," she said sympathetically. "You may have to wear long-sleeved dresses or a shawl for some time, I'm afraid."

The steward and Arden carefully hauled Mrs Van Meyerson to her feet. She was shaken but mobile, and the three of them accompanied her to her cabin, where her maid came and fussed around her.

"Well, I'll be darned, a lady doctor!" she said with a chuckle as she was settled in a plush armchair. "Just wait 'til I tell my friends. They'll be delighted. Thank you, my dear. Do you have a card?"

"Not with me," said Honora modestly. "But if you need me, I shall be glad to help. I have some arnica for your bruises in my cabin and will drop in to see you in the morning, if I may?"

"Oh, please do," said her patient.

"We will have to send for the ship's doctor," decided Arden. He turned to Honora. "I'm not doubting your professional skills for a moment," he told her. "It's purely procedure, and the Captain would insist on it."

She nodded. "Yes, of course," she said, meeting his eyes. "I understand."

They bid Mrs Van Meyerson goodnight, and Arden sent the steward to fetch the ship's doctor.

Now they were left alone in the corridor.

"So," said Arden, wondering what on earth to say to his old love. The ship rolled, and he automatically put out his arm to steady her. The moment the ship steadied, he dropped it self-consciously. "Thank you for your help," he said. "You arrived at an opportune moment."

"I wanted to go on deck but was dissuaded by the steward," she said, avoiding his eyes.

"It isn't safe," he told her. "And we wouldn't want one of our few lady doctors to go overboard. Jessie told me you would be going home to England when I was last at home."

"I'll be based in London," she said.

"I should warn you, though, that there is still a lot of ridiculous opposition to lady doctors," he told her. "But by Mrs Van Meyerson's reaction, I think you will have plenty of patients. She is a very influential woman on both sides of the Atlantic."

"I told you once, Mr Davenport, that I did not train to be a doctor to advise rich women to loosen their stays," she reminded him with a smile.

"I remember. It was on the night we went to the reception to meet Mr Lincoln and his wife."

"That was a wonderful night," said Honora, smiling as she remembered the crush in the White House and the cool walk home on Arden's arm.

She had abandoned his love and care for a phantom infatuation with one of her fellow students. Now as he stood beside her, kind and handsome, she knew she'd been a fool. If only she had not felt so lonely during his absences at sea.

"I'll accompany you back to your cabin," said Arden briskly. "We don't want another accident tonight."

They walked cautiously along the twisting and turning corridors until they reached her small cabin in second class. He was ever alert and caught her arm several times to steady her, but dropped it immediately whenever it was safe.

"Goodnight, Miss Darwen," he said formally.

"Goodnight, Arden," she said deliberately.

He smiled that she had called him by his first name. "Honora," he acknowledged with a small bow. "I hope to see you about ship."

"I'm sure you shall," she answered. "I should love to have the latest news of Jessie and her family."

Returning his formal nod, she went into her cabin with a smile.

Arden sought Honora out in the next few days. Luckily, the weather had calmed and, though there was still a swell upon the sea, it was safe to walk on deck. They politely asked of each other's health.

"I have taken this journey for my health," explained Honora. "I'm afraid I was working too hard at the hospital. My superior suggested I go to London to work with her sister at a training hospital for women."

"So you won't be going back to Gorbydale?" enquired Arden.

"I will of course visit," Honora told him, "but I'm not sure of a welcome at Overdale House. I'm sure my aunt is still angry with me for staying in America when I was needed at home. And Matthias does not readily forgive. I would dearly like to see Jessie again, and her family. I'm sure my cousin Robert will not reject me."

Arden looked at her thoughtfully. "I can offer myself as a go-between," he suggested. "I'll be heading for home once the ship docks in Liverpool."

"I'll be taking the train to London," she told him. "I'd like to establish myself in London before I return to Gorbydale. Doctor Blackwell is expecting me."

"I could ask Jessie how the land lies and write to you at your hospital. If your aunt is unwilling to see you, I'm sure you'll always have a welcome at my father's house."

"Even though we parted?" she asked in surprise.

"He remembers how good you were to my mother," Arden told her with a warm smile. "My family knows nothing of our previous understanding, especially as you seemed to wish it kept private. They knew I saw you in New York, and Jessie guessed my feelings for you, but I'm sure she never spoke of it to my father."

"I wouldn't want to put Jessie in a difficult situation," decided Honora. "It must be awkward enough for her living with Matthias."

"I'm sure your visit would be welcome. Jessie's friend Mary could even put you up in her boarding house at a pinch."

"Thank you, Arden," said Honora humbly. "You have been a great friend to me. I regret…"

He interrupted her. "Let's not speak of the past," he said. "It was an unsettling time for both of us, but it is the past. Let's hope that life will sail on an even keel for us from now on."

Honora smiled at him with gratitude. He saw a spark of hope in her eyes. Yet despite the unsettling appeal he'd felt when he heard her voice on that stormy night, Arden remembered the desolation of her rejection. Hardening his heart, he knew he didn't want to repeat the experience. He'd witnessed the fickleness of women on these transatlantic voyages, women whose husbands were also aboard, attempting to make romantic assignations with the handsome officers. Deep down he knew Honora was not like that, but her affections had drifted in his absence at sea. Could he trust her again? Suddenly, he decided to take a chance and hear her regrets.

"Honora…" he began.

To his frustration, they were interrupted by Mrs Van Meyerson's cry of delight. "Oh Officer Davenport, there you are. I've been searching for you in first class, and I didn't expect… Oh, Doctor Darwen, isn't it? I expect you were discussing my awful accident."

Arden acknowledged her with a polite nod and a wry smile. For ladies like Mrs Van Meyerson, the world revolved entirely around them. "We were just discussing our home town of Gorbydale, ma'am," he said firmly. "Doctor Darwen and I hail from the same small town in Lancashire."

The rich widow had been the last thing on his mind. He was suddenly eager to hear of Honora's regrets concerning him. But to his disappointment, she politely made her excuses and left him alone with Mrs Van Meyerson. He too made an excuse that he must return to his duties and, after escorting the widow back to first class, made his escape.

That night he slept badly, his churning thoughts ever turning to Honora's rejection of his love. In the morning, he decided that it was folly to rekindle their romance. How could he spend many months at sea and leave her open once again to temptation and still be sure of her enduring affection?

Over the rest of the voyage, they met as friends. Though they seemed as polite and easy with one another as they'd once been, a subtle chill had entered their relationship. Arden introduced Honora to the ship's doctor, but the man wasn't pleased to have a woman doctor intruding on his territory. She wasn't encouraged to repeat the visit.

When they reached Liverpool, Arden promised to write to the address she'd given him. Honora expressed the hope that she would see him again in Gorbydale. They were about to part with each other in hesitant politeness when once again they were interrupted by Mrs Van Meyerson. The widow thanked Arden for his company with noisy extravagance, then demanded Honora came to tea with her at the Dorchester hotel. Honora made a vague promise that she would and made to leave. For a moment she turned and hesitated. Arden smiled and nodded formally. With a heavy and confused heart, he watched her as she organised a porter to transport her luggage to the station. Then he turned back to the ship and his duties, wondering if he really could bear the pain of rejection once again.

CHAPTER 14: THE WANDERER RETURNS

Jessie was overjoyed to see her father coming up the drive to Overdale House with a welcome guest and rushed out to meet them.

"Welcome home," she greeted her brother with a kiss. "And you too, Father. You know you're always welcome. This is a rare visit. I only seem to see you at home these days."

Jacob paused and took a deep breath. "Aye lass, it's not surprising really. This drive takes it out of a fella. I'd forgotten how steep it was when Arden asked if I fancied a walk."

Matthias had been adamant that the whole town could witness his success when he built his mansion on the top of the rise overlooking Gorbydale. Now it was becoming a struggle for him to walk himself, he usually took the gig the short distance to the mill. Jessie was glad that Robert rode with him too to avoid the pain of his damaged leg. She too had found the drive steep lately. Whenever she paused for breath, she blamed her own lack of exercise.

Now Jessie noticed for the first time that her father was getting old. It was true he'd aged when he'd lost his beloved wife Nellie, but marrying Alice had renewed his vigour. Yet as she noticed the changes in her family and friends around her, she knew that time was never kind to anyone.

"Come along in and have some tea," she coaxed. "That'll revive you both."

Soon they were comfortable in her parlour and sipping tea. After they'd exchanged their pleasantries with much amusement about the antics of Jessie's children, Arden became serious.

"I met Honora aboard ship," he told Jessie.

"Oh! I hadn't realised she was coming so soon. And was everything all right?" she asked cautiously.

Arden nodded with a smile. "She's gone to London to help at a teaching hospital being set up for women," he said. "She'll be coming to visit Gorbydale once she's settled."

"I'll be so glad to see her," said Jessie warmly.

"I told her you would be," said her brother. "The thing is, she doesn't know what her welcome will be here at Overdale House. She knows it would put you in an awkward position if you offered her a bed here. Father and Alice have said they'll be glad to have her."

"Aye, me and Alice will make her welcome all right. But she's unsure what her aunt will think."

"Would you like me to ask Melissa in for a chat?" suggested Jessie.

"That would be a grand idea," said Jacob. "I always got on well with Mrs Overdale. Aye, we even quelled a riot together," he added, laughing.

Jessie had often heard the tale of how her mother-in-law and father, together with Uncle Eli, had quietened the situation when the unemployed mill workers rioted during the cotton famine.

"It were Eli who did the trick, really," Jacob told them. "He told the rioters that he might have to read the Riot Act and reminded them of what happened at Peterloo. 'And we don't want that to happen again, do we?' he warned them. They had plenty to riot about, poor devils. But it were common sense that prevailed, and we managed to sort out most of their grievances."

"It was brave all the same," said Arden. "My friend John was there, and he said he would never have faced such a mob."

"Aye, your mate was a good help," said Jacob. "Luckily, nobody got hurt. But I think most people trusted Eli, and the people from the chapel listened to me. And nobody wanted to cross Mrs Overdale. So everything worked out well."

"I'll go and get Melissa," said Jessie.

She found her mother-in-law dozing as usual. Gently she roused her.

"Father's here to see me with Arden. Would you like to come and have a cup of tea with us?"

Melissa looked groggy for a moment as she tried to focus her eyes. Then she smiled. "That would be nice, my dear," she said, holding out her hand for Jessie to help her out of her chair.

Jacob and Arden stood up to greet Melissa and, to their surprise, she kissed Jacob on both cheeks. Jessie thought at least she was in a good mood. Sometimes Melissa could be very irritable when she was woken up.

"Oh, this is nice," said Melissa, settling herself into one of Jessie's chairs. "This was my father's chair at Primrose Cottage many years ago. Matthias didn't think it was grand enough for our parlour, so it was stuck up in the attic. I'm glad to see it back in use, and with a lovely new cover too."

Comfortably seated, she chatted happily to Jacob. They had been old friends in their youth at the Endurance Mill, her brother Eli's factory. That was before her marriage to Matthias and before he'd risen in status and self-importance when he'd built the grand Invincible Mill at the head of the valley.

Then Jacob mentioned Arden's journey from America on the S.S. Baltic.

"I met Miss Darwen aboard ship," said Arden quietly. "She's come home to help at a teaching hospital for lady doctors in London."

"Will she be coming home here?" asked Melissa, suddenly alert.

"She'd like to come and see everyone, of course," said Jacob jovially. "I know you didn't approve of her staying in America, and it might be awkward for you. But she's very welcome to stay at our place. I just wanted to see that you're happy with that."

Melissa cast a suspicious eye round the three people waiting intently for a reply. "Well, I can't say I'm happy, can I?" she said tartly. "After all we'd done for her; offered her a home when she was destitute when her mother, my dear sister, died. I treated her like my own daughter, and what did she do but abandon us when Matthias was poorly? And what about when young Matthew was born? She might have been a help to Jessie then. But where was she? Why, swanning about in America of course. Am I happy? I don't think so."

Arden took a deep breath. "She's been working very hard in America to train to be a doctor," he said quietly. "It hasn't been easy for her with all the prejudice against women doctors, and she's had to train hard to prove herself. Her superior advised her to come to London because she was exhausted from working in New York. Yet even now she'll face opposition in England."

Melissa looked affronted by his defence of her niece, but Jacob intervened.

"You won't have to see the lass, you know, Mrs Overdale, if you don't want to," he said. "She'll be safe up Weavers Row if she does come to visit. I'm sure our Jessie would love to see her old friend. They went through a lot together in them

American hospitals. And between 'em they saved Robert's life — and his leg."

Melissa could only concede that they had indeed saved her precious only son. She paused and seemed to be remembering all that had happened as the girls went to find Robert, lost in the turmoil of the American war.

"I won't object to you housing my niece during her stay here," she said finally. "I'll not of course see her myself. Matthias wouldn't like it. Jessie must do as she pleases."

"Oh thank you, mother-in-law," said Jessie as she gave Melissa an impulsive kiss on the cheek.

Nothing more was said about the visit, and they drank their tea in quiet friendship.

As it happened, Jacob and Alice did not have their visitor. Jacob was now the manager of the Endurance, where he'd worked most of his life as a master weaver. Who else would Eli put in charge of his mill but his oldest and most trusted worker and friend? He'd decided to take life easier now he was plagued by arthritis, living as he was beside the Gorby river where a damp mist rose like a ghost in the mornings. Though Jacob missed weaving at his machine, he was not as dexterous as he had once been, and he found his new duties less onerous. He was chatting to Eli about Honora's proposed visit when his boss stopped him.

"She can come here, lad," said Eli. "She is my niece, after all. My housekeeper will look after her. I'm sure Mrs Corbett would like someone a bit younger round the house for a change. She must be fed up of looking after an old codger like me. Aye, tell the lass to come and stay with me. She'll be very welcome."

The visit was promptly arranged by letter. So when Honora finally came home some months after her arrival in England, Jessie hurried to meet her at her uncle's house. The friends greeted each other warmly.

"My, but you're proper thin," said Jessie, after hugging her friend and holding her at arm's length. "I reckon you've been working too hard."

"There's a lot to do," Honora told her with a wan smile. "But it feels strange to be home. I passed through Manchester on the way here. The slums down Angel Meadow seem to be worse than ever, if that were possible."

"Aye, the famine took a lot out of the city," said Jessie. "So many unemployed drifted to the city to find work where there was none and got stuck there. It's taken Gorbydale some time to recover too. But more cotton's coming in, and we're picking up," she added brightly. "And you'll no doubt hear about our cotton baroness Dolly Jacques, as she is now."

Honora fell silent for a moment. Jessie hadn't yet heard of her friend's suspicions that Clement Duplege might not be as dead as they once believed.

As the old friends chatted and caught up with their news, there was a knock on Eli's front door.

"You've some more visitors, Miss Honora," said Mrs Corbett with a smile as she opened the door to usher them in.

Helen bounced through the door, followed shyly by Matt and Jack. "Aunt Honora," said Helen, seizing Honora's hands. "I suppose I may call you that?" she asked, glancing at her mother for approval.

"Of course you may, my dear," said Honora with a bemused smile at Helen's confidence. "I am practically a sister to your dear mother."

"I told the boys to meet me directly from school so we could come and see you," said Helen. "Mama's told us so much about you."

"I hope you're not disappointed, then," said their visitor modestly. "And these two fine fellows must be Matthew and Jacob?"

The boys came forward with a shy smile.

"Ma says you come all the way from America," said Matt eagerly. "And you're staying in London. Perhaps Pa will bring us to visit you. I should dearly like to see the tower of London. Reverend Tyldesley has been telling us all about Henry the eighth, hasn't he, Jack?"

His brother nodded, his usual chatter silenced by shyness.

"I haven't seen it myself yet," said Honora, smiling at his enthusiasm. "We're very busy at the hospital. But perhaps if you come to visit, we could go and see it together."

"Oh can we, Mama?" cried Helen. "I should just love to see the ladies and their fashions in London."

"We'll see," said Jessie, laughing. "Your poor Aunt Honora has just arrived and already you've invited yourselves to go and see her in London. Honestly, what a trio of troublemakers you are!"

"It's just the enthusiasm of youth," Honora reminded. "You have three lovely children, and I'm very pleased to meet them."

"Will you all stay for tea?" asked Mrs Corbett, coming through the door. "Mr Eli will be home in a bit, and he's always glad to see you."

The boys looked hopeful at the mention of food, but Jessie rose to leave.

"Thank you for the invitation, Mrs Corbett," she said. "But I'm afraid I'll be needed at home to supervise there. We won't impose on you today. But we'd be pleased to come another day if that's all right? I was just so eager to see my old friend here, I just had to come and visit. The children invited themselves."

"You're welcome any time, Mrs Jessica," said the housekeeper. "Mr Eli loves to see the young 'uns."

They made their farewells and promised to visit again soon. They had left the house when Helen touched her mother's arm.

"I won't be coming home for tea," she told Jessie. "Dora has invited me to her house. It's Hadrian's last day before he returns to college, and they're having a little farewell tea before he leaves tomorrow. She only invited me this morning after art class. Is that all right?"

"I suppose so," said Jessie cautiously.

She wasn't happy about the amount of time her daughter spent with Dora Lightfoot, as she didn't like the girl and thought her sly. There seemed to be a lot of talk about this Hadrian too. She rightly suspected her daughter of being infatuated with him. Jessie was pleased to hear he was leaving.

CHAPTER 15: TEA AND UNDERSTANDING

As Helen reached the Lightfoots' house, to her delight, Hadrian Lightfoot opened the door to her. He had obviously pushed past the little maid, who hovered behind him, thwarted in her duties.

"Well, if it isn't the delightful Miss Overdale," he said, beaming as he ushered her into the house.

Helen was convinced he'd been watching at the bay window for her arrival, and a delicious feeling of pleasure engulfed her. She smiled her gratitude up at him. The moment she gazed into his startling blue eyes, she modestly lowered her own. All her friends knew it wasn't the done thing to appear too bold. The magazines and books on etiquette gave the same advice. All the same, Helen couldn't resist another sly peek to see if he was still attentive. He gave her a knowing grin. Her friend Dora came out to meet her and smirked like an artful cat up at her brother. Helen suspected there was some sort of conspiracy between them but she didn't care. Hadrian Lightfoot had smiled on her, and she was satiated with triumph. Gaining his approval was all she ever thought about in her waking moments.

"Are the girls here?" she asked. She fully expected Anna-Marie and Sabina to appear to witness her triumph.

"Oh, they haven't been invited," purred Dora, "only my special friend."

She linked Helen, and Dora's new 'special friend' felt blessed by her new status. If only their other friends had been present to see her elevation, life would have been perfect for Helen.

The Lightfoot family made her very welcome as they sat down to high tea. They spoke of how they would miss Hadrian once he went back to college.

"I hope you will miss me too, Miss Overdale," he murmured when he assumed the others were not listening.

"Oh yes," said Helen with enthusiasm, although blushing furiously.

If the others overheard, they did not object.

It was only later, when Mr Lightfoot senior began asking her about the Invincible Mill, that Helen began to feel awkward.

"Oh, Grandpapa says business is picking up," she told him confidently. She said nothing about the mortgage.

"And how is your crippled brother, my dear?" asked Mrs Lightfoot, with an insinuating smile.

Helen bit her lip. She knew well how angry her mother would have been to hear Matt called such a thing. "Our Matt is fine," she said firmly. "He's doing well with Reverend Tyldesley. Mama says he's a genius at mathematics."

This was a slight exaggeration on Helen's part. Matt had helped her with some homework, and her mother had mentioned how clever he was with figures. Her strategy worked.

"Oh," Dora's mother stared in surprise. "I didn't think… Would you like some tea, dear?" she said hurriedly to change the subject.

Helen smiled to herself, secretly pleased that she'd embarrassed the woman. Her mother's warning about the Lightfoots came back to her. They did indeed seem a bit too interested in her family's business. At once the ever open and candid Helen subtly learned to become discreet.

"I'm glad to see the mill is reviving," said Mr Lightfoot. "It was a great enterprise in this valley. A source of pride for us all."

Helen felt gratified by his praise of the Invincible. All the same, she was careful not to be carried away with pride in her family. She was eager to mention Honora's visit. "My father's cousin is visiting from London at present," she told them. "She is one of the very few lady doctors in England. She was trained in America, you know."

"How interesting," said Mr Lightfoot. "That would be Miss Honora."

"I'm sure I could not fully trust a lady doctor," sniffed his wife. "Why, our Doctor Braddock has years of experience behind him. I'm sure your aunt is very good, dear, but she's barely out of college."

"Yes, these ladies would be better tending to their homes and husbands," Mr Lightfoot asserted.

"I prefer Doctor Andrew to old Doctor Braddock," said Dora smartly. "He's so much more modern — and so handsome," she added with a giggle.

Helen was tempted to tell them that Honora had plenty of medical experience through working in the American Civil War, but she knew she was wasting her time. She recognised the older Lightfoots were firmly stuck with their ideas, and no amount of argument would budge them. She hoped Hadrian was more open to ideas.

"Shall we go out into the garden?" he suggested. "It's a lovely day, and Mother's roses are blooming beautifully."

Helen rose eagerly and followed him out into the long strip of greenery behind the house. Dora trailed behind them.

"Oh, I've just remembered something," said Dora brightly. "I'm sure you won't miss me for a moment or two."

The instant his sister had disappeared, Hadrian turned to Helen.

"And will you miss me when I return to Manchester, Miss Overdale?" he asked with a smile.

"Oh yes," said Helen eagerly. "I certainly will." Then she remembered to lower her eyes for a second and felt a warm glow rise in her cheeks.

"I don't suppose…? I hardly dare ask…?" began Hadrian. "Miss Overdale, Helen, would you write to me? A chap gets very homesick away from his people and friends. Just a little note maybe, from a pretty girl, would make all the difference."

"Oh, of course I will," said Helen eagerly. "Hadrian," she added shyly.

"Perhaps don't say anything to my sister just yet," he cautioned. "Or she will tease us mercifully."

At that moment Dora wandered out and Helen quickly nodded to him in conspiracy.

"Have you two been admiring the roses?" asked Dora with a sly smirk at her brother.

"Most certainly," said Hadrian. "Especially the ones in your cheeks," he murmured to Helen.

"I had better go and do some packing," he decided, much to Helen's disappointment. "I'll leave you girls to your gossiping."

Helen hardly listened as Dora chattered on in her usual way about nothing of consequence. Hadrian Lightfoot had asked her to write to him! It was wonderful. It was everything she had imagined in her girlish dreams. Then she worried where she would write to.

It was time for Helen to reluctantly go home. She was anxious that he had not reappeared, but just as Dora opened the door for her to leave, Hadrian rushed downstairs.

"I must say goodbye before you go, Miss Overdale," he said, formal once more. Then he slipped a piece of paper into her hand as he shook it, shielding their joined hands from his from his sister.

Helen gazed up into his eyes. "Goodbye, Mr Lightfoot. I hope we shall see you in Gorbydale soon."

She tripped home on airy feet. How would she survive without the tantalising excitement of seeing Hadrian every now and then to lighten her life? She'd promised to write but wondered if she must first receive one of his letters. Once out of sight of the Lightfoot house, she unscrolled the note clutched tightly in her hand.

Write soon, it said briefly, followed by his address at college.

She raised it to her lips and scurried home, filled with joy and anticipation.

CHAPTER 16: OLD FRIENDS

Though she had only visited her uncle's home as an occasional guest before, Honora felt quite at home with her Uncle Eli. Mrs Corbett made her very welcome. A tea party was arranged at the following weekend when Robert was free to join his family.

Matthias had been vehemently against seeing his niece, although Eli had invited him. He kept muttering about 'a viper in his bosom'. Melissa would not join them through loyalty to her husband.

"It's such a shame," Jessie told Robert. "I know Honora tried to help your father when she was at Overdale House, but he wouldn't listen to her advice anyway. I don't like to see conflict in the family."

"Can't be helped," said Robert. "You know how stubborn my father is. But I'm surprised at Mama. I thought she'd be more forgiving. And it's not as if Honora has disgraced the family. Being a doctor is an honourable profession."

Jessie hugged his arm. "It's a pity some people think it isn't honourable for a woman to be a doctor. More fool them."

They were welcomed into Mill House, Eli's home beside the Endurance. The old mill had been a water mill, powered by the Gorby river long before the Invincible had risen majestically in the valley. Matthias had been Eli's partner there when they'd first started in business. Mill House was where Matthias had met and married Eli's sister and where Robert had been born. Robert often told Jessie he felt more at home there than in the ornate rooms of Overdale House. The house was shabby but comfortable and clean, thanks to Mrs Corbett's efforts with the aid of a little maid of all work.

Jessie felt odd when she suggested that Honora stayed with the company as guest of honour, while Jessie herself helped Mrs Corbett the housekeeper to ferry in the tea. In Matthias's presence, Jessie was often reminded that she was a former mill girl. She'd travelled as Honora's companion to America and was always mindful of her position as an inferior. Now, as a woman married to the heir to the Invincible, she took social precedence. But deep down, she was still that mill girl.

"Please do sit down while I help Mrs Corbett," she said. "The children are eager to hear about your travels, and Robert has hardly seen you since you arrived."

Honora gave her a grateful smile. She had never knowingly treated her friend as an inferior and now looked on her as the sister she had never had.

Matt was very interested in hearing of America. "I should like to go one day," he said.

Jessie smiled at his ambition. "Perhaps you shall," she said. "After all, I never expected to travel so far."

"You never speak of it," her son complained. "Nor Pa either."

"Because America during a war and the unspeakable things men do to one another is not something I like to remember. You think Manchester is busy, you should see New York," she told him.

"I think it's even busier and noisier than when we first arrived there," said Honora with a chuckle. "You take your life in your hands trying to cross a road."

She told them something of her life in America and her work. She made them laugh telling them of the ludicrous things patients had said to her because she was a woman.

"I'm sure I should have reprimanded those idiots severely," protested Helen. "Or faced them with the biggest, sharpest syringe I could find."

"Unfortunately, it's better to keep the peace and impress them with your medical knowledge than berate them," said Honora with a chuckle. "If you told them off, they would only be convinced that you were very unwomanly and wanted to be a man."

"Will you return to America?" asked Robert.

Honora was thoughtful for a moment. "I don't honestly know," she said. "There's so much work to be done here. Though it's still difficult, women are more accepted in America."

Later, when they had a moment alone, Honora had a quiet word with Jessie.

"I know you must think me a fool for breaking my understanding with your brother Arden," she told her friend. "I sincerely do regret it. But my infatuation for…"

"For Ben Clark," finished her friend.

"You guessed!" gasped Honora.

"I did wonder," said Jessie. "You mentioned his name in your letters many times. I suspected he was 'your dear friend'."

"Unfortunately, he did not feel as I did. I was so infatuated that I deluded myself." Honora sighed.

"Is there any chance that you and Arden…?" began Jessie.

Honora shook her head. "He is, as you know, friendly and helpful to me, but there's a distinct coolness towards me. And I really don't blame him. I must really have hurt him."

Jessie regretted the broken romance between her favourite brother and her best friend. She would have been so pleased to have Honora as her sister-in-law. Naturally she wondered how or even if she could heal the rift between them. When she next saw Arden, she resolved to question him subtly.

Honora stayed for a few days before she resumed her work in London. She and Jessie went to tea with Jacob and Alice, and Jessie pointed out all the improvements to the town since her friend had left. They rested for a while in the municipal gardens while Jessie related proudly how Robert had helped with the works. She told Honora about the improvements to the privies and water supply in River Road.

"About time," said Honora. "The infections that spread from that swamp of filth were innumerable."

"The town couldn't have done it without Uncle Eli," Jessie told her. "Once he and Melissa took over the running of the Relief Committee, with Father helping of course, there was no end of improvements. But Eli put a considerable amount of his own savings in too."

"He's a good man," said Honora. "But what about Matthias? He always makes himself out to be one of the town's grandees. Didn't he help?"

Jessie was silent for a moment, wondering how much she should tell her friend. "He's not well, of course," she said cautiously. "But he doesn't have the money to back up his show of wealth. The mill is still in a lot of debt. Please don't say anything, but he overstretched himself during the cotton crisis. He tried trading with the South, but that Clement Duplege paid him in a lot of Confederate dollars and they were worthless."

Honora shivered at the name. "I received a letter from Dolly," she murmured in a low voice. "In it she says that Clement's old housekeeper was killed under a carriage. The woman said she'd been pushed just before she died."

"You surely don't suspect Clement?" gasped Jessie. "Surely he must be drowned. And if he were back from the dead, why would he kill his old housekeeper? It can't be right. You're just so fearful of his name."

"She had sold his house and disappeared with the money," said Honora flatly. "Oh, he would seek revenge all right. Look at poor Verity. I'm convinced he was the murderer. His body was never found."

"Oh, I do hope you're not right," Jessie told her.

"Ever since I received that letter, I've lived in fear," said Honora with a deep sigh. "I worked so hard to forget. That's the main reason why I'm in England. If he is alive, he'll need to work hard to find me here. I don't think I'll return to America if there's suspicion that he is alive."

The friends sat silently for a while, each consumed by their own thoughts. A sprinkling of rain pattered onto the leaves of the flowering shrubs, and they made to leave the gardens.

"I'm glad to see the town coming back to life," said Honora.

"So am I. The mill is picking up too. The price of raw cotton is falling, and hopefully we'll be out of debt soon. Though the merchants in Liverpool have decided to increase their charges now trade is increasing. Honestly, I wonder if we'll ever get straight."

Jessie took a growing interest in the commerce of the mill while listening to Matt try and explain the finances to Jack. Jack wasn't a bit bothered. He was more interested in going to play football with some friends in the town.

"I don't suppose I'll see anything of Aunt Melissa before I go back to London," sighed Honora. "I should have liked to thank her for taking me in when Mama died. I wanted to explain my reasons for staying in America, though I don't suppose she'd forgive me anyway."

"No, I'm sorry but she seems very bitter still," said Jessie. "I have tried now and again, but she just shuts me down the moment I open my mouth. She's very cantankerous these days. I expect it's that tincture she keeps swallowing like cordial."

"Did you water it down as I suggested?" asked her friend.

Jessie nodded. "She just seems to take more."

"It's a growing problem," admitted Honora. "It seems to have taken over from gin as an answer to people's problems — only it seems to cause more."

As the gardens were midway between the friends' destinations, they parted and promised to meet again the next day.

CHAPTER 17: A SURPRISE CALLER

A few days later, Honora was finishing her packing when the doorbell rang. There was a flurry of activity downstairs, and she went to her bedroom door to look. To her surprise, her aunt was just about to mount the staircase.

"Oh, do stay where you are, Aunt dear," called Honora. "I'll be down directly."

She hurried down the stairs full of trepidation to find Mrs Corbett escorting Melissa to a chair and offering her tea, which she refused.

"Well," said Melissa loudly. "I thought I'd better take a look at this doctor we have in the family."

"Yes Aunt, thank you Aunt," said Honora humbly. "I should have liked to come to Overdale House and thank you for all the kindness you showed me and the home you gave me when Mama died. But I didn't know if I would be welcome."

"Probably not by some," admitted Melissa. "But I wanted to see you for your dear mother's sake. She was my only sister, and we were dear friends and companions when we were young." To Honora's surprise, her aunt began to cry. "Dear friends and companions," she repeated in a whisper.

Honora too felt the tears prickling her eyes as she remembered her dear mother.

"She was such a gentle soul. She had such a kind heart," continued Melissa. "I didn't approve of her marrying a penniless doctor, but what could I say, she loved him very much. You're just like your father, always thinking you can save the world."

"Not save the world, Aunt, but if I can just save a handful of people; prevent them just fading away like dear Mama... Just fading away," she murmured as she remembered the wan face bathed in sweat as her mother struggled to breathe her last.

"So, I made up my mind to come and see you," said Melissa briskly. "I wish you well, despite all. And I want to thank you for saving Robert too. His leg is a mess, but that can't be helped. He can walk, and that's what counts."

"How is Uncle Matthias?" asked Honora politely.

"Well as can be expected," said Melissa abruptly. "He's a stubborn old goat, but he doesn't eat as much as he did. At least that bit of your advice got through to him, but not until old Braddock advised him of the same thing. I dare say if he'd listened to you earlier it might have prevented some of his problems. Come and give me a kiss, child."

Honora dutifully kissed her aunt on her downy cheek. "Thank you for coming, Aunt. I may be in London for some time. I do hope to come back to Manchester at some point. But I will call to Gorbydale whenever I can."

"I'm sure Jessica will inform me and we'll meet again," said Melissa, holding out an arm so her niece could help her to rise.

"Do you have a companion?" asked Honora, remembering all the little errands that she'd once run for her aunt.

"Lizzie is very good to me. She's the children's old nurse, and she's stayed on to help with the family. Matthew was a handful, as you can imagine. He's a good boy, though. Not like that villain Jack. The tricks he gets up to! How he slides down the hallway! He was in terrible trouble the other day when he knocked his mother's rose bowl off the mantelpiece with a football. Jessica was in tears. Oh, that devil knew what he'd done. He was nearly in tears himself. Luckily it was only in two pieces, and dear Robert managed to glue it together. It was her mother's, you know."

Honora nodded. She remembered the pretty china bowl, painted with roses on Nellie Davenport's mantelpiece so many years before. It seemed an age since she had tried to ease Nellie's breathing with eucalyptus oil and recalled the gratitude of the dying woman.

"Just fancy, that oil coming all the way from Australia," Nellie had said in wonder.

She would have been more amazed to witness her daughter and her friend travelling all the way to America, and her son Arden too, joining the Union Navy. Life was sometimes very strange and unexpected.

"You will keep in touch dear, won't you?" asked Melissa, looking anxious. "Jessica is very good to me. She relieves me of a lot of the burden of running the house. But family is family, and blood is thicker than water after all and … I do remember your dear mother with so much affection." She began weeping again, and Honora hastened to put a comforting arm around her aunt's shoulder.

"Of course I will, Aunt dear. Jessie always lets me know how you are, and Uncle Matthias and Eli too. I promise I will visit Gorbydale as often as I can. It's been a very pleasant few days' respite here, and Uncle Eli and Mrs Corbett have made me very welcome."

Melissa looked guilty. "Next time I will insist you stay with us," she said firmly.

"I think it would be easier all round if I stayed with Uncle Eli," Honora said quietly. "Really, I don't want to be a bother. And besides," she said brightly, "Uncle Eli might be offended if I suddenly spurned his hospitality. We can always meet here."

"I suppose so," Melissa agreed reluctantly.

They parted on good terms with many pledges of affection. Honora escorted her aunt out to her gig just as Jessie strolled up to Mill House. Jessie stopped in surprise.

"Why Jessica dear, why didn't you say you were coming to Eli's? I could have given you a lift in the gig," said Melissa pleasantly as she settled herself in the little vehicle.

"I er … I didn't know you were coming," stammered Jessie, glancing at Honora.

Her friend gave her a reassuring nod, and Melissa gave her a very smug smile. "Why of course, dear. I couldn't let Honora leave Gorbydale without saying goodbye, could I?"

"No, of course not," declared Jessie with a relieved smile.

"Time to go home," Melissa commanded Michael Jarvis, the groom's son, and they set off.

"Well, that was a surprise," said Jessie, turning to her friend, and Honora laughed. "For one moment I thought she'd come to tell you what an ungrateful wretch you are."

"So did I when I saw her heading up the stairs," admitted Honora. "But no. She came to say that she visited me for my dear mother's sake. They were very close as children."

"I'm very pleased for you both," said Jessie.

"She got very upset too when she remembered dear Mama," Honora told her. Her face was veiled in sadness for a moment, then she rallied. "Come and help me. With my surprise visit, I haven't finished my packing yet and I'll miss the train if I'm not careful."

The women hurried upstairs and, with cheerful banter to cover their sadness at parting, they finished their task. Mrs Corbett met them downstairs with a large packet of food for Honora to eat on her journey.

"Thank you so much," she told her uncle's housekeeper.

Mrs Corbett looked pleased when she received a hearty kiss on the cheek. "You're welcome anytime, my dear. I'm sorry Mr Eli isn't here to see you off, but he…"

At that moment, the door flew open and Eli burst into the hall.

"Oh good, you're still here. I got delayed at the mill. Are you ready, ladies? Come along, the gig is outside. Are you coming too, Jessie? I can drop you back at Overdale House."

Jessie thanked him and they bustled aboard the little gig, and Eli drove them off to the station.

"I'll be back soon," called Honora above the hissing engine.

Jessie watched her go with regret. They had been through such adventures together. Now Honora was out in the world and proving herself useful. Now Jessie's children had grown away from her, she felt restless. Of course, she was useful to the household, to her family. But her life had shrunk along with her horizons and, for all her experiences, she felt mired in domestication.

As they drove home, Eli chatted to her about the family. He asked many pertinent questions about Matt, and she spoke with pride about her son's progress.

CHAPTER 18: THE LITTLE FLOWER

Marguerite was a delightful baby. Even Jassy, who was married to Nathan's son David, was enchanted with her as she chuckled and blew bubbles from her rosebud lips. Jassy and Dolly maintained a civil though chilly relationship. Ever since the girl had exploded with wrath and jealousy when she heard that Dolly was to marry Nathan, Dolly had been wary of her. They had somehow managed to keep the peace between them for the sake of family harmony. It helped that David liked Dolly. He had always admired her tenacity as she struggled to revive the Amiens plantation, and he'd been very helpful to her and Barney. Once Dolly had held a secret infatuation for him, until she found love and peace with Nathan. The family rubbed along without arguments, but Dolly was always aware of the awful things Jassy had once called her in the height of her anger.

Jassy herself was now expecting a baby. She and David had been trying for a family for some time without success. To Dolly's surprise, Jassy followed her when she took her little daughter upstairs to change her. She carefully watched as Dolly tended to little Marguerite.

"Does it hurt having a baby?" she asked tentatively. "Mamma won't tell me."

Dolly smiled. "It's hard to explain," she said thoughtfully. "It sort of hurts, but it's more of an almighty urge to push that wracks your whole body. I suppose I was lucky, because my labour never lasted too long for me. I nearly had Albert as I ran home from work. They say the second baby is easier as the first one sort of opens the way out, if you know what I mean."

Jassy blushed. "Grandma says that all women must suffer because of the sin of Eve," she said gloomily.

Dolly laughed. "Oh, your grandma probably exaggerated her suffering to make your father feel guilty for being born. She says a lot of things that are a load of rubbish. Don't tell her I said that," she added with a chuckle. "She'll have me doomed to the fires of hell. She probably has already. You'll be fine. Your mother is a sensible woman, and I'll send Aunt Hattie over if you like. She's delivered lots of babies into the world."

"I'll wait and see at the time," decided Jassy. "Mamma should know what to do."

"Just keep Grandma out of the room," Dolly advised her.

"Oh, I will," said Jassy vehemently. "Anyway, she can't climb the stairs now. Mamma has made her a bedroom downstairs at the O'Neill place."

Dolly felt touched that the girl had confided in her. She tickled Marguerite under the chin and was rewarded with a beaming smile. This little girl had brought so much pleasure to them all. Once Dolly asked Jassy and David, along with Albert, to be Marguerite's godparents, Jassy had realised at last that Dolly was no threat to her and David's livelihood.

The Jacques and Amiens plantations were run separately, though the workers of both helped out when there was work to be done. The workers on the Jacques plantation were free men, and Nathan had never held slaves. Though the slaves of the Amiens plantation had been emancipated, there was often friction in town with those people who resented the South's defeat in the war. The folk on the plantations avoided Picardy Creek when they could, but those supplies that they could not grow or provide for themselves had to be brought in from the stores there. Dolly usually liked to drive in herself for a change of scenery and to pick up any gossip.

While she'd been pregnant, though, the journey had been too much for her. To the Jacques' dismay, two young men sent for supplies had been beaten up and had their purchases robbed. They arrived home bleeding and empty-handed. Nathan and David rode at once into town to complain to the sheriff but were met by sullen indifference and shifty-eyed silent guilt from the townsfolk.

"I'll go in myself next time," decided Nathan, furious that he would have to pay for their supplies all over again.

Accompanied by Zeb and a shotgun, he made sure that the supplies arrived safely. Dolly was always anxious until he arrived home.

She was anxious too about Albert. Nathan and Dolly, along with Jeremiah, accompanied him to Baton Rouge, where he was enrolled in the college. They decided that Jeremiah's sister Margaret lived too far from there. He introduced them to his old acquaintances from the college to reassure them that Albert would be fine.

Dolly watched as her once timid son eagerly drank in all the sights of his new life and settled into his room. She felt sad that he was so content to leave home and anxious to get on with his life.

"I'll be all right, Mam," he reassured her.

"Just remember what I told you," she murmured as she gave him a farewell hug. "Don't forget to write."

Dolly was reassured when a couple of boys came to introduce themselves to her son as she and Nathan left. He hardly seemed to notice her go as she raised her hand in farewell. As she turned to go, she missed the wistful look he gave her retreating back.

It was on the way home that her feelings overwhelmed her and she burst into tears.

"Albert will be fine," the two men hastened to comfort her.

"He's a young man now, my dear," said Nathan. "Boys grow up, and they don't always want their mothers. But he knows you're always waiting to welcome him home. He'll be back when Christmas comes."

Christmas seemed an age away for Dolly. Deep in her thoughts was the fear that Clement might be lurking around Baton Rouge. If he were alive, he would surely contact and upset her son's life. Then she tried to reassure herself that Clement was indeed dead and Amelia Kay's letter was just a tasteless joke to unsettle her. She'd met the woman twice and didn't like her anyway. With a deep sigh she hugged Nathan's arm and headed home to Marguerite, her little flower. That evening she wrote a letter to her mother Maggie, full of the joys and sorrows of being a mother. Maggie too had known all the misery of parting when Dolly had taken Albert to America.

When Albert arrived home at Christmas, he had grown taller and his figure had filled out. His once fiery red hair had darkened, and a golden bristle of moustache framed his upper lip. More than ever he resembled Clement. Dolly stared at her son. In his absence he'd become almost a stranger.

Dolly noticed him bridle when his old friends from the plantation teased him. It wasn't only his appearance that had changed. She wondered if the bigoted views of some sons of southern gentry would affect him. Gradually, as he settled back into his home, his air of superiority dissolved. As Nathan and David treated him as usual and Marguerite slavered on his suit, he discarded his air of privilege with his city clothes.

CHAPTER 19: A VISIT TO LIVERPOOL

Robert beamed as he came into the breakfast room holding up a letter on expensive-looking cream paper.

"It's from Gus," he told Jessie, handing her the letter. "He says it's high time we got together, so he's invited us over to stay with him and his family for the weekend after next. He has a ship being launched, and he thinks we'd enjoy the ceremony."

"Are all of us invited?" asked Jessie, scanning the letter.

"Oh yes. He especially mentions Helen; says he hasn't seen his goddaughter for some time. Would you like to go?"

"Oh yes, please!" shouted Helen, full of enthusiasm.

Jessie smiled at her daughter. Helen was very proud of her wealthy godfather and especially pleased to be mentioned. She'd been moping since Hadrian had returned to college. Jessie hoped a change of routine would do her good. Jessie suspected that Helen wrote to Hadrian constantly, though her daughter was disappointed that his letters were short and infrequent. Jessie hoped her daughter's infatuation and attachment to the Lightfoot family would gradually fade.

Augustus Kearsley often came to stay with the Overdales whenever he visited Manchester on business. The city hosted plenty of the engineering firms who supplied his shipyard. Robert and Jessie hadn't visited his palatial home in Liverpool since his wedding not long after their own marriage. Robert had been his best man, though he'd confessed to Jessie that he was surprised at his friend's choice of bride. The girl was the insipid daughter of a wealthy banker. Gus had previously been entangled with a beauty from the island of Nassau, the daughter of a shipping agent. He'd met the family while illegally trading with the American South during the civil war. Although the girl and her father had arrived in Liverpool with expectations, Gus's father had soon put a stop to that romance. The threat of being left penniless had brought Gus to his senses. Whenever he stayed with Robert and his family, he joked about escaping from his own. Jessie often wondered if he was actually joking, as he usually seemed reluctant to go home.

"Gus says Charles Augustus will be happy to show the young ones around. I expect the boy's lonely, being an only child," said Robert, beaming proudly at his own brood.

Jessie caught Matt and Jack grinning at each other. "And I don't want you two teasing the poor boy," she warned them. "You were both a pair of rascals last time when he came with his father. We'll be guests at his home, and you mustn't give the lad any grief. Do you hear?"

"Yes, Mama," they chorused obediently and then had a fit of sniggering.

"But he's so stupid," murmured Jack. "He believes anything you tell him."

"You've been warned," said his mother sternly. "Any tricks and you'll be sent home straight away."

"Yes, Mama," they repeated, their faces shining with an insincere innocence.

"Ignore them, Mama," said Helen. "They're very childish. I'll keep an eye on them and make sure they behave."

"Ooh, listen to Grandma," hooted Jack. "Oh, they're oh so very childish," he mimicked Helen in a silly voice.

"Mr Kearsley is my oldest friend, and I'll be very displeased indeed if you cause his son any trouble," said Robert sternly.

The boys were very rarely chastised by their father. They knew this was a final warning.

"Yes, Papa," they promised, serious at last.

The planned journey was anticipated with excitement, despite the warnings and Helen's dilemmas about which clothes to take.

They arrived by train to Liverpool and were met at the station by Gus's grand carriage. The children had never been to visit the Kearsleys before and were on their best behaviour. Helen was wearing another of her new dresses, remodelled from one of her grandmother's voluminous old gowns. Jessie was surprised and proud of the way her daughter had taken to sewing. Helen certainly had a talent for dressmaking, and her new lilac dress was very fetching as well as fashionable.

At the house Gus greeted them with his customary enthusiasm, though his wife and son were more reserved. Charles Augustus looked wary as the three Overdale children tumbled down from the carriage, Matt with a little help from the groom. Although he was unable to stand quite straight with his problems, Jessie noted that Matt was still taller than Gus's son. Like his father, Charles Augustus tended to be plump. Helen took charge of the situation and bounded up to him. She boldly took his hand and shook it vigorously.

"How lovely to see you again, Charles Augustus," she said, like a woman twice her age.

"Y-you too," said the boy, taken aback by her approach.

"How d'you do?" said Matt, following his sister's lead. He grinned at his parents to show he was making an effort to behave.

The adults greeted one another cordially. Jessie had the distinct impression that Gus's wife Amelia was not happy to be entertaining them. She was polite but cool and offered the briefest of handshakes as though her visitors had unwashed hands. Mrs Fitzpatrick, the buxom Irish housekeeper, stepped forward to introduce herself and showed them to their rooms with chatty goodwill.

"And will the boys be happy to share?" she asked.

"Yes, of course," said Jessie briskly. "Whatever's convenient. We don't want to put you out."

"Ach, you'll be no trouble at all," said the housekeeper warmly. "It'll be a nice change to have visitors. Look at this grand house now and hardly anybody in it. I'd better warn you, though, that the old missis is a bit odd these days," she told them, speaking of Gus's mother.

"I'm sorry to hear that, Mrs Fitz," said Robert. He had once been a frequent visitor to Gus's home, though rarely since his marriage.

"You'll see her at dinner," said Mrs Fitzpatrick. "The poor old soul does her best."

For what was left of the afternoon, Jessie was supervising her children in their rooms while Robert chatted to Gus in his library. They all trooped down to the dining room at the allotted time.

Old Mrs Kearsley was seated beside her son at the head of the table. "Who are all these people?" she demanded as the Overdales came to pay their respects and introduce themselves.

"It's Robert, Mother. You remember Robert, don't you?"

"Robert?" she said, shaking her head in puzzlement.

"She's a bit deaf," murmured Gus in apology.

Amelia snorted from the other end of the table.

"Never mind," said Robert politely. "Nice to see you again, Mrs Kearsley. This is Jessica, my wife, and the children." He didn't bother to give his children's names, knowing that it might just confuse the old lady.

Amelia was not happy with the company. "I should have insisted that the children eat in the nursery, but Augustus overruled me as usual," she said stiffly.

"Nonsense. Our guests are hardly children," said Gus jovially. "These are young adults, aren't you my dears? Anyway, Charles Augustus always eats his meals with us."

"And I dare say he eats plenty of them," Matt murmured to Jack beside him.

Jessie gave him a withering look.

"What did he say? What's up with the boy? Can't he speak up?" demanded Amelia. "I thought it was just his legs that are affected."

Jessie made an effort to curb her rising anger. They were so used to Matt's hesitant, quiet speech that they often forgot how others saw him.

"Our Matthew is quite shy," said Robert politely. "He's probably just overawed by the occasion."

Matt just nodded and hung his head in embarrassment. Robert gave Jessie a warning glance and she bit her tongue.

Robert and Gus began an animated conversation about the state of the country. The rest of the company fell into silence punctuated by intermittent complaints from old Mrs Kearsley.

"This meat's too tough," she grumbled.

"Would you like me to cut it up for you?" asked Jessie kindly.

"I'm not a baby," snapped Gus's mother. But she struggled with her food, and in the end she meekly allowed Jessie to help her.

After dinner, Charles Augustus was coaxed into playing the piano by his proud mother. He played a couple of timid pieces to polite applause. Helen took over the instrument and played a lively tune with a flourish, but with more enthusiasm than accuracy. She received livelier applause, especially from her brothers.

"I think perhaps you need a little more practice," commented her father with a chuckle.

The young ones were sent to bed early, and they slept well, tired after their long journey. Amelia pleaded a headache and retired. Old Mrs Kearsley was helped to bed by Mrs Fitzgerald and a maid. Left alone, Jessie felt neglected as the two old friends fell deep into conversation, and so she politely left them. She lay in bed remembering the first time she'd visited the Kearsley mansion. She and Kezia had accompanied the wounded Robert back from America. She and the freed slave had been banished to the kitchen to eat. Now she was an honoured guest — but still ignored. Musing on life's twists and turns, she slipped into sleep.

CHAPTER 20: THE LAUNCH

Next day, in their best clothes, the family went to attend the launch of the Kearsley's new ship. The adults rode in the carriage and the youngsters in a gig following. The ship to be launched was not one of the fine liners but a sturdy cargo ship for the trade in India. It was destined to sail along the newly built Suez Canal. Matt had surprised Gus the evening before by asking many pertinent questions about the ship and the canal. Though Matt's speech was quiet and halting, Gus listened patiently to the boy and answered all his questions as best he could.

"I've never sailed down the canal," he told Matt. "I had an opportunity a couple of years ago to go and see it, but of course the opening of the canal has been delayed by four years by cholera and the like and I wouldn't chance it."

"I should like to go and see it one day," said Matt. "They say it's the eighth wonder of the world."

Gus looked at him with growing admiration.

"Your lad is very determined despite his handicaps," he remarked to Robert later.

"Oh, he's stubborn like his mother," joked his friend. "He won't give up."

"He has an intelligence I never expected," said Gus. "I mean … I didn't mean to imply…" He floundered, trying to avoid insulting Robert's son.

"You needn't apologise, Gus," said Robert. "You wouldn't be the first one to underestimate Matthew. My own father barely acknowledges his intelligence. But he's got it all right."

"I wish Charles Augustus would take as much interest in our business as Matthew," admitted Gus. "But time will tell."

The launch was a wonderful affair with a band playing and bunting everywhere fluttering in a strong breeze. All the shipyard workers were lined up along the docks to see the ship sail for the first time. The public too were crowded around to see the spectacle. The ship stood motionless in the dry dock, propped up on enormous baulks of wood. It was held motionless by huge rusty chains, and Gus explained to Matt that the chains would prevent the ship sliding too quickly out into the river and becoming damaged.

Gus and his wife mounted a platform, and he handed her a bottle of champagne dangling from a rope and wreathed in flowers. "You know what to say," he prompted her.

She gave him a look of disdain and raised her chin the air. "I name this ship the *Osiris*," she cried loudly. "And God bless all who sail in her."

With that, she smashed the bottle against the ship's hull with a vehemence that surprised everyone. The crowd cheered as the baulks were driven away from the hull and the ship slipped down the muddy slope into the Mersey, slowed only by the slithering, rumbling chains.

"I think she was mentally aiming that bottle at Gus's head," Robert murmured to Jessie, and she gave him a wry smile.

Gus stopped and stared with a practised eye as his new ship bobbed upon the incoming tide. "She'll be having trials at sea for a few weeks to make sure she's seaworthy," he told Matt. "Then she'll sail out down the Suez canal with a cargo and arrive home in a few months full of tea. India is a fascinating place. The wealth of the maharajahs is a sight to behold, and yet so many of the people live in poverty. The journey to India took me months when I went the first time, and that was all the way around the Cape of Good Hope at the tip of South Africa. This canal will be a wonderful improvement to travel and cut the time in half."

"It's a pity you don't talk to your own son the way you talk to the idiot boy," murmured Amelia tartly as she passed.

Both Gus and Matt looked embarrassed at her rudeness.

"Charles Augustus doesn't seem interested," retorted Gus. "Just ignore her," he said kindly to the boy. "I apologise for her ignorance."

"There doesn't seem much love lost between Gus and his wife," said Jessie as she linked Robert's arm. "It's Charles I feel sorry for, stuck in the middle of it all."

"Yes, it's a pity Gus's father didn't let him marry Nadine. Can you imagine what a joyous occasion this would have been? She was full of life and she adored Gus."

The banquet that followed in the boardroom of Kearsley and Son was a happy occasion. Robert and Jessie were introduced to some of Gus's shareholders and the great and the good of Liverpool society who had come to celebrate the launch of the new ship. Amelia stayed aloof, talking merely to a couple of acquaintances. Jessie tried to be friendly to the woman but found her advances rebuffed. Always sociable, she had many interesting conversations with other guests. Amelia was the only one in the room who seemed to resent her for being a former mill girl.

Robert and Gus chatted about old times on the journey back to the mansion, but for Jessie the visit was strained.

CHAPTER 21: A FERRY ACROSS THE MERSEY

Next day, after breakfast, Gus gave his son some money and told him to take the Overdale children around Liverpool.

"I'll send the gig with you, of course," he told Charles Augustus. "We can't expect young Matt to walk far."

"Oh I can…" Matt was about to protest that he could walk farther that they expected, but Helen kicked his ankle.

"That would be lovely, Uncle Gus," she beamed.

The children piled aboard the spacious gig. Helen had hoped for a carriage but was satisfied with their transport nonetheless. Under Charles Augustus's supervision, the groom drove them around the city, seeing the tall ships unloading their endless cargo and the dockers swarming over them like flies.

"There is my father's shipyard," said Charles Augustus proudly.

The boys' eyes followed him along the docks to where tall cranes pierced the hazy skyline, but Helen was more interested in the people, some in fashionable dress, clambering aboard a small ship on a nearby dock.

"Where are they going?" she asked, pulling at their host's jacket.

"Oh, that's just the ferry to Birkenhead," he told her.

"Can we go?" she asked, smiling into his eyes.

He was too enchanted to deny her.

"Will you be all right wobbling about on a boat? You're wobbly enough already," Jack teased Matt.

"I'll hang on to the side," his brother told him, weighing up the situation. "Yes, I think I'll manage."

"Yes, we think we'll be all right, Charlie," said Jack with a cheeky grin.

After that the name stuck with the boys, and luckily Gus's son didn't object. He offered his arm to Helen as they boarded the ferry. The boys mingled with the crowd until Matt found a place to stay upright and watch the river. Charles Augustus guided Helen a little way away from the boys and found her a place by the rail.

"You can call me Charles," he murmured. "It's only my father who gives me my full title. I expect it's because I'm called after him. Mother only calls me 'son'. I expect that's because I'm her only one."

"Oh, that would be a blessing if you had two impudent brothers like mine," she said with a light laugh. "Sometimes they never give you a moment's peace."

"They shouldn't tease you," protested Charles. "You're so … so … pretty." A crimson blush rose up into his hairline, and he glanced away in embarrassment at his boldness.

Helen smiled to herself. She had made a conquest. "And you are…" She hesitated. Charles wasn't very handsome at all. Any fine features he may have had were lost in the plump shininess of his face. "Very distinguished," she added quickly, hoping her pause had not been too noticeable.

"I wonder if I might write to you when you return to Gorbydale?" asked Charles, emboldened by her praise.

"I should love that," said Helen, "but I'm afraid I already have a beau. He's studying at Owens College in Manchester," she added proudly. "But I should be happy to be your friend," she said, squeezing his arm in encouragement.

Charles nodded, looking disappointed. Helen flashed him a benign smile so as not to crush his aspirations altogether. While Matt and Jack took an interest in the workings of the boat and rest of the passengers, Charles hung close to Helen as she chatted amicably about everything and nothing.

Once the ferry had docked at Birkenhead, they decided to return back on the same ferry. Helen would have dearly loved to visit New Brighton along the coast.

"We have the groom and the gig waiting back in Liverpool," Charles pointed out. "And we mustn't be late for high tea or Mother will be most put out."

When they returned home, after a tour round Liverpool to see the grand new buildings, Amelia immediately noticed her son's attachment to Helen. She did not look pleased.

Mrs Fitzpatrick herded the children into the wide kitchen. "Your mother suggested it would be better for you to have your tea down here," she said with a smile. "The old missis is having one of her bad days, and you'll probably only annoy her. You'll be more comfortable down here, and Mrs Cook will look after you." She settled them at a table set up in one corner for them.

The boys were so hungry after their day in the open air that they didn't care where they ate. Helen complained that she wasn't allowed to eat with the adults, but the boys just ignored her and tucked into a plate of sandwiches without question.

"Are all cooks called Cook?" Matt asked the red-faced woman who approached them with another plate of dainty sandwiches.

"I'm sure I don't know, duck," she said with a smile. "I know I am, though my proper name's Mularky."

"Mularky!" cried Jack. "Always up for a lark."

"I don't know about that — though I'm always up with the lark," said the cook, laughing. "You look as though you're always up for a lark."

"Oh, he is," confirmed Matt, and Jack nodded vigorously, his mouth full of bread.

"Would you like more sandwiches?" she asked.

"Yes please, Cook," said Charles, though he politely offered the plate to Helen first.

To Helen's annoyance, their dinner was taken in the kitchen too. She had put on her best dress to eat all the same and was passing Gus's study when she heard his wife's strident voice. Though she knew it was wrong to eavesdrop, she silently paused by the door.

"I'm sorry, but my nerves will not stand another meal with those children. What with that boy mumbling like an idiot and that girl making eyes at my son."

"*Our* son," Gus gently corrected her, though Amelia ignored him and just snorted.

"It's bad enough having to eat while your mother is making an exhibition of herself."

"They are my guests, dear, and it is my mother's house," Gus tried to pacify her.

But she was beyond soothing. "I hope I shan't be seeing that crowd in my house again," she snapped.

"My mother's house," muttered Gus again, but he had not won the argument.

Helen was adamant she would not set foot in the house again and was determined to tell her mother about the overheard conversation. She hesitated. Her mama would be most upset to hear Matt called an idiot, and it was downright insulting to suggest that she was making eyes at Charles when she was wholly devoted to Hadrian.

Contrary to her feelings, Helen decided to disarm the obnoxious Amelia with charm. She behaved very graciously to her detractor and in the process enchanted Charles even more. His mother grimaced when he expressed a desire to accompany the family to the railway station as they left. Unfortunately for Charles, there was no room in the carriage.

In the following months, he accompanied his father to Gorbydale whenever he could, to see Helen, oblivious to her brother's teasing.

CHAPTER 22: A KISS ON THE HAND

"I'll have to report you to Hadrian," teased Dora. "I'm appalled to see you flirting with Charles Kearsley while my brother is away studying."

"I'm certainly not flirting," protested Helen. "Charles's father is my papa's oldest friend. He's practically family. You know my heart is devoted to Hadrian."

"Hmm," mused Dora. "We'll see."

Selena and Anna-Marie giggled.

"I wouldn't blame you if you did fancy that Kearsley boy," said Selena, whose father worked for an insurance company. "Charles Kearsley will be very rich one day, my pa says. His grandfather was practically a lord but for some illegal boat business with America."

Helen knew Selena had her eye on Hadrian herself and would be only too glad to divert him from Helen's affections.

"Charles Kearsley's not very handsome though, is he?" remarked Anna-Marie, glancing at Hadrian's portrait, prominent on the mantelpiece.

Helen suspected that Dora had indeed written to her brother, because Hadrian arrived home one weekend. He rarely bothered to visit his home during term time. Now Helen was invited to tea once again.

"Tea isn't quite ready yet," said Hadrian. "It's such a lovely day, perhaps we might walk in the garden."

They stepped out into warm sunshine, and Hadrian led them through a pergola to a fragrant display of roses. Almost immediately Dora made herself scarce with some flimsy excuse, and Hadrian and Helen were left alone.

"What's all this I hear about you losing your heart to a rich shipping merchant's son?" he teased her.

"A *shipbuilder's* son," she corrected him with a coquettish smile. "Oh, Charles is a darling. He's devoted to me."

"And you're devoted to him?" demanded Hadrian, looking annoyed.

Helen gave a light laugh. She had been learning to flirt and enjoyed it. She'd had plenty of opportunity to practise on Charles. It pleased her to think that Hadrian was jealous; that she was not his abject slave. All the same, she did not want to alienate his feelings for her. "Oh, you know who I'm devoted to," she said, smiling up into his eyes.

She expected Hadrian to look pleased with her confession, but for a moment he glared at her. Helen looked puzzled, but then his face softened and he was instantly his usual charming self.

"I hope you don't write to him," he said with a strained smile. "I do so look forward to your letters."

Helen's letters were chatty but, despite her overwhelming feelings for Hadrian, she did not pour her heart out to him in writing. She guessed correctly that he would probably show them to his friends. She'd had it drummed into her by her mother that a girl had to retain her modesty or men would despise her.

"It just wouldn't be right for me to write to Charles," she admitted. "Though he did ask me to."

Once again, the dark cloud passed over Hadrian's brow. He was indeed jealous, she knew and that pleased her. But in the next moment she knew she had gone too far in teasing him. She was alarmed when he turned his back on her to master his feelings. She tentatively touched his shoulder.

"Oh Hadrian, you know it's you who holds all my affections," she whispered.

In an instant he swirled round and, grasping her hand, dragged her behind a blowsy hydrangea. He grabbed her shoulders and was just about to kiss her roughly when she gasped and pulled herself from his grasp.

"Hadrian!" she cried in shock. "How could you?"

He realised he had gone too far and began his excuses. She backed away when he reached for her hand, but he persisted and took it tenderly, almost reverently, in his own. Humbly he raised it to his lips and pressed it in a gentle kiss. "I'm so sorry, Miss Overdale, dear Helen," he murmured. "I was just so overcome by my feelings for you. I could not bear to lose you to another man. Please, please forgive me. What can I do to make you forgive me?"

Helen had been shocked by his vehemence and loss of control. She was after all only sixteen and felt overwhelmed by the situation. Deep down it was thrilling to have had such an effect on her beau, but it had frightened her all the same. Now he was sorry and anxious to make amends. She softened and smiled. "You could write more letters to me," she said with a playful smile. "But you mustn't be jealous of Charles. He is a dear friend, but he does not hold my heart."

"I promise I will write more," said Hadrian, taking her hands and kissing each one. "But it's so dashed busy at college, and there's a ream of stuff to learn and study. You will forgive me if I slip up now and again, won't you?"

"We'll see," said Helen demurely. She yearned for his letters, and often when they arrived there was little in them to satisfy her.

"Perhaps you and Dora could come to town and have tea with me one day," he suggested. "I'm sure there are lots of shops you would like to visit too."

Helen's eyes lit up. There was a fabric shop in Manchester where she loved to go. All the same, she didn't want her friends to know that she made her own clothes. To see Helen wearing a dress of the fabric she'd bought would certainly give the game away. "What a splendid idea," she said. "I'm sure Dora would come with me."

His sister was certainly pleased with the plan when she arrived in the garden moments later. "Tea's ready," she said brightly. "What have you two been up to?"

"Admiring the beauty in the garden," said Hadrian smartly.

Helen was entranced. Her emotions fluctuated all through the high tea. She caught Hadrian's eyes on her many times but glanced down, modestly sipping her tea and nibbling the sandwiches and cakes in a ladylike manner. She trembled inwardly when she remembered Hadrian's passion, yet at the same time was secretly pleased that she had had such an effect on him.

For a few months his letters arrived more frequently, but the content left her sadly disappointed.

"I am aware that your mother may read my notes," he excused himself when they next met. Helen had to be satisfied with the morsels he sent.

CHAPTER 23: THE JUNIOR CLERK

"I've been watching this lad of yours, young Matt," Uncle Eli told Robert after a hearty Sunday dinner at Overdale House.

The rest of the family had settled down, but Eli suggested that he and his nephew took a stroll on the terrace to let their food settle. Robert sensed that his uncle wanted a private word away from Matthias.

"He's got a good brain on him," said Eli. "He might not be as physically able as other lads, but he'll do all right in the thinking department. Have you got any plans for him?"

Robert shook his head. "He's still being taught by Reverend Tyldesley. He's a good scholar all right."

"Do you think he'd like to come and work for me at the Endurance?" asked Eli.

Robert looked surprised. He thought for a moment. "He has problems with his writing," he said quietly. "He can write. He's good at figures and the like, but he's slow and awkward with his hands as they are. Jessie's brother John was trying to devise a pen that would be easier for him to grasp."

"A mate of mine has his daughter working for him," said Eli. "She's learning the bookkeeper's work over at the Dahlia Mill in Rawtenstall. I could get a little lass or a lad in to do the writing for our Matt, 'cos I'm sure he can work out all the figures and the costings. What do you think?"

"I can ask him," decided Robert. "Jessie doesn't want him to go college. She doesn't think he would cope, and young men can be very cruel."

"Aye, she's right there," said Eli. "I had to sack a lad the other day for some nasty trick he played on one poor soul.

Young Norbert is a bit slow, but he's a wonder with a broom and he's a help clearing up in the grounds and the mill. It's important, 'cos there's too many accidents in an untidy mill. But there's no need to be cruel to them as has problems anyway. I'd keep an eye on your lad."

Robert called Matt outside. Jessie glanced up in curiosity. The three men walked to the edge of the terrace to talk.

"This looks very serious," said Matt. "Have I done something wrong?"

"Quite the opposite, lad," said Eli with a grin. "I'm offering you the opportunity of a position at my mill. What's your opinion of working with an old codger like me, in an old and antiquated mill, and under the thumb of your grandad who's my manager?"

"Sounds perfect," said Matt, laughing. "What could you find for me to do, Uncle Eli?"

"Well, I've noticed you've got a good brain on you, and your Dad says you're good at figures. My bookkeeper Josiah Greenhalgh has been with me years, and I've noticed him slipping up a bit. He needs an assistant, and I'm thinking he'll be retiring soon. What about it?"

"I could try it out and see if it suits you," said Matt thoughtfully.

"I was thinking more if it would suit you," said Eli. "But that's a good suggestion. I told you he had a good head on him, our Robert. That's a wise thought is that, lad. I reckon we'll get on fine."

"You can ride over to the Endurance on the little cob," suggested Robert. "It's not that far."

"And there's the salary, of course," said Eli. "We'll pay you a bit less while you're learning. That's only fair on the other lads. We don't want any accusations of nepotism."

"What's that when it's at home?" asked Matt.

"Jobs for the boys," Eli told him. "Getting your family in top jobs, even when they know nowt. It causes resentment among the other workers. But I think Josiah would be glad of the help. But you'd have to be tactful, mind; make sure he doesn't feel you're pushing him out."

"I wouldn't do that, Uncle Eli. I'd just be happy to get any work," said Matt. "Me, a wage-earner! Let's go and tell Grandpapa. He thinks I'm useless."

Robert and Eli grinned at one another. Matthias had underestimated them both in the past, and they knew just how young Matt felt.

Jessie was so proud when Matt made his announcement. Helen was impressed and of course Jack teased him. He immediately asked with a grin if he might borrow money. When Matthias was told, he and Melissa gave each other a sly glance. Matt was immediately determined to prove his grandfather's doubts to be groundless.

He started work the following Monday.

"Good morning, Mr Overdale," said Jacob, shaking his hand formally. "I hope you'll be very happy working with us?"

Matt was taken aback by his grandfather's formality. "Er, good morning, Mr Davenport. I'm sure I shall," he replied, equally formal.

"Good lad," murmured Jacob. "Best keep it professional," he added with a wink.

At first Matt was set to shadowing Josiah Greenhalgh, Eli's bookkeeper. There was a lot to learn about the mill's complicated accounting methods. The old man was suspicious at first and gave Matt a hard time. But gradually, as he recognised the boy's abilities, he gave him more work to do and between them the workload eased.

"The lad's all right," Josiah confessed to Eli. "I'll feel happier going over to my sister's in Helmshore now I know my books are in good hands. When the time's right, of course. I feel I've got a bit of steam in me yet."

All the same, Josiah wasn't happy to hear that Eli intended to hire a young woman as Matt's assistant.

"The lasses are fine with the weaving," he moaned. "But with figures and such — well, I don't know."

"If a lass has got a good brain, what's the point in wasting it, I say," Eli defended his plans. "Look at Crawshaw's lass over at the Dahlia. She's doing fine. Saved her old dad a packet so I hear, after his last bookkeeper tried to diddle him."

"I just hope you're right," said Josiah gloomily.

"We must move with the times," said Eli stoutly. "And anyway, I'll be paying a lass less. That should appeal to your bookkeeper's heart."

So Miss Charity Fitch was employed to be an assistant to Matt. She was the daughter of a newly widowed mother and needed to work to help the family finances. A few years older than Matt, she had a plain but kind face. She impressed Eli with her neat writing and figures. He subtly discovered that she had no sweetheart and was not likely to leave them in the near future. So she got the job.

Charity quickly deciphered Matt's erratic writing and transposed it into orderly script. After a few weeks, even Josiah was impressed with her quiet efficiency. For all her serene demeanour, Charity had a steely heart. One morning, Matt arrived in the office looking miserable. He was usually cheerful when he arrived at the mill. He enjoyed his work and every morning, as he left his pony with Norbert, he felt a growing sense of achievement. Charity noticed his mood immediately.

"You're very quiet, Mr Overdale," she said softly. "Has something upset you?"

His very hesitation confirmed her suspicion. "No, no nothing," he denied.

"Are you sure?" she asked. "It's not like you to be miserable first thing. You usually wait until Mr Greenhalgh drops all his work on you before you lose your smile."

Matt remained quiet. He bit his lip and stared at his desk.

Charity wasn't a girl to give up easily. She liked Matt and they worked well together. She didn't like to see him troubled. "What is it that's upset you?" she tried again. "Don't they say a problem shared is a problem halved?"

He raised his head and glanced at her with a troubled smile. "It isn't the kind of problem that can be shared," he said quietly.

"Has someone upset you?" she insisted.

His silence again gave her the clue she needed.

"It isn't your Granddad Davenport, because he's very protective where you're concerned. He wouldn't upset you if he could help it. It can't be your brother, because you both tease each other all the time. Not Mr Greenhalgh, because he's very sensitive towards you because of your uncle. So is it someone else here?"

Matt reddened.

"Right," decided Charity firmly. "Then it's just a case of who."

"Please don't say anything," pleaded Matt. "I'm used to people making unkind remarks. I shouldn't have been eavesdropping — well, not really eavesdropping, but I was nearby when I heard him."

"So it's a him," said Charity thoughtfully. "It'll be that Mac Barry. He always has something to say for himself. He usually makes some tart remark whenever he sees me. I just ignore him. But I don't like the idea of him picking on you."

Matt looked alarmed. "Please don't say anything, Miss Fitch. It will only make things worse," he begged. "He was just saying as how I was a cripple and I was pushing Mr Greenhalgh out of work because I was related to Mr Gorman. Of course, I do have problems. But I do my best and help Mr Greenhalgh all I can."

"You do indeed," said Charity. "You're more of an asset to the mill than that lazy beggar. Mr Gorman only employs him in the warehouse because his mother is a widow and she worked here for years."

They both knew that Eli was very good to his loyal employees.

"Please don't say anything," Matt asked again.

"Just take no notice of him," advised Charity. "He's not worth getting upset about."

Matt nodded. He seemed relieved that, though he hadn't actually told his assistant who had mocked him, she knew and supported him.

It was a couple of days later as she made her way to the counting office that Mac Barry caught her eye.

"And how's Master Overdale's pretty nurse?" he sniggered.

She beckoned him to the side of the room with a polite smile. He mistook her demeanour for encouragement and joined her eagerly, winking over at one of his mates. He was soon enlightened. Her smile abruptly disappeared.

"If I hear that you have insulted Mr Overdale again, I shall report you to Mr Davenport and Mr Gorman shall hear of it. It's only because Mr Overdale has instructed me not to say anything that prevents me from reporting you now. You have Mr Overdale to thank for you keeping your job here, because I would have no hesitation in telling the mill manager, his grandfather, what you said. Do you understand?"

He nodded, his eyes wide with anxiety.

"And if you give me any more cheek, I shall recall and act on this threat. Right?"

"Yes Miss, sorry Miss," he said humbly.

"And I think you owe Mr Overdale an apology," she added.

"Yes Miss, sorry Miss."

Matt was surprised when Mac Barry arrived at the door of his office clutching his cap in his hands.

"Sorry, Mr Overdale," he mumbled and rapidly disappeared.

"Did you say something to Mac Barry?" Matt asked Charity.

She concentrated on sharpening her pencil. "Some things have to be done," she said primly. "He won't give you or me any trouble again."

Matt had found a friend and champion. Together the two companions worked well, and Matt thrived on his work for the Endurance. Even his writing improved.

CHAPTER 24: MELISSA

Jessie was just coming out from the kitchen when she heard the heavy thud and the cry. She rushed to the bottom of the staircase, where she found Melissa lying prone along the carpet. She seemed dazed and stared up at Jessie in confusion.

"Are you all right, Mother-in-law?" asked Jessie, kneeling beside her, though it was plainly obvious that Melissa wasn't.

Melissa just groaned and closed her eyes.

Jessie ran to the kitchen corridor and called loudly for help. Her cries alerted Lizzie, who emerged from the dining room. Cook and Maggie hurried from the kitchen.

"Whatever's the matter, Mrs Jessie?" asked the cook as she came into the hallway. Then she spotted Melissa's dress crumpled at the bottom of the stairs. "Oh dear me, it's the mistress. Is she badly hurt?"

"I can't tell yet," Jessie told her. "I've only just found her. She seems to have knocked herself out. We'd better get the doctor."

"I'll go," volunteered Lizzie. "I'll be quickest."

"Go and see Michael at the stables," suggested Jessie. "He can go for the doctor on Robert's mare." She felt her mother-in-law's pulse. "Her heart's still beating," she said. "Melissa, can you hear me?"

A faint groan issued from Melissa's lips.

"Should we get her up to bed?" asked Cook.

"No, not until the doctor has seen her," said Jessie. "She may have broken something." She'd seen too many factures worsened by moving the patient in her time nursing.

"Shall I go for Master Overdale and Mr Robert?" asked Maggie timidly.

"Oh, would you? Thank you, Maggie," said Jessie, glancing up at her. "Try not to alarm them. Just say she's had a fall."

Left alone with the cook, she tried again for some response from Melissa but with little success. Lizzie hurried back into the house.

"Michael's gone right away," she said. "He didn't even stop to put on a saddle."

Despite her worries, Jessie noticed that Lizzie's face was flushed crimson and assumed it was because she'd been rushing.

It wasn't long before Robert arrived, followed by Matthias, puffing with effort.

"What happened?" asked Robert.

Jessie shook her head in uncertainty. "I heard a thump and found your mother here at the foot of the stairs. She must have fallen down, but I don't know how far down. She's alive, but I can't get any response from her. She must have hit her head."

"Let's get her up to bed, then," Matthias butted in and bent down to help.

"No, no you mustn't." Jessie laid a restraining hand on his arm.

"She'll be much more comfortable in bed," asserted Matthias, annoyed at being checked.

"If she has broken anything, especially her back, we would make things worse by moving her," said Jessie firmly. "Believe me, I know. We must wait for the doctor. Lizzie, would you go and fetch a blanket to keep Mrs Overdale warm?"

Lizzie hurried away on her task as Matthias stepped back, grumbling 'better in bed'.

It wasn't until Doctor Andrew arrived that he stopped complaining to Robert.

"You've done the right thing, keeping her still," the doctor told Jessie. "I must check if there's anything broken." They watched anxiously as he checked all her limbs. "Mrs Overdale's limbs seem intact. I'm unable to check her spine through her clothes and corset. Is there anything I can use as a stretcher?" he asked Michael, who had stayed to help if he could.

It was at that moment Jessie turned and noticed Lizzie move away from the groom's side, and she began to wonder.

Michael thought for a moment. "There's a hurdle in the stables that might do. I'll go and fetch it."

As he hurried away, he glanced back at Lizzie and a faint smile curved the girl's lips. Jessie's suspicions were confirmed. Lizzie loved Michael, and by the warm look he gave her in return, their love was mutual. Jessie was pleased for them.

When he returned, they very gently lifted Melissa onto the wooden hurdle. She gave a sharp cry as she was moved, though her eyes were closed fast and she showed no signs of waking up. Matthias darted forward and clutched her hand.

"We're here, Lissy dear," he cried. "We'll have you right in no time. We'll try not to hurt you."

Carefully carrying the hurdle, they moved awkwardly up the stairs, Matthias still holding Melissa's hand firm. Jessie hurried ahead to organise the bedroom. On the bedside cabinet she noticed the cursed bottle of laudanum. Melissa had seemed quite normal at breakfast, but Jessie wondered if she had slipped upstairs to take a sly dose of her tincture. She wondered whether she should have moved the bottle to save Melissa's dignity but thought better of it. When Doctor Andrew had entered the room, he had glanced at the bottle too. Though he had frowned, he had said nothing.

Gingerly they laid the hurdle on the bed and with some awkward manoeuvring, managed to slide Melissa's prone body onto the mattress. She was still unconscious, but small whimpers escaped from her as they worked.

Doctor Andrew removed her lace cap and examined her head as best he could.

"Will she live?" asked Matthias anxiously.

The doctor gave him a sympathetic smile. "I won't know until I can find where she's hurt," he said. "I'm afraid I can't promise you anything. I suspect she's fallen on her head and is concussed. We will have to wait and see if she wakens. She may be able to tell us where she hurts and if she's able to move her limbs."

"Should I send for Doctor Braddock? Will he know?" demanded Matthias tactlessly.

"No one can know until we can examine her properly," insisted the doctor. "Her pulse is very weak. You could try putting smelling salts under her nose to bring her round, but if she is concussed that will make no difference. And if she wakes, she may be in a lot of pain."

"What about the juice of the poppy?" asked Matthias, anxious to do something.

Doctor Andrew picked up the bottle of laudanum and showed it to him. "It may be the juice of the poppy that has caused this accident," he said sternly. "It dulls the senses, and your wife may not have been quite alert as she descended the stairs."

"But it's only a drop of tincture," blustered Matthias.

"It's highly addictive," the doctor told him. "Who prescribed this for her?"

Matthias was silent, knowing well it might have been Doctor Braddock. When her father-in-law left the room for a moment, Jessie urgently whispered to the doctor.

"I was worried that Melissa was having too much," she said quietly. "I didn't like the way it made her so drowsy. I suggested she should cut down, but my mother-in-law refused. Her niece Honora suggested I watered it down with some wine, and I did that. Then she just seemed to take more."

The doctor nodded. "I've witnessed this so many times in my patients. Let's hope that for the moment it eases her pain, but to withdraw from the foul stuff is painful indeed."

Matthias was reluctant to leave his wife, but Jessie persuaded him to go while she and Lizzie gently removed Melissa's dress and loosed her corset under the doctor's supervision. He hoped that the corset might hold her spine in place until he could examine it better. Melissa moaned and groaned, her face contorted in pain, but not once did she open her eyes.

"I can't say I'm happy with how limp her legs seem," murmured the doctor, feeling for the pulse in Melissa feet.

Jessie touched her legs. They were icy. "Should I get a hot water bottle, do you think?" she asked.

"It might help," said the doctor with a sigh.

When the women had finished, Robert fetched a chair for his father and the old man began his vigil beside Melissa, holding his wife's limp hand. He refused anything to eat but accepted a cup of tea from Jessie.

The others took turns to sit beside him, quietly watching for any signs of life in the patient. Doctor Andrew promised to call again in the morning, and they promised to call him if there was any improvement in Melissa's condition.

"I think we should send for Braddock," said Matthias when Robert came to sit beside him after supper.

"It's that old fool that's got her into this mess in the first place with his damn tincture," growled Robert.

"Don't swear in front of your mother," snapped Matthias, but he had heard his son's protest.

There was no more mention of Braddock.

Through the night the family took turns to keep vigil beside Melissa's bed until they were too tired to stay awake. Matthias refused to go to bed, but in the morning he opened his eyes to find a blanket wrapped round him. Jessie smiled at him across the bed.

"Would you like a cup of tea, Father-in-law?" she asked. "Maybe you could eat a small bowl of porridge? You need to keep your strength up for when Melissa is better."

"Do you think she'll get better?" he asked, his eyes bleary with unshed tears.

"It's in the hands of God now," said Jessie, anxiously gazing at the inert body of her mother-in-law. She had been praying all her waking moments. "But she does seem to be sleeping more than unconscious, somehow. Look, she seems to be snoring gently."

Matthias stared intently at his wife. "Aye, happen you're right. The doc will be able to tell us when he arrives. I will have a drop o' tea and a spoon or two of porridge, then. I'm fair clemmed," he admitted. He moved a little in his chair. "By heck, I'm that stiff an' all."

"We could bring the day bed into the room if you'd like?" suggested Jessie, ever practical. "Then you can have a lie down if you're feeling tired."

He nodded. "Aye, all right. But I'm not leaving her," he asserted.

"I know. But you need your rest too," she said as she left to arrange things.

There was little progress all the next day. Doctor Andrew called in the morning and again tested Melissa's legs and ankles. By the grim expression on his face, Jessie knew there was no progress. She too had felt the icy flesh and noted the missing pulse.

It was nearly lunchtime when Doctor Braddock came blustering into the room. "And how is my patient?" he demanded. He dropped his bag on Melissa's dressing table and marched towards the bed.

"She's not to be moved," growled Matthias, glaring at Braddock.

"Nonsense. I know what's best for…"

He got no further. Matthew put a firm hand in front of him. "Like that bloody tincture!" he said, completely forgetting his reprimand to his son.

"It was merely for nerves," blustered the doctor. "A little drop now and again is…"

"Highly addictive, I've been told. My Melissa never had no 'nerves'. Remember how she faced that mob at the workhouse? Nerves! Poppycock!"

Hearing the row, Jessie hurried into the room. "Perhaps you would like to come down for a cup of tea, Doctor Braddock," she said quietly.

"No, no, I must see my patient," began the doctor.

"Doctor Braddock, I insist you come down for a cup of tea." Jessie's gaze was steely, and for a moment the doctor wavered.

"Very well, then," he said, tilting his nose in the air. "On your head be it."

She led him into the morning room.

"Doctor Andrew's orders are that Mrs Overdale should not be moved except under strict supervision. He suspects that her spine may be broken. And I suspect that too," she added.

"You? How on earth would a chit like you know?" protested Braddock.

Jessie bridled. She was a competent wife and mother of three children. She was not going to be called a chit by anybody. She visibly swelled to her full height. "Because I served as a nurse in a military hospital in Washington during the war with the American South," said Jessie firmly. "I dare to suggest that I have seen more damaged bones than you, doctor, hundreds and hundreds of them, including spines. Many men damaged by cannon fire. Mrs Overdale's legs and feet are deathly cold. I can feel no pulse in her feet. She must not be moved."

"So between you and that impudent puppy my nephew, you have decided…"

"I venture to suggest that Doctor Andrew has learnt many new improved techniques developed in the medical schools since you were a student — all those many years ago," she reminded him. "I certainly trust him, and I'm sure my husband and father-in-law do too."

Faced by her vehement opposition, the doctor backed down. "Well, I bid you good day then," he said, firmly placing his hat on his head. "No doubt you will need me before the week is out."

As it happened there was no need of the doctor, or any doctor. In the lonely hours of the following morning, Matthias woke with a jolt to find his wife silent and cold. Robert sat holding his mother's hand on a silent watch.

"Why didn't you wake me?" demanded his father.

"It only happened a few moments ago," explained Robert, wiping a tear from his eye with his free hand. He could not let go of Melissa, as if he might yet feel a faint pulse. "I didn't want to let go of her hand in case there was any sign of life. But I'm so sorry, Papa; I think she's gone."

"She can't be," wailed Matthias, desperately clutching Melissa's cold and lifeless hand.

Jessie, woken from a fitful sleep by her father-in-law's cries, hurried in wearing her nightdress and wrapped in a quickly snatched shawl. She checked Melissa for a pulse and nodded to Robert. "She's gone," she confirmed. "God rest her soul."

The old man was inconsolable. Robert and Jessie hovered like wraiths around him as he gave in to his grief. They carried on the work of the home and the mill in a state of numbness themselves. Trying to coax him to eat was hopeless. It was hard for them all to grasp that Melissa was gone.

Doctor Andrew arrived and examined her body and, in his uncle's presence, confirmed that her back was indeed broken and that she had also damaged her neck in the fall. He wanted no doubts as to why she had died, and Doctor Braddock reluctantly agreed with him. Matthias nodded at their conclusions, barely hearing the words.

"I should send for Honora," suggested Jessie to Matthias.

He looked affronted. "I'm not having that ungrateful…" he began, but Jessie stopped him.

"Melissa came to see Honora when she came home and stayed with Eli," she told him. "She didn't say anything to you because she knew you'd be upset. But they made their peace. You must know that Melissa loved Honora for her sister's sake. Please let her come?"

He stared at her for a moment with red-rimmed eyes. "Aye, all right then," he sighed. "She's a right to pay her respects to her aunt. Honora was good to her, and I reckon she was fond of the girl too. Tell her to come, then."

"Oh thank you, Father-in-law," said Jessie.

To Matthias's surprise, she gave him a grateful kiss on the cheek.

Jessie went straight away to write and convey the sad news to her friend. Honora wrote back immediately and promised to come.

I'm so glad we made our peace before my aunt died, she added at the end of her reply. *I'm only sorry she could not understand my longing to become a doctor and the sacrifices I have had to make to follow my calling.*

Jessie and Helen set about looking for mourning clothes for the funeral. Jessie found her old black dress in the bottom of a trunk.

"It certainly won't fit me anymore," she decided, holding it against herself. "Will it fit you, dear?"

Helen looked critically at the old-fashioned garment. Though she loved to have new clothes, black wasn't a colour she'd have chosen. Yet she had to look respectable at her grandmother's funeral. She twisted the garment around, scrutinising the stitching, estimating the amount of fabric. "I think I could do something with this now we've got the sewing machine," she decided.

"Good girl," said Jessie warmly. "We can't really afford new clothes just yet. Now I'll see what we've got in Grandmama's chest. She didn't often wear black, but I know she's got some black frock somewhere."

Conscious of Matthias's feelings, she asked his permission to look in his deceased wife's wardrobe. There she found a black dress that might be suitable. It was very loose when she tried it on but, like her daughter, she knew it could be altered. Once the evening meal was finished, they commandeered the dining table and spent the evening companionably altering their dresses.

Jessie merely altered her dress to fit her, regardless of the fashion. She was sure she could hide any of the old-fashioned details beneath the black silk shawl she found among Melissa's things. Helen, though, had almost dismantled her mother's old dress, carefully unpicking the tiny hand stitches. Jessie watched with some regret, remembering the nights she'd spent sewing before her mother's funeral. In silent admiration she saw Helen poring over the sewing machine and refashioning the swathes of material until she produced something very becoming.

"You know, you have a real talent for fashion," said Jessie as Helen tried on the dress.

She smiled as Helen preened and posed in front of her grandmother's cheval mirror, the only full length mirror in the house.

"That dress is beautiful, as nice as anything in a Manchester shop. I'm really proud of you," she told her daughter. "It's such a pity that it's in black. I don't suppose many people at the funeral will notice it."

Helen smiled to herself. There was one person she wanted to impress, and she was sure the black dress would make her look more mature.

CHAPTER 25: PRECIOUS THINGS

The mill was closed on the day of Melissa's funeral. Honora arrived with Eli, supporting the old man in his grief.

"She were a good 'un," he said, shaking Matthias's and Robert's hands as he joined them behind the coffin. "One of the best."

Jack walked behind the hearse, following his grandfather and father. He looked young and anxious, walking solemnly beside his Grandad Jacob.

Honora joined Jessie in the black-draped carriage that followed the hearse. Matthias had insisted that Matt travelled with them.

"I don't want folk staring and pointing at him," he grumbled, although his grandson was often seen about the town.

Matt was such a frequent sight that few people even bothered to notice him, except to mention his nice manners and friendly lopsided smile.

The crowds gathered in and around the church and in respectful silence witnessed Melissa's last journey. Many were weeping. She had been popular in the town and supported the workers in their troubles. She'd even faced an angry mob to set their grievances right. The sewing classes for the unemployed girls in her own home had been very popular. She'd insisted that the Relief Committee gave money to help poor folk redeem their blankets from the pawn brokers in that cold winter during the cotton famine. All these things were remembered and discussed in the homes and shops and alehouses of Gorbydale. Her name was blessed around the town.

Honora looked nervous as Robert and Jessie insisted she come back for the funeral meal at Overdale House. "Do you think it will be all right?" she asked.

They nodded in agreement.

Matthias greeted her at the door.

"I'm so very sorry for your loss," she said as she tentatively offered her hand. "My aunt was so kind. I will miss her terribly. Everyone will miss her."

"Aye," said Matthias. "Aye." It was as if he'd lost his power of speech, but to her surprise he gave her a hug.

The funeral was a very grand affair that Jessie knew would have greatly gratified Melissa.

Honora had to catch the evening train back to Manchester, and Jessie accompanied her to the station in Eli's gig. She'd had little time to talk to her friend as she dispensed the hospitality required for the day among the invited mourners.

"Couldn't Arden come?" Honora asked Jessie shyly. "I was talking to John and Elsie, but I didn't see him."

Jessie smiled. Perhaps her friend still had feelings for her brother, and it was such a shame that Arden had lost his faith in Honora. He'd never married, although he mentioned meeting different women on his travels when Jessie pressed him.

"He's on the other side of the Atlantic at the moment. Eddie is taking exams and couldn't come either. He's hoping to graduate as a schoolmaster this summer." She added her news about her younger brother so that Honora wouldn't feel too embarrassed for showing interest in Arden. "How are things at the hospital?"

"We're very busy. And we're gradually getting there, despite the setbacks," admitted Honora. "We have many girls come to be trained as doctors, but some are discouraged by the opposition and the difficulty of the training. The more determined students seem to be older women who have already trained as nurses. At least they know what to expect."

"Like you and me," said Jessie with a smile. "But I honestly couldn't have faced all the study and hardship you've endured."

"You have a family to support, and I daresay a business too, by Robert's side."

"That's true," admitted Jessie. "But the family are growing up. They don't need me as much as they did. Matt is now a working man, and Helen looks on me as something ancient. She's always been an independent madam. Now Jack is at the grammar school, he has to travel to Manchester by train each day. He keeps mithering his father to go as a boarder. But we don't have the money for school fees at present. Matthias is on at him to go for a scholarship."

"He'll be fine," said Honora. "He's a bright lad. And his future's assured with the mill."

"Let's hope so," said her friend.

Jessie hugged Honora before she boarded the train. It seemed strange that once she'd been Honora's companion, inferior in social status, but now they felt like sisters in all but name.

"Don't forget to write," she called as she waved her friend goodbye.

Matthias was lost in grief for weeks, despite Jessie's coaxing. One morning, he ventured with Robert towards the mill but returned home almost straightaway.

"I've had a breath of fresh air anyways," he muttered to Jessie as she hurried to help him down from the gig.

Then he retreated to his study and only emerged for meals. He ate little and visibly shrank before the eyes of the family.

Finally he decided that something must be done with his wife's belongings. He brought her jewellery box down to his study and summoned the family. "I'd like you and Helen to have her precious things," he told Jessie. "Maybe you might choose something to send to Honora in remembrance of her aunt." Reverently he opened the pretty japanned box. Then his mouth dropped open. "There's nowt here," he gasped. "What's happened to all that nice stuff I bought her? I asked her why she didn't wear her necklaces, and she said she had trouble with the clasps. But where are they?"

Jessie moved beside him and peered into the box. It was indeed empty but for some folded pieces of paper. She gently picked one out and carefully unfolded it.

"It's a pawn ticket," she said in surprise. "It's from some firm in Liverpool, and it says…" She murmured the writing as she read then handed it to Matthias.

"I can't read it, lass. I haven't got me spectacles," he said, his once strong Lancashire accent revived by his grief. "What's it say?"

"It's a list of her jewellery," said Jessie cautiously.

"What's the date?" asked Matthias.

Jessie told him.

"Aye, that's about right," said Matthias wearily. "I know where her stuff's gone. The mortgage was due. She said she'd go to Liverpool to see old man Kearsley to ask if he'd cash them Confederate dollars for me. I thought at the time she'd got a lot for them. Them dollars that Clement Duplege paid me with were virtually worthless. I thought Kearsley was just being generous, feeling sorry for me. No, it was Melissa who was generous, giving up her precious things for me, to save the mill. God rest her soul." He began to cry, and Helen hurried to his side and put her arm round his shoulder.

"You mustn't cry for Grandmama," she coaxed him. "She's in a better place now. And she saved the mill for you. That's all the more precious to us now."

He nodded sadly. "Aye, you're right, pet. I'm just crying for meself. What will I do without her?"

"You've got us to support you," said Helen. "We'll always be here to look after you."

"I'm the one who should be looking after you, pet," said Matthias, stroking her hair. "But I'm growing old now, an old broken-down workhorse. Only fit to follow your grandmamma to the grave." He looked ready to weep again.

"Nonsense, Papa," said Robert, trying to rally him. "In a week or so, you'll be at the mill, wondering what a mess I've made of it in your absence."

Matthias gave a wan smile. They both knew that the mill was running quite smoothly without him. "Aye, happen you're right," he admitted. "But maybe I'll give it a day or two. I wouldn't want to be crying like a babby in front of the workers. But I'm that shaken up by your mother's…"

Jessie was distressed to see the once strong Matthias reduced to misery. She'd felt the same debilitating grief when her mother Nellie died. But Jessie was practical above all things. She rallied the family and ran the house efficiently as ever, as she had done during Melissa's descent into laudanum addiction. She treated Matthias with as much sympathy as she could muster, although she despaired at his lack of progress. Her father Jacob had grieved for her mother Nellie but supressed his sorrow by keeping busy.

"Why don't you go fishing with Eli?" she asked one morning. She'd been racking her brain to think of something to revive her father-in-law and something her son had mentioned gave her an idea. "Matt tells me Eli likes to go fishing on the Gorby whenever he can now he's semi-retired. Father manages the mill mostly these days."

"What, in that mucky river?" protested Matthias.

"Matt says he goes up the valley where there's no mills and the water's clean. It would be a breath of fresh air for you," she suggested.

Matthias sat staring into space for a few moments. "Aye, that might be an idea. We used to go fishing in the Gorby when we were nippers, me and Eli and your Dad. Your Dad pulled me out once when I'd been a bit bold at the edge of the bank and fell in. Saved my life, he did, by grabbing the top of me hair. It hurt like billy-o, mind, but at least I wasn't drowned. When I arrived home like a drowned rat, my Dad took us all to the river and made sure we could swim. Aye — happy days."

Jessie had heard this story from her father numerous times but never from Matthias's mouth. "Shall I ask Uncle Eli then?" she tried.

"Happen I'll go over and see him meself," said Matthias thoughtfully. "I'll see what tackle he's using. I've got some old stuff in the attic somewhere. That's if it's fit to use."

Jessie was pleased to see some spark of enthusiasm in him. From the large window in her parlour, she watched him trudging slowly down the valley towards the old Endurance Mill. As he reached the main street he visibly straightened up, keeping up appearances among the townsfolk. When Matt arrived home from work, he told her how his grandfather had arrived at the mill to see Eli.

"He saw me working at my desk," he told his mother, "and he said 'I'm glad to see you're making yourself useful'. I think they've arranged to go fishing in a couple of days, if the weather's fine."

Jessie was pleased that Matthias was at last taking some notice of her son. "How are you getting on with Charity Fitch?" she asked, looking away and pretending to be busy. She had noticed her son taking an unusual amount of time tidying his hair in the mirror a couple of mornings before he went to work. She'd become curious as to how her son was coping at Eli's mill with a girl as an assistant.

"Oh, she's grand," said Matt with a secret smile to himself. "A real help. She's showing me how to hold the pen a different way, see if I can make my figures clearer. She wraps some wadding round it to make it easier to hold. She's grand."

"Oh good," said Jessie with relief.

She could not know that Matt thought Charity so much more than grand. He loved to watch her poring over the figures as she tried to decipher his scrawl to translate them into her own neat columns. He even enjoyed her good-natured scolding when she struggled to recognise a number. Matt assessed himself in the tall mirror of his wardrobe and sighed. He wasn't a bad looking lad, inheriting some of his father's good looks, but his ready smile was lopsided. He walked with difficulty, his gait awkward and clumsy, especially when he was tired. Norbert had to help him onto the pony at the end of the day. What could he offer a sweet girl like Charity? He wouldn't even dare. It would be unlike her to laugh at him, but when she rejected any of his advances it would cause embarrassment between them, and he would hate her to leave the mill because of him. She needed her wages to keep herself and her widowed mother. Matt had to be content to quietly admire his secret love.

CHAPTER 26: A FISHING EXPEDITION

Matt had never mentioned the incident with Mac Barry to anyone in the family, keeping that embarrassing moment firmly to himself. Only he, Charity Fitch and Mac knew of it. Charity never mentioned it either. Always encouraging and continually trying to help Matt improve his writing, she carried on work with quiet efficiency. Charity treated Matt in much the same way Helen did, a way that could only be described as friendly tolerance. But she was protective too. She even suggested to Mr Greenhalgh that he was leaving too much of his work to Matt. He eyed her with affronted surprise but said nothing. All the same, Matt's workload decreased.

His champion remained ever vigilant for any slight to the boy who was technically her superior. Matt had no notion of treating her as inferior. He treated her as a friend. Every day he looked forward to seeing her.

On the other hand, he treated Mac Barry with caution. He had a distinct impression that the other boy still sniggered behind his back, but to Matt's face he was deferential. His mates must have heard of the incident because they began to show Matt a grudging respect.

Eli and Jacob watched their progress with quiet amusement.

"You did right by our Matt there," Jacob told his boss. "He's coming on grand."

"He's a good lad," said Eli. "I can trust him with the figures, and the lass is doing well translating them. I'm pleased with them both. Josiah Greenhalgh is pleased with them too. Like me, he's happy to delegate and that's what I'll be doing to you more in the future. Matthias is coming over today and we're going fishing."

"Lovely day for it," said Jacob enviously.

"Aye, it'll get him out of the house," said Eli with a sigh. "Perhaps it'll chivvy him up. Remember we used to have some fun when we were lads, dabbling about in the river. Mind it was a damn sight cleaner when we were nippers."

"It's not so bad higher up the valley," Jacob told him. "I was up there with the Rambling Club the other week."

It wasn't long before Matthias appeared. He'd arrived in his gig with Michael driving and all his ancient gear piled in the back.

"I didn't realise it was an expedition," Eli murmured to Jacob. "I was hoping for just a couple of rods and a bit of bait."

They set out anyway once Eli had retrieved his rods from his office.

The day was warm and they left the gig on an old drovers' road and scrambled down the riverbank. Michael followed with Matthias's rods and tackle.

"Me leg was playing me up," Matthias excused himself to Eli when he'd seen his brother-in-law's glance of disbelief.

They settled themselves down and Michael left, promising to return for them later.

"How are you keeping, then?" asked Eli. "I know it must be hard."

"Damn hard," grunted Matthias. "The whole house speaks to me of her. The mill reminds me of all the times she supported me. She saved it with her jewellery, you know. She flogged her precious bits and pieces to save the mill."

"Aye, our Robert mentioned it," said his brother-in-law. "You could have come to me, you know. I had a bit put by."

Matthias looked at him. In the misty sunlight over the river he could see the resemblance between the brother and sister, the soft crown of white hair, the plump cheeks and the kind, intelligent eyes. To Eli's embarrassment, Matthias began to cry.

"It were pride," he said. "Damn pride. I thought I were king of the valley. But I were nothing but an old fool. I wanted her to be the queen, but she ended up without a bit of jewellery except her wedding ring. An old fool, that's what I was," he added bitterly.

"But the mill's doing all right?" queried Eli, patting his back in sympathy. "Now cotton's back on track, you'll be picking up?"

"I wish I was," sighed his brother-in-law. "I got a bit behind with the mortgage during the war. Taylor Walmsley put money into the business and now he wants it back. I don't know where I'm going to get that from. He's in India at the moment. Says he's trying to improve the cotton quality so we're not reliant on the American crop. But I reckon, and so does Robert, that he's trying to track down his wife and that plant fella she ran off with."

"Well, if he's gallivanting round India, he won't want his money just yet, then," said Eli with a grin. "It's a big place."

Matthias just sighed and put his head in his hands.

Eli began to prepare his rod for a cast and tied a lead weight to the line. Then he attached his bait. He swung his rod in a graceful arc and the line arched high over the river and fell into the lazily flowing water with a loud splash.

Beside him there was another splash, but a louder, larger, more disturbing splash.

"You old fool!" shouted Eli as he grabbed for the disappearing head of Matthias.

The hair flowed up through the murky water as it floated away, and Eli had no choice but to fling his rod away and jump in after the sinking body of his brother-in-law. Lunging forward, he managed to hook his arm round his friend's neck and haul his head spluttering from the churning water.

"Let me be," gasped Matthias.

"Shut up and kick your legs or you'll have us both under," snapped Eli. "Do you want my drowning on your conscience before you meet your maker?"

Faced with that prospect, Matthias could do nothing but co-operate.

They reached the bank and Eli grabbed a branch from an overhanging tree that was trailing in the river. He hauled them both to the side. As he clung grimly to the branch, he managed to push Matthias to safety and then scrambled up through the scratching foliage himself.

"What the bloody hell were you thinking of?" he snarled. "You nearly got us both drowned."

"You should have left me," whimpered Matthias. "I wanted to be with Lissy."

"And what do you think the family would have thought of me, leaving you to drown? Lucky I was always the better swimmer or we'd have both had it."

"I'm sorry, Eli. I'm right sorry. I was just… I was just…" Matthias couldn't finish. He just gave way to his grief.

Eli put an arm around him. "Never mind, owd lad, we're both safe now. I know just how you feel. I felt the same way when I lost my Ruth. I thought there was no point in living."

Matthias stared at him in surprise. "You mean that lass you were engaged to years ago?"

"Aye. When I lost her to diphtheria, I thought my world had ended," admitted Eli, staring far into the past.

"An' you never found another?" queried his friend, shaking his head in disbelief.

"Not to match her, no. Aye, and there were plenty trying to charm me when I was younger, but they couldn't match my Ruth. I admit I had thought to do away with myself just like you. But I thought about me Mam and Dad and me sisters. They'd have been devastated. It would have ruined their lives too. They didn't deserve that. And neither do your lot. So I just thought I'd try and do a bit of good in the world, just like Ruth would have had me do."

"You do that, all right. The locals think you're some kind of saint," snorted Matthias.

"Some saint — with a rusty, battered halo!" joked Eli. "But look at us, though. We're like a right couple of drowned rats. I don't know how we're going to explain all this — do you? A big fish dragged us in, do you think?" he suggested with a chuckle. "We saw a mermaid and she lured us in?"

"That's the sea," muttered Matthias, looking pathetic.

"Oh aye, so they wouldn't believe that one, then!" remarked Eli.

Matthias glanced up and noticed his friend's grinning face. Then they both set off laughing.

"A ruddy mermaid!" said Eli, gasping with laughter. "'Scuse the language."

They both laughed until they were exhausted at the absurdity of it all. Eli took a deep breath.

"Come on, let's get dried a bit before we get pneumonia," he suggested, wiping his eyes.

They staggered to their feet and trailed back to where they'd left their equipment. It was a surprising way away, although the river appeared to be moving so slowly. Chivvied by Eli, Matthias had to shape himself. They wrung out whatever clothes they could easily do and before long they heard the jingle of harness along the road.

Michael was surprised at their appearance. Eli mumbled something about 'a bit of an accident'. The groom wrapped Matthias in an old horse blanket and gave his jacket to Eli. Then they drove to Mill House, where the housekeeper Mrs Corbett sorted them both out so they could send Matthias home looking respectable. Eli was surprised that his clothes fit his brother-in-law. He hadn't realised how much weight Matthias had lost in his grief. Mrs Corbett gave them both a searching look when they cobbled together some excuse for their appearance.

The two men sat by the fire, thoughtfully sipping a reviving brandy.

"Please don't mention this to anyone," Matthias pleaded.

"Well, promise me you won't try anything so daft again, then," demanded Eli. "Do you think Melissa would have wanted the shame of you drowning yourself on the family?"

"No, she wouldn't," admitted his brother-in-law wearily. "I promise I won't do anything so foolish again."

"Very well then, I won't say owt," promised Eli. He paused for a serious moment. "But I'll have to think twice about taking you fishing again. You frightened off all the fish!"

Despite their scare and the awful consequences the two old friends could have faced, they began to laugh. They laughed even harder when Mrs Corbett arrived with more brandy. She gave them both an incredulous stare and shook her head as she walked away.

CHAPTER 27: THE INVITATION

Helen watched Jessie carefully open the letter that Lizzie had brought to the breakfast table.

"It isn't Honora's writing, or Arden's spidery hand," she said, glancing at the envelope. She quickly skimmed through the note.

"Oh, we're invited to John and Elsie's for Sunday tea to celebrate Eleanor's engagement." Then she read the letter with more care. "Eleanor is becoming betrothed to someone called Reginald Pemberton. It seems he's a lad who works with John at the railway engineering works. He was one of our John's apprentices, and he's a good lad, our John says, honest and sober. How old is Eleanor now? She seems very young to be thinking of getting engaged."

"She's nineteen," said Helen. "She's two years and a bit older than me."

"So she is," said her mother. "She seems younger. I expect she'll wait a year or two to get married. Although Elsie was very young."

"Oh Mama, what does age matter?" snapped Helen. "If you're ready to get married, you're ready."

Her father laughed. "Listen to the voice of experience, my dear," Robert chided Jessie with a grin. "Luckily, she doesn't know the half of it. Marriage is a very serious business, my pet, as you'll no doubt find out one day."

Helen scowled. Hadrian Lightfoot was home from college, and she was fretting that she hadn't yet received an invitation to tea at the Lightfoots' house. She'd watched the letter arrive with eager anticipation, only to have her hopes dashed. Now she'd learnt that her unassuming cousin Eleanor was about to get engaged. She chafed to go to the Lightfoots' but didn't want to seem too eager. The very day before, Sabina and Anna-Marie had called at Overdale House, giggling with gossip.

"We just called to see Dora, but the maid wouldn't let us in," said Sabina, grinning at Anna-Marie. "Very hoity-toity she was too. 'Miss Dora Lightfoot is not at home to visitors today,' says she."

"I expect she got her monthlies," decided Anna-Marie. "She's always a miserable b… very irritable when she's got the curse."

"Would your friends like to stay for tea?" asked Jessie, popping her head around Helen's bedroom door.

"Yes please," chorused the girls.

They were always assured of a good feed at Overdale House, although it didn't hold the attraction of Hadrian Lightfoot.

Helen had planned to brood in her bedroom on her lack of invitation to the Lightfoot house, but instead she went along with her mother's suggestion. While her friends chattered and chewed, she thought about her dilemma. She decided then that she wouldn't risk the humiliation of being turned away from the Lightfoots' door.

It was frustrating, especially since she'd heard of her cousin's engagement. Eleanor was a milliner, making silk flowers for hats. She always wore the latest in bonnets, which framed her golden curls around her pretty face. Here was Helen, frustrated in seeing the man she wanted to dedicate her life to. He hadn't even written to say he was coming home. If she'd spoken of her love to her friends or her mother, they might have pointed out to the besotted girl that Hadrian didn't seem as ardent as she was. Helen constantly made excuses to herself for her beau.

When Sunday came, the family went as usual to church in the morning. Matthias hadn't joined them since his wife's death. As they entered into the hushed portals of the church, Helen immediately glanced to where the Lightfoots had their pew. It was empty. She wondered if perhaps they were late, but the service started with no sign of the family. All through the sermon she speculated. It wasn't until the congregation filed out, politely shaking the minister's hand, that she heard a heard a man in a knot of worshippers mention the familiar name.

"I'm always tempted to call them 'Lightfeet'," he said with a chuckle.

His wife nudged him and they turned and bowed politely to the Overdale family.

"Good day," said Robert, politely tipping his hat as Jessie nodded to them.

The family moved on towards the gig but Helen tried to hang back, pretending to tie a shoelace of her Sunday best boots. To her frustration, the worshippers turned away and she could not hear their murmured conversation.

"Come along dear, we have to go to Doveton this afternoon, remember," said Jessie, hanging back for her daughter.

Helen could not forget. "Do you think something has happened to the Lightfoots?" she tried, hoping her mother might have heard something. "They weren't in church this morning."

"I'm sure Lizzie will be able to tell us, if she knows anything. It's quite surprising what that family of hers hears. There are so many of them in all corners around the town that very little gossip escapes them," said Jessie, laughing. "I suppose you're worried about your friend Dora? Perhaps Sabina or Anna-Marie might know."

"Perhaps," agreed Helen and fell into silent reverie.

"I reckon Dora has run off with a horse trader and the family are hiding with shame," joked Jack.

"No, she's broken open old Lightfoot's safe and run off with all the clients' money," added Matt, who was more interested in the financial aspect.

"Now that's enough, boys," scolded Jessie as Robert smothered a smile. "If the Lightfoots are in trouble, then we should pity them. You've just come out of church, remember."

"Yes, Mama," chorused the boys and dissolved into chuckles.

Helen gave them a piercing scowl which made them laugh all the more.

Lizzie knew nothing when Helen quizzed her. "I'll let you know if I find out anything," she promised. "Our Sarah is a scullery maid in the house next door but one to the Lightfoots. She'll know."

So Helen went with her parents and brothers to Doveton and the railway house where her Uncle Jack's family lived, still speculating about the fate of her fancy.

The house, though larger than its neighbours, was full of people. Helen congratulated her cousin Eleanor with a kiss and was introduced to Reginald and the rest of the Pembertons. They seemed a dull crowd and quiet as deemed suitable for a Sunday. Although her grandfather was a chapel man too, he wasn't opposed to merriment and toasted the happy couple with fruit punch.

"As head of the family, I'm proper chuffed to see my first grandchild embarking on the road to matrimony. It's a grand road, though difficult at times. I should know, I've done it twice," he joked, lifting his glass to Alice, his second wife, who smiled and raised her glass in return.

Mrs Pemberton sniffed as she glanced in disapproval at her husband.

"And I wish Eleanor and Reginald every happiness," continued Jacob. "She's named for her Granny and she were a good 'un, so you'll be well looked-after, Reginald."

Reginald raised his glass too, avoiding his mother's unyielding face. "I'm sure I will, Mr Davenport," he said, smiling as he slipped his arm round his fiancé's waist. "And my fiancé and I thank you all for your kind good wishes."

Everybody cheered and wished them well.

Helen wondered if ever she would stand beside Hadrian Lightfoot to receive the congratulations of her family. The celebration would have to be held in the spacious rooms of Overdale House, and she would ensure that it was a great occasion. She could almost see the banquet she had supervised personally and how she would wallow in the envy of Dora and her friends.

They arrived home before it became too dark. Although Robert had helped to redesign the centre of Gorbydale with funds from the Relief Committee during the Cotton Famine, the street lighting was still poor.

Lizzie helped them remove their travelling clothes and ushered them into their parlour for a hot drink.

"The Master's long gone to bed, Mrs Jessie, so I took the liberty of lighting the fire," she said. "I thought there was a chill in the air."

"Lizzie, you're a wonder," said Jessie warmly. "What would we do without you?"

"Oh, and I've heard a bit of news about the Lightfoots," she told them. "Their son Hadrian has been thrown out of college.

There's been some goings-on in the city, and he's said to be in the thick of it. There were complaints to the college and he's out on his ear."

"So that's why they didn't show up at church this morning," said Matt with a grin. "And I was sure it was because of Dora."

Helen was silent, her busy brain already making excuses. She knew there must be some mistake. Hadrian would surely explain to her at the earliest opportunity. Perhaps he was too embarrassed to face her. She would go to him and tell him she did not believe the gossip.

"Still, he'll have a position in his father's business to fall back on, no doubt. You don't need articles or a degree to be a clerk," said Robert with a shrug.

"Would his father's clients trust him, though?" queried Jessie.

"Young men do stupid things," said her husband with a knowing look at his wife. "They're forgotten in time. Old man Lightfoot will see him right. I don't suppose we'll be changing our lawyer. He's the only one for miles."

"I suppose you're right," she admitted. "But I'd keep a keen eye on the accounts if I were you."

Helen slept fitfully that night. She was all the more determined to go to the Lightfoots' whether she was admitted or not.

The rumours circulating about Hadrian Lightfoot were quite true and, through Lizzie's grapevine, gradually emerged. One of her cousins knew a potboy in Manchester. The 'goings-on' had occurred on a drunken evening Hadrian had spent celebrating with his friends. He'd cornered a nubile barmaid who, with fistfuls of flagons, hadn't been able to avoid his advances. Unfortunately for Hadrian, she was the daughter of the landlord and the fiancé of a local blacksmith. Hadrian's friends had persuaded the girl's beau not to beat him to pulp. They suggested to the landlord that he might lose a lot of custom from the college. It wasn't the first time Hadrian had caused trouble, and his friends were getting tired of his antics. There were complaints made to the college and the list was not a short one. As he hadn't bothered to attend many lectures, he was asked to leave.

The college had written to his father, sparing no details. His father had appealed, to no avail.

"The landlord said it was only in consideration of Hadrian's friends that he hadn't complained loads of times before," said Lizzie, shaking her head. "Hadrian said his father would pay him and promised not to misbehave again, but they weren't having it."

Sarah, from her vantage point two doors away from the Lightfoots, was a fount of information. She'd joined their little maid to go shopping and gathered all the relevant details with enthusiasm. Helen soaked in every word. Hadrian's father was furious. His first act was to cut off his son's allowance. Penniless and in disgrace, Hadrian was confined to the house. None of his Gorbydale friends were likely to fund him; he was the one most often with his hand in his pocket. So he lay sulking in his room, away from his father's fury and his mother's tears at the disgrace.

Helen was anxious about her beau and burning to help him. Risking the humiliation of being excluded from the house, she tapped tentatively at the Lightfoots' front door. Luckily, Dora had been reading in the bay window. She rushed to the door before the maid, who'd been instructed to say that the family were not available for visitors.

Dora opened the door and waited until the maid disappeared back to the scullery. Then she beckoned Helen in with a finger to her lips. "Come on upstairs," she whispered.

They hurried up to Dora's bedroom and closed the door.

"I expect you've heard?" said Dora with a tragic sigh.

"You mean about Hadrian?" asked Helen. "I heard some rumours — but I wasn't sure if I believed them."

"You are quite right not to," stated her friend. "Some silly barmaid said Hadrian had molested her when he had only bumped into her by accident. Her father was the landlord, and he complained to the college. Poor Hadrian is distraught, and my father is furious."

"Surely he could appeal?" suggested Helen.

Dora shook her head. "They have very strict rules at Owens. He shouldn't have been in an alehouse in the first place, but his friends persuaded him."

Helen hesitated for a moment, remembering the afternoon that she'd passed Hadrian and his friends drinking at the Bridge Inn in Gorbydale. He didn't look as though he'd needed much persuasion.

"Papa is furious at the moment, but Mama's hoping that she can persuade him to take my brother on at his firm. I'm sure her tears would persuade me, but my father has hardened his heart against poor Hadrian at the moment. He says my brother's disgrace would discourage his clients."

"Oh dear," said Helen, unsure what to say. "I'm sure my Grandpapa and Papa wouldn't take their business away if I explained."

"Best not say anything," Dora warned her hurriedly. "I'm sure it will soon blow over. It's not as if anyone would see Hadrian anyway if he was beavering away in the back office. He has beautiful handwriting."

She'd obviously forgotten, or didn't know, that he'd been writing to Helen and she wasn't unduly impressed by his scrawl.

"Would you like to speak to him?" asked Dora.

Helen's heart leapt. "Would it be all right?"

"We must be quiet, though," warned her friend. She ushered Helen out onto the landing and tapped gently on her brother's bedroom door. Quietly she opened it. "I've got a visitor for you," she whispered.

"Don't want to see anyone," Helen heard Hadrian growl.

"Oh, I think you'll like this one," coaxed Dora.

She beckoned Helen into the room. Hadrian had been lying on the bed, his hair tousled, his shirt half buttoned. Helen thought he looked like Lord Byron. He leapt to his feet and clasped her hands. She thought he looked adorable.

"Oh Miss Overdale, you are a sight for sore eyes; a breath of fresh air in my fetid room of misery." He spoke so poetically, how could she fail to be touched? She'd longed to see him, and now she knew she'd brought him a little comfort.

"Poor Mr Lightfoot," she said. "Dora has been telling me of all your troubles." As she modestly lowered her eyes, she did not notice the questioning look he gave his sister, or the impatient shake of his sister's head that warned him not to ask any awkward questions.

"Never mind," he said, slipping an arm round her shoulder. "This will soon pass. And how have you been? I'm so sorry I forgot to write. As you can guess, I've been exceptionally busy these last few weeks."

His sister's eyes widened with understanding. Helen had kept her letter writing a close and delicious secret.

"Well, you're home now, and no doubt Papa will relent and find you a position in his office," said Dora. "We'd better go.

Helen isn't supposed to be here. It won't help to annoy our parents if they see her."

She gave Helen a searching glance and jerked her head towards the door. Dora disappeared through it and Helen made to follow. The moment before she left, she felt a hand on her shoulder. As she gazed up in adoration at Hadrian, to her delight and surprise he gave her a swift kiss on the lips.

"Bless you for coming," he murmured. Then he quickly shooed her out of the door, fleetingly touching her fingers as she left. Helen gazed back at him in longing.

"Hurry up," ordered Dora in a sharp whisper and slipped downstairs.

Helen followed as ordered.

"You're a dark horse," said her friend with a sly smile. "I didn't know you were writing to my brother. Anyway, I hope to see you soon with some news." With that, she urged her visitor quickly out of the front door.

Helen hurried away from the Lightfoots'. Her heart was singing as she tripped home, convinced that Hadrian cared for her.

CHAPTER 28: THE WAKES FAIR

Wakes Week had arrived, and the mills were closed. Everyone in Gorbydale was in a holiday mood. Helen had agreed to meet Sabina and Anna-Marie at the fair.

The Lightfoot family were still keeping a low profile, to Helen's annoyance. She had dreamt herself walking arm in arm with Hadrian for all the world to see, although that was unlikely to happen at the best of times. Her parents would not have approved, and Hadrian seemed very cautious in his displays of affection.

"Sabina is calling for me," said Anna-Marie, who lived nearest to the fairground. "Will you call too?"

"I'll meet you there," decided Helen.

She wanted a quick look round the fair without her two giggling friends holding her back. There was a slim chance that Hadrian might have slipped away from his parents' house, and she didn't want the girls spoiling their meeting and making sly remarks.

The field was buzzing with the townsfolk and loud with the cries of hawkers and fairground workers. The reedy music of barrel organs tinkled around the gaily-coloured stalls. The townsfolk too were in their Sunday best. Despite the deprivation of the cotton famine years, they had slowly refurbished their homes and wardrobes and put on a fine show for the fair.

There was no sign of Helen's friends, and she wandered aimlessly through the gaudy stalls until she saw the roundabout. Entranced by the brightly-painted horses, she stopped to watch. The noise and the hiss of the steam engine fascinated her. She was determined to go on it herself when her friends joined her. Girls cried out in excitement, clutching their skirts as it whirled around. Suddenly she felt someone beside her and smelt him too.

"Spare a copper for an old soldier, little miss," came a gravelly voice.

Helen turned in alarm and saw a grim-looking man beside her. He shook a chipped enamel mug at her and leered, showing two blackened teeth. Helen stepped back in fear, but he lumbered forward too. She wanted to scream and run but didn't want to make a spectacle of herself.

"I … I…" she stuttered, afraid to look in her purse for a small coin in case he should snatch it. Now she was annoyed with herself that she had boldly decided to go to the fair alone. She froze with indecision, but the man's grimace grew wider.

Then she heard a voice beside her. It wasn't a Gorbydale voice. It made her think of visitors from America when she was young.

"Is this man bothering you, miss?"

The 'old soldier' turned to the intruder with a snarl. Then his face dropped in eye-popping surprise.

"Hello, Seth," said Helen's saviour pleasantly. "Fancy seeing you here. I understood from my grandmother that you were still in jail."

"Damn my eyes. It's you, you little runt. I'd recognise that damn hair anywhere," said the villain. "I just got out. I was hoping for a crust. The house is gone. Mam warned me not to go near that Overdale place or she'd be out on her ear. What's a man to do?"

The red-haired young man drew some money out of his pocket. "Here, take this and go and get yourself something to eat. But don't expect any more. Now leave the fair and don't bother this young lady or any other again, or they'll have the police on you."

"I won't, lad. Albert, wasn't it? Damn my eyes. Fancy seeing you here. Thanks anyway." With that, he slunk off between the stalls and out of sight.

Helen turned to her rescuer and saw a tall, slim young man with hair the colour of a summer fox. His fine moustache was fairer and framed a kind smile.

"Oh thank you," she said. "I was really afraid for a moment. That man just said you were Albert. Are you Maggie's grandson? Albert from America?"

"That's right," he told her with a smile. "I've come to visit my grandmother up at Overdale House."

"Oh, I remember you now. Do you remember me? I'm Helen Overdale. You came to visit us with Dolly, your mother, and Mr Jacques, who does business with my papa."

"Yes, I remember," said Albert with a beaming smile. "I remember it very well. I apologise for my Uncle Seth. He was always a bad one. I thought he was in jail, though."

"No need for you to apologise," said Helen, smiling up at him. "But I'm so glad you arrived when you did. I was so frightened. I thought he was going to snatch my purse."

"Well, you are safe now," he told her.

They hesitated, wondering how to proceed.

"Are you going up to Overdale House to see Maggie?" she asked.

"Oh yes. I just came from the hotel and thought I'd take a look at the Wakes fair. I often came with Mam when I was little. Though we didn't have much money to spend, she always gave me a penny to buy a toffee apple."

"Shall we go and buy some now and then go up to the house?" said Helen with a giggle.

"Yes, we shall!" said Albert, offering her his arm. He gallantly paid for two sticky toffee apples and they headed for Overdale House.

"The fair is on again tomorrow too," Helen told him. "We can come and have a proper look around. That's if you want to?" she added anxiously.

"I surely do," said Albert, laughing.

"We could stay now, but I'm sure Maggie will be anxious to see you. And I know you'll want to see her too. She tells us all about you. Mama writes her letters for her, you know."

"Yes, I know," admitted her new friend. "How is she?"

"Well, of course she's getting older and a bit slower too, but Lizzie is helping out. And Mama does a lot in the house, though Grandpapa objects and says she should leave it to the servants. But Mama doesn't like to be idle, she says." She was chattering away as if she had known him all her life, and in a way she had.

Their hands were very sticky from the toffee apples, and it prevented Albert from offering her his arm. All the same, they were walking very close. It was this closeness that Sabina and Anna-Marie reported back to Dora when they arrived at the fair to find their friend walking away with a tall, auburn-haired man and forgetting them entirely. Obviously Hadrian would have to be informed.

Maggie was overjoyed to see Albert. She kissed and hugged him and scolded him for not letting her know he was coming. Jessie insisted she had the day off and invited them both to tea in her parlour. She knew that Matthias might grumble, but Albert was after all the son of Robert's old friend Nathan Jacques. It was Jacques cotton than ran the Invincible Mill.

Albert was invited to stay.

"I have a room at the hotel," he told Jessie. "I didn't presume on your hospitality."

"Nonsense," she told him. "You'll be very welcome here. Robert wouldn't hear of you staying in a hotel. It would be an insult to your dear father. Helen, go and see Michael; Albert's bags must be brought here."

Helen nodded and hurried off, smiling broadly. A visitor from America was so exciting.

CHAPTER 29: RIVER ROAD

It wasn't until the evening that Albert told his grandmother that Seth was out of prison and in the town. He'd led her out onto the terrace for a quiet word. The lights and faint music drifted up from the fairground below to remind him. He'd noticed that Helen had said nothing to her parents about the incident at the fair.

Maggie groaned. "I thought they'd locked him away for good," she said, sinking wearily onto a wooden bench where Jessie often came to have a breath of fresh air. "He was safer in there, and so were we. I know he's my son, but he's a wrong 'un. He always was. He won't dare come here, though. I've warned him I'll lose my job if he starts any shenanigans round here." She began to weep. "I've had enough," she murmured. "I'm too old to be mithered. They're very good to me here. I can't work like I used to, but I do me best. They even got me a young girl to help me. Mrs Jessie and Cook know how I'm fixed. But they're very good to me."

Albert sat beside her and took her hand. "Why don't you come back to America with me, Mam? I'll look after you. Mam will too, you know I mean Dolly. It's very confusing," he added with a chuckle. "You were 'Mam' until I was hauled off to America, and now I call her Mam."

She patted his hand. "It's very good of you, love, but I'm too old. I've lived in Gorbydale all my life. What would I do in America?"

"Sit on a cushion and sew a fine seam?" he said, laughing. "Remember that? You used to sing it to me when I was little. Then you'd say 'I wish I had the time'. Well, you'd have the time at the Jacques' place. You'd see little Marguerite too. She's a peach."

"Has she got red hair like you?" asked Maggie and then remembered Albert's parentage. Clement had had auburn red hair. "Oh no … I didn't mean to…"

Albert laughed. "No, Mam. She has fair hair like I expect Dolly had when she was young."

"Aye, she did that. She was white blonde when she was a tot. But no, our Albert, I'm best here. I'm too old."

"I wouldn't mind going to see the old place," said Albert thoughtfully. "Is it as bad as it used to be?"

"Oh no. It's not there. Our half of River Road's been knocked down," Maggie told him. "I thought you knew. The row nearest the river is gone. The council said it was er … insanitary, that's it. They rebuilt the privies on the other side of the road, but our side was knocked down. There's a wider road there now so they can bring more wagons up into the town from the Doveton railway."

"We'll have to go and see it," said Albert.

"You go," said Maggie. "I don't want to be reminded."

Helen came bursting out of the door to find Albert. Her mother had warned her to leave him and his grandmother in peace but in her eagerness, she reckoned they'd had enough time to chat.

"Oh look, the fair's still going. Will we go and see it properly tomorrow?" she asked, gazing down over the valley.

"If you like?" said Albert.

"Oh yes I should," Helen told him with a merry laugh. "We hardly saw it today because…" She turned to Maggie. "Well you know, when I saw Albert I knew he'd want to come and see you right away."

Albert smiled at her tact and unbounded enthusiasm. Maggie glanced at them both.

"It's getting a bit chilly," she said quietly. "You don't mind if I go in, do you? I think I'll go to bed. I've had enough excitement for one day."

Albert kissed her papery cheek. It was covered in soft wrinkles, and he realised how she'd aged since he last saw her.

In the early morning, Albert slipped down to the River Road. It had indeed changed beyond recognition. The remaining houses looked respectable for once, fronted by a broad road. There was a walkway along the river where his grandmother's back yard would have been, and even the river looked cleaner. Long green strands of weed flowed like drowned maiden's hair along the water. Albert stood where his old home must have been and remembered all that had happened there. As he stared into the rippling river, a figure rose in the corner of his eye. What he had assumed was a bundle of rags lying on the river bank mutated into the hunched figure of a man.

"Morning Albert. What are you doing here? Come to see yer old uncle, have yer?"

"I didn't know you were here, Seth."

"You don't have a bob or two so as I can get a morsel to eat, have yer?" asked Seth.

"Not on me," Albert told him. "I came out without any money." He didn't like lying, but sometimes it was necessary.

"Come for old times' sake, eh? They wasn't bad old times," said his uncle.

"That's not what I remember," replied Albert grimly.

Though he'd been a small child, he remembered being terrified of his grandfather Tommo, and Seth too. His grandmother's skirts had been his one refuge.

"Perhaps you could tell the old queen to come and meet me down here?" suggested Seth.

Albert thought for a moment. "Why don't you just leave her alone?" he said, though he was uncertain what Seth's reaction might be. "She's happy in her job at the Overdales'. She's got a home, and they're good to her. Why don't you leave her in peace and clear off? They don't know you in Manchester. You could get a job. No one will employ you round here."

"She's my mam," said Seth bluntly. "She wasn't your mam. Our Dolly fell on her feet with that American bloke. You've done all right."

"You don't know the half of it," thought Albert to himself, but said nothing of Dolly's life with the drunken Clement.

He tried to appeal to anything that remained of Seth's attachment to his mother. "Why don't you be a good son for once and leave Maggie alone?" he insisted, standing his ground in spite of Seth's reputation. "I'll give you some money. You could make a new start in Manchester." He suspected he was wasting his time. Seth would take the money, just go to the local pub and get drunk. But it was worth a try.

"Ok then," agreed Seth. "Bring me the cash and I'll clear off. There's nowt for me here, anyway. Folks see me coming and get out of the way. That's no way to pick pockets," he added with a filthy laugh.

Albert pretended to search in his pockets and drew out his wallet. "I thought I'd left it behind," he said. "I've got a bit with me."

Seth went to grab the wallet. Albert was too quick for him. He jumped aside. As Seth lunged, the momentum catapulted him forward. Flying past Albert, he missed the edge of the riverbank and lurched into mid-air. Flailing wildly, he plunged into the river.

Albert stared in horror at his uncle's thrashing arms. For a moment he was stunned. Then he began to shout loudly. "Help, help!" he cried, stumbling along the river bank as Seth was dragged away by the current.

Albert wildly glanced around for something to cast out to Seth. Alerted by his cries, people tumbled out of the houses. Some were ready to go to work, others half-dressed. They hurried towards Albert and one man threw a rope towards the sinking man.

"This happens all the time round here," said one woman. "Where's Jimmy?"

A man was removing his boots as he ran forward. Without hesitation he dived into the river and swam strongly towards Seth. The next moment they appeared to be grappling in the river. To the horror of the onlookers, the pair sank. To everyone's relief as they followed down the riverbank, the pair bobbed up again out of the water. The man with the rope tried again to throw it out. This time the swimmer grasped it strongly and the crowd pulled him to the side. He was dragging the lifeless lump of Seth.

"The silly bugger nearly drowned me," he gasped. "He nearly drowned us both." He was hauled onto the riverbank and rolled Seth's limp body beside him. "Best get to work on him, then," he said and tried pumping Seth's chest with determination.

"It's that Seth Tate," mumbled someone. "Nasty piece of work. Best let him be. He'll be no loss."

Albert secretly agreed with him but watched, fascinated as the man called Jimmy worked on.

Suddenly, Seth gave a splutter and spewed water from his mouth. He groaned and opened his eyes. Then he closed them again and groaned once more. With a huge sigh he seemed to tense, his face contorted. Then he sagged, limp and lifeless.

"His heart must have given out," murmured someone.

"If he had one!" sneered a woman. "He crippled our Len with his clogs."

"Best call the bobbies," suggested someone else.

Albert was tempted to sneak away but waited with the others until a policeman was called.

"Not another one," sighed the constable. "You'd think they'd avoid the river when they've had a drink. Who is he, then?"

"Seth Tate," they all chorused.

"Oh, him. I thought he was inside," he said.

"He was trying to grab this young fella's wallet," volunteered the woman with the crippled relative. "This fella ducked and Seth fell in. I saw it all when I opened my curtains. That Seth's been sleeping rough here on the bank all night."

"He's just come out of prison," explained Albert. "I … I'm his nephew." He thought it better to confess right away than have it discovered later.

"You're not from round here, though, are you?" questioned the policeman on hearing his accent.

"Here, you're not little Albert?" asked the woman in surprise.

Albert nodded.

"Why, it's little Albert what went to America with Dolly Tate. Well, look at you. You're a proper nob now. Here, it's little Albert," she told everyone. "Maggie Tate's er… You know, what lived with Maggie. Fancy that."

The policeman sighed. "Well, what do you want doing with the body, seeing as you're related?"

Albert didn't have a clue what to do.

"If what this lady says is true, it looks like an accident, sir," said the officer. "I can get in touch with an undertaker if you like. Unless you want to take him home or something?"

"I'm a guest at Overdale House," explained Albert.

The crowd buzzed with amazement.

"Fancy that!"

"Well I never!"

"Little Albert!"

"It wouldn't be suitable," decided Albert. "Yes, perhaps if you know of a reasonable undertaker."

He waited with the body until Seth was carted away. The crowd drifted about their business, though a few women hung about asking him about Maggie and Dolly. He answered pleasantly with as little information as he could. Then he hurried back to Overdale House, where the family were at their breakfast. They seemed pleased to see him, as they'd been puzzled by his disappearance. He quickly told them what had happened and then went to the kitchen to tell Maggie the strange news.

She listened to him, stunned. "Our Seth?" she kept asking pathetically. "Our Seth? You're sure it was our Seth?"

Albert reassured her there had been no mistake. Eventually she had to believe him and sank limply onto a kitchen chair. The cook brought her a cup of strong sweet tea, which she sipped in a daze.

"Poor old girl's had a bad shock," murmured the cook.

Jessie arrived in the kitchen to offer help. "Would you like to go and have a lie down?" she asked kindly.

Maggie looked up blankly. "I can't believe it. He were a bad 'un, I know, but he didn't deserve this. An' trying to rob our Albert an' all."

She began to cry. Her heartrending wail echoed around the kitchen. Albert was immediately transported, taken back to a miserable day in a Liverpool railway station, the day he'd been wrenched from his grandmother to travel to America with his mother and newly discovered father. She'd been heartbroken then as she was now. For all his faults and failings, Seth had been her son.

Seth was buried in a pauper's grave like his father Tommo before him. There was only Maggie at the graveside to witness his burial. She could not weep for the brute he'd become, a man who'd died trying to rob his nephew. There was little chance of him growing honest and kind with Tommo as a father. But she wept for the curly-haired child of her memory and arrived back at Overdale House like a broken rag doll. Jessie had insisted that Maggie went to her son's funeral in the gig, as the cemetery was some way out of town. Albert had waited with Michael in the vehicle to support her. She was still very tired when she arrived back and went up to her bed to mourn.

Albert climbed the three flights of stairs up to the attic and tapped on her bedroom door. "Can I come in, Mam?" he called softly.

"Aye, lad. All right," came the reply.

The room was surprisingly cosy with a warm coverlet on the small bed and a colourful rag rug at the bedside. It was also neat, which surprised him. Their home in River Road had been one of squalor. He supposed his grandmother had despaired of the effort of keeping it clean with Tommo and Seth and their filthy ways. Maggie propped herself up in bed. She looked frail and her eyes were red-rimmed.

"Jessie sent me up with a cup of tea for you and some bread and jam to keep your strength up," he said, placing the cup on a small bedside table.

He was touched to see a photograph of Dolly and the family on it. She was seated in front of Nathan, who stood with a protective hand on her shoulder. Marguerite was on her lap and Albert standing beside her. They looked like any other family, posing solemnly for the camera. No one could have guessed the trauma behind their staring eyes.

"I'm going to write to my mother and tell her what's happened."

"Aye, she'd best be told," said Maggie sadly. "Though I expect, like most folk, she won't regret his passing. Where did I go wrong?" she sobbed and her tears flowed again.

"You didn't go wrong, Mam," Albert told her sternly. "He had bad blood, just like Tommo. I've turned out all right, and so's Dolly."

"Because you both escaped," murmured Maggie.

"Yes, escaped Tommo and Seth — and Clement," said Albert, wondering if he'd said too much.

"Clement?" asked his grandmother in surprise.

"Yes, Mam. Oh, he was good to me all right. I was his precious son. But he wasn't always good to Dolly. She had to work hard to get the plantation up and running. And he drank like a fish."

"I didn't know," said Maggie, shaking her head in bewilderment.

"We didn't want you to know," Albert told her. "But you know now, and Dolly's fallen on her feet. Nathan's a good man. She deserves to be happy, and Marguerite's a little poppet. You must come and live with us. You'd be happy too."

"I'm too old." Maggie huddled her blankets around her. "I'm too old. I'd get seasick going all that way. I even felt sickly on Hollingworth Lake when I was a girl."

Albert stayed silent, remembering the misery of his first crossing of the Atlantic. He was much better at sea now but still very queasy in a swell.

"Think about it, Mam," urged Albert. "I've been invited to stay for another week, and then I'm going to Liverpool for a few days to meet some cotton merchants before I sail home. Young Mr Overdale has arranged it."

Maggie shook her head. "You write to our Dolly," she decided. "Tell her I'm well. At least I don't have the big worry of Seth popping up at the house anymore. Give her my love."

So Albert sat down and wrote to his mother. He didn't give her the full details of her brother's death. He would do that when he returned home.

CHAPTER 30: DOLLY

As Maggie had predicted, Dolly was not sorry that her brother had left this world. He'd been a bully and a constant threat to her in her youth. It was only Tommo's scant protection of his only daughter that had saved her.

She read the letter and sighed. It was the end of an era, and she had survived it. She glanced round the comfort of her home and was grateful. But fancy Seth dying in a drowning accident. She shivered and remembered Clement in his watery grave. At least she hoped he was in his watery grave. Despite Nathan's sensible reassurances, she was still wary of strangers approaching the house.

"I'm sorry your brother has died, but from what you tell me, he'll not be missed," said her husband.

"You're right there," said Dolly. "But Mam will be sad, though. Despite everything, he was her son, and she often spoke about him being a sweet child. That was before Tommo got his hands on him and turned him into a rogue."

Marguerite toddled up to her, holding out her hands to be lifted onto her mother's knee. The little girl was becoming plump. Dolly knew her daughter was spoiled, but she was determined that she would have all the things that Dolly had missed as a child. She remembered staring in the window of the local sweetshop, her eyes round as they drank in all the delights on display. She'd had to cajole and bully the local children into sharing their sweets if ever they had a rare treat. Her cousin Elsie had sometimes had boiled sweets when her father was paid on Friday, and Dolly had naturally called to play on that day to cadge something from the timid girl.

"Mam read," said Marguerite, thrusting a well-pawed children's book at her mother.

"I'll be off to the fields," said Nathan and bent down to kiss her. "See you later."

Dolly sat down and opened the book and showed her little daughter the pictures. Marguerite knew every one by heart and was most indignant if Dolly skipped a page. Dolly tried to teach her the simple words on the page too.

She was determined that the child should learn to read and write. They finished the book and, with her plans in mind, she took Marguerite's hand and strolled over to the village school. She found Jeremiah sitting with his pupils under the shade of a nearby tree. He looked quite content in his open-necked shirt, sitting on an old chair, teaching the children from both plantations. He rose to his feet when he saw her and encouraged the children to do the same.

"Good morning, Mrs Dolly," he said formally, and the children chorused after him, "Good morning, Mrs Dolly," in their high sing-song voices.

"Good morning, children," she said with a bow and smiled to herself. Never in her lifetime had she expected to be greeted with such enthusiastic formality.

"Please sit down, Mr Leach," she said, smiling. "I'm sorry to disturb you. I just thought I'd come over with Marguerite to see how the boys and girls are getting along."

"Oh, we're just fine," Jeremiah told her. "Aren't we, children?"

"Yes, Mr Leach," they all chorused.

"We come out 'cos it was so hot in the classroom," one girl ventured.

"In this heat you'd boil like puddens in there," said Dolly.

"What's a pudden, Mr Leach?" asked the girl, looking puzzled.

"Perhaps Mrs Dolly would like to tell us?" suggested their schoolteacher with a smile.

"A pudding is something you eat," she told them, remembering the hot and tasty suet puddings that the cook at Overdale House used to make. "It's usually made with suet pastry, and you can put meat or dried fruit it. Then you put it in a cotton bag and boil it in a big pot of water. It tastes very nice."

"I was just telling the children about our country, Mrs Dolly," said Jeremiah. "How it was broken in two and now it's back together in the Union. Though some folks still resent that."

"My daddy was a slave," one boy told Dolly earnestly. "But he ain't no more."

"He isn't anymore," corrected the teacher.

"Yes sir, that's just what I said," the boy reassured him.

Dolly and Jeremiah grinned.

"They'll learn with time," she said. "I had to squash my Lancashire dialect 'cos nobody understood me. How you speak depends on who you're talking to."

"You are right of course, Mrs Dolly," conceded Jeremiah. "I shouldn't expect my pupils to speak like Southern gentlemen."

"As long as they can read and write," said Dolly. "Do you hear that, children? If you can read and write, no one can fool you so easily. Speaking of reading and writing, I was wondering if you had any spare schoolbooks so I can teach Marguerite a few simple words. She loves her picture books, but most of the words are too hard."

"I'll bring some over to your house when school is finished," he agreed.

"Then you must stay for supper," she insisted, and he didn't argue with that.

Over in the shade of the schoolhouse, a young woman was sitting with a group of older girls. Jeremiah noticed Dolly's glance in her direction.

"You must come and meet Ambrosia," he decided. "I'm training her to be my new assistant. She's teaching some of the older girls to sew at the moment, but I can assure you she is quite competent in teaching reading and writing skills too. Now be very good, children, while Mrs Dolly and I say hello to Miss Peters."

The children murmured agreement.

"You noticed her name?" Jeremiah asked Dolly. "She's from the Amiens plantation."

"Oh yes, I remember," agreed Dolly. "Isn't she one of Barney's granddaughters?"

"That's right," said her friend. "She didn't want to take the name Amiens like many of the slaves had to do. I suggested she did like the Icelanders and took her father's name. But Petersdottir sounded a bit outlandish, so she shortened it to Peters."

"You know so much, Jeremiah," said Dolly, laughing. "How on earth do you know what the Icelanders call themselves?"

"I was with one in college," he told her with a smile. "It sounds a fascinating place."

"Very cold, I expect," said Dolly, shivering despite the heat of the day.

Ambrosia Peters was a very pleasant young woman. At her prompting, her pupils all stood up and greeted Dolly. As they sat down again, Marguerite went and settled herself beside the other children and was reluctant to leave. Dolly hesitated to leave her ewe lamb behind but had plenty of things to do at home.

"We'll look after her," one little girl reassured her.

"We surely will," said Ambrosia.

"I can bring her home safely with me," said Jeremiah.

Seeing her daughter was quite happy, Dolly left the little girl with the other children and slowly came away. With Albert gone and Marguerite happy to leave her, Dolly felt lonely. As she walked the dusty, dry road to her home, she imagined the cool wastes of Iceland. A stray breath of air blew an eerie wisp of dust into the air and she became suddenly aware of her isolation. She heard rustling among the cotton fields at her side and froze. Though anxious and alert, she jumped in fright when a bird fluttered out and soared into the sky. Then she cursed herself for a fool to be frightened by a bird. Squinting along the dusty road, she looked for any signs of life, but she was quite alone. Dolly quickened her steps. She felt as if someone was watching her, though it was plain that the road was lonely and abandoned.

"Clement is dead," she told herself firmly. "Clement is dead, and the crocodiles got him."

She felt foolish to be so spooked just because she was alone but hurried along all the same. It was a huge relief when the chimney of her home came into view. Her heart slowed down as she strolled casually towards the house.

Their housekeeper Julia was on the front porch, shelling peas. "You all right, Mrs Dolly?" she asked in concern. "You looked in a mighty hurry to get here. And where's Miss Marguerite? You ain't lost her, have you?"

"I'm fine," said Dolly, laughing in relief. "I've just been over to the schoolhouse. Marguerite wanted to stay with the children, so I let her. She doesn't often get the chance to meet children of her own age. Jeremiah will be coming over for supper and bringing her back."

"Better shell more peas then," decided Julia with a smile.

Dolly sat down next to Julia and began to pop peas into the bowl. It was good to be doing some ordinary task, and she felt foolish for her groundless fears. Though the spectre of Clement was pushed to the back of her mind, he never disappeared entirely. Now Seth had gone in the same watery manner, it had released all the bitter memories she had so carefully quashed.

Jeremiah arrived back later, riding on his mule with Marguerite sitting up before him. Nathan lifted her down and she was so excited, babbling about her afternoon with the other children. Dolly noticed with regret that Jeremiah was getting old. Over supper, he mentioned that he was ready to retire sometime.

"Once Ambrosia is ready to run the school on her own, I'll hand over the reins to her," he said. "The children are good on the whole, but one or two bigger boys are a handful. They don't want to be in school, but their parents insist that they should make the most of their education. Ambrosia is very capable, though. She whips 'em good if they try any of their tricks on me. With a cane, of course," he added when he saw Dolly's horrified look. "Not with one of those cruel whips the overseers used. All the same, she shows them one of those whips now and again to remind the children of what her people had to endure. Then she points out how important education is."

"What will you do when you retire?" asked Nathan. "We can build a place here for you on the plantation."

"I might throw myself on my sister's hospitality," decided Jeremiah. "She's asked me often enough. But whether she'll like me under her feet if I accept is another matter."

"You know you're always welcome here. I'd be sorry to see you go," said Dolly. "You've been with me through thick and thin. It would be the end of an era."

A new era was about to begin. To the delight of the Jacques and O'Neill families, Jassy produced a baby boy. But as one life entered the world, another left it. As Jassy was whisked up to the bedroom at Jacinta Springs, Grandma O'Neill decided she must go too to supervise the birth. David and his father were waiting anxiously in the drawing room as Dolly and Jassy's mother Clara helped Jassy through her labour. Aunt Hattie had arrived to take charge, but no one noticed Grandma. Although she had not been upstairs for months, she stubbornly decided to tackle the stairs on her own. As she laboured upwards, halfway up her struggles had come to an end and her old heart had given out. Mrs O'Neill found her mother-in-law lying on the treads, her lips blue and cold, as she hurried down to tell David of the new arrival. So there was rejoicing and sadness at Jacinta Springs.

Dolly was respectful and silent at the funeral. She was glad the old woman with her sharp tongue had gone, sure that Grandma had poisoned Jassy's mind against her.

Wandering into the kitchen, she found Mrs O'Neill and offered to help. She sympathised with her for the loss of her mother. The woman was silent for a moment. She turned and looked directly at Dolly as if trying to assess her. Then she spoke quietly and carefully.

"Look, I know we ain't been very friendly afore. Ma was a force of nature, I know that. She squashed me down many a time if I tried to go agin her. She never thought I was good enough for her son. It was better to keep my mouth shut to keep the peace. But she tried to squash my Jassy too, and I didn't like that. You was good to Jassy when she was havin' the baby. Ma was always telling her terrible things about how a woman should suffer and frightening her. I didn't have an easy time with my three, so I was no help. But you put my girl straight. And Ma didn't like the idea of Aunt Hattie bein' at the birthin'. That's why she was headin' up those stairs to take charge. I was as nervous as a cat, but Hattie was so calm and so much help. I want to thank you. We'll start again. You call me Clara. We don't want no more of this Mrs O'Neill business."

Dolly was so touched that she gave Clara a hug. It surprised them both and they began to laugh with embarrassment. Clara's husband came into the kitchen, surprised by the sound, and found the two women working amicably together.

Dolly may have been missing her son, but she had found a new friend. After the day of Grandma O'Neill's funeral, there was a new friendliness between the two families and so harmony reigned over the new grandchild.

CHAPTER 31: A FAREWELL

It was time for Albert to leave Gorbydale. He had been a welcome diversion at Overdale House, but he accepted the offer of travelling back to Liverpool with Gus and Charles. They'd arrived unexpectedly as they had business in Doveton and had taken the opportunity to visit their friends.

Robert shook Albert's hand and sent his very best wishes to Nathan. Jessie kissed his cheek and furnished him with some sandwiches for his journey. Matt and Jack wished him well. They'd questioned him keenly about America and found him good company whenever they could part him from their sister. His grandmother Maggie clung to him like a limpet, bravely holding back her tears.

"I don't know if I'll ever see you again," she sobbed into his shoulder.

"Don't say that, Mam. I'll come and visit you when I can. Once I've finished with the college, I'll be a free man."

"You know you're welcome here any time," said Robert and Jessie together and chuckled that they'd both said the same thing at the same time.

Helen held his hands longer than was necessary as she wished him a safe journey and told him she hoped he would come again. She'd enjoyed his visit. He'd been easy to talk to and, as she wasn't remotely romantically engaged with him, she'd enjoyed mildly flirting with him. Whenever she was with Hadrian, she hung on his every word, seeking his approval. It didn't help conversation. In the same way, she knew that Charles admired her by the avid way he listened to her. She recognised the symptoms in herself. Albert's visit had been a welcome diversion, starved as she was of Hadrian's company.

Her friends had reported that her beau was still lying low until his father decided what to do with him. Without his allowance, Hadrian was robbed of the means of enjoying himself.

Days after Albert left, Sabina and Anna-Marie arrived with the welcome news that Hadrian was working in his father's office, copying documents.

"Dora said Mr Lightfoot has assured his clients that Hadrian will not be let loose on their business," said Sabina smugly. "My Pa said he'd better not be, or he'll take his business elsewhere."

Helen felt affronted on Hadrian's behalf. At least he was working, even if it was a lowly clerk's job. Though it was not the prestigious career in the law she'd envisaged for him.

"Dora says that at least things will soon go back to normal, and he'll be out and about," added Anna-Marie, who was still a champion of Hadrian.

Sabina seemed to have lost interest in him altogether.

Anna-Marie's prediction proved right. As Helen sat on the terrace reading a book and wearing a becoming straw hat to protect her complexion from the sun, she noticed a movement down the slope that led to Gorbydale. She stared in surprise and noticed that it was Hadrian waving a white handkerchief. She quickly glanced round to see if anyone was watching her. She knew her mother was busy in the house and her brothers had gone to town. Papa of course was at the mill, along with her grandfather. She put down her book and slipped quickly along the flowering bushes that led to the path into town.

Hadrian grinned as she joined him. "Well, you're a sight for sore eyes," he said, smiling. "How pretty your hat is."

"Oh, this old thing?" said Helen, modestly blushing and preening herself.

"I had to come and talk to you," said Hadrian, looking serious. "I heard you've lost your heart to an American boy now. First the Liverpool shipbuilder's heir and now an American. No wonder I'm torn apart with jealousy, and me just a humble clerk."

Helen gave him a coquettish smile. "You know you have no need to be jealous," she told him demurely. "Albert is a dear friend of the family, and Charles is such a dull boy — though of course he is devoted to me," she added mischievously.

Hadrian looked momentarily annoyed, but his smile returned instantly. "I've been waiting here an age for you to notice me," he said. "I didn't want any of your family to notice me."

"Why ever not?" protested Helen.

"Because my reputation is mud round here at the moment," sighed Hadrian. "You should hear the rumours going round about me. A pack of lies of course, but you know how people love to gossip. Anyway, I thought your family might chase me away."

"Why ever should they?" asked Helen. "They don't think like that. Mama was once a spinner at the Invincible."

"And she landed on her feet when she ensnared the heir to the mill," chuckled her admirer.

Helen didn't like the sneering tone of his voice but ignored the jibe.

"And you, my darling girl, are an heiress, and I am a penniless clerk," said Hadrian, looking forlorn.

"Don't be silly," Helen scolded him. She didn't enlighten him that the mill was in debt and, though trade was beginning to pick up once again, the folk at Overdale House were still careful with their money.

"While I was waiting for you to notice me, I noticed that little white building in the bushes up there on the hill," said Hadrian. "What is it?"

"Oh, that's Grandpapa's temple," Helen told him. "We used to go up there to play when we were children. Grandpapa never goes there now. It's very neglected these days." She didn't tell him that there wasn't the money to have it maintained.

"It looks very interesting. Perhaps we could go and see it. Your people wouldn't see us together up there, I'm sure."

"I've told you, they aren't..." Helen began to protest, but Hadrian had grabbed her hand and coaxed her through the bushes and up to Overdale's Folly, as the townsfolk called the temple.

When they reached it, Helen panting for breath, they found it full of leaves and debris. Some of the plaster had crumbled, revealing plain brick under the once pristine white stucco.

"It's ideal," said Hadrian with a sly smile. Before she could protest, he pulled her into his arms and crushed her to him. She gave a little cry as he kissed her hard on the lips but, despite herself, she melted into his embrace. Bewildering moments later, she gasped for breath and pushed him away.

"You shouldn't have done that," she challenged him.

"Oh, come on. You know you liked it," said Hadrian, starting towards her again.

She stepped back and stood firm, looking fierce and forbidding him to repeat his behaviour. "My parents would indeed chase you away if they knew what you'd just done," she hissed.

"But you won't tell them, will you?"

Hadrian smiled, sure of her devotion to him. Then, when he saw the determined look on her face, he became instantly apologetic. “I’m sorry, my darling girl. I was so eaten up with jealousy, I just couldn’t help myself. You understand, don’t you?” he pleaded. “A man’s feelings sometimes get the better of him. You look so lovely in that hat.”

She too had once been eaten up with the same frustrating feelings. Seeing his abashed features, she softened. “Yes, I understand,” she admitted quietly. “But you mustn’t let it happen again.”

“I promise I’ll treat you with the utmost respect,” he told her, gently taking her hand and reverently kissing it. “Please forgive me.”

She nodded. “We’d better go back,” she said.

He took her hand once more as he led her down to the path where he could slip away to Gorbydale. Before he slipped through the overgrown bushes to leave, he turned to her and smiled in conspiracy.

“But that is a capital place to meet, though, isn’t it?” he said, his eyes shining. “Could we meet there sometimes, if I promise to behave myself?”

“We might,” conceded Helen with a cautionary smile.

It was the perfect place for a tryst, if only Hadrian would contain his ardour. Helen was confused. She didn’t know if she should be shocked or pleased at his behaviour. It was overwhelming to have such power over a young man’s emotions.

CHAPTER 32: A TRIP TO THE SHOPS

Dolly was anxious most of the time that Albert was away. He'd written to her to tell her of her brother's death but tactfully omitted the details. She knew he was heading home to finish his studies after his trip. Restless until she saw him again, she decided that a trip to Baton Rouge was necessary. In some way she felt she would be nearer to him, although he had promised he would return to the plantation before he went back to college. Life on the plantation was fine, but she was a town girl at heart. Deep inside she was longing to look in some shops, tired of buying her clothes through catalogues. Often they didn't fit or were of poor quality. She put her suggestion to Nathan.

"You don't want me to go with you, do you?" he asked in alarm.

"No, of course not," she told him, "but I was wondering if Jeremiah would like to come with me and visit his sister."

"Will you take Marguerite?" asked Nathan.

"I think it's too far for her to travel just yet," decided Dolly. "I should take Clemmie, though. The change will do her good. She's been very quiet and mopey since Albert went to college and now he's away in England, she hardly says a word."

Aunt Hattie did her best for the girl, but she wasn't Albert. He had taken to Clemmie the very moment he'd met her. The quiet child dragged away from his home in Lancashire and the war-traumatised girl had an odd affinity. But he was a young man now, ready to take his place in the world, and Clementine Duplege was approaching middle age and still locked in a twilight world of trauma. Her sister Delia never bothered to contact her or enquire how she was.

"Will you be all right with Clemmie?" asked Nathan.

"Yes, I think so. She doesn't panic anymore. She's very docile, and I think the change will do her good. We might visit the college where Albert studies, so she'll know where he'll be when he comes back home."

Clemmie wasn't the only one missing Albert.

Dolly consulted Jeremiah about her plans and he was eager to accompany her.

"If we're going to the college, I might meet up with some of my old friends. And I can consult with my sister Margaret about my future plans," he said with delight.

They set off in the cool of the morning as the mists trailed up from the overhanging trees. Dolly was momentarily hesitant when Marguerite appeared tearful, but Aunt Hattie coaxed the little girl with the promise of treats to come.

It was a long and dusty journey, but they reached Margaret's home before nightfall and she was delighted to see them. Dolly had bought some food on the way, as they were not expected and over their evening meal they swapped their news. Jeremiah's sister was pleased to hear that Dolly's daughter shared a similar name.

"Let's hope she doesn't get called Maggie like I was," she said.

"That's what Mam's called," Dolly told her. "I never heard her called anything else."

After initially glancing fearfully round her, Clemmie began to relax. She helped the two women in the kitchen as Aunt Hattie had trained her to do.

"Poor child," said Margaret. "She wasn't trained to do chores in that big house with slaves to wait on her. They say that it was terrible in Vicksburg towards the end of the siege."

Though Clemmie was anything but a child, they pitied her in her childlike state.

"You're happy with us, aren't you Clem?" asked Dolly. "She's very good with Marguerite, and Albert will be home soon."

Clemmie nodded happily and continued drying the dishes.

Next day, they drove into the city. They planned for Jeremiah to leave Dolly and Clemmie at the stores, while he drove to the college, hoping to see his friends. They would be picked up later and driven again to the college for Clemmie to see where Albert studied.

"If any of my old friends are here, I'm sure they will show us around. That's if they're still alive," said Jeremiah with a sigh, conscious of his own advancing age. "I get so little news out at the plantation. I'm sure some of them will even object to me teaching negro children."

"Perhaps you should come with us to the stores and buy a new jacket," suggested Dolly, glancing at his dusty and rusty old black coat.

He ruefully glanced down at it. "I've never been a dandy," he admitted. "Though Esther always made sure I was tidy."

He rarely mentioned his late wife, but Dolly knew he'd turned to drink when she'd died. Arriving at the Amiens plantation to teach Albert had saved him.

They were driving towards the stores through ever increasing traffic. Dolly had never seen Baton Rouge so busy, but business had certainly picked up since the war had ended. They'd almost reached the stores when they were hailed by a loud voice.

"Jeremiah! Jeremiah!"

He pulled the horse to a standstill and glanced round. A plump and extravagantly dressed woman approached them. Dolly's blood ran cold. She immediately recognised Amelia Kay, though the woman had certainly aged and put on some weight.

"Jeremiah, I thought it was you. I hope you are keeping well?"

"Very well, thank you," said Jeremiah politely. "And you yourself? You look well."

The woman turned her attention to Dolly and their eyes met. "Why, Mrs Duplege?" said Amelia with a kind of sneering pleasantry. "How nice to see you. And looking well too." She spoke as if she had expected Dolly to look withered by the worries she herself had inflicted on her.

"Mrs Kay," said Dolly with a small bow. "Though I myself am now Mrs Jacques. However, your letter did reach me eventually. Unfortunately, the Amiens plantation house is no more. It was destroyed in a hurricane. But the mail man found me all right."

"And what did you think of my note?" asked Amelia slyly.

"At first I found it very worrying," admitted Dolly, "but of course my husband and kind friends," she nodded towards Jeremiah, "have persuaded me that Clement's resurrection was nothing but a silly rumour. He would surely have come to find his son Albert were he alive."

"You have a point," said Amelia with false sweetness. "All the same, I thought I should warn you. He was always a tricky devil. He was vehement at the time, that he would take revenge on poor Alice Domain for stealing his house. And her dying words were very strange."

"Yes, I'm sure they were — if they had been heard correctly," said Dolly abruptly. "Now if you'll excuse us, we have a very busy day ahead."

They made their brief goodbyes and hastily drove away.

"That woman just wants to cause nothing but trouble," snorted Dolly. Yet she couldn't help glancing back to where Amelia Kay stood watching them from the sidewalk with a smirk on her face.

Once again, Dolly tried to dismiss what she had said. She had almost forgotten what Clement looked like. As she'd explained to Albert, there were no images of her dead husband to remind her.

"Are you all right, Clemmie?" she said, turning her attention to her. "We'll go to the shops very soon and buy you a nice dress. Would you like that?"

Clemmie nodded, though she took little interest in the clothes she wore. Her mind seemed locked in some private limbo brought about by the trauma of the Civil War. It was only Albert who had coaxed her out of it, and, now he was away in England, she had retreated into her torpor once again.

Dolly busied herself with shopping. It was an effort to get Clemmie to try on any clothes, but they emerged from their expedition with a dress apiece. She noticed there were many war veterans about the streets, many with missing limbs. Some were begging, but many just struggled along with day to day life. She thought of Robert Overdale and his damaged leg, the result of the war. Her life in Gorbydale had been one of drudgery, and now she was living comfortably on the Jacques plantation. Yet though she tried to dismiss it, Amelia's presence had unsettled her. Away at the plantation she had longed for a bit of civilisation. Now she just wanted to return to the comfort and safety of her home.

Jeremiah met them with the wagon at the appointed hour. They had arranged to get something to eat, but now he told them that one of his old pupils, Leon Porteus, now a tutor at the college, had invited them to take some refreshment with him. Dolly was eager to see where Albert studied and to show Clemmie too. She hoped it would ease the woman's mind. They drove towards the college and were just about to pass the gates when Clemmie cried out.

"Uncle Clement!" she gasped.

"Stop, stop," Dolly urged Jeremiah.

He immediately came to a halt, to the annoyance of a carriage behind them. The driver shouted angrily as he tried to manoeuvre around the dusty wagon. Dolly looked frantically around but could see no one resembling her late husband.

"Where, Clemmie?" she demanded. "Where did you see him? Where did you see your Uncle Clement?" She shook the girl for some answer.

Clemmie was staring down the street. "He's gone," she whimpered. "Can't see him no more."

Dolly turned frantically to Jeremiah. "We should drive back and see if we can see him."

He laid a calming hand on her arm. "Dear lady," he said quietly. "We both know your husband drowned in the river. There were witnesses. Miss Clementine is uneasy in the big city. She has no doubt been unsettled by all this talk of her uncle from Mrs Kay; all this silly talk of him trying to find Albert. You must know he is gone. If he had been standing on the street, I am sure one of us would have noticed him."

"Clemmie noticed him," groaned Dolly.

"Miss Clementine noticed someone she thought was her uncle. Remember he was a spy. Remember there was a bounty man after him before he died. Didn't you once mention that there was a substantial reward offered by the father of the girl who was murdered?"

"Verity Cain," murmured Dolly as all the grim details came pouring back to her.

"Do you think Mr Duplege would appear as himself in a place where he was well known? He would surely be in disguise. If he was indeed here, Miss Clementine would not have recognised him. Calm yourself, dear lady. We'll go and have something nice to eat with Porteus and forget all about it."

Though Dolly could see the sense of his arguments, she couldn't banish her anxieties from her mind. Mr Porteus greeted them warmly and led them into the college. There were few people about as it was the vacation. All through the meal, Jeremiah and his old pupil chatted and laughed about old times.

Clemmie quietly ate her meal, now and then glancing up nervously. She had lost some weight since Albert had left, no doubt through anxiety at his loss. Though she was getting older, she had regained some of her old prettiness. Porteus was very gallant to her when they first met but soon came to realise that Clemmie was not as ordinary women. Her strange shyness and silence confused him, but he was kind and polite all the same.

Dolly ate little, distracted by her thoughts. Jeremiah tried to include her in the conversation but soon realised her mind was elsewhere. It was only when he mentioned Albert that she gave him any attention. Porteus didn't tutor Albert but had met him through Jeremiah and had found him a very friendly young man.

"I hear from my colleagues that he is doing very well. Jeremiah here is a very good teacher as I can vouch for myself.

I have never been to England, Mrs Jacques," said Porteus, "but I'm sure it will be a very good experience for the boy. And as Jeremiah says, he will learn much about the cotton industry from your friends."

"We had a letter from him from London," Dolly proudly told him. "He wished to go to Paris, but his friend has run out of funds. I expect he'll be home soon."

"No doubt he'll be back for the beginning of term," said Jeremiah.

"Albert coming home soon," Clemmie murmured with a beam of satisfaction.

Once they had left the college, after thanking and saying goodbye to Porteus, all Dolly's anxieties came flooding back. All the way to Margaret's house she nervously scrutinised the roads and alleyways for some hint of what Clemmie had seen. There was no sight of anyone resembling Clement, and she had to admit that Jeremiah was right. Surely Clemmie had been overexcited by Amelia Kay's interference. The woman was nothing but a spiteful menace. Dolly reasoned that if Clement were alive, he would hardly haunt the college during vacation time, when Albert was likely to be at home on the plantation. That thought made her wary all the way back to the plantation when they travelled home the next morning. As they rumbled along, she barely listened as Jeremiah outlined the plans for his future.

"Much as I would like the convenience of living near a town, Mrs Dolly, I think I prefer the informality of life on the plantation. I have felt the restrictions of wearing a shirt and stiff collar these last few days. Not to mention a jacket, which is very irksome. If Mr Jacques agrees, I would like to stay on at the schoolhouse and teach until my faculties decline and I am unable to. I'm sure Ambrosia would be willing to live at home with her parents until she marries. I don't suppose she'll have to leave just because she is married."

"Of course not. I always thought that was a daft idea," admitted Dolly, suddenly taking notice. She wasn't sure what faculties were, but she could take a guess. "Supposing you don't have kids. There were plenty of married women at t'mill that didn't. And plenty that did and all. I'm sure Nathan will agree with me."

They were greeted with great excitement when they arrived home. Marguerite hugged her mother and would not let go. Dolly realised that her daughter had hardly been out of her sight before this trip.

"We've missed you," said Nathan, hugging her too, though he wasn't usually so demonstrative in public.

She suddenly noticed that he was getting old. Though he was some years older than her, he was always very active, and she'd never noticed before. She hugged him with deep enthusiasm, feeling safe once more.

"I've missed you too," she said. "I'm so glad to be home."

CHAPTER 33: PLANS AND STRATAGEMS

The twins' seventeenth birthday was approaching. Usually the celebration was just a family affair, but Helen had hinted at a tea party for her friends several times. Jessie wondered if she should go ahead and invite more than the family to Overdale House. Helen had plenty of friends, but Jessie didn't want Matt to feel left out. She knew he thought his sister's friends were annoying. What she didn't suspect was that Helen was planning to invite Hadrian, if only she could persuade her mother to arrange a tea party. Nor did Jessie suspect that her daughter was meeting her beau on the sly at Overdale's Folly.

Jessie broached the idea of the party with Robert one evening after he'd had a particularly heavy day at the mill. His father had been interfering once again, and money was again the cause of their argument.

"Can we afford it?" Robert asked tetchily. "I've had the old man on at me all afternoon about cutting expenses. No doubt Helen wants to invite half of Gorbydale. And how will our Matt feel with all those silly wittering girls in the house? Let's just keep it to the family as usual, eh? There's enough of them as it is."

"I suppose so," sighed Jessie.

"She'll be wanting a ball next," complained Robert. "We're not made of money, Jess. You know that."

"Yes, I know," she admitted. "It was just that she's set her heart on it."

"Well, she can just unset it, then," said Robert firmly. "She can have what she wants when we get on our feet. She's been spoilt from the moment she was born, especially by my mother and father."

"Yes, I suppose she has," admitted Jessie. "Your mother told me once that she always wanted a daughter. I suppose I didn't quite fit the bill."

"You're all right for me," said her husband, giving her a hug. "I'm sorry to disappoint you, love, but you know how we're fixed. Can you imagine Papa with a house full of giggling girls? He's grumpy enough as it is."

Jessie knew Robert had been wary of Helen's friends ever since he'd overheard a careless remark of Sabina's. Once, when Helen had left the room, her friend had mentioned the 'crippled boy' and added, "I suppose their Pa's a cripple too, when you think about it."

"Inviting family will be enough," he decided firmly.

"Should we invite Reginald, Eleanor's fiancé, do you think?" asked Jessie. "I suppose he is one of the family now."

"Oh, why not?" conceded Robert with a chuckle. "He doesn't look as if he eats much."

Helen was livid that her cousin's fiancé was invited and not her friends. Her plans to show Hadrian off to the family were thwarted. She was sick of lurking in the shrubbery waiting for him to arrive at their trysts. He wasn't always punctual, though she excused his sometimes dubious excuses. She wanted him to call at the house and to go walking with her for everyone to see. Hadrian, though, had persuaded her that her parents would not approve of him with all the rumours that were rumbling round the town. He was sure they would forbid her to see him, and deep down she suspected he might be right.

Her father would complain that she was too young anyway to have a beau. He still thought of her as a child. She'd even tried to coax her grandfather into suggesting a tea party with her friends, but he hadn't fallen for her plan. It was all very frustrating.

Helen wasn't the only one with a secret longing. Matt inwardly groaned when he heard his sister pleading for her party. Her friends drove him silly when they appeared at Overdale House, giggling and gossiping in a huddle. Whenever he appeared, they stared at him suspiciously. It was only the bold Dora that ever addressed him with a supercilious 'good day, Master Matthew'. Then the other girls would start giggling and whispering behind their hands. He'd heard them murmur that they couldn't understand a word he said.

Charity Fitch was so different. She was calm and patient with him and, every time he looked at her sweet face, he loved her more. But he knew his longing was to remain a secret. If he told her of his feelings, he would surely embarrass them both. She might even leave the mill office because of it, and he would hate that. So he stayed frustratingly silent. Matt had decided that someone as sweet as Charity would never want to love someone like him. So they stayed friendly colleagues and worked amicably together. She rarely scolded him if he was clumsy and, if ever she couldn't read his figures, she asked him quietly to clarify them.

Then he got the idea that if Helen had her way over the tea party, he would invite Charity as his friend. What could be more appropriate than that?

Preparations for the tea party went ahead with only the family invited. Helen sulked but was ignored by her mother.

"You know how we're fixed," she scolded Helen. "Let that be an end to it. Anyway, I've just had a letter from your Aunt Honora and she'll be coming. So that's another guest to feed."

"You always do mountains of food anyway," complained Helen. "I'm sure my friends wouldn't eat much."

"Don't aggravate your grandpapa, Helen," warned Jessie. "He's grumpy enough with the thought of my family arriving. Anyway, what about a new dress?" she suggested, changing the subject. "I've found a lovely blue silk dress of your grandmother's at the back of her wardrobe. There's yards of material in it. Perhaps we could plan something from it."

"My dead grandmama's clothes," complained Helen, looking horrified. But when she saw the shiny rippling silk in hyacinth blue, she was enchanted.

"There is some fading at the edge of some gathers, but I'm sure we can work round it," said Jessie, examining the shimmering swathes of the skirt. "We'd better check with your Grandpapa," she decided. "I don't suppose he'll remember the dress. I doubt Melissa had worn it for some time. I've never seen her in it, and your father and I have been married nearly twenty years. She must have been very slim. But I shouldn't want your grandfather to be upset."

At first Matthias grumbled about 'robbing the dead'. Then, seeing the disappointment in Helen's face, he relented. "Aye, you're welcome to it lass," he said. "Waste not, want not. Your Grandmama looked a picture in that dress, and I'm sure you will too."

Helen ran and hugged her grandfather and he looked very pleased. She was always his favourite.

All the same, she was very disappointed that her friends would not be invited to the party to see her in her new dress. Nor did she have the opportunity to bring her liaison with Hadrian out into the open. She complained about it when she next met him at the temple.

"Don't fret about it, my sweetheart," he reassured her tenderly. "I must prove myself first before I face the scrutiny of your family. It will all come right in time."

Though the time was shorter than they expected.

CHAPTER 34: THE BIRTHDAY TEA

Helen's dress was a triumph. Jessie and Helen had worked from early morning to take advantage of the light as they fashioned the delicate silk. Helen had definite ideas of how it should look and sketched a design similar to one in her magazine but with subtle changes that astonished Jessie. Her daughter certainly had an eye for fashion.

She watched Helen enthusiastically greet the family and the admiration that shone in their eyes. Her daughter was growing up into a lovely young woman, and Jessie knew with regret that she had been treating Helen as a spoilt child. No one seeing her daughter's lively welcome to her relatives would suspect that she was disappointed that her own friends would not witness her triumph.

"Well, here's a pretty sight," said Jacob, taking his granddaughter's hands and showing her to the company. "How about a kiss for your old grandad, then?"

Helen kissed his soft old cheek and smiled. Matthias glowered, jealous that some old weaver could claim *his* granddaughter's affection.

"And here's our Matt looking very smart too," said Jacob, holding out his hands to his grandson.

Matt made a valiant effort to walk straight to his grandfather, leaning heavily on his stick. He had been secretly exercising in his bedroom, to the amusement of Jack, who shared it with him. Matt was making a determined effort to impress Charity. When Jessie had heard of his efforts through Jack's teasing, she'd arranged for her youngest son to move into a smaller room nearby.

"It's time Matt had his own bedroom," she'd told Matthias, who of course grumbled about the expense.

"What if he falls over?" suggested her father-in-law.

"He's got a voice, hasn't he?" said Jessie, sharper than she'd intended. "He can call for help. Anyway, he hasn't fallen in ages."

Now here was her son shyly greeting his birthday guests.

"Here's the working man," said Jacob proudly as he shook Matt's hand. "Congratulations, lad. I'm right proud of you for all you've achieved."

Matthias uncomfortably cleared his throat. Jessie glanced at him. He'd been ready to condemn Matt to an asylum when he'd been born less than perfect.

Matt smiled and welcomed everyone with his sister, and then Robert shepherded them all into the dining room. A feast awaited them. Beneath all the fancy garnish was plain fare, but Jessie and Lizzie had decorated the cook's everyday dishes with gusto and Helen had added the fancier touches. There were roses carved from radish and carrot, tomato water lilies and scallion curls, and everyone was delighted with the display.

"I wonder where Honora has got to?" Jessie asked Robert. "She said in her letter she'd be here by now and there's no sign of her. Do you think we should start?"

"We can't keep the company waiting forever," Robert told her. "What if she doesn't come?"

They'd just settled themselves at the table when they heard wheels rattling on the gravel, and moments later Honora came rushing in, full of apologies. Jessie rose to meet her.

"I'm so sorry I'm late," said her friend, pausing for breath. "The Manchester train was delayed when some cows got on the line."

"You might have had an extra piece of beef to bring with you," joked Jacob.

"Luckily, it wasn't that serious," said Honora. "But the silly creatures just kept walking along the line when they tried to herd them back into the field."

"Never mind. You're here now," said Jessie warmly. "Come and have something to eat."

Honora called her congratulations to Helen and Matt down the table, and everyone settled to the meal. The company soon demolished the feast.

Jessie glanced round the room and smiled at her guests. Her father Jacob and Alice were there, along with her brother John and his wife Elsie and their two sons James and Alan. Reginald Pemberton, Eleanor's fiancé, had stuck beside her like glue. Eddie, Jessie's younger brother, was present too. Gus and Charles had also been invited, and Charles proudly presented his family's gift to Helen and hung beside her as she opened it.

"It's lovely," she told him with a smile as she held a delicate golden locket up to the light.

Charles looked suitably pleased. "I chose it," he murmured with a smile just for Helen.

They all moved into the parlour after their high tea.

"Incidentally," Honora told Jessie later when they had all settled down, "I thought I saw someone up in that little temple on top of the hill, the one they call Overdale's Folly."

Helen immediately looked alert.

"Well, they're very silly if they go up there," said Jessie. "It was crumbling last time I walked up there. They might get hurt by falling lumps of plaster. Perhaps it was one of the boys."

"The lads and I can take a stroll up there afterwards, if you're worried," suggested Eddie.

Helen listened intently to their exchanges and grew anxious. She of course could not leave her own party. "When do you plan to get married?" she asked her cousin Eleanor to distract herself.

Her cousin blushed and smiled up at her fiancé. Reginald nodded at her in approval.

"We thought the year after next, Miss Overdale," he said quietly. "So as we can save a bit of money together, like. Give ourselves a bit of a head start."

"Sensible young fella," said Jacob. "Some of the couples nowadays haven't got a pot to…" He caught the alarm in his wife's eyes. "Haven't got two brass farthings to rub together," he finished.

Alice nodded in approval. 'A pot to piss in' wasn't acceptable in polite company.

Robert smiled. Jessie was surprised how her chapel-going father's language had coarsened. He had been so strict with them when they were younger.

"The old man's getting racy in his old age," murmured Eddie in her ear with a chuckle. "He's beginning to sound like the lads at my school." After leaving grammar school, he was now teaching boys at a Ragged School in Manchester.

As the afternoon wore on, the company began to depart. Gus and Charles left early, as they had the long journey back to Liverpool. John and Elsie and their boys were heading for the new omnibus service that had begun in the town, along with Eleanor and her fiancé. Eddie was leaving with them to catch his train in Doveton to return to his lodgings near his school. Honora and Uncle Eli were to give Jacob and Alice a lift home in Eli's gig.

"I'll call and see you tomorrow, if I may?" Honora asked Jessie. "It's been ages since we talked to one another."

"Oh, please do," said her friend. "We had hardly any time together today. I long for some conversation that isn't about Gorbydale."

As Jessie and Robert waved goodbye to their family and friends, Jack slipped past them. He'd already changed out of his best clothes.

"I'm just off to see a couple of mates," he muttered.

"Off you go, then," said Jessie, smiling. To his embarrassment, she caught him and kissed his forehead. "You've been very well-behaved this afternoon. I've been proud of you. Go out and let off some steam."

"Aye, he's the only one with any vigour," complained Matthias as he went by. "The rest of us are all cripples."

"What about me and Helen, then?" demanded Jessie.

"Well, you're only women. That doesn't count," grumbled her father-in-law. "I was talking about Overdale menfolk."

"You menfolk do very well despite your problems," insisted Jessie. "It takes determination and strength not to just give up if you've trouble with your legs."

Robert, with his arm around her waist, hugged her to his side. "And we wouldn't dare give up with tough Overdale women beside us," he said, laughing.

They were interrupted by Helen as she slipped down the stairs.

"Did you enjoy your party?" Jessie asked. "And you too, Matt?"

"Very much so," replied Matt. "Uncle Eli gave me a nice pocket watch. It's gold-plated, but he said he'd give me a solid gold one for my twenty-first."

"He gave me a silver charm bracelet," said Helen, displaying it on her arm. "I'm just popping out for some fresh air."

"Aren't you going to change your new dress?" asked Jessie.

"There's no need. I won't be long," insisted her daughter.

They couldn't know that Helen intended to investigate Honora's sighting of someone at the temple. She was convinced it was Hadrian, and she wanted him to see her in her best dress.

CHAPTER 35: OVERDALE'S FOLLY

Helen hurried towards the little temple. In her rush her dress was caught by a bush, and she sighed at the mark on the delicate silk, but she was desperate to see Hadrian. She'd been right and he was waiting for her. At least he hadn't left as he had done once before. Instead he was smiling in welcome and hadn't scolded. Helen was delighted that he was as anxious to see her as she was to see him. He drew her to him with tender passion and kissed her hair.

"Oh Helen, I thought you'd abandoned me," he said breathlessly. "I saw that shipbuilder's boy arrive with his father and thought you would never come. Oh Helen, I'm so glad you're here."

"Hadrian, you know I'd never abandon you," she reassured him, hugging him tightly. She was filled with joy and relief that he'd missed her. It felt so different from the times when he was tetchy that she'd been late.

"It's just that I get so jealous," he murmured, nibbling her ear.

"You should never be jealous," Helen said, pulling him closer.

"Oh Helen, I wish I could claim you for my own," said Hadrian, steering her gently towards the wall. "To make you wholly mine alone."

As he pressed her back, a flurry of loose plaster scattered down. Her first thought was that she must brush her clothes before she left. But the ardour of his welcome delighted and bemused her as he caressed her and she sank deeper into his embrace. She felt his hand slip beneath her skirt and its warmth on the cool skin above her stocking.

"Hadrian," she murmured. "Oh Hadrian."

"I'll be gentle, my love," he murmured into her ear.

Helen was slipping deeper and deliciously under his spell.

"Helen! What's he doing to you?"

The loud shout snapped the lovers out of their enchantment. They leapt apart and stared at Jack, standing at the temple entrance with two of his friends.

"I'm going to tell Papa," he said angrily.

Helen quickly straightened her dress and, darting towards her brother, grabbed his arm. "No, please don't, Jack. Please don't," she begged.

"I'll give you some money," said Hadrian without hesitation.

Jack looked disgustedly at him. "Trying to bribe me won't work with me you … you cad. You're that Hadrian Lightfoot, aren't you? I won't let you treat my sister like that — like some…" He turned red at his unspoken implication. "I'm going to tell Papa. Come on lads, I've got to tell my dad."

"Please don't?" Helen tried once more.

But he ignored her. With that, he turned and left. His friends stared in curiosity at the pair for a moment and then disappeared after Jack into the gathering twilight.

"What will we do?" asked Helen anxiously. "You must come up to the house and explain. You must tell them we plan to get married when I'm a little older."

Hadrian looked taken aback. "Er … yes, yes, of course," he stammered. Then he took a deep breath to reassure himself. "But your father will be very angry when he hears what we've been up to. I … I'd rather not face him at the moment. Perhaps you can talk to him and … and calm him down. I'll perhaps come and see him soon and … you know. I'd better go." With that, he gave her a swift peck on the cheek and disappeared into the darkness.

Helen slumped down on the seat. Of all the awful things to happen. She saw her brother's horrified face; behind him the two boys, staring in shock tainted by curiosity. She sat there wondering what to do, reluctant to face her father's anger and her mother's disappointment in her. She didn't have to wait long. In the quiet evening she heard the thump of her father's stick on the path, followed by her mother's anxious voice. They appeared at the temple and stared at her. Her father was red-faced with the effort of climbing the hill. Helen noticed he clutched a riding crop in his hand. Her mother was breathless and anxious.

"So he's scarpered, has he?" growled her father. "And what about you, miss? Have you finished with shaming the family for tonight? It's bad enough our Jack having to witness your shenanigans, but his friends had to see it all too. No doubt right now they'll be telling all their families what you've been up to. Get back to the house at once and go to your room. We'll deal with you in the morning."

"We're going to get married when I'm older," protested Helen defiantly.

"Are you now?" snorted her father. "We'll have to see about that. I notice lover boy hasn't hung around to verify that."

"He will," said Helen, now close to tears, despite her bravado. "He said he's going to call on you."

Her mother shook her head in dismay. "Oh Helen, how could you let us down like that? I thought you'd have had more sense," said Jessie.

Helen hurried past them and almost ran all the way to the house, stumbling in the dark. Her parents followed at a slower speed, pausing to rest Robert's leg now and again.

Jack was standing with Matt at the French windows, awaiting the arrivals. They looked anxious.

"Traitor," Helen hissed at Jack as she dashed into the house.

"Slut," he shouted at her retreating back as she hurried towards her bedroom.

"That's enough," said Matt calmly.

Helen fell on her bed and wept. Her brother had utterly ruined the most momentous moment of her life. She had been about to give herself to Hadrian Lightfoot to make herself wholly his.

She was awake most of the night, and so she was still restlessly asleep when her father left in the morning on an angry errand.

CHAPTER 36: A CONFRONTATION

Robert presented himself at Lightfoot and Co., Solicitor at Law and demanded to see Hadrian's father. He could see no sign of the seducer but sounds of activity came from an adjoining room. Mr Lightfoot was surprised to see Robert and ushered him into his office.

"I don't suppose your son has told you what happened last night?" demanded Robert.

The solicitor looked blank. "No," he answered cautiously.

"To put it mildly, he was caught trying to seduce my daughter," said Robert angrily. "My daughter maintains he wishes to marry her. I should like to know what you are going to do about it?"

Mr Lightfoot looked wary. "Hadrian and your daughter? Are you sure, sir?"

"Of course I am. Do you think I would come here on a wild goose chase? There were witnesses. My son and his friends saw what was happening and he is not prone to lying."

"I understand," conceded the lawyer, looking disconcerted. "I suppose I'd better call him in."

Angry words rose from the adjoining office and then Hadrian was led in, looking very subdued.

"I … I was going to call on you, Mr Overdale," he muttered.

"So my daughter mentioned," said Robert. "It's a pity that you didn't stay to explain yourself last night. Though perhaps it's as well, as I was about to thrash you." Despite his lame leg, he looked as if he was quite capable and angry enough to do so.

"I'm sorry, Mr Overdale. We fully intend to get married," Hadrian excused himself. "It was just that we were a bit carried away."

"My wife and I think that because of the scandal involved and the fact that there were witnesses, the wedding should take place quite soon. It would be much sooner than we would have wished. I should hate for my daughter to be maligned around the town."

"You could offer the lads some money to keep quiet," Hadrian blurted out.

Even his father looked disgusted with him. Robert had already heard what he had suggested to Jack and bit his lip.

"If you are man enough, you should be prepared to marry her and save her reputation," snapped Robert, his fist tensed as if clutching that riding crop.

Hadrian shrank back against his father's desk.

"If those were your intentions, Hadrian, you must of course honour them. We must make arrangements as soon as possible," decided Mr Lightfoot. "I can assure you my son will of course do his duty, Mr Overdale. I'll make sure of that. The reputation of both the young people and our families are at stake."

Robert wasn't sure if Hadrian had much of a reputation left but said nothing. "Perhaps we might meet at Overdale House and discuss matters," he suggested. "I suggest this evening after dinner you must come, so we can get this tawdry business over as soon as possible."

"Certainly," said Mr Lightfoot humbly. "I'll bring him and see he gets there. Should I bring my wife?"

"That's for you to decide," said Robert. "I'm sure Mrs Overdale will wish to be there."

There was the problem of what to tell his father. He would want to know what was happening when the Lightfoots arrived that evening.

Robert and Jessie knocked tentatively at Matthias's study door and entered at his call.

"What's up?" demanded Matthias, immediately suspicious. "You don't often knock and wait. More often than not you just barge in. Is summat up?"

"We don't want to upset you, Father-in-law," ventured Jessie, "but there's something we must tell you."

"Spit it out, then." Matthias folded his hands over his stomach and leaned back in his chair. "Have you overspent the budget on some fancy folderols for this party?"

"It's not that," sighed Robert. "You know our Jessie is always careful with money. I almost wish it was. No, our Helen's got herself into a spot of bother."

"Helen?" Matthias looked surprised.

"She's been caught kissing and cuddling with the Lightfoot boy up in your temple," said Robert.

Matthias chuckled. "Well, we all did a bit of that, lad. When we were younger, of course. She's growing into a proper young lady. We all saw that at the party. The Lightfoot pup, eh? I don't suppose it's serious."

"Helen insists they're going to get married when she's older," Jessie told him.

Matthias pondered this for a moment. "So they were doing a bit more than kissing and cuddling, I take it," he guessed.

"Jack and his friends saw them," said Robert, shaking his head. "No doubt it will be the talk of the town soon. I've asked the Lightfoots to call this evening. My daughter's reputation is at stake here."

"Daft little madam," growled Matthias. "I thought she'd have more sense."

"So did we," said Jessie.

"I reckon this lad has led her on," decided Matthias. "Well, we'll have to see what can be done. What time are they coming?"

"You don't need to be there," said Robert hastily.

"As head of the family, I will most certainly be there. I reckon I'll have something to say to that philanderer," snapped his father. "I'll have a think about what's to be done. No doubt he's after her money." He began to laugh. "It's a pity she's got none. He's in for a shock."

Jessie glanced at Robert in alarm. "It's not funny, Father-in-law," she said in exasperation.

"No, you're right lass," he said, looking serious. "It's anything but funny. I had a letter from Taylor Walmsley the other day. He wrote to remind that he'd like repayment on what he put into t'mill. We're making a profit all right, and we've nearly paid off the arrears on the mortgage. But Walmsley will want paying off all the same, and we're putting what we can on one side to do just that. He seems to be doing well at the moment over in India, trading with the East India Company. But when he comes back, he'll want his money."

"You never mentioned it," said Robert, looking annoyed.

"I er … forgot," mumbled Matthias, looking sheepish. "But we'll have to tighten our belts a bit longer."

"Yes, I'm sorry, Father-in-law. I know we have to watch what we spend," said Jessie.

"All the same, we'll do what we can for our lass," said Matthias. "She a mite young to get wed, though. But like you say, we'll have to insist that he makes an honest woman of her."

"I don't suppose we could send her away, perhaps to stay with Honora for a while, until it all blows over," suggested Jessie.

"It's a good suggestion. Sadly, I don't think she'd agree," sighed Robert. "You saw how defiant she was last night. She'll stick by him."

"I suppose you're right," conceded his wife. "But will he stick by her? I don't trust any of those Lightfoots, especially after all the recent rumours about Hadrian. How could she have been so stupid?"

"I don't trust them either," said Matthias. "They don't call lawyers 'shysters' for nothing. Anyway, if the lad tries to back out, we'll stick him with a charge of 'breach of promise'."

"I sincerely wish it would all just blow over," Jessie said, shaking her head. "She's made a silly mistake. I'll mention about staying with Honora. Seeing all the sights in London might take her mind off Hadrian. I'm sure she'd change her mind about marrying so young." She wasn't hopeful about her daughter agreeing to that.

Jessie went to tell Helen about her father's visit to the Lightfoots' office. She mentioned London, but as she expected Helen was defiant despite her predicament.

"Hadrian loves me and I'm going to marry him," she insisted.

"You're very young," her mother told her gently. "Marriage is a very serious business. It takes work and commitment. It's not all fun and parties. You're young to be tied down with children if and when they come."

But she got nowhere with her daughter.

Honora arrived just after they had finished their talk. She had come to say goodbye to her friend before she travelled back to London. She immediately guessed that something was wrong when she saw Jessie's troubled face as she came through the parlour door. Despite her intentions to keep the affair quiet, Jessie sat down and poured out her troubles to her friend over cup of tea. Honora listened patiently, silently weighing up her friend's predicament.

"And how did she take your suggestion that she should come and stay with me until it all blew over?" she said eventually.

"Not as I'd have liked. I hope you don't mind," said Jessie with a tired sigh. "I don't even know how you are situated and whether you'd have room for Helen."

"I'd have enjoyed having her stay," said Honora, squeezing her friend's hand for support. "It would have been a perfect solution. Although I am very busy, I would have made time for her. She might even have decided to help in the clinic and come to appreciate the work we do there."

Jessie smiled at her friend's enthusiasm for medicine and secretly doubted if Helen would have been able to cope with blood and sickness. "She might have done," she said.

"But you say she's adamant that she wants to marry him?" asked Honora.

"Unfortunately yes, and you know how stubborn she can be," said Jessie sadly.

"And what about this Hadrian?" asked her friend. "Is he as keen to be saddled with a wife?"

Jessie still secretly hoped that her plan to send Helen away might work, if only Hadrian proved reluctant to marry. "We shall find that out tonight," she said quietly.

"Let me know if there is anything I can do?" Honora offered. "She's not got the ring on her finger yet, and she may yet change her mind."

"Thank you," said Jessie. "But I don't hold out much hope. Anyway, what are your plans? We've hardly had any time to talk this visit. Will you return to America?"

Honora shook her head. "I don't think so. There is so much work to do here in England. I am hoping that we might establish a women's clinic here in Manchester. Elizabeth (Miss Blackwell) is keen to expand her work.

"There is another reason why I'd rather remain in England. Do you remember that letter that I sent you about Clement Duplege, saying that I feared my life might be in danger?"

"Oddly enough, I still have it safe," said Jessie. "I know that Clement drowned, but I never threw the letter away."

Then Honora told Jessie about the letter that Dolly had received from Amelia Kay with her suspicions.

"You mean you suspect that Clement is still alive?" asked Jessie in surprise.

"I know it sounds ridiculous," admitted her friend. "If my friend hadn't been murdered, I would have dismissed the rumour as ridiculous. But I can't help feeling uneasy. I'd feel safer in England."

"Oh Honora, I'm so glad you'll hopefully be nearer home," said Jessie, giving her friend a heartfelt hug. "Anyway, you'll be able to come to the wedding."

"If it goes ahead," said Honora cautiously.

Jessie shook her head in exasperation. "Oh, unfortunately I'm sure it will."

CHAPTER 37: A SETTLEMENT OF SORTS

The Lightfoots arrived soon after the Overdales had finished their evening meal. Jessie had suggested the main parlour for the meeting. The visitors were led there by Lizzie, who made her disapproval known by showing them little of her usual friendliness.

Jessie felt anxious as she told her two sons to make themselves scarce. "And no eavesdropping," she warned.

Then the Overdales joined their guests, Matthias insisting on leading the way as the head of the family. Mrs Lightfoot was present, along with her husband and Hadrian. Hadrian looked downcast and hardly glanced at Helen when she entered. If she was hoping for some spark of feeling from him, she was to be disappointed. The atmosphere was chilly, and Matthias made matters worse by insisting Mr Lightfoot vacate his favourite chair.

"I'm afraid you'll have to move," he insisted. "That's the only chair that's right for my back."

Their visitor hurriedly scrambled from the large leather armchair. He apologised for his mistake but looked irritated. Finally they were all settled and Robert was about to speak when his father began.

"I'd like an apology from you, young man, for bringing shame on my granddaughter. You've caused our family great distress by your actions, and we fully expect you to do the right thing."

"Yes, of course, Mr Overdale," said Hadrian, glancing at his father. "I do most humbly apologise for what's happened. Helen was in no way to blame. I forced myself on her in my ardour." He took a deep breath and hesitated. If Helen was expecting a declaration of undying love and a proposal of marriage, she would have to wait. It seemed apparent to Jessie that he was trying to wriggle out of his predicament.

"Yes, of course my son will do the right thing by Miss Overdale," said his father, glaring at his son. "An engagement should be announced as soon as possible."

Jessie glanced at her daughter. Helen was pale and looked sick. This was no way for a romantic girl to hear that she was going to become engaged to be married. Jessie felt very sorry for her. If only Helen hadn't been so adamant that Hadrian would marry her, she could have gone to stay with Honora and carried on with her life.

"Of course, I expect there will be some kind of marriage settlement," suggested Mr Lightfoot. "I propose that your granddaughter should have an income of…"

"Now hang on there," said Matthias. "Am I to understand that your son is earning a salary at your office?"

"Why yes, of course," said Mr Lightfoot.

"Well, then *he* can keep his wife, just like everyone else has to do," said Matthias. "I'm not paying some fella for seducing my granddaughter." The Lightfoots were shocked into silence. "Now here's what I propose. They can live in the old manager's house, rent free. Now our Robert's managing t'mill, it's been empty for a bit. But it can be aired, and there are a few sticks of furniture in it and curtains and things. My last manager went to a smaller house when he retired and left some stuff. And I'll give her a couple of hundred as a dowry."

"A couple of…?" Mr Lightfoot looked astounded and Hadrian bit his lip.

"And I'm sure you'll put something into the pot," said Matthias with a benign smile. "Of course, her father will have the expense of the wedding but in the circumstances, given the recent rumours surrounding your son, we won't be having an extravagant one, will we?"

"No, I suppose not," Mr Lightfoot reluctantly agreed.

"But…" began Mrs Lightfoot.

Her husband tapped her hand to silence her. "Certainly a house, rent free, is a generous offer and a help to expenses," he conceded. "We are to hope that my son advances in our profession and will keep the young lady in the manner she is accustomed to."

"I think they should do well enough," said Jessie. "Helen is quite practical. She can cook and sew. I've made sure of that."

Mrs Lightfoot sniffed.

"Would you like some tea?" asked Jessie, ignoring the woman's glare of disapproval. Everyone in Gorbydale knew that Jessie once worked as a spinner in the mill.

They sipped their tea in silence.

"Perhaps you two young people would like a private word with one another," Jessie suggested as she noticed her daughter looking near to tears.

Hadrian glanced up from the carpet where he had continually fixed his gaze. "Yes, thank you, Mrs Overdale. That would be a good idea. Would you come and talk to me, Helen?" He held out his hand, his faint smile loaded with regret. Helen took it eagerly and they hurried out of the room.

"And no misbehaving, mind," Matthias's voice boomed across the room and echoed round the house.

Hadrian glanced angrily at Helen. "The old skinflint," he muttered.

"Are you so unhappy?" she asked.

In all the confusion of their discovery, she'd had little time to reflect. But in the silence of her bedroom, her mother's suggestion of a stay in London had drifted into her mind. She had dismissed the thought, remembering her beau's ardent embraces. His ardour seemed to have cooled when confronted by the disapproval of their families.

"Oh, I'm not unhappy, my darling," he said. "Just angry with myself for putting you in this awful position. It was all my fault. I was just so carried away with my love for you. I really wouldn't blame you if you cast me aside." He paused hopefully for her answer but had underestimated the strength of her feelings for him.

"Oh Hadrian, I can't think of anything nicer than to be married to you," said Helen, placing her head on his chest. "It will be lovely. I promise you I'll make you a good wife."

"Lovely," he echoed quietly.

So it was settled apart from the smaller details. The young couple were to go to the vicar the next day and arrange a date.

"But I'll be working at the office," Hadrian tried to excuse himself.

"You can have the morning off," snapped his father.

Helen smiled wanly at her beau. "We could have a look at the manager's house after we've been to the church," she suggested.

"I suppose so," said Hadrian with a shrug.

"There's more furniture if you need it, in our attic and in one of the stables," Jessie told them, practical as ever. "We found some nice pieces up there for our parlour."

Mrs Lightfoot smothered a sneer and glanced at her husband. "I'm sure we can contribute to the bedding and household goods," she simpered.

Jessie ordered more tea, and the Lightfoots drank it quickly and made to depart.

"I'm glad that's over with," murmured Robert as they stood at the door to wave them off.

Hadrian lingered behind and blew a half-hearted kiss towards his bride-to-be. Helen pretended to catch it and raised it to her lips, but her beau had disappeared into the darkness before she could return it.

"Are you happy with the arrangements?" asked Jessie.

Helen just nodded, too bewildered by all that had happened in so short a time. She wished that Hadrian had shown some of the passion he'd displayed at the little temple. Now his ardour had disappeared along with the discovery of their tryst. It was time to face the reality of young love.

"It will be lovely," Helen murmured, as though to convince herself.

CHAPTER 38: OVERDALE LODGE

Helen rose fresh and eager next morning. She'd had trouble getting to sleep with all that was tumbling about in her thoughts. But in that sleepless hour, her plans began to hatch, and she was eager to share them with her mother.

"I was thinking about my bridesmaids," she said. "Of course, I must have Dora and Sabina and Anna-Marie. I wonder what colour they should wear? I thought perhaps blue. And my dress of course would be white."

Jessie stared at her. "I don't think the family can afford a lavish affair, love. Perhaps limit yourself to two bridesmaids. What about Dora, as she's Hadrian's sister, and your cousin Elsie? That's a bridesmaid from both families. That way, you won't have to choose between Sabina and Anna-Marie. I'm sure Dora and Elsie both already have pretty dresses they can wear."

Helen looked appalled. "I can make their dresses," she protested.

"Will we have time?" asked her mother.

"Perhaps not," decided Helen with a sigh. "I know Dora has a pretty blue dress. Perhaps Eleanor will have one too."

"You always have your new blue silk that you could lend her," suggested Jessie.

Her daughter gasped. The thought of her cousin in her beautiful silk dress was too much. "She's much slighter than me," she insisted.

"We can put a few tucks in it," said Jessie firmly. "You're much the same height."

All Helen's plans were melting away. "What about my dress?" she asked anxiously.

Her mother thought for a moment. "I don't think your grandmother had a white dress in her wardrobe that we could use," she said quietly. "I'll ask your grandpapa if I may look though the chests. I know she kept some clothes in there that didn't fit her anymore. There may be some material that would be suitable."

Not even a new dress for her wedding! Helen was crestfallen.

Matthias grudgingly gave his permission before he headed out to the mill. He kissed Helen's forehead. "We'll do our best for you, lass, but you know we haven't got a lot of brass to spare. If circumstances were more favourable, you know we'd have planned to make a better show."

"Yes, Grandpapa," said Helen humbly. "Thank you for letting us have the manager's house."

"It will be in my name, mind you," warned Matthias. "Then it can't be sold to pay any debts. You'll always have a roof over your head."

Helen blushed, annoyed at her grandfather's assumptions that the young couple would run up debts. "Yes, of course, Grandpapa," she agreed with a tight smile.

Jessie nodded her approval. "And you don't mind if we take a look through Grandmama's belongings?" she confirmed.

"If it's of any use, you go ahead," said Matthias wearily. "She has no use for them now. She'd be happy enough to see her granddaughter in one of her frocks for her wedding. Anyway, we'll see you later."

Robert kissed his wife and then planted a kiss on Helen's brow. "Best of luck," he said simply. He gave his wife a telling glance as he left.

"What time will Hadrian be calling?" Jessie asked Helen.

Her daughter shrugged. "When he arrives, I suppose."

Their arrangements had always seemed loose. He was often late for their trysts, yet chastised her if he had to wait for her to arrive.

"Then let's go and look in your Grandmama's chests before he comes. Lizzie will give us a call when he arrives. We might find something useful," suggested her mother.

If they hoped for a few yards of white silk or satin, they were to be disappointed. They did however find a copious white lace shawl. It was yellowing at one corner, but Jessie was sure she could remedy that.

"We could go to Manchester and buy some white material for a dress and cover the bodice in this lace," suggested Helen, her natural creativity inspired by the sight of the material.

They were interrupted by a loud banging on the front door. They heard Lizzie admitting Hadrian and made to hurry down. Jessie snatched the lace from Helen and tossed it into her bedroom.

"Mustn't let the bridegroom see the dress," she said with a smile.

"You mean the bit of the dress," said Helen, laughing. She was pleased with their find. The thought of the glorious dress she would fashion had elated her despite the disruption of all her other plans.

With growing enthusiasm she coaxed Hadrian to see the vicar. When they arrived at the vicarage, the maid told them he was in a meeting with his curate, the Reverend Tyldesley. Of course, Helen had met her brothers' old tutor many times. As he emerged from the vicar's study, he greeted her with a smile and nodded briefly towards Hadrian.

"How is Matthew?" he asked. "I hear he's in gainful employment at your uncle's mill nowadays. Does he enjoy it?"

"He's very enthusiastic about it and full of ideas," Helen told him. Her head had been so full of Hadrian that she'd taken little notice of her twin. Now she suddenly realised how much she'd absorbed when Matt told her about his new job.

"I'm very pleased for him," said Reverend Tyldesley. "And how is young Jacob doing at the grammar school?"

Helen hesitated for a moment before she realised he was referring to Jack's proper name. "I know he's doing well at sport, but he hardly says anything about lessons," said Helen with a chuckle.

Hadrian pulled out his watch and pointedly stared at it.

"I'm sorry, I mustn't keep you," apologised the curate. "Please give my regards to your brothers."

"I will," she promised, blushing hard at Hadrian's rudeness.

The curate glanced at Hadrian, then back at Helen as if evaluating the purpose of their visit. "Goodbye for now, Miss Overdale," he said. "Mr Lightfoot." With that, he left them.

"Insolent dog! Did you see the way he sneered at us?" grumbled Hadrian.

"No, I didn't," said Helen. "I don't think he sneered. I've always thought he was very nice. My brothers liked him."

"What would they know?" scoffed her beau. He muttered something under his breath. Helen couldn't ask him to repeat it as the vicar summoned them into his study. She realised it was just as well. Hadrian did not seem as eager as she had expected.

Throughout their meeting, the vicar had asked them several times if they were sure they wished to get married.

"Yes, of course," Hadrian told him abruptly.

The vicar didn't seem totally convinced. All the same, the arrangements for the wedding were made.

Hadrian strode ahead in silence towards the mill manager's old house. Helen thought that now they were engaged, he might offer her his arm. Nevertheless, she scurried beside him to keep up. As they both reached the front door, she handed him the large brass key from her pocket and they went in.

It was gloomy in the hallway and smelt of musty neglect. The house brightened when they opened the shutters, though a myriad of dust motes danced in the pale sunlight. There was some heavy, dusty furniture in the room at the front of the house.

"This would probably be our parlour," said Helen, almost in a whisper. With surprise, she caught her reflection in the grimy glass of a tall spindly dresser. She looked pale and ghostly. Hadrian's face appeared behind her, impassive and grim. For a moment, her enthusiasm for this wedding faltered. Perhaps she was making a terrible mistake after all. But Hadrian slipped his arm round her waist.

"I wonder if there's a bed upstairs," he whispered in her ear.

"Hadrian!" she protested.

"Well, we're engaged now, aren't we?" he said with a smirk. "Such things are permitted. We practically managed it when we weren't engaged."

"And look at the trouble it's caused," she scolded him, trying to wriggle free.

Hadrian was not letting go. She blushed at the memory of her behaviour in the temple. Now here she was alone with Hadrian and he seemed very determined to finish his seduction.

They jumped apart when there was a brief knock on the door and they heard it open with a creak.

"Anybody home?" came her mother's voice.

"I should have locked that damn door," hissed Hadrian angrily.

Helen was very relieved he hadn't.

Her mother, followed by Lizzie, came into the room. "I thought I'd find you here," said Jessie lightly. "Lizzie spotted you coming along the road from the church. We've come to see how much work needs doing to make the house habitable. It doesn't seem too bad," she said, glancing around. "We'll need to do plenty of dusting and sweeping, though."

"I'm sure Mama can arrange for our maid to come and help," said Hadrian sweetly.

"That would be good of her," replied Jessie with a taut smile. "Incidentally, I found out that the house is called Overdale Lodge. I caught a glimpse of the deeds."

"Overdale Lodge," murmured Hadrian. "Not Lightfoot Lodge, then?"

They explored all the rooms. The kitchen was the worst place in the house. Though built at the same time as Overdale House, it had never been modernised.

"Perhaps we could persuade your grandfather to put in a modern range," suggested Jessie. "We might stress how dangerous an open fire is. He won't want his precious granddaughter burnt. What do you think?"

Helen nodded in approval. She'd never cooked on an open hearth.

Hadrian disappeared into the rest of the house, and she hesitated before following him.

"At least the privy is indoors," he called, emerging from a doorway in a small corridor leading to the back door.

"That's good," said Helen.

He dipped back through the door and they heard the sound of water on porcelain.

"He could have closed the door," muttered Lizzie.

The sound of a chain being yanked was not followed by a flush of water.

"There's no damned water," complained Hadrian.

"I expect the water was turned off at the mains to prevent any bursts," said Jessie. "Let's have a look for the stopcock."

She discovered it in a cupboard near the front door and, with a bit of difficulty, turned it on. Instantly they heard the sound of rushing water in the kitchen and privy.

"I'd better go and turn off the tap," said Lizzie, hurrying away.

"At least you have a convenient supply of water. We'll need plenty of it to clean the place up," Jessie decided.

"How do you know where all these things are?" asked Helen in amazement.

"Because I was brought up in a home where we had to do things for ourselves," said her mother, smiling. "We couldn't afford a tradesman every time something went wrong. Besides, we had two engineers in the house. The boys were always interested in how things worked."

They examined the rest of the house, with Hadrian trailing behind. There was a large bed in the main bedroom whose springs creaked like a wailing banshee when Helen perched on it.

"You'll need a new mattress," decided Jessie.

There was also a copious wardrobe and a chest of drawers with wide heavy drawers.

"You could do with a washstand," she suggested. "There might be one in the attic at home."

A small bed was the only item in another bedroom, and the other was empty.

"I could use this as my sewing room," said Helen. "If you'll let me borrow the sewing machine from time to time, Mama?"

"You're welcome, dear. Your father and I might buy you one as a wedding present."

"Sewing?" asked Hadrian.

Helen nodded proudly. "I make all my own clothes," she told him.

He looked appalled.

"I could probably make you a shirt if I had a pattern, and certainly cravats," Helen teased him.

Hadrian snorted. This was hardly the grand lifestyle he had obviously envisaged with a mill owner's granddaughter.

They were learning something new about each other all the time. Helen had learnt that her husband-to-be was not always the even-tempered and sweet-natured man who had cast his spell over her. She wondered about that proposed visit to London that her mother had suggested. But it was all too late. The banns for her wedding would be read out for the first time in church on the next Sunday.

CHAPTER 39: THE RETURN

Albert had returned home for a short visit before he began his studies once more. His mother was shocked when he finally told her how Seth had died.

"He always was a bad 'un," she said angrily. Then she became anxious. "And he could have drowned you, my love. Oh Albert, I've been so anxious while you were away in England. I'd have been worse if I'd known what had happened with Seth. You'll settle down in America now, though, won't you?"

He could not reassure her. "The Overdales made me feel very welcome," he said. "I learnt a lot about the cotton business. And then there's Mam. She got so upset when I was leaving. She thought she would never see me again. Perhaps... Who knows... I may feel I need to go back and see her."

"You're like your father, with itchy feet," said Dolly with a sigh. "Perhaps you might meet a nice girl and settle down."

Albert laughed at her anxiety and couldn't help teasing her. "Oh, there are lots of nice girls in England too, Mam. Helen Overdale is very pretty," he told her.

Dolly noted his enthusiasm with dismay. When Albert returned to college, she started feeling apprehensive. Her son's 'itchy feet' had unsettled her. She asked one of the boys to prepare a wagon and, securing Marguerite next to her, she headed over to the Amiens plantation. She felt she must check on her son's inheritance in his absence and see how the cotton was growing in the fields. The toddler was wearing a cotton bonnet against the sun, as Dolly was herself.

There was little left of the Amiens mansion. It had not fared well when the tail of a hurricane had battered Louisiana. One fearful night the wind had begun to howl and the rain lashed the windows of their home. Dolly had clung desperately to Nathan and begged him not to go out to secure things around their house. In the morning, the chairs from the porch had been found some way away. One of the workers had been hit by some falling debris from his roof, and many of the other rooves needed repair.

The once grand Amiens mansion was wrecked. The two white pillars that had once graced the entrance now stood alone like the remaining teeth in an empty skull. Dolly, with Albert's permission, had given the plantation workers leave to use any useful timber from the house to improve their shacks.

"No one can live in that wreck," she'd said. "And it would take too much money and effort to repair it. We'll build you a new house, a modern house, when you're ready to get married."

"If I get married in America," Albert had answered with an enigmatic smile.

Dolly knew with sadness that he was growing away from her, his horizons and hopes drifting from her plans for his future. He had matured beyond her expectations now he was away at college. Though she knew he had been bullied at first, he had risen above it. It was not surprising when she remembered how her son had survived Tommo's taunting. Jeremiah Cain had been right to suggest Albert went away. The old man was quite content to potter round the Jacques plantation, teaching the children from both plantations. Albert was daily witnessing a different way of life and she knew he wanted to travel, especially to see Maggie in Gorbydale. He often spoke of his grandmother and how she had shielded him from Tommo and

Seth's excesses. Dolly felt guilty for leaving him for her mother to raise but she'd had little choice. As the sole breadwinner in the house, she'd had to protect her job at all costs.

Tethering the gig to one of the white pillars, she hauled Marguerite down from her seat. The little girl was quite sturdy on her feet and clutched Dolly's hand as her mother cautiously walked into the ruins of her old home. The Jacques house had suffered little damage in the storm, being in good repair. As the wind had hurtled through the Amiens mansion, with its broken and missing windows, the roof had flown off like a kite and the walls collapsed at the onslaught. Much of it had been found some fields away. Dolly wondered how she would have survived if she'd still lived in the old place.

The house had been positioned away from the old slave village behind a row of trees. It lay like a broken crate, discarded among the broken branches, surrounded by debris, haunted by the ghosts of past Dupleges. Their lifestyles had been buoyed on the sufferings of slaves. Now Albert was the only male left to make his own way in the world.

Surveying the diminishing state of her old home, Dolly turned to go with a sigh. She planned to visit the village and her workers. It was the height of the noonday sun and there was no one about. The workers would be away from the fields, eating their midday meal. She was surprised to see a figure emerging from the trees. In the haze of heat she could not see clearly who it was. The man was taller than Barney, her overseer, and for a moment Dolly felt anxious. Her heart began to beat faster as the figure became clearer. She blinked hard, unwilling to believe her eyes.

"Clement!" she finally gasped.

To an outsider he looked like one of the itinerant veterans of the war that sometimes wandered into the plantation. He was gaunt, his hair greying, but Dolly would recognise her husband anywhere. His clothes were shabby workmen's clothes, so different from the dandified outfits he once wore, even in his most drunken states. The alligators had not got him after all.

"Pretty little girl," he said with a tight smile.

Dolly pulled Marguerite closer to her. "I thought you were dead," she hissed.

"So do the authorities," Clement smirked.

"You never sent any word that you were alive," she protested. "Not even to your son."

Clement began to look serious. "I came to see Albert. I want to see my son."

"Well, you won't see him here," Dolly told him. "He's gone off to college like you wanted him to. He's happy there, seeing a bit of the world. He thinks you're dead. Why don't you leave it that way? Why not just leave him alone?"

"He's my son," said Clement simply. "You have a child of your own here. I suppose she's David Jacques' girl?"

"David? No, I'm married to Nathan," protested Dolly. Though she could see why Clement would suspect she'd be married to the younger man. He had known she had once been infatuated with Nathan's son.

"Nathan?" said Clement in surprise.

"He's a good man. He's kind to me. He was a good dad to Albert; a good father; treated him as his own."

"But he isn't his father. I would like to see my son," insisted Clement.

Dolly hesitated. She didn't want to tell him of Albert's whereabouts. She could have told him that Albert was in England and at least have a chance to make her son aware that his father was alive and looking for him.

"Why ruin his life? Why don't you leave him in peace? Why drag him into your intrigues?" she pleaded.

He took a deliberate step towards her. She automatically pushed Marguerite behind her.

"I suppose you're going to kill me," she stammered, trembling with fear. "Please don't harm the child. She hasn't done you any harm. She's just an innocent."

Clement looked alarmed. "I ain't going to kill you," he said in surprise. "Why would I kill you? You done the best you could by me. Why woman, you even brought my plantation alive again. Look at it thriving now. I know I gave you a hard time, but I wouldn't harm you."

Dolly breathed deeply with relief, though her heart was still beating rapidly. She knew he was implicated in the death of Verity Cain and had instantly assumed that would be her fate too. She thought fast. "The plantation is being worked for Albert now," she told him quickly. "For your son." Then she played her trump card. "And the plantation doesn't rightly belong to you or Albert," she added in a low voice. "I found your brother's will. Henri left the plantation to his daughters, Delia and Clementine. Clemmie had the will hidden in her corsets. When I found it, I burnt it. I did it for Albert."

Clement's eyes widened in surprise. "A will?"

"Yes, and I had to go to court and swear Albert was legitimate because Delia was trying to claim he wasn't. Honora Darwen wrote a letter to the court for me to swear she knew you were his father. She helped secure the plantation for Albert."

"That bitch! Well, I suppose I have to thank her for that," said Clement thoughtfully.

Dolly hoped she had won a reprieve for Honora. She, too, had Honora to thank for her son's inheritance, shaky though his claim was. All the same, she could not write to warn Honora that Clement was alive. Too many complications had arisen with his appearance.

Clement glanced over the ruins of his old home. "I don't suppose you could save the mansion?" he asked.

"We were just lucky we weren't living in it when the hurricane came," said Dolly. "It was like matchsticks the next morning."

"About Albert?" Clement persisted.

"Why don't you just leave him alone?" Dolly pleaded again. "Please, Clement?" She almost felt sorry for him when his face fell.

"I can't. He's my son. I went all the way to England to find him. I can't lose him now."

"If I tell you, will you just go and look at him? Please don't talk to him. He's happy where he is. He wants to travel. Please don't let him go about with that burden round his neck?" She was in tears with her desperate appeal. Marguerite began to whimper, clinging to her mother's skirt.

"I'll see," he conceded. "I don't really want him to see me like this anyhow."

Dolly bit her lip and decided to tell him some version of the truth. "He's been in England to see his grandmother. He was very fond of her," she said quietly. "He's doing very well. He's had enough upset in his young life. I wasn't a very good mother to him to begin with. I'm doing my best now."

"When will he be back?"

"I don't know," she lied. "He's got itchy feet like you."

Clement nodded and turned to go. "I don't suppose I'll see you again," he said. "But thanks for looking out for my son — our son. I hope you'll be happy with Jacques. He's a better man than I ever was." He shook his head. "I wouldn't have killed you, Dolly. You done me no harm." With that, he faded into the trees.

Dolly watched him go and hugged her daughter to her with relief. She did not know what Clement would do. Hopefully he would see sense and not embroil Albert in his problems.

"Let's go and see Uncle Barney," she said, brightening her voice to calm her child.

Despite her enforced jollity, Dolly was trembling and troubled. What could she do? If she betrayed Clement to the authorities, her marriage to Nathan would be called into question. Albert would bear the stigma of a murderer for a father. Clement's prior claim on the plantation might be forfeit. Dolly was weary with it all. She would say nothing and let fate take its course.

Barney was not in the village. Neither were many of the other men. Dolly was puzzled. She had not seen them in the fields. She asked Aunt Ida, who was sitting in the sun by her door.

"Don't rightly know," she said when Dolly enquired where everyone was. "My eyesight ain't what it used to be. Hearin's not so good either."

Dolly went back to her wagon and secured Marguerite back in her place. Driving out from the village, she was met by Barney and a few other men on the dusty road through the trees. "Oh, I was looking for you," she called. "I wondered where you were."

Barney approached the gig. The other men hung back, their faces grim and unspeaking.

"Just doin' some business, Mrs Dolly," said Barney with a stiff smile. "Just doin' some business. Nothin' for you to worry about."

His manner didn't invite questions, so Dolly didn't ask further. The rest of the men drifted away, some with awkward backward glances towards Barney. Something had happened, but the men often solved disputes among themselves and she trusted Barney to be a fair man. So Dolly merely made a few enquiries about the progress of the Amiens plantation.

"I've been meaning to drive over, but I've had a lot to do this last week. And this little madam takes a lot of my time," she excused herself, smiling back at Marguerite.

The little girl giggled at Barney, who wiggled his fingers at her.

"No need to worry, Mrs Dolly. The plantation is in fine order. You know you can trust me."

"I couldn't do without you, Barney," she told him. "You're my saviour right enough."

He murmured something under his breath that Dolly couldn't quite catch. He didn't repeat it and she didn't ask.

Marguerite became fractious, and Dolly made her excuses and drove home. She briefly wondered what had happened at the village but forgot all about it as her daughter whined for her attention. She deliberately did not tell Nathan of her meeting with Clement, and the following days were occupied as her little girl cut her double teeth with misery and sleeplessness. Dolly anxiously wondered if Clement would track down their son to Baton Rouge. She was fearful that Albert would write about an encounter with his father. It was with great relief that she read his next letter and it contained nothing but his college activities. Perhaps Clement had done as she had pleaded and, if he had discovered where Albert was staying, had seen but not spoken to his son.

Dolly longed to unburden herself to Nathan but knew she could not. It was bad enough to know that she might not legally be married to him. She had been so happy, so contented with her new life. With Clement's reappearance, all her achievements threatened to collapse in ruins around her and she could do nothing about it.

CHAPTER 40: RUMOURS

Jessie, accompanied by Lizzie, armed with brooms and dusters and scrubbing brushes, set out for Overdale Lodge. Covered in copious aprons, they were determined to banish the months of neglect from the house. The first thing Jessie did was light the fire. There was a small coalhole in the back yard, and she scraped enough of the remaining lumps of coal to make a steady blaze in the kitchen grate. Then she filled a large kettle with water.

"That slop stone's not much good," she told Lizzie, pointing to a shallow trough of chipped earthenware that stood for a sink. "Let's see if there are any bowls in the cupboards."

They found a large enamel bowl and several battered saucepans that had been abandoned when the mill manager had moved. Jessie filled them to hasten the supply of hot water for their task.

First they hauled a worn carpet out into the back yard and manhandled it over a washing line. Jessie tested the rope first.

"Do you think it will hold?" asked Lizzie doubtfully.

"It's going to have to," said Jessie with a chuckle. "It doesn't seem too bad. We can leave it for the wind to blow some dust away and then come and give it a good bashing. I noticed a carpet beater hung on the back of the pantry door."

They went back into the house and began to dust and sweep. Jessie climbed on a chair and began to clean the windows with scrunched up newspaper and a bottle of vinegar.

"This will get the worst of the muck off," she said, surveying her work with satisfaction. "This room looks brighter already. I reckon we might finish the parlour and the main bedroom today."

"It smells like a chip shop, though," said Lizzie, laughing.

"That will soon fade," Jessie told her with a smile. "Hopefully we'll have Helen with us tomorrow. I left her sewing her wedding dress. She said she'd come to a tricky bit, so I took pity on her."

She and Helen had made a trip to Manchester and, avoiding the more expensive stores, found a bolt of white crepe in a small backstreet shop. It had yellowed along the edges of the roll, but Jessie had remedied that with careful washing.

"I might get the lads to beat that carpet for us on Saturday afternoon," she decided. "I don't think I've got the energy for that today. The weather should hold until then, so it will have a good airing."

She hadn't worked so hard for some time, but she was determined to make the house presentable for her daughter. Slowly the parlour was taking shape, the old wooden furniture gleaming and the sharp smell of the vinegar drowned by the warm smell of beeswax.

"I'm sure I could run up some cushion covers for this old sofa to brighten it up," said Jessie, surveying the sagging old upholstery.

"That's if you can get near the sewing machine," chuckled Lizzie.

"Aye, you're right," sighed Jessie. "Helen's putting her heart and soul into this dress. But I'm sure she'll help us tomorrow."

She felt guilty about asking Lizzie to help her clean Helen's new home. As Maggie grew older and less capable, the girl had so much more to do, helping in the kitchen as well as the house. Lizzie was totally loyal to Jessie, though, and would always help her in any way she could.

Helen was delighted with the progress when she came to help the next day. Then her head was filled with plans to sew soft furnishings. The boys took great delight in beating the carpet, though the washing line broke with their efforts. Michael had to rig up another one, watched by an admiring Lizzie. Jessie hoped that they would soon get together. Over the next few days, the house became habitable.

There were two days to go before the wedding when Lizzie hovered by Jessie after breakfast. Instead of clearing away the dirty dishes with Maggie, she waited until everyone had left the room.

"Could I have a quiet word with you, Mrs Jessie?" she asked nervously.

Jessie was immediately alerted by her anxious manner, and all sorts of notions came into her head. Had Lizzie found another job and was about to leave them? Had she had enough of Matthias's mood swings? Were the boys being cheeky to her or playing tricks on her as they had once done? Robert had soon put a stop to that. Jessie quietly closed the door to the breakfast room and beckoned Lizzie to her.

"I don't think we'll be disturbed," she said. "Robert and his father have gone to the mill, and Matt is at Eli's. Jack's gone to school, and Helen is going through her trousseau yet again. What's wrong, Lizzie? I hope it's nothing serious?"

Lizzie hesitated for a moment. "It's young Mr Lightfoot," she blurted out. "My brother Reuben called this morning with the groceries. He said there was a right to-do last night down at the Bridge Inn. Mr Lightfoot and his friends got a bit rowdy, and the barman got his arm broken." Her words all tumbled out in a breathless rush. She glanced at Jessie. "They say he was like a raging bull when he was drunk and insulting everyone. His friends couldn't stop him."

A surge of anger rose in Jessie. She was ready to defend her darling daughter and about to snap that Lizzie shouldn't repeat such gossip. Lizzie sensed it, looking uneasy; Lizzie who was always reliable and loyal to the family.

"Perhaps he's just a nervous groom letting off steam before he settled down," said Lizzie quietly. "I didn't know if I should say anything, but I thought it would be better coming from me, rather than you hearing it from someone like Mrs Walmsley. Reuben said Hadrian's father was seen to pay the innkeeper for the damage caused and slipped the barman a few bob to keep the affair quiet. They managed to whisk Master Hadrian away before the bobbies arrived."

Jessie looked at her honest face, and her anger sank into a tight knot in her stomach. She felt sick. "Yes, of course you should have told me, Lizzie. You're quite right. Old Ma Walmsley would love a nasty bit of gossip like that to taunt me with. I suppose it's all over the town?"

"It was in a crowded inn," said Lizzie. "Our Reuben was there with his mates. Some of the lads suggested they go and see 'the toffs misbehaving themselves', as he said. Lawyer Lightfoot may have paid to keep it quiet, but they all saw what happened and it's bound to get out."

Jessie sat heavily on a chair. She shook her head in despair. "What do I do, Lizzie? Should I tell Helen?"

"I doubt she'd believe you, or if she did, she'd defend him," said Lizzie. "She's that stubborn. She's besotted with him. She'll marry him whatever."

Lizzie had been with the children as babies. She'd seen them nearly every day of their lives. She knew exactly what Helen was like and the extent of her stubbornness.

"I don't know whether to tell Robert," said Jessie, weighing up the consequences.

"I don't know what to say, Mrs Jessie." Lizzie hesitated. "Would it make any difference? It could only cause bad feeling between him and the groom. That wouldn't help family harmony much."

Jessie held her hand. "Thank you, Lizzie, for telling me. And you give good advice. You always have done. What would I do without you? What would we all do without you?"

"I've always loved working here at Overdale House," Lizzie told her with a modest smile. "You saved me from a life of squalor, and you've always treated me like one of the family. The Master can get cranky and, before she died, the Mistress got a bit mazy with that medicine of hers, but I could cope with that. But I'll always do my best for the family. I'll keep my eye on Miss Helen. I can always pop over to their house and help out if needs be."

"Thank you, Lizzie. You'll always have a home here while I'm alive," said Jessie.

After Lizzie went back to her work, Jessie sat gazing out into the garden for a while, wondering what her daughter was about to marry into. Jessie had never warmed to Hadrian, or any of the Lightfoots for that matter. But for her daughter to marry a drunkard and a bully was just appalling. Lizzie was right, though. Helen would marry her choice whatever her mother said, and if Jessie objected she was sure she would alienate her daughter. That was the last thing she wanted to do.

CHAPTER 41: THE WEDDING

The wedding was to be a quiet affair. Helen looked beautiful in her high-necked dress with a bodice of white lace and a bustle and short train of the remaining delicate fabric falling down the back of her full skirt. She and her mother had laboured long over its intricate folds to hide the joins, but it was as beautiful as anything in the Manchester bridal shops. Lizzie followed behind, carefully carrying Helen's trailing veil.

Robert squeezed Jessie's hand as his daughter descended the stairs from her bedroom. "She's a beauty, is our girl," he said, his voice emotional with pride. "Just like her mother," he added in a whisper.

"Aye, she's bonny right enough," said her grandfather. "Despite her age, I reckon she'll do all right with young Lightfoot. He is, after all, a gentleman's son. It's less than I hoped for, but the shipbuilder's lad was a bit slow coming forward."

Jessie raised an eyebrow at Robert and he suppressed a chuckle.

Gus's father had never received the peerage that had been rumoured. Through the grapevine, the Overdales heard that a government inspector had discovered a blockade runner for the Southern states being built in the Kearsley shipyard. The low, grey painted boats had been used to smuggle supplies and arms to the South. As Britain was nominally neutral in the American Civil War, his efforts had been frowned upon. Since Gus had inherited his father's business, he had hinted to his old friend Robert that he hoped his son might marry into the aristocracy. Jessie silently wished him luck. Charles Augustus may be the heir to a prosperous shipbuilding business, but he was rather a dull boy.

Matthias was, for all his years, still chafing that he was not regarded as a gentleman, merely trade.

"There's no telling young folks who to marry these days, Papa," Robert told his father.

"Or in my time either," snorted Matthias with a pointed glance at Jessie.

Robert slipped an arm round his wife's waist. "We've done all right," he said, smiling. "And just look at our handsome children."

Matt and Jack watched their sister with pride, looking very smart in their new suits. Matt had a cane to assist in his walking. It was topped with the smooth carved head of a noble-looking dog, and he was very proud of it. It had been given to him by his Uncle Eli and had been his great grandfather's. His grandfather, though, refused to use a stick. As they entered the church before the bride, he clung doggedly to Jessie's arm. Then he began to brace himself against the church furniture.

"He'd have been better using a stick than lurching along like drunk," murmured Jessie to Matt.

"You know Grandpapa," whispered her son with a grin. "His pride prevents any display of weakness."

Jacob and Alice were sitting with Uncle Eli and Honora dressed in their finest as Jessie and her boys entered their pew at the front. Then came John and his family with Eddie and Eleanor's fiancé Reginald. Behind the family sat Gus and Charles Augustus. As Helen's godfather Gus was determined to be there, although Amelia was missing, with a plea of some mysterious ailment.

The wheezy organ blew into action, and they all stood to greet the bride. Robert was walking with the aid of a silver-topped cane that Jessie had spotted in a second-hand shop. Once black and tarnished, it had been lovingly polished by Jessie for her husband. No one would have guessed she had paid pennies for it. On his arm Helen looked flushed and excited. Dora and Eleanor followed her, wearing pale blue.

The groom and his family turned to watch their approach. They had already observed the ungainly entrance of the Davenports with a barely hidden distain. Jessie lifted her chin in defiance. She may have once been a mill girl, but she felt herself every bit as worthy as the Lightfoots.

Hadrian nodded as his bride approached him, his face a mask of seriousness. Jessie watched him carefully. She hoped he would be loving and kind towards her daughter, but she could not help thinking about what Lizzie had told her.

Lizzie, who had waited at the back of the church to help Helen with her dress, slipped into the back pews beside Michael and his father and mother.

The service was quiet as the organ wheezed to a stop and the service began. Hadrian's answers to the vicar's questions were mumbled and hesitant. In contrast Helen spoke her responses determinedly, her clear voice ringing round the rising arches of the church. There was a hush as the vicar asked the age-old question: 'Has anyone any just cause…?' Mrs Lightfoot cleared her throat noisily. Jessie held her breath. The silence hung for a long moment, until the vicar carried determinedly on with the service. There was an audible sigh of relief as Hadrian at last smiled and kissed his wife. Helen's anxious face relaxed as they went out hand in hand into the sunshine, followed by their relieved relatives. The deed was done.

The wedding breakfast at Overdale House was a mixed affair. The Davenports were as lively as ever. Even Reginald seemed more animated in their presence. The Lightfoots with their few relatives had been sparse on their side of the church. Now they seemed determined to be critical. The elderly aunts continually demanded attention from a harassed Lizzie. She had recruited two of her sisters to help at the occasion, but Eleanor and Alice were kind enough to be helpful too.

"Who the hell do they think they are?" demanded Matthias in a whisper loud enough to be heard. "I didn't expect to be entertaining royalty."

A display of the wedding gifts was laid out on a table at one side of the room. The Davenports had given practical gifts of bed linen and kitchen goods. A new sewing machine, with its elaborate golden decoration, was Jessie's gift. The Lightfoots' offerings were a silver-plated tea set and elaborate vases, of little use to the couple. Uncle Eli ushered Jessie to one side and gave her a heavy bag of coins.

"Put that safe," he murmured. "It's fifty gold sovereigns. I didn't want to give it to the groom. I've heard odd rumours. You mention it to our Helen, and it's to be used for her when she needs it. You understand, don't you?"

"I certainly do. It's very good of you, Uncle Eli," she told him with a hearty kiss. "I can't thank you enough. It's good for a girl to have her own money to fall back on."

She watched Eleanor and Reginald and the loving way they treated each other. She noticed the way Michael helped Lizzie, their hands brushing and their secret smiles whenever their eyes met. Hadrian, on the other side of the room from Helen, was chatting to his family. However, his efforts to rally them were doomed. His jokes continually fell flat with the disapproving aunts, and he drank all the more to cover his embarrassment. Helen was chatting to Sabina and Anna-Marie as they admired her gown.

"Go and be nice to Hadrian's aunts," Jessie murmured to her. She knew how her daughter could charm people when she put her mind to it. "Then go and put your grandfather in a better mood," she suggested.

With a radiant smile, Helen reluctantly went to do her duty by her guests and soon the aunts had thawed. Jessie, who was adept at lip-reading from her days at the mill, saw them say what a charming girl her daughter was and how very polite. Matthias, too, mellowed a little when Helen went to make a fuss of him.

The aunts were the first to leave, taking the Lightfoots' small carriage to Doveton station. Then John reluctantly gathered his family together. Eleanor slipped upstairs with Helen to her bedroom and helped her change into her trousseau. Jessie thanked her niece when she arrived back downstairs dressed in her own clothes, Helen's blue dress left draped carefully on the bed.

"You looked proper lovely, my love," she told Eleanor. She was very fond of her niece and had helped to deliver her into the world. Eleanor was so different from her cousin. She was fair and fine-boned like her mother Elsie, so unlike Helen's robust dark beauty. Yet the blue dress had suited both girls.

Reginald heartily agreed with Jessie. "She looked a proper peach," he said proudly and added, "It'll be us next."

Helen descended the stairs looking as lovely in her plum velvet suit as she did in her wedding dress.

"The gig's waiting to take you to the station," said Matthias, glancing out through the window. "I reckon you'll reach Lytham by evening."

"Couldn't we have had the carriage?" Hadrian complained to his father.

His mother's face froze in prim disapproval.

"Mr Overdale is good enough to offer his gig," said his father sternly. "The carriage is needed to convey your sister and mother home. Anyway, it's only five miles to Doveton. You won't be in the gig for long."

Hadrian sniffed and stared out of the window. Jessie noticed that not once had he complimented Helen on her appearance. She remembered the bag of sovereigns slipped into the sideboard and wondered if she should mention them to her daughter before she left. Despite her natural inclination to share the news, she decided not to. She had an awful premonition that the scales would soon fall from her besotted daughter's eyes and Helen would see Hadrian as he really was.

CHAPTER 42: HONEYMOON HOTEL

The couple were tired by the time they reached the hotel at Lytham. Hadrian had slept for most of the train journey. He had snored loudly, to the fascination of the little boy in the carriage and the annoyance of the boy's mother.

"Is he drunk?" asked the child.

His mother hushed him.

"He had a late night," Helen apologised with an embarrassed smile, although the reek of alcohol filling the carriage told a different story.

There was very little polite conversation until they reached St Anne's station.

Helen roused her new husband, and he glared at her in annoyance. "We've arrived, dear," she murmured.

The mother quickly grabbed her son and hurried away, leaving the young couple to sort themselves out. They found a porter, then a hansom cab that took them the short journey to the St Anne's Hotel, newly built and gleaming. Helen admired its fashionable decoration.

"My father recommended it," said Hadrian. "He stayed here when he came to rearrange the will of some old hag who'd moved from Gorbydale to be by the sea. Of course, he put the expense of his stay on her bill. It's not bad, is it?"

Helen blushed as her new husband signed the register, writing her unfamiliar new name. The manager at the reception smiled, and she felt everyone must know they were a honeymoon couple. They were shown to their room, and she was about to unpack when Hadrian dumped their case on the floor and grabbed her around the waist.

"Come on then, let's get the deed done," he said with a cynical laugh. "I can't wait to finish the job I started in that folly thing. I've waited long enough."

Pushing her onto the bed, he pulled her clothes aside and took her virginity with little finesse. Then he rolled to one side of the bed and began snoring loudly. Helen stared at the ceiling in disbelief. Where was the burning passion she had felt in the little temple when she had been so eager to give herself to her beau? Now she felt frozen in disbelief at his brusqueness.

Quietly she left the bed and removed her clothes. The skirt of her velvet suit was torn, and she wondered how she would mend it without any sewing materials. Her underwear lay discarded on the floor. She picked up the delicate silk garments she'd trimmed lovingly with lace and smoothed and folded them for the morning. Then she opened her case and removed the pretty cotton nightdress that her mother had sewn and embroidered for her. Holding the fine cotton to her cheek, she inhaled the faint scent of lavender in its folds. Helen had once imagined dressing shyly in her nightgown and presenting herself to her new husband, virginal and pure. Now she felt soiled and used. There was a watery bloodstain on her petticoat, and she wondered how she could soak it overnight. Going to the washstand, she poured some cold water in the basin. First she washed her face, then gently rubbed the stain from the garment in the water. There was a faint hint of pink left as she draped her petticoat over a chair, hoping it would be dry in the morning. In a daze she slipped into her nightdress. Hadrian lay fully clothed on the bed. Hesitating at first, Helen decided to at least remove his shoes, which she did very carefully to avoid waking him. Then, seeing he was still snoring loudly, she undid his cravat, first removing the pearl pin.

The sheets were cold but calming in their smooth softness. Her mind still numb with shock, Helen lay awake listening to the unfamiliar sounds of the hotel around her, wondering what her future held. Her eagerness in Overdale's Folly now seemed an embarrassing dream. Though her every thought had seemed to focus on Hadrian, she realised she hardly knew him at all. His moods changed like quicksilver, and she realised with dismay that she would be constantly making excuses for him 'until death do us part'. Now she had a lifetime to wonder at her own folly in marrying so young.

The next morning he was a different man, sweet and charming. He admired her nightdress and kissed her tenderly. He lent her his tie pin to secure her torn skirt until she could buy some cotton and thread in the town. He was pleasant to the other hotel guests in the dining room as they took breakfast. Helen began to revive after her restless night and thought that perhaps married life might not be so bad after all.

They took a stroll through the town and admired the new buildings rising around and passed a newly built terrace of smart villas lining the road.

"I should like to live in a house like that," he said. "Though I don't suppose that's likely any time soon, not with Grandpa Scrooge in charge of the finances. So when is the old goat going to come up with this two hundred pounds?"

"He's put it in a bank account for me," said Helen. "He gave me the bank book at our wedding breakfast."

"You kept that quiet," snorted Hadrian.

"I was going to tell you on the train as a surprise, but you were asleep," she excused herself.

"So have you got the bank book with you?" he asked. "There's bound to be a branch of the bank here in St. Anne's, and we can get our hands on a bit of cash."

"I left it at home for safety," Helen explained.

"A fat lot of good that is," said her new husband angrily.

"But we'll need it at home to pay bills," tried Helen. "Anyway, my mother gave me ten pounds to spend. We're not without money. And I suppose you have some too?" she suggested quietly.

"That's my business," he said abruptly.

Helen had never had to budget for herself in her life, but she knew her parents were always careful with money. With Hadrian so secretive about his finances, she now discovered how hard that might be.

They had stopped before a haberdashery shop with some beautiful soft furnishings in the window. Helen stared at the prices of the cushion covers.

"I could easily make stuff like that," she thought aloud. "And prettier too."

"What? You mean you want to sew furnishings like some mean little seamstress?" sneered Hadrian. "You don't mean you want to sell things like that too? Oh well, once in trade, always in trade, I suppose. I hope you're not thinking of selling door to door. I didn't imagine I'd shackled myself to some pedlar."

Stung by the word 'shackled', Helen defended herself quietly. "I was only thinking about it. Shall we go and see the sea?" she asked to change the subject.

They strolled down towards the seashore and breathed in the fresh sea-washed air. The subject of her sewing was abandoned, but Helen's thoughts were busy with possibilities.

It wasn't until they were back in their room at the hotel that Hadrian began again to criticise her grandfather for stinginess.

"I'd expected him to cough up a lot more than two hundred," he said. "I don't suppose it's for each year?"

Helen shook her head. "I don't think so."

"I guessed as much," snapped Hadrian. "I thought you told me you were his favourite grandchild. A man like him wouldn't favour the cripple anyway, and I don't suppose that kid Jack pays him much attention."

Helen bit her lip to hear Matt called a cripple. "My brother is doing very well at the Endurance Mill," she defended. "He's now in charge of Uncle Eli's accounts since his old bookkeeper retired."

"And I'll bet he's got his hand in the till," laughed Hadrian.

"That's a foul slander," hissed Helen. "Matt is very honest." Her husband had gone too far in criticising her family. Her instinct to continually placate him was slowly dissolving.

Hadrian stared at her in surprise. "Don't take that tone with me," he warned. "I didn't expect to be saddled with a silly bitch like you without at least some cash attached."

"How can you be so cruel? At least I'm bringing some money into the marriage. If you'd stuck at your studies, you might have got a better position in a decent law firm," she snapped back at him.

The slap knocked her sideways. Helen tumbled and banged her head on the washstand. Stunned, she tentatively raised her hand to the pain and saw a trickle of blood staining her fingers.

Hadrian was instantly contrite. "Oh my darling, oh my darling, I didn't mean to do it," he cried, hauling her to her feet and holding her close. "Are you all right? Let me see?" He pulled a towel from the towel rail and, dousing it in water, dabbed it on her head. With growing panic he tried to staunch the blood, but it would not stop. "I'm so sorry, so sorry," he kept pleading, almost in tears.

Helen felt sick and lightheaded. He helped her to a chair by the dressing table. Finally the blood ceased to flow, though the towel was a mess. Later, when she had recovered somewhat, she rinsed the towel through in cold water so the hotel staff would not witness her shame. The bruise on her cheek, however, was not so easily washed away. Helen sat next to a wall in the dining room so that the other guests would not see her face. She walked with her head down and held a handkerchief up to her cheek as she left the room. Whenever she went out for the rest of the week, she wore a veil on her hat.

That night, Hadrian was tenderness itself with her. He made love to her gently and thoughtfully, and Helen began to wonder about her marriage. If she could resist provoking her new husband, perhaps her life would run smoothly.

On her return home, however, her mother remarked on the lingering yellow mark on her daughter's cheek.

"I walked into a door in the dark," said Helen. "I was half asleep, and of course the room was unfamiliar."

Jessie didn't look convinced.

CHAPTER 43: HOME LIFE

Life settled into a routine for Helen in her new home. Hadrian went to his father's office every morning and she set herself to housework. She spent weeks getting the house the way she wanted it. They had found some furniture in the attic in her old home which fitted into Overdale Lodge perfectly. Helen examined a small, battered table and found it sturdy enough. With some difficulty, she had manhandled it up into a small unused bedroom and set up her sewing machine. The ideas that had taken root in St Anne's were still buzzing round her head. Her next task was to find some fabric. With that in mind she went to see her mother, remembering the wealth of material that was tied up in her late grandmother's wardrobe.

Jessie was intrigued with her daughter's ideas. "Do you think it will pay?" she asked.

"Oh Mama, you should have seen the prices in the shops at St. Anne's. Even if I make a shilling or two making cushion covers, it will help with the housekeeping. But I need to keep my costs down."

"You're very enterprising," said her mother with a chuckle. "The Overdale lust for commerce certainly runs in your veins."

Helen laughed. "Do you think I'll grow a big belly like Grandpapa?"

"One day you might," said Jessie. "But not through overeating. When the little ones start to arrive, there'll be a change round your waistline."

Helen blushed to hear her mother speak about pregnancy.

"I know, I've remembered just the thing," said Jessie suddenly. "There was the end of a bolt of calico left over from the sewing classes. Nobody seemed bothered with it once the classes had finished, and I put it to one side. I think it's in the bottom of the bedding chest in my bedroom."

They went and found the fabric under all the bedding. It was plain white and not exactly what Helen was hoping for.

"The girls used it to make aprons," explained her mother.

And then Helen remembered a café in St Anne's. The café was busy and, ignoring Hadrian's grumblings, Helen had watched the waitresses as they waited for their tea. They had all worn white aprons and caps but trimmed in red gingham to match the tablecloths. Once again, her busy mind began designing.

"I'll take it," she said.

All the housewives wore aprons to protect their clothes. She was sure the young ones would rather wear pretty ones.

"Do you need any of Uncle Eli's money?" asked Jessie.

Helen hesitated. She had never mentioned her uncle's gift to Hadrian. The way he'd appropriated the money her grandfather had given them into his own bank account still rankled with her. She'd expected that they would budget for their home together as her parents did, but Hadrian had other ideas. He'd left her with very little for herself.

"I'll take one sovereign," she said. "That should be plenty to buy me some thread and some trimmings to get me started."

The clock in the hallway began chiming twelve o'clock. Helen stopped still.

"I hadn't realised it was so late," she said. "I'd better get back to make Hadrian's dinner."

Grabbing the calico and a pair of good scissors that her mother had offered her, she hurried down the hill and dashed into the kitchen. Her husband was sitting at the table with a mug of ale in his hand.

"Oh, there you are. Gallivanting back up to your mother's again, I see," he drawled. "We'll have to put a stop to that. And what's all that you've got there?"

She tentatively showed him the bolt of cloth. "It's calico," she said. "I was thinking of er…" Suddenly she didn't want to tell him of her plans. He would surely sneer at them. "Some pillowcases," she said with a pert smile, pleased at her subterfuge. "I didn't expect you home so early," she said as she stirred a pot of stew she'd made the previous day.

"Things were slack at the office this morning," said Hadrian. "The old man has some big job he wants me to do this afternoon. I might be a bit late this evening."

Helen nodded and dished out his meal.

There was a jug of ale on the table, and Hadrian refilled his mug. "I thought I'd get something decent to drink with my dinner," he said. "I'm sick of tea, and I'm sick of brewing it for the old man's clients. I'm treated like nothing but a skivvy at that place," he complained.

Helen was tempted to say that he was lucky to have a job, especially as Hadrian's father seemed barely able to tolerate him. She and her new husband had been invited to tea when they arrived home from their honeymoon. She had sent his parents postcards from St. Anne's and brought little gifts. These were accepted politely, but she was treated coolly and had the impression that they thought she had trapped Hadrian into marriage and under the false pretence that she was a wealthy heiress. Throughout the high tea, little niggling remarks were fired in her direction. Mr Lightfoot then asked his son when he would return to work.

"Honeymoon means a month, surely," joked Hadrian flippantly.

"I think you'll find that I expect you back in the office on Monday at nine o'clock sharp," snapped his father.

They had little to say to each other after that. Mrs Lightfoot and Dora kept the conversation going with gossip about their neighbours. Helen was increasingly anxious to go home.

Thereafter Hadrian visited his family alone, usually when he knew his father was away on business. He was always sure of a welcome from his mother and sister, who doted on him. The friendship between Helen and Dora slowly faded, though Dora sometimes popped into the lodge to see her brother and especially when there was any gossip rumbling round.

"Father never tells us anything about his business," she complained to Helen as she sipped tea, poured from the silver-plated teapot.

"That's because it's private," her brother rebuked her, then proceeded to tell her any personal gossip he'd gleaned.

Helen was dismayed by the way they talked about their father's clients. She resolved to warn her family to change their lawyers. It was a pity that the nearest law firm was in Doveton, and the Lightfoots might look on any change as a snub.

In the following days, she kept her sewing activities quiet from Hadrian's family and he took little interest in it himself. He just assumed she was sewing for their home, especially when pretty cushions appeared to brighten their old sofa, or she wore a becoming apron. But slowly Helen had a batch of offerings that she could show for sale. She used her sovereign to buy some more material and trimmings, going to a fent shop in the town to buy ends of rolls and lace and ribbon. Her ingenuity with these small remnants impressed her mother when she called to see Helen.

Her daughter proudly showed her what she had been doing.

"You really have a gift," said Jessie, examining a cushion cover that was rimmed with small ribbon roses. "This is lovely."

"I was wondering where to sell my efforts," admitted Helen. "If I take them locally, people might tell the Lightfoots and they'll start making remarks about 'tinkers' and 'people in trade'. No doubt they'll think that's beneath their dignity." She had often wondered about her grandfather's obsession with 'the gentry'. Now she knew how he felt. It was galling to be patronised by the Lightfoots.

"That's their problem if they object to people earning an honest living through their own efforts," Jessie told her daughter. "I can't be doing with such snobbery. But then I'm only an ignorant mill girl!"

"You have more brains and courage than any of Hadrian's lot," said Helen, hugging her mother. "I can't see Madame Lightfoot nursing soldiers in the middle of a war."

"That was a long time ago," sighed Jessie, remembering her adventures in America. "I wonder how Honora is doing in London. She owes me a letter. But I expect she's been too busy to write."

Helen wondered what her life would have been like if she had acted on her mother's suggestion that she should go and stay with Honora. But she'd desperately wanted to marry Hadrian. Now she had to live with that decision.

"Take no notice of the silly scandalmongers," her mother told her as she drew on her shawl to leave. "And I might mention to your papa and grandfather about changing their lawyers."

She had been shocked by what she'd heard of Hadrian's indiscretions.

CHAPTER 44: OLD FRIENDS

Honora had indeed been too busy to write to her friends. She'd worked so hard at the clinic that most evenings she fell asleep almost as soon as she had eaten her supper. Elizabeth Blackwell called her into her office for a quiet word.

"Doctor Darwen, I've watched you these past months and you are working your fingers to the bone."

"But there's so much to be done," protested Honora.

"And exactly how many patients did your father cure once he'd caught cholera?" asked Elizabeth, who knew of Honora's history.

Honora took a deep breath and looked close to tears when she remembered her dear father toiling away over the poverty-stricken masses of the Manchester slums.

"You see my point, dear," said Elizabeth kindly. "We are not immune to the diseases of the patients we treat and, if we are overworked and tired, we are more susceptible to them. I myself am a case in point."

Honora stared at her in surprise. She couldn't remember her mentor being ill, except for minor ailments.

"You know of course that I am virtually blind in one eye because I caught purulent ophthalmia from one of my patients in Paris." Honora had noticed Elizabeth's eye but been too polite to mention it. "That is why I am so very insistent on good hygiene. You must know that I intend to retire soon. Most people expect Doctor Jex-Blake to take over, but I know she wishes to return to Edinburgh. Her friend that followed her here from Edinburgh University would make a more suitable director, I'm sure. She is, how can I say, more diplomatic." She gave Honora a knowing glance.

"I know exactly what you mean," admitted Honora with a smile.

Doctor Jex-Blake could be very abrupt, and that wasn't helpful when the future of women doctors needed all the help it could get.

"Of course, I rely on you not to repeat our little conversation," said her mentor.

"I'll be the soul of discretion," promised Honora.

"So, my dear, I noticed that you seemed somewhat refreshed by the short break you took for your niece's wedding. So, despite the fact that we are of course very busy, I suggest you take some time to go and visit your family. We're always busy here, and there is never a good time to go. So 'carpe diem', seize the day and come back to us with renewed vigour."

"If you insist," said Honora quietly. Her head spun with all she had to do, yet she had to admit she was feeling exhausted.

"I insist," said Doctor Blackwell.

Honora finished her clinic and then wrote to her Uncle Eli, asking if she might come and stay. She was still unsure if she would receive a welcome at Overdale House with Matthias in residence. He had been polite but cool with her at Helen's wedding, and she didn't want to cause any awkwardness for Jessie. Her old friend would willingly accommodate her. Days later, she received a letter saying Eli would gladly welcome her to the Mill House.

The journey by train would be long and tedious and, once she was seated, she took one of her medical books from her bag and began to read. The carriage was full. A plump woman with a little girl sat beside her, and she smiled at the little one and hoped that the sticky lollipop the child was eating would not drop onto her velvet skirt. An elderly man sat in the corner near the door and a middle-aged couple sat in front of her. The man opposite was bored as his wife sat looking out of the window. He took a great interest in her book.

"Medical stuff, eh? I should have thought a nice novel would be more in your line. Something by one those Brontë ladies, perhaps."

He obviously hadn't read any of the Brontë books with their tangled tales of relationships. Honora gave a trite smile and continued with her reading. The man didn't take the hint in his quest to find some distraction.

"I don't hold with any of this lady doctor malarkey," he said. "It's unnatural. What lady wants to go dabbling in blood, for goodness' sake?"

Honora held her breath and tried to ignore him. Her annoyance got the better of her. "So your wife has never cooked liver or kidneys?" she asked politely.

Her fellow passenger blustered at the challenge.

"I like a good steak and kidney pie," said the plump woman. "And you're right, dear. There's plenty of blood comes off that offal. Ooh, and stuffed lambs hearts are very tasty; one of my favourites."

"But medicine's a different matter," snapped the man. "I mean, a woman hasn't got the same brain capacity as a man. It's been proven."

"Did you know that Doctor Elizabeth Blackwell, who founded my infirmary in London, had the highest marks, above all the male students, at her medical school? Not bad for a woman with a small brain," said Honora as she tried to concentrate on her book once again.

"Well, I think it's unnatural," stated the man loudly.

"So you'd rather have a strange man examining your wife's private parts, would you?" said Honora calmly.

"That's a disgusting thing to say," protested her antagonist. "What do you think?" he appealed to the elderly passenger in the corner.

The old man glanced at him sternly. "My wife was a very private and modest woman," he said quietly. "She had some lady's problems, but she wouldn't go to the doctor because she was too embarrassed. It was too late for her when she finally went to see him. He found she had ovarian cancer. If we had had a lady doctor, I'm sure my dear wife would have gone to be examined much earlier and might have had a chance to be cured. And I wouldn't be on my own now." He turned to Honora. "You keep up the good work, miss."

"Thank you," said Honora, grateful for his support. "I'm very sorry for your loss."

"She was a grand woman," he said sadly. "A grand woman, taken from me too soon."

With that, he sank into reverie and Honora turned back to her book with a barely supressed smile. Her protagonist grumbled quietly to his wife.

"I'm sure I shouldn't like a strange man poking about in my bits," she heard the woman murmur very quietly so as not to embarrass her husband.

The rest of the journey was quietly uneventful but for the chatter of the little girl, who was eventually lulled to sleep with the rhythm of the wheels.

When they arrived in Manchester, Honora stretched her cramped limbs as she reached for her case and headed for the train for Doveton. As she reached the platform, she stopped in surprise. There in front of her was a familiar figure she had once longed to see but now only confused her. He must have sensed someone watching him and turned towards her before she could slip into the ladies' waiting room.

"Honora?" asked Arden Davenport. "Fancy seeing you here. Are you heading for Gorbydale too?"

"I'll be staying for a few days with my Uncle Eli," she told him.

"Good," he said with a smile. "We can travel together, then." He hesitated for a second. "If that's all right with you?"

"Of course it is. We can catch up on old times. I had expected to see you at Helen's wedding," she said.

"Afraid I was halfway across the Atlantic at the time. It was all a bit sudden. Is there anything I should know?" he asked with a knowing glance.

"Helen isn't with child, if that's what you mean?" said Honora with a wry smile. "Jessie told me quietly that they married so hastily to prevent some embarrassing gossip getting out. She wanted Helen to come and stay with me until the rumours died down. But you know Helen. She wanted to marry Hadrian Lightfoot, the lawyer's son, and once she's made up her mind, there's no changing it."

"Is this Hadrian bloke all right?" asked Arden.

Honora paused for a moment. "He's very charming," she said in Hadrian's favour. "I'm not sure Jessie and Robert know him very well. Matthias positively detests him for seducing his precious granddaughter," she added with a laugh.

"She always was his favourite," admitted Arden. "She could always wrap the old man round her little finger, even when she was a tot. Anyway, how are you? Still working too hard?"

"That's why I've been ordered to come home for a rest," she admitted.

The Doveton train chugged into the station and he helped her aboard with her case. Once again the carriage was crowded, so they had little opportunity for private conversation.

"Will we share a hansom?" asked Arden when they reached Doveton. "I can drop you off at Eli's and carry on up to Weavers Row."

Honora agreed but immediately felt embarrassed by their closeness in the narrow cab.

"It's good to see you," said Arden. "I often think about you and the times I visited you in New York. It seems a lifetime away."

"So much has happened since then," Honora admitted. "Though not much has happened for us women doctors. I'm still not recognised in Britain. I've just had an argument with a man on the London train."

"I'll bet you won," Arden laughed.

"I did, in fact," chuckled Honora. "With the help of a very nice old man who'd lost his wife."

Their conversation lulled as the hansom trundled the five miles to Gorbydale. Then they both began talking at once and laughed.

"You go first," said Honora.

Arden cleared his throat and paused for a moment. "I was wondering if perhaps I could call and see you while we are both in town?" he asked quietly.

"I'm sure we'll see each other..." Honora started to say, then changed her mind. "Yes, please do. It would be good to catch up."

Honora visited Jessie, and the old friends lost no time in catching up with each other's news.

"When will you be able to come and practise in Gorbydale?" asked Jessie, linking her old friend as they strolled down to see Helen in her new home.

"Not anytime soon," said Honora with a sigh. "Doctor Blackwell has retired, and Mrs Isobel Thorne is our new director. I'll stay for a while until the new regime settles down and then perhaps look around. There are rumours that we women will soon be accepted to practise. And then I'll see."

"Well, we're very proud of you, whatever you do," Jessie told her.

Helen was very pleased to see Honora and proud to show her what she was doing. She gave her one of her prettiest cushion covers.

"It will brighten up your room, wherever you are," said Helen, laughing, "and then you can remember us in Gorbydale."

"I always think of you in Gorbydale," Honora told her. "All my best friends and family are here."

Arden called a few days later once they had both been reunited with their families and settled in. She was pleased to see him; she'd been wondering if he'd made the suggestion to visit just to be polite and would not follow up on it.

"It's a lovely day," he said. "Do you fancy going out for a walk?"

She called to Mrs Corbett and told her their plans.

"That'll be lovely dear," said Eli's housekeeper, with an expressive smile that suggested an assignation rather than just a walk with an old friend. "Will I make some extra dinner for Mr Davenport?"

"That would be kind," Arden told her. "If Mr Gorman wouldn't mind?"

"Oh no, he'd love to see you. He always says he likes a visit from the young folks."

"Not so young anymore," admitted Arden.

He offered Honora his arm as they left the house and she gratefully took it. She hadn't meant to, but she was still tired after her long journey from London in the cramped carriage.

"Would a stroll up to the old fort be too much for you?" asked Arden. "We can take it slowly. The air is so much fresher up there, and it would do your lungs good. I find the atmosphere round here very smoky after life at sea, even in the engine room."

They took their time, pausing to gaze over the Gorbydale valley as they climbed up the hill. The broken ruins at the peak were thought to be the remains of a Roman fort, and Arden had once found an old coin there. But its true past had long been lost in history. The view of two valleys was breathtaking and with the fresher air, also breath-giving. Honora sat to rest on a remaining broken wall.

"So what are your plans?" asked Arden. "Will you eventually go back to America?"

Honora hesitated. Then she told him all about Clement, how she suspected him of murdering her friend Verity by mistake and how she'd lived in fear of his revenge until she'd heard the news of his death.

"And now you're free from his malice," Arden reassured her. "Don't forget I've sailed on the Mississippi and witnessed those alligators. They're voracious." He shuddered as he remembered.

"I thought I was free," said Honora. "Then Dolly received a letter from one of Clement's old friends. His old housekeeper died in a curious accident and, in her dying breath, said she'd been pushed under a carriage."

"Why would they suspect Clement?" asked Arden, puzzled.

"Because she'd sold his house and kept the money," said Honora. "As we know, he likes his revenge."

"So you feel safer in England?" Arden decided.

Honora nodded.

"Do you think you will ever return to Gorbydale?" he asked.

"There's work to be done here, but I doubt if I'd have the opportunity to set up a clinic," admitted Honora. "And would people come to my surgery? There's such a prejudice against us women doctors. It's beyond understanding."

"Oh, men will think you're standing on their toes and taking their business," said Arden with a laugh. "It will be nothing to do with your competence, only protection of their doctor's fees. Your day will surely come."

"I do hope you're right," sighed Honora.

She gazed up at him as he examined the remains of his old haunting ground, high above his parents' house. Arden was still as handsome as ever, though a tell-tale streak of grey flecked his dark hair. He was sunburned too from life at sea. She wondered if they would have married, if she hadn't been so foolish as to fall in love with another man who didn't want her.

He turned and smiled. "I wonder how our lives would have been if we had married and settled down here in Gorbydale?"

"I suppose we should have managed," she said. "Though I wouldn't have been able to practise as a doctor. Didn't your mother Nellie always say, 'Whatever is meant for you won't pass you by'?"

"So she did," said Arden with a chuckle. "Fancy remembering that. But I think that ship has passed us by, don't you? There might have been a time..."

"But I was so wrapped up in my work, and you were far away at sea," Honora mused. "You should have married someone else," she added. "You still can."

"And so could you," he said.

"I'm probably too old to have children now," sighed Honora. "But you..."

"But I could marry and leave my wife and any children alone while I'm at sea," said Arden. "It isn't ideal. No, I'm quite resigned to my life on board. And if I get lonely, there are plenty of wealthy widows who take to a man in uniform. That reminds me, did Mrs Van Meyerson get in touch with you? I remember she promised to find you some wealthy patients. She didn't mention it when I saw her last, and I forgot to ask."

Honora shook her head, remembering the rich widow she had helped on her voyage back to England. She also recalled how attracted the woman was to Arden. "I doubted she'd contact me. Our clinic is not in the most salubrious part of town," she said with a chuckle. "Perhaps she might call if I ever get to Harley Street! But that's not likely."

"You never know," said Arden, smiling.

From their vantage point above the town, they could see the smoking chimney of Jacob's cottage just below them.

"Shall we call and get a cup of tea from Alice?" suggested Arden. "I'm sure she'd like to see you. She mentioned you the other day, and I can tell her I'll be eating with you and Eli at dinnertime. Father will be hard at work at the Endurance."

Honora agreed. It had been a long time since she'd visited Weavers Row. She'd helped to relieve Jessie's mother Nellie before she'd died of cotton lung; a result of her childhood days working in a mill. Alice, Jacob's second wife, welcomed her warmly. As with Mrs Corbett, Alice was under the impression that Honora and Arden were more than friends.

"Will you be having a word with her Uncle Eli?" Honora heard Alice whisper.

"What about?" asked Arden, oblivious to his stepmother's hints.

"You know!" urged Alice.

Her insinuations suddenly dawned on Arden. "Oh no, Alice, you mustn't dust off your wedding hat," he told her quietly in the hope that Honora would not hear. "Miss Honora and I are just good friends. Please be assured of that."

Honora felt a pang of disappointment at his protests. She wondered what it would have been like to be welcomed into the Davenport family, but it was obvious now that she and Arden would only ever be friends. As he had mentioned, the ship of their romance had long since sailed.

CHAPTER 45: THE SALESWOMAN

Helen had been proud to show her mother and Honora all her sewing efforts and was reassured when Honora said how professional and attractive they were. Now Helen was eager to put her plans into place. She waited until Hadrian had left for work. The previous day, he hadn't arrived home for his dinner. His excuse, when he eventually arrived home in the evening, was that he had called into the Bridge Inn on the way home for a jug of ale and met an old friend there.

"He was in Gorbydale for the funeral of a relative. He was eating alone and he looked a bit miserable, so I thought I'd keep him company," said Hadrian, oblivious that his wife had waited ages for him to arrive and then had to eat alone when he didn't show up.

"You could have brought him home here and I'd have given him something to eat," Helen told him.

"What, more of that damned stew? I didn't want to embarrass myself — or you," sneered Hadrian.

She reheated the stew for his tea anyway and ate some bread and cheese herself. He ate the stew up with relish. In previous days she would have cooked him something fresh, but a small hard core of resistance was growing in the heart that had once been so tender and forgiving towards him.

"How long is your friend in Gorbydale for?" she asked nonchalantly.

"Couple of days, I think," said Hadrian, wiping his plate clean with a morsel of bread. He'd eaten as if he'd had no food for a couple of days.

"Will you be eating with him tomorrow?" Helen was silently planning.

"Yes, I might. In fact, I probably will," he said, grinning up at her. Then he added, "You don't mind, do you?"

"Not if it helps your friend," said Helen calmly.

The way was free for her to go to Doveton.

She packed her wares in the case they had used for their honeymoon and went to catch the Doveton bus in the town square. She was feeling excited and also smug that she had kept her secret from her husband. Buoyed with hope, she heard the steady clip-clop of horses and the bus appeared over the bridge. As she was just about to board, she froze as someone tapped her on the shoulder.

"Hello, Helen. Are you running away from home with your suitcase?" giggled Anna-Marie.

Helen stumbled onto the bus and slumped down into a seat. Anna-Marie and Sabina slipped into the seat in front of her and to her horror, Dora sat down beside her.

"We're going to catch the train in Doveton and have a day out in Manchester, aren't we girls?"

"Oh yes," chorused the two girls.

"And we're having tea in Kendal Milne's," said Sabina proudly.

"So are you leaving town, then?" asked Dora pertly.

Helen thought fast. "My mother asked me to take some of Jack's old clothes to my uncle's house," she said quickly. "He's grown so fast, and Elsie's boys are a bit smaller."

"Oh, hand-me-downs," sniffed Dora. "Being an only girl, I was spared that indignity."

Sabina stayed silent, as she had two older sisters and no doubt wore their cast-offs.

"We send our old clothes to my cousins," said Anna-Marie. "They're very glad of them."

"I expect you wore Hadrian's old baby clothes, though," remarked Helen to Dora. "Baby boys and girls wear the same things anyway. I remember my mother brought our layettes out for Jack when he was born."

"Oh, Dora was too young to be appalled then," joked Sabina, and the two girls in front started giggling.

Helen bit her lip to smother a smirk. Dora remained in silent disapproval of her friends' treachery.

Mercifully, they were diverted from any disagreements as the journey to Doveton was busy with passengers getting on and off. The bus was very crowded by the time they reached the town.

"Goodbye, then. Have a lovely time in Manchester," said Helen as she left them to continue their journey to the station. She hoped they would not remember that her uncle, an engineer on the railways, lived in a house not far from the station.

As she left the bus stop, she noticed a draper's nearby. Glancing at the goods in the window, she decided that her wares would certainly fit in and thought she'd try her luck.

The woman behind the counter was very interested, though she was continually interrupted by customers. Then she offered Helen paltry price for the pinafores and cushion covers.

"Couldn't you give me a bit more?" asked Helen, almost insulted by the offer, especially when she'd seen the prices the woman charged for plainer goods.

"I've got to make a profit myself," said the shopkeeper. "Take it or leave it."

Helen hesitated. "I'll need to think about it," she said, knowing there were more shops she could try.

"Well, I've got customers waiting," said the woman abruptly and turned to the mill girl waiting at the counter.

Packing her goods into the case, she bid the woman 'good day' and went out into the street. Disheartened by her first tentative effort, she glanced around to see where she might try next.

"Excuse me," said a voice behind her.

She turned to find the mill girl from the shop beside her.

"Perhaps I can help you," said the girl. "I noticed those things you were packing away and you've got some lovely stuff."

"Thank you," said Helen.

"Have you thought about having a market stall?" asked the girl.

"I … I couldn't," Helen sighed. "My husband wouldn't approve."

"Oh, you've got one of them, have you?" chuckled the girl. "No offence meant, though," she added hastily when she saw the look on Helen's face. "Listen, I work at the Dove Mill up the road. Our girls would fight to get their hands on nice stuff like that. A couple of cushion covers like yours would really brighten up a room. You'd definitely make a lot more money than that old biddy was offering."

Helen became interested.

The girl hesitated as she looked over Helen's clothes. "I can see that you might be a bit er … wary of dealing with us mill girls," she said.

"My Ma … mother was a mill girl," Helen told her. "It's not that. I don't think I'd have the time. I'd have to get home."

"Oh, the husband?" said the girl, raising her eyebrows. "Look, my name's Lorna, Lorna Napier. I could sell the stuff if you like."

Helen didn't hesitate. "And I could give you a percentage?" she suggested. "Do you think you could do it?"

"Easy, with nice stuff like that. A percentage, eh?" Lorna's eyes lit up. "I was just going to ask for a couple of bob."

"Oh no, a percentage would be fairer," decided her new partner. "I could give you ten percent of everything you sell. That's er … two shillings in the pound."

The girl held out her hand and Helen shook it heartily. "I'd best get back to work," said Lorna. "Give us your case."

Helen hesitated.

"Come on, walk with me towards the mill. I'll show you where I live on the way," said Lorna. "You can call when you like and collect your money, say in a couple of days. I reckon we'll do all right with this lot. Lasses are always selling stuff in our dinner hour. We don't always have time to go looking round the shops, except Saturday afternoon, see. Then it's mostly shopping for grub."

As they hurried along the streets, they heard the factory hooter for the end of the dinner break.

"That's my house at the end of Anita Street," said Lorna, pointing to the end of a terrace. "Number 8. I'll have to dash, but just go and knock for my Mam. She'll tell you I live there." With that, she headed off for the mill carrying Helen's case. She turned and waved just before she disappeared into the mill gates.

Helen stopped in the middle of the street and stared. She had just trusted a complete stranger with all her hard work. It had all happened so fast and, if she hadn't been so disappointed by the draper's meagre offer, she would never have fallen in with the girl's suggestion. Reluctantly she went to the house that Lorna had pointed out and knocked hesitantly on the door. There was no answer. She knocked again, her heart trembling. There was an ominous silence. Helen waited for a long moment, then turned to go, feeling such a fool. She felt like crying, sure she had lost all her wares. How would she ever find Lorna, if that's what she was called, in a mill full of women? How was she going to explain the loss of the case to Hadrian?

"Hang on, I'm coming," she heard the faint voice call from behind the front door.

The door was flung open and a plump woman in a pinafore stood there, gasping for breath.

"I was just in the privy out back, love. I heard someone at t'door but had to adjust meself — if you know what I mean," she added with a wink. "Now, what can I do you for? If you're collecting for the temperance, I'm afraid I've nowt to spare. I don't drink much anyway."

"I was wondering if Lorna lives here," asked Helen tentatively.

"Our Lorna, oh aye, but she's at t'mill right now, love. You'll get her after six o'clock. She's not in any trouble, is she?"

"No, no, not at all," said Helen, laughing with relief. "Just tell her Helen called, the woman with the case. She'll know what you mean. Thank you, thank you very much." With that, she waved goodbye, leaving Lorna's mother looking puzzled.

She laughed to herself on the way home. Would their enterprise really pay off? She hoped with all her heart that her hard work would benefit both her and Lorna.

If Lorna could sell her wares for even pennies more than the draper had offered, it would be an achievement. And the praise she'd had for the aprons and cushion covers had reassured Helen.

"You've got some lovely stuff," Lorna had said.

Helen smiled to herself as she sat on the bus home. Now she had to devise a way to visit Lorna without Hadrian suspecting what she was doing.

Hadrian arrived home that evening in a terrible mood. He complained about everything, about the food, about the house, about her appearance.

"Is your friend all right?" she was eventually tempted to ask.

"Friend?" asked Hadrian, looking puzzled.

"At the Bridge Inn; the one who'd come for the family funeral," she said.

"Oh, er … yes," stuttered her husband. "Well, you know, as well as can be expected. Anyway, he's gone home."

"So has something happened at the office?"

He stared at her in surprise as if she was reading his mind. "Well, I'd only had a little drink, you know, I mean with my friend, at the er … Bridge Inn, and my father hauled me into his office and complained about my drinking. Old fool," he muttered.

"Oh," said Helen, unsure of what to say, fearful that any of her remarks might further stoke his annoyance. "Well, now your friend's gone home, you can come home for your dinner," she finished with a smile.

It was the last thing she wanted, as she'd planned to meet Lorna at midday to see about their arrangement. There was no way that Helen could go to Doveton after six o'clock in the evening without arousing her husband's suspicion.

A couple of days later, she had her chance.

"The old man has asked me to go to St Anne's to get some documents signed tomorrow. He just needs some signatures, or he'd go himself," said Hadrian. "It'll give me a chance to get out of the office. He's watching me like a hawk. Anyway, I'll be going early but it'll probably take all day. I'd have taken you with me, but Father wouldn't cover the expense."

"That's fine," said Helen. "I'll have plenty to do. Go and enjoy a bit of fresh air while you can."

Once he'd gone the next day, she waited until she knew his train from Doveton had left and then headed that way herself on the omnibus. She heard the hooter from the mill as she walked towards Anita Street. Moments later, she saw Lorna heading towards her home. She waved and Lorna hurried to meet her.

"Am I glad to see you," she said with a grin. "We've done really well, and I've actually got some more orders. I told you they'd sell like hot cakes. Come on in." She ushered Helen into the terraced cottage. "Hi Mam, I'm home and I've got someone with me," she called.

Mrs Napier bustled out of the kitchen. "Hello, love, called for your money, have you? Our Lorna's right chuffed. Did she tell you how well she'd done?"

Helen nodded with a smile.

"Have you had anything to eat?" asked Lorna's mother. "I've done plenty, and I can put another bowl out."

Helen was about to refuse out of politeness, but the aroma of the thick pea and ham soup was too much of a temptation. "Oooh, that smells good," she confessed. "I'll have some, please, if I'm not robbing anyone."

"You're welcome, lass," said Mrs Napier, laughing.

Lorna went to a cupboard by the chimney breast and took out a glass jar. She unscrewed the lid and tipped the contents onto the table, bright florins and shillings and a couple of half-crowns.

"What about that, then?" she asked with pride. "Two pounds, three shillings and sixpence."

"That's wonderful," said Helen. "You must have worked so hard."

"Not a bit of it," said Lorna. "When I showed them what I'd got, they couldn't wait to get their hands on the stuff. And the ones that missed out wanted to know when I could bring some more."

"You know, I could have brought some stuff with me today," confessed Helen. "I just wasn't sure how things were going."

"You should have some confidence in yourself," Lorna urged her. "You've got a real talent there. The girls were saying they loved the colours and how pretty your stuff was. The cushion covers went quickest. Can you make them in pairs? People like matching covers."

"Yes, of course I can," said Helen.

"And is it too fiddly to make heart shapes?" asked her new friend. "One of the girls asked for some to give as a wedding present. She'd seen some in Manchester that she fancied, but they were dear and she didn't have enough money. We could charge more for heart shapes."

Helen stared at the money and ideas buzzed round her head. "What colours do the girls prefer?" she asked.

"Red and pink and floral sold quickest," said Lorna. "But blue's popular too."

Helen nodded. "I'll remember that. Now, I'd better sort your money out for you." She tried to calculate the ten per cent in her head. "I think it's four shillings and fourpence and another couple of pence." She handed Lorna four shillings and sixpence. "Is that all right?"

"Lovely, since I was only going to ask for a couple of bob," said Lorna, laughing. "I mean, you've done all the hard work, sewing and stuff. And you'll have to buy more material."

Helen had some ideas on that too. "Do you think the girls would like cotton damask?"

"In the right colours, they'd like anything," said Lorna. "Oooh look, here's our grub. Better tuck in before the hooter goes."

Accompanied by crusty bread, the soup was delicious. After thanking Mrs Napier, Helen accompanied Lorna back to the mill. The two girls were well pleased with their business arrangements and promised to meet soon. Then Helen left to have a quick look around town. She found a fent shop and bought a large bag of scraps of ribbon and lace for pennies.

The bus back to Gorbydale stopped in the middle of town, and it was only a short walk to the old Endurance Mill. She hesitated as she entered the mill. Her grandfather spotted her and hurried over to meet her.

"Is anything wrong, love?" he asked anxiously.

"No, no," she reassured him. "I've er … just come to have a look round. Listen, can I have a quiet word?"

He steered her towards the counting office.

Matt looked up with a surprised smile. "Hello, Sissy," he said. "What are you doing here?"

Charity glanced up, and Matt immediately introduced her.

"This is Miss Charity Fitch, my assistant," he said proudly.

Helen nodded. "Hello," she said. "Nice to meet you, Miss Fitch. My brother is always praising you."

Charity smiled at Helen and then turned her shy smile to Matt. Only his twin might have noticed the faintest blush that touched Matt's cheeks.

Then Helen remembered her business and turned to Jacob. "Do they have many fents here at the mill, you know, ends of rolls, mistakes and the like?"

"Aye, we've a few," he admitted. "One of the engineering firms sometimes buys them for rags and dusters and stuff. We've a paper mill that buys them too."

"Could I buy some of the bigger pieces?" she asked, to her grandfather's surprise.

"I don't see why not," he said. "We couldn't give you them free, of course, but we'd ask a fair price."

"I'd be grateful if you didn't mention it to anyone just yet," said Helen, glancing at Matt. She looked at Charity, who nodded her head. "I'm not sure if my husband or his family would approve."

"Enough said," said Jacob with a chuckle. "They won't hear anything from any of us, will they?"

Matt and Charity assured her they would keep her secret, and Helen went home with a parcel of useful pieces of cotton damask for a very reasonable price.

CHAPTER 46: HEARTS AND HUMILIATION

On the way home, Helen called into the butcher's shop for something to make for Hadrian's tea when he arrived back from the office. She gave her order to a young man, and he had almost finished wrapping it when the owner of the shop confronted her.

"When will your husband be paying the butcher's bill?" he demanded. "We've already sent him one reminder."

Helen remembered the money in her pocket but had no idea how much the bill would be. She did not want to start discussing what she could pay in front of the other customers. "I'll have a word with him," she told the butcher humbly. "I'll just take the mince, then."

Reluctantly he gave her a pound of minced meat, and she paid him for it from her small earnings. The butcher slipped the chops and sausage back onto his shelves. The other customers gave her a pitying glance as she left the shop.

Helen was furious at her humiliation. She had never even heard of the butcher's reminder. When Hadrian arrived home that evening, she was determined to confront him.

When she reached Overdale Lodge, she sat down with a cup of tea and wondered what she must do. First she decided to put her remaining money away separately in a moneybox. As a child, she had been given the pottery owl by Grandad Jacob.

"You be like that wise old owl and save up for a rainy day," he'd told her. "Pop your spare pennies in there and you'll soon be rich."

Helen had never had any pennies to spare, as she always liked to spend them. Matt, who'd received a pottery squirrel from Jacob, regularly squirrelled away any money he was given, unlike his sister. Now she had a reason to save.

Once, her parents and grandparents had provided for her every need. Now she was on her own and her husband controlled all the money, including the dowry her grandfather had given her. Helen had kept Uncle Eli's sovereigns a secret from her husband with good reason. Somehow, their bills were always paid late.

Helen put the owl on a high shelf in the room she now called her sewing room. Hadrian rarely, if ever, went in there. Then she reviewed her purchases. The cotton damask was all white, but she planned to dye it in the most popular colours. Sketching out a large heart on an old newspaper, she carefully cut it out to use as a template. Then she experimented with lace and ribbon. 'Matching pairs' Lorna had suggested, so Helen would have to plan carefully to eke out her stock of trimmings.

She sat back, pleased with her day's work, her head busy with plans. Hadrian might be secretive about his salary, but Helen could learn to be secretive too. Her initial fury had dispersed as she worked on her ideas. All the same, she was determined to face her husband, stressing her humiliation in front of the folk of Gorbydale. No doubt it would be the talk of the town that the granddaughter of the master of the Invincible could not pay her debts, or that the son of the town's only solicitor was hard-up.

When Hadrian arrived home, tired but jubilant and smelling of beer, she placed a plate of mince and potatoes in front of him.

"What's all this muck?" he demanded sourly. "You've been lolling about the house all day and could only come up with this? What's up with you, you lazy slut?"

"I did go to the butcher's to buy some nice chops," said Helen primly. "But the butcher wasn't willing to let me have much, as our bill hasn't been paid."

"Oh, that!" said Hadrian, looking guilty. "I'll er … pay it on the way to work in the morning."

"I felt very humiliated in front of a queue of customers," said Helen quietly.

"So what? It'll give the old cats something to talk about. The high and mighty Overdales can't pay their bills." Hadrian chuckled as he sneered at her.

"I'm a Lightfoot now," she pointed out coolly. "And the butcher did deliberately say 'your husband' hadn't paid the bill and that he'd sent you a note. My mother is a valued customer there, and he usually asks after her and sends his regards." She hadn't meant to provoke her husband, but his face turned from a sneer to crimson fury.

"Oh, the damned Overdales, bloody hypocrites and skinflints. 'Oh, I taught my daughter to cook,' says the old mill hand," he mimicked in a high-pitched voice. "Well, you should be able to cook something better that this shite."

With that, he threw the plate at her. It caught her cheek as it flew and shattered on the floor, splaying mince and potatoes all over the threadbare carpet. Helen's hand flew to her face in horror. It was covered in blood and gravy as she reached for a towel.

Hadrian was instantly repentant. "Oh I'm sorry, I'm sorry. I didn't mean to do that. I've had such a tiring day, and when I gave my stuff in at the office, the old man had a go at me again for having a drink, when I'd travelled all that way on a bumpy coach to see that grumpy old cat and she never so much as offered me a cup of tea."

Helen stared at him and coldly turned towards the sink. She rinsed the blood from her hand and, dampening a corner of the towel, staunched the blood from her cheekbone.

"I'll clean the carpet," offered Hadrian, looking stricken at what he'd done. He tried mopping the mess on the floor with a dishcloth, making more mess as he ineffectually dabbed at the spoilt meal.

"Leave it for me," ordered Helen quietly. "I'll do it in a minute." She sat down on a chair, feeling dazed. Her cheek stung, and she knew a bruise would mar her face in the morning. Hadrian took her hand and knelt beside her.

"I'm so, so sorry, my love," he almost sobbed. "Please forgive me. I'll never do that again, honestly I won't. Please, please don't tell your mother or your family. She's a grand woman, honestly she is. And you're like her. I promise I'll pay the butcher's bill. I'll go first thing in the morning."

He rambled on with his apologies and promises as Helen stared blankly at the mess on the floor. She had had such a wonderful day with so many prospects before her. Now her girlish dreams for her marriage were as shattered as the dinner plate on the floor.

"I'll clear it up," she said, wearily rising from her chair, "before it gets trodden into the carpet."

CHAPTER 47: AN ECHO FROM THE PAST

It was months later, and Matthias was still complaining about the expense of the wedding. The installation of a proper range in Helen's kitchen had been his greatest expense. Yet since he owned the house, Jessie thought it reasonable that he should pay for it. The rest of the festivities had been paid for from Robert and Jessie's savings.

"But you wouldn't like Helen's death on your conscience if she got burnt on the open range, would you?" Jessie reasoned with him.

So many women died when their long skirts brushed against the fire or red hot embers fell from the grate.

"Aye, I expect you're right," grumbled Matthias. "But money doesn't grow on trees, you know."

"At least there'll be no more weddings for a while," Jessie reassured him.

"Aye, young Jack will have more sense than to get married 'til he's good and ready," he said.

So Matthias had convinced himself that Matt would never be married. Jessie acknowledged that it might be difficult for her son to find a bride, but she still had hopes that someone would appreciate his sensitivity and kind heart, not to mention his mischievous sense of humour.

An unexpected letter added to Matthias's monetary worries. Jessie stared at the envelope from India. It was in a familiar hand, but she couldn't quite place it. Her eyes flew to the signature the moment she opened it.

"Amisha!" she read with surprise. She hurriedly read the rest of the letter.

"What is it about?" asked Robert.

Jessie shook her head as if she couldn't understand its contents and then reread the letter carefully. "Taylor Walmsley is dead," she said quietly. "Amisha says he's dead. I can't believe it." She reread the pages one more time. "Yes, he's died in India. Amisha has written to tell me. She says that Taylor went to track down her and Crispin Pettigrew in India, no doubt to get his revenge for their eloping. But he was in a terrible state when he found them in Lahore. He was burning up with some fever. Amisha took him in and nursed him, but he was beyond recovery. She was with him when he died at their house. How awful for her."

"I wonder if his mother knows?" said Robert.

"Should we go and tell her?" wondered Jessie.

They stared at each other in disbelief.

"Who's Taylor Walmsley?" inquired Jack, nonchalantly eating his breakfast.

"He was one of our overseers who made good. He has shares in the mill," his father told him. "Or had shares," he corrected himself. "I wonder what that will mean for the Invincible?"

Matthias ambled up to the breakfast table. "What's all this about the Invincible?" he demanded, alerted by the mention of his beloved mill.

"Taylor Walmsley has died in India," explained Jessie. "I've just had a letter from Amisha. She nursed him in his last days, but she wasn't able to save him."

"By heck, that's a surprise," said Matthias, looking stunned. "How will that affect t'mill?"

"We don't know yet if Mrs Walmsley knows about Taylor," said Robert. "Do we go and tell her or what?"

"I suppose we should," Jessie murmured. "At least we can give our condolences."

"You're right. We'll go together this morning," decided Robert. "We'll go in the gig when we've dropped Papa off at the mill."

"Aye, and er … send her my sympathies and all," said his father. "I can't abide the woman, but it wouldn't do to alienate her in case Walmsley's left her t'shares in t'mill."

Jessie smiled at his obsession and went to change into a dark coloured dress.

"We've come to see Mrs Walmsley," said Jessie when the door had eventually opened at the Walmsley house.

"I'll see if she's available," a timid-looking maid told them.

She kept them waiting at the door for several minutes before she arrived back, looking anxious. "You'd better come in," she said quietly. "The missis has had some bad news, you know. She's in a terrible state."

They nodded and went into a darkened parlour.

Mrs Walmsley stared up at them, her eyes visibly red even in the gloom. "I expect you've come to gloat," she snapped. "My poor, poor boy." Then she burst into chest-heaving sobs.

Jessie immediately sat on a footstool near her chair and took her hand. "Oh no, Mrs Walmsley. We wouldn't do that. We're really sorry for what's happened. It must be terrible for you, and with Taylor so far away."

"It was that woman that did it," she hissed between her sobs. "The East India Company wrote to me. They said he died at her home; her with her fancy man. I'll bet she's poisoned my Taylor. I don't know why he even married her."

Because he thought Amisha was biddable and he could control her, thought Jessie to herself, but stayed diplomatically silent on that subject. All the same, she felt she had to defend her friend. "Oh no, Mrs Walmsley. Don't think that. Amisha's not like that. She wrote to me. She said she nursed him in his last illness but, though he revived a little, she couldn't save him. He had a terrible fever."

"Aye, she would say that. Why would she want to save him? It's all her fault. If she hadn't run away with that … with that … snake-in-the-grass, Pettiwhatever, our Taylor wouldn't have gone chasing after her. It's a killer country, is that India. The white man's grave, that's what they call it. Well, it's my poor son's grave now." With a wail, she sobbed loudly into her handkerchief.

They didn't dare point out that it was Africa that was called 'the white man's grave'.

"Is there anything we can do, Mrs Walmsley?" asked Jessie. "Would you like a cup of tea?" She felt genuinely sorry for the woman and thought how she would feel herself if anything happened to any of her children.

"I'd like you to go," said the grieving woman stiffly. "You should have married him by rights," she added, glaring at Jessie. "If he'd been settled at home, then he wouldn't have gone gallivanting off to India. I reckon you thought he wasn't good enough for you, didn't you, Miss High and Mighty?"

"It wasn't like that," said Jessie quietly. "Taylor didn't get round to asking me. He shilly-shallied until it was too late, and by then I'd fallen in love with someone else — my Robert." She held out her hand, and he helped her up from the stool.

"I'm very sorry for your loss, Mrs Walmsley," said Robert. "And my father was most particular in sending his condolences too. If there's anything we can do, please let us know. Perhaps as your son is buried in Lahore, you could have a memorial service for him at the church in Gorbydale?" he suggested.

"We're chapel," she sniffed. "Aye, that's an idea though. I'll get on to the preacher. You'll be welcome if you can bother to come. I see you've turned church these days, Mrs Overdale. We don't see you at the chapel anymore."

"I worship with my husband," said Jessie quietly. "But of course we'll come and commemorate your son when it's arranged."

They were just about to leave when she called to them, "And I'll be in touch with my lawyer about the shares in the mill."

At this parting barb, Robert gave Jessie an uneasy glance.

"Do we tell Papa or not?" he asked as they left the house.

"I suppose he should be warned," said Jessie. "Do you suppose Taylor left a will?"

"Well, we'll soon find out," said Robert with a sigh as he helped her into the gig.

CHAPTER 48: THE LAWYER'S OFFICE

Mrs Walmsley lost no time in heading towards the Lightfoots' office the next day. She arrived and demanded to see the solicitor immediately. As he was the only solicitor in town, his business dealt with most of Gorbydale's problems with the law.

"Do you have an appointment?" asked the clerk at the counter.

"I've had no time to make an appointment, young man," she snapped. "Will he see me or not?"

Moments later, she was ushered into Lightfoot's office and shown to a comfortable chair.

"I understand you have had a distressing bereavement, Mrs Walmsley. I am of course very sorry for your trouble," began the solicitor.

"Aye, of course you'll know. Your lad is married to the Overdale girl, though I wasn't invited to the wedding," sneered his client. "No doubt that's where you'll have heard of my poor son's demise." She gave a deep sob, then delved to recover a lace handkerchief from her reticule. Sniffing into it, she recovered her composure. A strong whiff of smelling salts drifted into the room. "I'd like to see his will," she said. "I'm sure he came once and made a will with you."

"We'll see," said Lightfoot. He banged a counter bell on his desk and the clerk from the front office came scurrying in. "Get someone to search for a will in the name of Taylor Walmsley, will you, Moore?" he asked. "And would you like a cup of tea, Mrs Walmsley, to revive you while we're waiting?"

"Might as well," she said.

The clerk hurried away on his errands. That someone ordered to retrieve the will was Hadrian. As it happened, his curiosity had got the better of him and he'd already delved into the will records. So he knew precisely where to retrieve the Walmsley will. The will arrived with the tea.

Mr Lightfoot carefully examined the seal on the large brown envelope, then gently removed the will. He laid it on his desk and perused it slowly.

"Well?" demanded Mrs Walmsley. "What's it say?"

He glanced up at her cautiously, as if reluctant to reveal its contents. "I'm afraid you might be disappointed, Mrs Walmsley," he said.

"What's it say?" she urged him again.

"You son was married to an Indian lady, I believe," he tried.

"Yes, yes, of course. But everyone knows she ran off with a blackguard and left our Taylor. We told people that she'd gone back to India to look after her sick mother, but nobody believed that."

"Did they ever divorce?" he asked. "I have no recollection of preparing a divorce case at this office. Would he have consulted another solicitor to your knowledge?"

She stared at him. "I've no idea. I thought he always came to you. What does it say? Tell me, for goodness' sake."

Lightfoot cleared his throat. "*I, Taylor Arthur Walmsley, being of sound mind…*"

"Never mind all that business," snapped Mrs Walmsley. "Give me the guts of it. What's it say?"

"He leaves and bequeaths to Mrs Amy (aka) which means 'also known as'…"

"I know what it means," she shouted at him, impatient to hear the contents of the will.

"To Mrs Amy (aka Amisha) Walmsley and her heirs all his worldly goods, notably the house in Gorbydale, his bank account and shares in the Invincible Mill."

"He can't do." Her face fell in disbelief. "She'd deserted him. Surely that's grounds for divorce?"

"But if he didn't apply for a divorce, Mrs Walmsley, the will still stands," said Lightfoot. "For all legal purposes, Mrs Amy (or Amisha) Walmsley is still his wife and entitled to the contents of this will."

"There's no justice," shouted Mrs Walmsley. "I'll find another solicitor. I'll fight the will."

"Please calm yourself, Mrs Walmsley," tried the solicitor. "I can assure you that if there is no divorce, the marriage still stands. It could be argued that perhaps your son went to India to be reconciled with his wife."

"Never!" She collapsed into the chair and seemed to shrink. Then she took a deep breath, a cunning look suffused her face and she became revitalised. "What if you were to say that a divorce had been procured?" she asked, staring hard at Lightfoot. "I'm sure I could make it worth your while, and that slut in India would never know."

He hesitated for a moment. "I would not do it, Mrs Walmsley. I'm surprised you asked," he said stiffly.

"No, of course you can't do it," sneered the woman. "You're all tied up with that Overdale lot now your lad has wed into that nest of vipers. I suppose he got a nice settlement from them for making the Overdale wench respectable. The whole town knows there's been some funny goings-on up at that Overdale's Folly. It's a right scandal."

Mr Lightfoot rose to his full height and towered over the woman. "Mrs Walmsley, I may be in my rights to take out a case for libel against you if you impugn the good name of my son or his wife. I have revealed the contents of your son's will to you against my better judgement. Now please leave my premises."

Grumbling under her breath, Mrs Walmsley walked home. People stopped her along the way and offered their sympathy and condolences. She was not a popular woman, but the people of Gorbydale were always sympathetic to the bereaved, even those who remembered the tyranny of her son when he was an overseer at the mill.

Once she had left, Mr Lightfoot asked his son to come into his office. "I suppose you took a look at the will?" he asked.

Hadrian looked immediately guilty but said nothing.

"I thought as much. The seal looked as if it had been recently glued down. Don't try that again. Anyway, I want you to go to the Overdales'. I need to find the address of Taylor Walmsley's wife. I believe young Mrs Overdale was a friend of hers, and no doubt they may have been in contact."

Hadrian hurried up to Overdale House, calling in on the way to the lodge. He found Helen sewing in her kitchen.

"Great news, my love," he said and, to her surprise, gave her a hearty kiss. "Walmsley's not left a penny to that old bag, his mother. It's all gone to his wife in India, and I know she was a great friend of your mother. The mill won't have to cough up after all. Maybe that old skinflint of a grandfather could be coaxed to give us more money. Anyway, I'd best be off." With that, he waved her goodbye and sped up to see Jessie.

Helen stared at the work she'd been doing. She had usually packed up all her sewing before Hadrian arrived home. The only fire in the house during the day was in the kitchen, and she sewed there for warmth. She wondered if he had noticed the pile of cushion covers on the table and realised they would not appear in their own house.

Jessie was surprised to see Hadrian, breathing heavily after his dash with the news.

"Of course I'll give you Amisha's address," she said when he explained his errand. "You say Taylor Walmsley has left all his money and goods to her? I wonder how she will take it? I'll bet his mother is livid."

"She looked furious as she left the offices," said Hadrian with a chuckle, "especially as my Pa ordered her out for libelling Helen and me."

"How do you mean?" asked Jessie cautiously.

Hadrian shrugged. "Well, you know... That business up at the folly... People talk. Well, let them. Stupid peasants."

Jessie stared at him. She would never entirely trust him, especially after what Lizzie had told her before the wedding. Then there was the day she had found her daughter with a large bruise on her cheek. Helen of course had made some excuse about a cupboard door, but Jessie had her suspicions.

She found Amisha's address and wrote it down in bold letters for the solicitor, making sure there would be no mistake. Then she handed it to Hadrian and he gleefully hurried away. She watched her son-in-law racing down the drive and wondered about his enthusiasm. He seemed delighted that Mrs Walmsley would be left without a penny of her son's estate. She knew that would be exactly Matthias's attitude. It didn't seem quite right to her. Amisha had deserted her husband and yet would benefit from all his hard work. His mother, who had brought him up and supported him when he was laid off at the mill, would have nothing. She wondered what her friend would do. Amisha was now free to marry with her heart, and she certainly might need the money.

The talk over the dinner table that evening was of the will and its consequences.

"You might write to your friend and tell her that we will of course pay the dividends into an account for her. Such as them dividends are, but trade will soon pick up," said Matthias confidently.

"What if she wants to have the money from the shares?" asked Jessie.

Matthias looked horrified. "You must talk her out of it. You were very good to her when she was a stranger here. Surely she'd take your advice," he insisted.

"I'm not sure what she'll do," Jessie told him. "We will just have to wait. I'll write to her, though. How strange that she should have nursed Taylor Walmsley in his last illness. I'm very surprised that that he allowed her to do it. He must have been very ill indeed."

They realised it would be some months before the estate could be settled. Some weeks later, Jessie received a letter from Amisha.

My dearest friend Jessie,

I hope you and your family are well, especially young Matthew. I am happy here with my dear love Crispin, and we are joined in matrimony now that I am free to do so. I expect you will have had all the news about Taylor's will by now. Lawyer Lightfoot has of course written to me, thanks to your help. I do not feel that I can accept all this good fortune after the heartache and trouble that I caused poor Taylor. It was a sad but heartfelt service that I gave him at the end so that he would not die alone.

Because of all the bitterness that his death has caused, I have renounced any claim to his house. I was not happy there and have asked Lawyer

Lightfoot to transfer the deeds to Taylor's mother. She never liked me, but nevertheless I feel it is only right to give her Taylor's house. The money in his bank I will keep and also his salary owing from the East India Company. This is not for myself but for the child I am carrying. It will make our lives easier and help dear Crispin in his research. The shares from the Invincible Mill I have asked Lawyer Lightfoot to transfer into Matthew's name. He writes that they will be held in trust, as he is not yet of age. It will help him in his struggle through life. I hope you will accept them on his behalf. I will write to you again soon when all these things have been settled.

Your loving and grateful friend,
Amisha Pettigrew.

Matt looked stunned. "She's given the shares in the mill to me?"

His mother smiled at him. "Yes, you're a man of means now," she told him. "Amisha was very fond of you and took a great deal of interest in your progress. I think she's given you the shares to help because of your disability. She'd be very proud if she could see you now."

"Perhaps I could write to her to thank her and send her a photograph," he suggested.

"That would be a good idea," said his mother. "I know she'd appreciate it."

"At least I don't have to worry about finding the money to pay you off, lad," said Matthias, satisfied with the outcome of Taylor Walmsley's will. "I dreaded having to deal with his dragon of a mother. And you've a stake in our business now, lad. If we thrive, you'll thrive too. Good to keep it in the family."

"It was good of Amisha to let Mrs Walmsley keep his house," said Robert. "She didn't have to, and by all accounts that old madam led the poor girl a merry dance, always interfering."

Yet Taylor's mother did not benefit from owning his house. One evening, the dark sky over Gorbydale was bright with flames. The clanging bells of the fire brigade echoed around the valley. Someone's house was on fire.

Jessie watched the flames with fascination from her parlour window. "I wonder whose house that is?" she asked. "The poor souls, I hope nobody is hurt."

It was next morning that they found out whose house had been destroyed. It had belonged to Taylor Walmsley.

Mrs Walmsley looked very pleased with herself as she was served her breakfast.

"Any news of the fire?" she asked her maid with a smirk. "I hope nobody was hurt."

"Just a fireman, ma'am. He tripped over a hose in all the confusion, but he's all right," said her maid.

They heard the letterbox flap, and the maid hurried to fetch the post.

"It's from that shark Lightfoot," decided Mrs Walmsley, examining the envelope. "I wonder what he wants?"

From the kitchen the maid heard her horrendous howl. Her mistress looked stupefied, clutching her letter as the maid hurried in to clear the breakfast things.

"Is there anything I can do, ma'am?" she asked cautiously.

Mrs Walmsley turned blank eyes towards her and shook her head like an automaton.

As she returned to the kitchen, the maid noticed that the keys to Taylor Walmsley's house were hung on a hook on the hall stand. Her mistress had often left them there so she could enter her son's home whenever the fancy took her. She was a stickler for tidiness, and the keys had been shoved away in the small drawer of the hall stand for months while her son was in India.

The letter from the lawyer's office informing Taylor's mother that she now owned her late son's house had arrived just too late.

CHAPTER 49: STITCH AND SAVE

If Helen thought that Hadrian had no inkling of what she was doing behind his back, she was very much mistaken. He had been very gentle with her since the incident with the plate of mince. Now, however, he began to wonder what his wife had been sewing in the kitchen. He had taken great interest in the instructions from Amisha to his father. Now he became jealous that Matt had received the shares in the mill, while his wife, although Matt's twin, had received nothing.

"Why did you get nothing from that Indian woman?" he asked casually.

"My mother says Amisha was very helpful when Matt was born. He was very wobbly, and Amisha taught Mama how to exercise Matt's legs to strengthen them. I expect she thought that Matt needed the money more than me."

"Yes, I expect she thought a cripple wouldn't have any prospects," sneered Hadrian. "She didn't expect old Matt would have his sticky fingers in your decrepit old uncle's moneybox."

"Don't say that; it's not true," Helen warned him. She'd become tentatively bolder since witnessing her husband's remorse after the incident with the plate of mince. "Matt has done very well, despite his handicaps. I'm very glad that Amisha has given him the shares. It will save Grandpapa a lot of worry too. He was very worried that Taylor Walmsley would demand his money back or sell the shares to a bank. Anyway, the shares aren't worth much at the moment, but they will be soon. The trade's picking up."

"And then Old Skinflint might cough up a bit more in our direction," suggested Hadrian. He suddenly had a thought about the day he had rushed home with the news of Amisha's inheritance. There had been a lot of fabric on the table, and he hadn't given his wife any money to buy it. "Trade's picking up, eh? So that's why you had a lot of old rags on the kitchen table, was it? Now they have rags to spare at that cockeyed old mill. So what were you doing with them?"

Helen looked immediately guilty. She stayed silent as she rapidly devised her excuses.

"So what's going on in that sewing room of yours?" demanded Hadrian.

Before she had time to answer, he'd jumped to his feet and was racing up the stairs. She tore after him but was too late to stop him entering her sanctuary. A pile of deep red damask hearts lay on the top of an old chest of drawers, waiting to be embellished with her ribbons and lace. She had dyed the fabric in an old saucepan in the kitchen. The smell of the chemical dye had lingered, and she was sure Hadrian might be suspicious then. But he'd suspected nothing. Now here was the evidence of her secret efforts. Then, to her dismay, she noticed that she had not replaced the pottery owl to his usual niche on a shelf. As he tossed about the crimson hearts, Hadrian's hand accidentally glanced against the owl. An ominous chink of metal echoed round the room. Hadrian picked up the moneybox and shook it. It rattled with the money she'd saved. He tipped it up and shook it violently, but only a couple of silver threepenny bits rolled out onto the floor. Enraged by his inability to release the money, Hadrian angrily flung the owl onto the floor. It smashed into a myriad shards of pottery, mingled with silver and copper coins.

"You've got a nice little hoard here, haven't you?" he confronted her. "Keeping secrets from your husband are you, you deceitful madam? You've got a proper little sewing factory going on here right under my nose."

"I was only using my spare time sewing to make some extra money," she said firmly but calmly. "I thought it would help with the household bills."

"Flogging knick-knacks on the high street like a pedlar to show me up, are you?" raged her husband. "Trying to show me up. I shouldn't expect any better from a tradesman's daughter. Well, you kept it a nice little secret from me. I'm your husband and therefore entitled to this money." He bent and picked Helen's hard-earned money from the floor, leaving the smashed pottery for her to clean up. Then he put the coins in his pocket. "Well, we'll put a stop to this right now. My wife the huckster! I'll be the laughing stock of the town," he snapped.

Helen thought how much she enjoyed the sewing: designing and making her own pretty pieces. She took pride in her work and would miss it. Not to mention the increasing sum of money she'd squirreled into her pottery owl. She decided to bargain with him. "I don't sell any of my wares in Gorbydale," she explained quietly. "I take them to a friend in Doveton, and she sells them at the mill where she works. They're very popular. I've a few orders, and I've promised to fulfil them. Nobody knows I'm related to you. I'm surprised you object to me making extra money. As you say, you're entitled to it too."

Hadrian pulled out a handful of coins from his pocket and swiftly assessed his haul. "You say nobody knows it's you?" he questioned her cautiously.

"Why would they? They're only interested in the Dove Mill and its doings. Nobody's interested in what goes on in Gorbydale."

He stared at the coins again. "I expect you're right. All right, then. You can carry on with what you're doing. But don't go on trying to deceive me. I'm not stupid. And don't bring my name into it."

"Of course I won't. Anyway, I'll stop sewing if and when I..." Helen blushed and hesitated. "You know, start to have a baby."

Hadrian stared at her, assessing his wife with a critical eye. "Er, yes, about that. I think it's too soon to think about a family just yet. I have a method I might try so you don't become pregnant. A friend of mine advised me. We'll see."

In the following days he produced a sheath of some sort of animal skin. Helen found it uncomfortable, and using it made Hadrian irritable. She kept diplomatically quiet, and their strained relationship soldiered on with a subtle underlying pressure. Helen avoided provoking Hadrian's volatile nature at all costs. He was his charming self until he'd had a drink. Then he was as explosive as a firework, and she stayed silent and submissive. Though against her own determined nature, it was the easiest and safest thing to do.

Helen continued her sewing activities and Lorna sold all her efforts. Between them they gauged the tastes of the mill workers and, as Christmas approached, they branched out into smaller knick-knacks like pin cushions and lavender bags. The goods sold with increasing popularity. When she was very busy with orders, Jessie came down to the lodge during the day and helped her daughter to hand-sew the trimmings. They worked companionably together, more in harmony than they'd ever been at Overdale House.

Jessie laughingly refused any money for her work. "I enjoy it," she told Helen. "It gets very quiet at home during the day once Jack goes to school and the men are at the mill. You can pay me in cups of tea."

Helen carefully avoided her mother's subtle questions about starting a family. In a way, she was relieved that she didn't have to worry about protecting a child when Hadrian was behaving so erratically.

Now her tactics changed. Helen put half her earnings in a clear glass jar for her husband to see. The rest she stowed away in one of her grandfather's old cigar boxes under a piece of stiff card and a covering of lace and ribbon fragments. If her husband queried why her earnings were so small, she insisted she had to buy more supplies of ribbon and lace. Secretly she counted her growing stash of money and made sure the cigar box was well hidden.

CHAPTER 50: JACK

It was twelve o'clock, and Jack still hadn't left his bed. Robert rapped on his bedroom door and went in. His son groaned and reluctantly sat up, his hair tousled and standing on end. Robert knew his son was restless. Jack had complained to his mother that travelling to Manchester every day was tiring. He had to leave Gorbydale early in the morning, and as a growing boy he felt he needed more sleep.

"I'm tired. I need my sleep. Why can't I board at the grammar school like my friends?" he demanded irritably as he shifted himself to sit at the edge of the bed. "Then I wouldn't be so tired. I'd only have to travel at weekends."

"What about all your friends here in Gorbydale?" said Robert. "Anyway, I'm not sure we can afford the fees."

His son remained grumpy and defiant. "I'm worn out with all this to-ing and fro-ing," he tried. "I can't concentrate when I get to school. Why can't we afford the fees? We've got a dirty great mill there churning out thread all day."

"We've got a dirty great mortgage too," snapped his father. "Well, it's not as bad as it was, but we're not out of the woods yet. I was hoping one day we'd be able to branch out into weaving the thread we 'churn out'. Those weaving looms are expensive, though. The new mills are bigger and have both spinning and weaving. If we don't act soon, we won't be able to compete with our yarn."

Jack was still looking sulky when his grandfather passed the bedroom in the middle of the conversation.

"What's up with the lad?" Matthias asked. "He's got a face like a bulldog chewing a wasp."

"He wants to board at the grammar school like his friends," said Robert with a sigh. "I've explained that money's tight."

"Well, he should board with his friends," said Matthias grandly. "He should learn to become a gentleman like his friends. His sister's married to a gentleman, and our Jack should have his chance too. He'll be running this mill one day, and he won't have to kowtow to the likes of them that think themselves superior. 'Liverpool *gentlemen* and Manchester *men*,' they say. Well, I'm not having it. Us Overdales are as good as anybody."

Robert knew his father's grievance was of long standing. The chip on Matthias's shoulder had never disappeared. It seemed to grow larger as he grew older. "It's not like that anymore, Papa," Robert pointed out to Matthias. "Business men have more respect nowadays."

"Don't let 'em fool you," snorted his father. "The gentry will treat you with respect only when they're after your money."

Robert shook his head but didn't bother to argue. He had felt the scorn of those who considered themselves socially superior when he'd been sent away to boarding school.

"Surely we can find some money to let the lad board?" coaxed Matthias. "It'll only be for a few years anyway, and then he can come into t'mill."

"That's if he wants to," said his son, glancing at Jack.

The boy's face had changed from surly to a radiant beam at his grandfather's backing.

Robert knew that Jack wasn't interested in books like Matt, but he loved sport and the outdoors. He'd shown little interest in the workings of the mill, preferring to play football with his friends or go fishing in the Gorby river. Robert knew, though, that Jack was his grandfather's great hope for the future of the Invincible Mill.

"I'll look into our finances," said Robert with a resigned sigh. "Then we can contact the school and see what can be done. There might be bursaries and the like. Though I expect that's only for poorer pupils."

"Aye, and the sons of clergymen," muttered Matthias. "Gentleman — pah!"

Jack jumped up and gave his father a rare hug. "Thanks, Papa," he cried and went off to tell Matt his good news.

The brothers were close despite the difference in their ages and circumstances. Jack had always been very protective of Matt, and Matt often slipped his young brother some spending money from his wages.

Jessie was dubious when Robert told her of the plans. "I suppose that will mean less money for your plans for the mill," she said. "Your father is very short-sighted. All the same, Jack does get tired travelling backwards and forwards. He's growing like a weed just now. His trousers don't seem to fit him for long." She smiled at her worried husband. "On the plus side, that will be one less mouth to feed. He eats like a horse. Anyway, he'll be home for the weekends."

Jessie gave her husband a reassuring hug. He continually worried about money, and his children bewildered him.

"Don't worry about our Jack," she coaxed. "Our Eddie was just like him when he was growing up. I know Jack's changed from the friendly little boy he once was. He's just at the grunting stage now. But Eddie's turned out all right, and so will Jack."

Robert reluctantly agreed and gave her a half-hearted hug. His children were growing up and away from home. He knew Jessie felt that she too was becoming redundant. She slipped down the drive to help Helen whenever she could. She'd confessed that she was uneasy about Hadrian and his treatment of Helen.

"If he lays a finger on her, he'll have me to answer to," said Robert fiercely.

So the money was found for Jack to become a boarder in Manchester. To Robert's surprise, his son also joined the Rifle Corps. The following Christmas, Jack asked for a shotgun as a gift. Robert baulked at the expense, but Jessie quietly went into Manchester and negotiated a good price on a second-hand firearm at a gunsmiths. Now whenever Jack was home, he went shooting in the hills around Gorbydale and brought home rabbits for the pot.

"I remember trapping rabbits to eat up at the fort, during the Cotton Crisis," said Jessie.

She and her young brother Eddie had caught the poor animals to feed the family, though she was never easy with the idea. But hard times had brought hard solutions. Her children had had a much easier life, though she was anxious about Helen. Despite his problems, Matt seemed to be thriving and was forever cheerful with his impish sense of humour. He was the only one who could connect with Jack at times.

"I'll miss you and your disgusting habits," he'd teased his brother when he heard Jack was going to board. "But I suppose you'll bring worse ones back with you at weekends."

The family had expected Jack to be home each weekend, but somehow there was always a match to play or some event to attend. To Matthias's delight, Jack was slowly assuming the habits of a gentleman. In his pride in his grandson, he hadn't noticed Jack slowly distancing himself from the mill.

"Isn't the lad home?" asked Matthias one Saturday morning.

"Matt's gone down to have a look round the Invincible with Robert," said Jessie. She placed a cup of tea beside her father-in-law and stepped back to assess him. The cup rattled in the saucer as he lifted it up from a small table beside him. He was becoming very frail, and he'd spent little time at his beloved mill in the recent days. All the same, he felt he was still in charge and Robert seethed with frustration at some of his father's decisions.

"I meant Jack," said Matthias, glancing up at her.

Jessie knew precisely who he meant. Her father-in-law forever overlooked his eldest grandson. "Jack sent a note to say he has a rugby match today, and then he's going to tea with his friends. Then he might stay with his friend in Cheetham Hill overnight. He wrote that it would be quicker to get back to school on Monday morning."

"So he's not bothering to come home, then," grumbled Matthias.

"I think his friend has two pretty sisters," chuckled Jessie. "I heard him talking about them to Matt."

"Chasing girls at his age!" growled her father-in-law.

"He is nearly seventeen," Jessie told him. "Helen was married at seventeen. She's been married nearly four years now. How time flies."

Matthias sipped his tea, looking glum. "Well, so long as he doesn't get married before he comes into t'mill. We can't afford a big enough wage for him to keep a wife."

Matthias idolised his second grandson and saw him as the natural heir to the mill. He had obviously decided that Matt's disability was a bar to his succession. He would not even acknowledge his eldest grandson's interest in all things relating to cotton. At that moment, Matt was discussing weaving looms with his father at the mill.

At the old Endurance, Eli was considering buying new looms with more adaptability. Many people in the towns were abandoning their old and uncomfortable wooden settles for upholstered chairs, and the damask that Eli's mill produced was in greater demand. Matt knew his father wanted to expand into weaving, and he'd suggested that Robert should buy Eli's old machines as a start. They'd gone to the mill to assess where the looms could be located.

When they finally returned home for their midday meal, Jessie was pleased to see her husband and son talking so animatedly. Although Matt's voice was low and hesitant, his father had great patience with him and listened with interest to what his son was saying. However, Matthias was not happy to hear them making plans for his mill without him.

"Buying Eli's old rubbish," he complained. "What would you want to do that for?"

"The looms aren't rubbish, Grandpapa," Matt defended his idea. "They're in good working order. Uncle Eli sees to that. But he needs to produce a thicker quality of damask for the furniture industry, so he's buying some new ones. Some of our older looms aren't capable of it. But they'd be fine for weaving plain calico once they were adjusted to take the coarser thread."

"And where's the money for these looms going to come from, then?" snapped Matthias, annoyed to be contradicted by the young man he'd once consigned as an idiot.

"Buying Eli's looms would be a start," sighed Robert. "I'm sure he would give us a fair price. We could hire some weavers and train some of our workers on the looms. Then when we can afford to expand, we'd buy more modern machines."

"We should stick to what we know," Matthias obstinately maintained.

"Then we'll be left behind," said his son, equally obstinate. "The new mills are much bigger than the Invincible, and they're both spinning and weaving the cotton. They won't want to buy our yarn in a while."

"We'll see," grumbled Matthias.

Jessie raised her eyes to her husband. Matthias would not be budged. The trouble was that when anything happened to him, as it inevitably would, their trade might have fallen.

"Let's have something to eat before it gets cold," she suggested sensibly. She gave Matt a warning glance as he seemed just about to argue with his grandfather. He nodded and sat resignedly in his place at the table.

"Maybe Jack will be here next weekend," said Matthias, staring hopefully at his grandson's empty place.

The following Saturday, Jack was again missing. Jessie had received a note in the week from him asking for some warm clothes, and the usual request for money:

Dear Mama,

The Rifle Corps will be training with the Lancashire Fusiliers this weekend up on the moors. I don't want to miss the opportunity. I also wonder if you could spare some funds for the expedition. I know you will be disappointed, but I promise to be home next week. Regards to the family.

Your loving son, Jack.

She showed the letter to Robert. He read it with an exasperated sigh.

"He needs more money, eh? He's already spent this month's allowance. I'm sure he thinks it grows on trees. And he seems to be taking a great interest in all this military stuff," he said doubtfully.

"I suppose he needs the extra money for this camping trip. But surely the military stuff is just boys' games," decided Jessie. "It's a bit of adventure. You know what he's like when he's home, always wanting to be out and about. Matt is still annoyed with him for taking his pony Bob without permission and wearing the poor creature out."

"Perhaps we could get him a horse of his own," suggested Robert. "I know it's more expense, but I was always eager to come home and ride Surefoot whenever I could. With his own horse, Jack might be tempted to come home more at the weekends."

Jessie was doubtful if even the lure of his own horse would tempt Jack back to Gorbydale. She suspected her son preferred the excitement of life in the city with his friends, rather than the dull provincial life of the mill town. They all missed Jack's breezy, happy-go-lucky presence at the weekend, especially his grandfather. With Helen living in her own home, she was not around to fuss him as often whenever he was in a grumpy mood. Matthias's mood was becoming more tetchy with the frustration of age.

CHAPTER 51: REVELATIONS AND RESERVATIONS

Jack arrived home the following weekend. Jessie thought how tall and handsome he looked, even after a couple of weeks' absence. She had always thought of him as a schoolboy but now he was a young man, taller than his father and with an air of polish that none of the family had achieved. His confident manner reminded her of her brother Arden when he had returned from America.

He was buzzing with news and couldn't wait to tell them. They were seated round the dining room table. Matthias had insisted his grandson sit next to him.

"I had a marvellous time with the Fusiliers on the moors," said Jack proudly. "The sergeant told me I'm a crack-shot. I want to join up once I've left the grammar school. They'd train me as an officer."

"I thought you wanted to go to Owens College," said his father, looking surprised.

Jessie bit her lip and dreaded what she would hear next.

"You and Mama want me to go to Owens, but you know I'm not bookish like our Matt," said Jack, looking wary that his news had not been well accepted.

"Nay lad, you can't join the army," protested Matthias. "You're to come to t'mill." He began to cough. Jack quickly passed him a glass of water, but his grandfather struggled for breath. He grabbed at the glass but spilt the contents all over the table. "Nay lad," he croaked. "Nay."

"Get a drop of brandy," Jessie ordered Robert. She bundled Jack out of the way and tried to calm Matthias. "Don't upset yourself, Father-in-Law," she said quietly. "Here, have a sip of brandy. It'll help you."

Matthias turned bloodshot eyes towards her. His breath was shallow and laboured. "I don't feel so good," he muttered.

"We'll get you upstairs for a lie down," suggested Jessie. "Matt, go and fetch Lizzie and Michael if he's about."

Michael was often drawn to the kitchen and Lizzie when he was not working.

The sip of brandy revived Matthias a little but he still looked pale, with beads of sweat on his brow. There was a blue tinge to his lips.

"Perhaps we could settle Grandpapa in his parlour," suggested Matt. "It would be easier than struggling with him upstairs."

"Good idea," said his mother.

"I'll go and fetch a pillow and blanket," said her son, ever practical.

"Let me go," said Jack. "I'll be quicker." He looked shocked at the trouble he'd caused with his casual announcement.

Between them they settled Matthias on a sofa, with a pillow behind his head and a blanket over him. Once he was quieter, a little colour returned to his cheeks.

"Do you think we should get a doctor?" asked Robert.

"Yes, that would be wise," said Jessie.

"I don't want that old fool Braddock," growled Matthias, his breathing still laboured. Though his voice was slurred, they understood him well enough. "Get me the young lad, Doctor Andrew. He'll have more idea what's wrong with me."

Jessie was just about to say that Matthias had had a shock, but she stopped herself in time. It was the thought of Jack joining the army that had upset his grandfather, and she didn't want Matthias to be reminded of it. She wondered what to think of it herself. The subject of Jack's career was abandoned for the moment.

"You've been overdoing it, I think," said the doctor when he'd finally arrived. "I recommend bed rest, or at least parlour rest."

"I can't be doing with lying about," muttered Matthias. "I've work to do."

"Not for a week or two," suggested Doctor Andrew sympathetically. "You don't want to bring on another stroke, do you?"

"A stroke! I can't do. It's years since I had my last one," protested the old man.

"You might just have had a mild one — a warning if you like. A warning to take it easy for a while," reasoned the doctor.

Matthias wasn't happy but reluctantly lay back on the sofa. He looked anxious, as if he would receive another attack any moment.

"Would you like a cup of tea, Doctor?" Jessie offered. "I'm sure you'd like one, Father-in-Law."

"Aye, all right," said Matthias with a sigh. "If I'm to be an invalid, I might as well be a pampered one."

Jessie smiled and led the doctor out of the room. "How bad is he?" she asked quietly.

"He's a good age, I think?" said Doctor Andrew.

"Well into his seventies," Jessie told him.

"Then he's a good age for these parts. Living up above the smoke of the town helps. The poor wretches below are breathing foul air all day," he told her. "But old age takes its toll. If he takes things easy, he'll recover."

Jessie doubted that Matthias was capable of taking things easy. When Honora had last visited, she'd been surprised at the amount of rich food Matthias devoured. Now her father-in-law was settled, Jessie put her mind to Jack's disturbing announcement.

Helen came up to the house and sat with her grandfather while Robert and Jessie talked to their son. Their parlour was on the other side of the house and away from Matthias's hearing. Jessie asked Matt to leave them, but Jack protested.

"He's all right to stay. I want someone on my side."

Matt shrugged and sat down to listen.

"You know you're too young to join the army without our permission," said Robert.

"I won't be in a few years," Jack said defiantly. "And by then lads younger than me will have got their commissions and been promoted, and they'll all be senior to me. So you'll have blighted my career."

"Where did you get this crazy idea from?" asked Jessie quietly.

"It's not crazy. I'm a good shot. I really enjoyed last weekend, living in tents and everything. I'm sure I'd like the army life."

"In tents, in summer sunshine, with your friends around you. Who wouldn't enjoy it?" said his father. "But think about camping in a cramped tent in the rain, the cold, the damp fog and the mud. Or even in the blazing heat of the desert. With guns going off and the dead and the wounded. The smell. Have you ever smelt death?"

Jack shook his head but stayed determined.

"Ask your mother," said Robert, nodding towards Jessie. "She's seen what fighting can do. It's not all 'half a league, half a league, half a league onwards' and glory. Those poor deluded men from the Crimean war are dead too. Blown to bits. Or patched up like I was. Or worse, losing a limb. You've read the books. Do you think that's what we want for you?"

His son looked chastened for a moment. "I want to serve my country," he said defiantly. "Uncle Arden joined the navy, not for us, mind, but he was a hero in the American war. Nobody stopped him joining."

"He didn't have much choice," his mother told him. "It was go to America or starve here."

"He didn't have to join the Union navy, though," argued Jack. "He said himself he could have got work on the steamships crossing the Atlantic. He told me he'd made some sort of promise to his mother to help free the slaves. I want to fight for my country." He crossed his arms and hugged his defiance to himself.

"How long would you have to sign up for?" asked Matt.

Jack turned with relief to his brother. "Three years, I think."

"You could sign up for the minimum and then come home to the mill," suggested Matt. "If I know you, you'd probably be fed up with it by then anyway. I know you don't want him to go," he added, turning to his parents. "But it would be a solution and stop him running away and lying about his age."

When Jack turned crimson and would not face his parents, Jessie knew that was exactly what he'd planned to do.

"Your father and I need to talk about this," she said calmly. "But promise me you will make no rash decisions. If your hero Uncle Arden can make a promise to his mother, then I'm sure you can. We have your sick grandfather on our hands at the moment, and your revelation hasn't helped."

"It probably caused it," said Robert and earned a frown from his wife.

Jack looked guilty. "All right. I promise I won't do anything rash," he said. "But I can't wait forever. My friends will be joining the army training college after the summer holidays. I was hoping to go too."

"And who's going to pay all your expenses?" asked Robert. "You'll need a uniform and a load of equipment. That doesn't come cheap."

That stumped Jack. For a moment it looked as if he hadn't considered what training as an officer entailed, though he'd found out more than his parents suspected. "But I won't have to purchase my commission anymore," he argued. "Cardwell has put a stop to that. The sergeant was telling me. He says the army will get better officers now. Our army will be every bit as good as the Prussians. You might have to pay for Sandhurst, but then you'd be paying for me to go to Owens anyway."

Robert sighed. "You and this sergeant have it all worked out, it seems. A pity this sergeant isn't paying the bills."

Jessie watched her son, and his eagerness to join the army was genuine. Whatever he did, even as a young child, he did with enthusiasm and persistence. She'd even noticed books on soldiers and war in his bedroom, and he was not a natural reader. But she'd never expected he'd go as far as to join the army.

"We have all this trouble with your Grandpapa right now," she said calmly. "We can't make any instant decisions. Your father and I will have a talk about it and, when you come home next weekend, we'll all have a talk. Your grandfather might be feeling better next week and able to cope with whatever we decide. Please don't do anything rash."

Jack nodded. "I'm serious, Mama," he said sincerely. "I need to go out into the world and do something with my life. You and Papa did when you were young."

"And it wasn't an easy experience," admitted Jessie. "It was damned hard most of the time. The blood and the suffering were everywhere."

Both Jack and Robert stared in surprise at her vehement words.

"Oops!" said Matt with a chuckle. "I never expected that from Mama." He had been listening quietly in a corner.

"Excuse my language," Jessie apologised, looking chastened.

"Perhaps this once," said Robert, laughing and giving his wife a hug round her shoulders.

The mood lightened. Jack promised not to do anything hasty until he had spoken with his parents the following week.

Next morning he headed back to the grammar school, and Robert and Jessie were left with a sick Matthias and a decision to make.

CHAPTER 52: THE MASTER OF THE INVINCIBLE

The mild stroke had knocked the confidence of Matthias Overdale. He tried to rest as the doctor had ordered, but idleness didn't sit well with him. Jessie sat quietly sewing as he lay on his sofa. She could tell his thoughts were agitated.

"Will you ask Robert to come and have a little chat when he comes home from t'mill?" he asked.

She had noticed that as he grew older his speech had slid back into the accents of his youth. The refined tones he'd miserably failed to master had disappeared. At least he sounded more natural.

"Yes, of course," said Jessie. "Would you like a nice cup of tea?"

"Aye, all right then."

All thoughts of tea were abandoned when Helen arrived to see her grandfather.

"Poor Grandpapa," she sympathised. "Matt called before he went to work to say you'd been poorly. I've brought you some chicken broth."

Matthias immediately perked up as she pulled up a footstool and sat down beside him.

"Are you all right while I go to the kitchen?" asked Jessie. "Do you still want some tea?"

"It's coming out of my ears," joked Matthias. "I'll wait and have some of this lovely broth. Oh, you're such a sweetheart to think of your old Grandpapa," he told Helen with a fond smile.

Jessie chuckled to herself and left her daughter to make a fuss of the old man. Helen was always his favourite and could wind him round her little finger. When she returned, Jessie asked her daughter if she wanted to stay for dinner.

"I'd better get home," said Helen with a sigh. "Hadrian will be expecting something on the table. I've some broth for him too."

Jessie left them together and went about her own business. She had been helping out in the kitchen as Maggie became slower. She really hadn't the heart to tell the poor woman to retire. There would be no place for Maggie but the workhouse and, while she could help a little in the kitchen, Jessie would make sure she would have a home at Overdale House.

Later, when Helen went home, Jessie warmed the broth and took it in to her father-in-law.

"Is the lass all right?" he asked. "She was looking a bit peaky to me. Her hand was proper bony. Is that husband of hers treating her all right?"

"As far as I know," admitted Jessie. "He's been spoilt and can be a bit demanding from what I can tell. But they seem to jog on along together all right." Jessie had her suspicions but kept them to herself.

"What is it — three years or four since they've been married and no sign of any little ones yet? Is everything all right?" persisted Matthias.

Jessie gave a wry smile. "You should know, Father-in-Law, that Helen keeps her private life very private. I wouldn't tell you if I knew meself — and I don't."

"Aye, that's right and proper, I suppose," admitted Matthias, leaning back with a big sigh. "Nobody tells me owt anyway."

"Do you think it's any different for me?" asked Jessie, laughing.

She wondered what he wanted to speak to Robert about. Was he fretting about the Invincible or had he remembered Jack's plans to join the army?

Uncle Eli called to see the invalid that afternoon. He was in there a good hour before they asked for tea.

"You'll remember to tell Robert I want a word, won't you?" Matthias reminded Jessie as she showed Eli out.

"I'm sure he'll be all right," Eli reassured her as he left her at the door. "Perhaps he'll learn to take it easy, for a while at any rate."

Robert went in to see his father straight away when he came home and promised the old man he would speak with him that evening after dinner.

"He's fretting about something," he told Jessie. "But he hasn't mentioned Jack, so I don't think it's that."

"And what will we do about our son?" she asked.

They had avoided the subject themselves, but were both privately mulling over the problem.

"Perhaps we should just let him join," sighed Robert. "He might not even pass the tests. He might not survive the training. He'll only fret and do something stupid like join up as an ordinary soldier if we forbid him. At least he'd be trained as an officer."

"I'm glad you decided that," said Jessie, hugging his arm as she led him to the table. "We can't make him live his life the way we want, or even his grandfather wants. At least he'll have our support and backing to do the best he can. I just hope we can afford it. But we don't have to tell Matthias yet, do we?"

"God forbid!" Robert shook his head. "We'll speak to Jack first. Then we'll decide when to tell my father. We don't want a relapse."

Robert went in to his father after his evening meal and pulled an armchair up to the sofa. "So, what's worrying you, Papa?" he asked gently. "You know you mustn't worry. The mill's in good hands. The mortgage is nearly paid off. Trade is picking up and the workforce is content for now."

"Aye, lad, it's none of those things. It's me. I'm getting old, lad. I thought I was invincible like my mill, but I'm not, am I?"

"We're none of us getting any younger," admitted Robert. "You have plenty of years ahead of you — if you take things easy."

"I don't think so, lad. I've felt the hand of mortality on my shoulder and it's fair shaken me." Matthias gazed at his son with rheumy eyes. "I had a long chat with Eli this afternoon. He's had the right idea. He's left the running of the Endurance to your father-in-law Jacob and given himself some leisure, fishing and the like. Another thing he's done is put me in the way of another lawyer, a fellow in Doveton that was recommended to him. He doesn't trust Lightfoot. Says he had his doubts when there was some wrangling over what was left of the Relief Fund from the Cotton Crisis. Lightfoot suggested some dubious scheme, whereas Eli insisted it be used for the people of the town. That's when he changed his lawyer."

"Yes, I remember. The public baths were refurbished and a laundry added with the remaining money from the Fund," said Robert, who had helped with the scheme.

"I don't feel right dealing with the Lightfoots, not with young Hadrian able to delve into my affairs. When I'm feeling a bit better, would you come with me to Doveton?"

"Yes, of course, Papa," agreed Robert.

The next Friday, Matthias revived when Jack came home for the weekend.

"Please don't mention the army," his mother warned him before Jack went in to see his grandfather.

Jack look defiant, but Jessie put a finger to her lips.

"Not a word. We'll talk about it later, but I don't want Matthias upset. Wait to hear what your father and I have to say."

"All right, then," agreed Jack, still looking surly. "But I'm determined to go, you know."

"We know," said his mother. "I'll speak to you when your father gets home."

He seemed to sense a change in her attitude and nodded. "I won't say a word," he promised.

"Would you like some tea, Grandpapa?" she asked as she led her son in. "Look who's home for the weekend."

"Our Jack! Welcome home, lad," said Matthias, looking pleased. "And what have you been up to?"

Jessie left them. If only her father-in-law could treat Matt with the same fondness that he lavished on Jack and Helen. He had never once given her eldest son a few shillings in the same way he treated her other two children. She had always tried to treat her offspring equally, though she had to admit to spending more of her time with Matt when he was younger. Now she was worried about Jack and what the future might hold for him.

He was elated when his parents told him they would agree to his joining the army. He hugged his mother and shook his father's hand vigorously. "You won't regret it," he said. "I'll make you proud of me."

"I know you will, son," said Robert, his arm round his wife's waist to support her.

She'd been upset the night before, anxious about whether they were doing the right thing. But they had both agreed that their son had to decide his own future.

"We only want you to be safe," Jessie told Jack earnestly.

"Oh, I'll keep my head down all right," he said, laughing. "I must go and tell Matt. He thinks I'm quite mad, but I know he'll be pleased for me."

"Not a word to your grandfather," Jessie warned him. "And tell Matt to say nothing too."

"To hear is to obey, General," said her son with a mock salute.

"Go on with you!" said Jessie, shaking her head at his frivolity. "I hope we've done the right thing," she said, stifling a sob as her son dashed off to tell his brother his news. She laid her head on Robert's shoulder.

"You mustn't worry. He'll be all right," he reassured her. "I just hope Papa will be fine when we eventually give him the news."

It was a couple of weeks before Matthias felt able to travel to Doveton with his son. Jessie made sure he was wrapped up warm as they helped him into the gig. Michael drove carefully for the five miles into the town.

Hadrian was furious. "Did you know your grandfather was going to change his lawyers?" he demanded of Helen.

"Has he?" she asked in surprise. "How would I know? Anyway, where is the nearest lawyer? There's no other in town."

He could not mistake her genuine surprise, but Hadrian's anger took no prisoners. "You must have known. You're his little pet. 'Yes, Grandpapa, no, Grandpapa,'" he mimicked in a high voice. "Don't tell me you didn't know." He grabbed her wrist and she gasped at the stinging pain. "What's he done that for? What have you told him?"

Helen tried to be calm. "I haven't told him anything. What is there to tell? I don't know anything about it," she insisted quietly but firmly. "I don't know anything about the business of the mill. Do you want me to ask him?"

Hadrian calmed down a little and loosed his grip. "I don't know. I'll have to think about that. I would have thought he'd like to keep his business in the family. And I am part of the family, like it or lump it."

"Perhaps he doesn't want everyone in the family knowing his business," said Helen. "He's very secretive about his finances. I've heard my mother mention it before."

"Perhaps he's going bust, then, and doesn't want us to know about it," said her husband, clutching at wild and desperate straws.

Helen shook her head. "No, no!" she protested. "I'd have known about that. Papa wants to invest in some weaving machines. They wouldn't be doing that if they were going bust. It's impossible."

"Well, I hope you're right," said Hadrian, dropping her wrist. "I didn't expect to get trapped into marriage by a bunch of paupers."

Helen rubbed her painful wrist. She suspected a bruise might appear on her pale skin and knew she might have to wear her blouse with the long frilled cuffs once again. She was stung by her husband's remarks. How could she have trapped him when her mother wanted her to go to Honora in London to be away from him? Once she'd thought he loved her, but she had long since been disillusioned. It had become very clear that he'd only been interested in her because he thought her family had money. It was unfortunate that her grandpapa had changed his lawyer, but it was really none of her business. Nevertheless, she would once more be blamed.

CHAPTER 53: AN INVITATION TO DINNER

Plans went ahead for Jack to join the army. Jessie stayed home when Robert accompanied their son to his school, and the headmaster agreed that he should attend the Royal Military Academy at Sandhurst the following school year.

"He should have no problems with the academic side of things, providing he applies himself," he warned.

"Oh, I will, sir," said Jack eagerly. "Especially as it will be subjects I'm interested in."

The headmaster raised his eyebrows and Robert cleared his throat.

They still hadn't told Matthias of his grandson's plans. He was recovering well and even ventured out in the gig with Jessie for some fresh air. Her head was full of her son's intended career, and she found it very hard to stay silent about it to Matthias. The old man had wanted to visit the Invincible, but Doctor Andrew advised it would be too noisy and the atmosphere too tainted by cotton dust in his present state.

"Wait until you're a bit stronger," advised the doctor. "I'd recommend some fresh air so that your lungs will be strong to compensate the weakness of your heart."

Reluctantly Matthias agreed with him. So he and Jessie travelled out along the river until they found Eli happy at his beloved fishing.

"Hello, old lad," Eli greeted his brother-in-law. "Come to frighten my fish, have you?"

Matthias chuckled and shook his head. "This lass won't let me," he complained, gesturing to Jessie. "She's treating me like a babby. I'm all wrapped up in blankets against the cold."

"We only want to get you better," Jessie scolded him.

Her father-in-law gave her a rare fond smile. "I know, lass. I'm only teasing. I'm better looked after than the Widow of Windsor," he admitted, referring to the queen, who had retired to her castle.

Matthias was very tired when they returned home and retreated to his sofa for a nap. Jessie covered him with a woollen rug. He seemed very frail, his skin pale and with a sheen of sweat from the effort of climbing down from the gig. Soon he would have to be told of Jack's acceptance by Sandhurst. As Matt had suggested, Jack was going to serve for the minimum number of years. Leaving the army while still in his twenties, he would have plenty of time to learn the business of the Invincible. All the same, Jessie knew how hurt Matthias would be.

"We should invite Helen and Hadrian to Sunday dinner," she told Robert that evening. "Jack said he would be home, and it would be nice for us all to be together. We haven't been together in an age."

Next day, Jessie called on Helen with her invitation. They sat in the kitchen and chatted while Helen handstitched some lace onto a pretty christening gown. A delighted Jessie was about to ask if the tiny garment was for Helen herself until her daughter mentioned that one of the mill girls had ordered it.

"I can see you're expanding your range," said Jessie, admiring her daughter's work.

"This is the second one I've made," Helen told her, holding up the delicate gown to the light from the window. "They don't take much fabric, although they're fiddly to make. I've had to refuse an order for a wedding dress, though. It would take too much time and involve measuring and fitting the bride. Babies are much the same size."

"I'm really proud of you," Jessie told her. "Of all of you." Then she told Helen of Jack's plans.

Her daughter was shocked. "But what does Grandpapa think?" she asked. "Surely he'll object."

"What do you think brought on his attack?" sighed her mother. "But your father and I were worried that Jack would run away and join up as a private. He did threaten to. At least this way he'll train as an officer."

"Yes, I suppose so," Helen agreed. "But I'm really surprised. I suppose joining the Rifle Corps has given him the idea."

"And two of his friends are keen to go too," said Jessie. "Please don't say anything at all to your grandfather yet. It's such a strain trying to keep the secret. He'll be so upset. But there will be plenty of time for Jack to come back to the mill."

"He might find life in Gorbydale too mundane," said Helen. "He's never really shown any interest in the mill at all. Not like Matt."

"Who knows what the future will bring?" said Jessie, gathering her shawl round her. "Speaking of the future, will you be making a christening robe of your own sometime?" She knew it was intrusive to ask, but Matthias's comments had worried her. Jessie was troubled by the momentary look of misery on her daughter's face. But Helen soon recovered.

"I'm young yet," she said jauntily. "Are you in such a hurry to become a granny?"

On Sunday, the family assembled for a roast dinner. Jessie had warned them to be careful with Matthias and on no account to mention Jack's plans. The meal was, as ever, delicious and plentiful. Jessie had been busy in the kitchen with the cook and Lizzie. Maggie had helped with the vegetables and the soup, but this had tired her, and she was sitting at the kitchen table decorating a trifle with glace cherries.

"I'll get Helen to help me serve," Jessie told Lizzie. "You go and get ready."

Lizzie had confided to Jessie that she was invited to eat with Michael's parents. Sunday was her day off, but she had agreed to help out when she found out that Jessie had invited the family.

"Of course, I know them all well, but it seems more important when I've been formally invited to Sunday dinner," Lizzie confessed.

"You go and enjoy yourself," said Jessie. "I'm delighted for you both. His parents love you anyway."

Jessie and her daughter carried the food to the table.

"Where's Lizzie?" queried Matthias.

"Gone courting!" said Jessie with a chuckle.

"Who with?" he demanded.

"Michael, of course."

"Oh, that's all right then," said Matthias, settling back into his chair. "Couldn't Maggie help out?"

"The poor old thing is worn out," Helen told him.

Matthias looked affronted. "That 'poor old thing' is only the same age as me," he grumbled.

"She's had a much harder life, though," said Jessie quickly to keep the peace.

They settled down to eat.

Jack was bursting with his news but kept a wary eye on his grandfather. Jessie knew how much he wanted to talk to the family about his plans. It was such a strain to keep his secret, and she knew Matthias had to be told soon. They had all finished the beef and were admiring the trifle.

"It looks too good to eat," said Jack.

"Better make the most of it. You won't get such good grub in the army," said Hadrian loudly.

Everyone at the table stared at him. Helen looked horrified and grabbed her husband's sleeve to warn him. He shook her hand away and smirked at her.

"Eh, what was that?" demanded Matthias at the other end of the table. "Am I hearing things?"

Jessie glared at Hadrian. There was no avoiding Jack's news now. "Please don't fret yourself, Grandpapa," she said quietly, glaring with annoyance at Hadrian. "We were going to have a little announcement after dinner. That's why we've invited everybody." With all her heart she was sorry that Hadrian had been invited. She had a deep suspicion that he'd deliberately revealed the secret to upset the family.

"Surely the lad's not going into the army after all I said?" muttered Matthias, his face turning red with agitation.

"We can talk about it after we've eaten," suggested Robert. "When we've settled down."

"What have you been keeping from me?" growled his father. "All of you. All of you know what's happening. Nobody tells me nowt."

"Surely that's a double negative," said Hadrian glibly.

"You've done enough damage," hissed Helen, glaring at her husband in pure hatred. "And you promised me you wouldn't say anything."

"It just slipped out," he said with a shrug.

"We didn't want to worry you, Papa. Anyway, Jack won't be away for long," said Robert, trying to soothe his father.

Jessie poured Matthias a sip of brandy. "You mustn't distress yourself," she said kindly.

"Distress myself, distress myself!" Matthias's voice rose in anger. "Not distress myself when all my family's plotting behind my back?" His lips were alarmingly dull blue. His hand flew to his chest. "I don't feel so good," he gasped as he slumped forward.

"Jack, go for the doctor," ordered Jessie, hurrying to Matthias's side.

"Take Bob," called Matt, as his brother rushed to the door. "Go for Andrew."

"I hope you're pleased with yourself," Helen snapped at Hadrian.

"I think you should go home," Robert ordered him angrily.

"But perhaps I can be of help," murmured his daughter, anxious to be useful and help her grandfather.

"You can help by taking him home before I hit him," snapped her father, glaring at his son-in-law.

"Come on." Hadrian grabbed his wife's arm. "I know when I'm not wanted. I don't like damned trifle anyway."

The others tried to revive Matthias. Matt brought his medicine, but it was of no use. By now he was barely conscious and breathing laboriously. They laid him on the floor with a cushion under his head. Matt slipped a throw from the sofa over him.

"He didn't let us explain," sobbed Jessie. "He would have been told that Jack would be coming home in a few years."

"He may be all right," Robert tried to comfort her.

But when Doctor Andrew arrived, he held out little hope for Matthias. His already weakened heart might not survive the shock of his favourite grandson's imminent departure. He lingered all evening but in the cold hours of the night, with

Robert and Jessie holding vigil by his bedside, Matthias Overdale, the Master of the Invincible left this life.

The family was shocked.

"It's all my fault. I won't join the army," said a stunned Jack.

"That's all too late now," sighed his mother. "The damage is done. If Hadrian had kept his big gob shut, we might have had a chance to explain. But Matthias would have had to know sometime. Don't forget he lived a long life, son. We can't live other people's lives for them. They must choose their own. Matthias wouldn't have chosen me to marry your father, but we had other plans. Go and live your life as you wish to."

CHAPTER 54: A FAREWELL

The funeral of the Master of the Invincible was a grand affair. The Invincible was closed for the day, and the workforce stood respectfully outside its walls as Matthias's hearse, pulled by black plumed horses, drove solemnly past the great monument to his enterprise. It was the end of an era. True that many of his workmen and women resented his petty rules and hoped for a better regime from his son, but the church was packed and mourners from the town lined the streets. The vicar spoke of Matthias Overdale's importance to the town and how he would be missed by his family. But of all the many people that offered their condolences to Robert and the family, not one spoke of his kindness. He had been cantankerous, obstinate and self-centred to everyone but his late wife and his two favourite grandchildren. All the same, the family would miss him. He had been a large figure in their lives.

"I expect it'll be us next," said Eli, standing beside Jacob at the graveside.

"Hardly worth going home, then!" joked his old friend, and the chuckling pair earned a disapproving look from the vicar.

Robert smiled at his uncle and father-in-law. They may not have had many years left, but they were determined to live them to the full. Matthias had spent so much of his life being miserable. Jack was full of remorse, though determined to go on with his plans for the army. Matt looked dolefully into the grave, no doubt wondering what his future might be.

Jessie and Helen, with the other female members of the family and invited friends waited at Overdale House. As was the custom, it was thought unfitting for ladies to be present at the graveside, lest they be overcome with the emotion of the occasion. Honora was sitting by Helen quietly chatting, while Jessie made sure that everyone was provided with tea. Hadrian had been politely told he would not be needed at the funeral.

When Helen had quietly told him of her parents' request, he was furious.

"How dare they!" he shouted. "I'm a member of the family, same as anyone else."

"What did you expect?" she asked sarcastically. "I did warn you. You promised me you wouldn't say anything about Jack joining the army. And look what happened when you did."

The crockery rattled as she gripped the dresser as the stinging slap sent her off balance.

"And I didn't appreciate the way you talked to me that night at your parents' house," snapped Hadrian. "Just watch it, my girl. You may sauce me in front of them, but I'll have respect in my own home. The old skinflint had lived long enough anyway. With a bit of luck he's left you this house."

But the house remained as part of the estate. Matthias had left everything, including the remaining mortgage, to Robert. Robert was not about to relinquish Overdale Lodge to Helen so that Hadrian could get his hands on it.

A new regime was about to begin at the mill. Robert waited a couple of weeks out of respect for his father, then abolished the rule where his workers would have their wages docked if they were late with a genuine excuse.

"But the excuse must be genuine," he told the overseers who had gathered to hear him. "If anyone takes advantage with flimsy excuses, their pay will be docked after three instances. I think that's only fair, don't you?"

They all nodded in agreement. The workers were delighted, especially those with children or ailing family members who often faced an emergency in the mornings. Robert's popularity went up immediately. When Jessie accompanied him round town, she noticed his workers smiled and touched their caps in greeting when they saw him, a sharp difference to the begrudging acknowledgement of Matthias. She mentioned it one night over dinner.

"That's because they rely on me for their livelihood," said Robert modestly.

But Jessie knew it was something much deeper than that.

"Uncle Eli says it's a good idea not to make enemies of your workforce," said Matt, tucking into his meal. "People work better if their employer is fair with them."

"But won't people take advantage of a weak boss?" protested Jack, almost an echo of his grandfather.

"The odd one might," said his brother. "But most people appreciate fairness. Most of Uncle Eli's workers have been with him ages. I was reading an article in the newspaper saying that cotton production in America is improving now that men are free and getting paid for their work."

"Nathan has always said that," Robert told his sons. "I'm pleased you're taking an interest in such things," he told Matt.

Jessie watched her sons as they tucked into their food. They were growing into young men before her eyes. They were so different in their outlook but good friends all the same, despite their teasing. Soon Jack would leave them. She presumed that at least Matt would always be with them. Her home was slowly emptying. Melissa and now Matthias were gone. Helen was married and at least was nearby. Lizzie had hinted that she might soon be married to Michael and leave her room upstairs, though she would be living over the stables with her in-laws once she was wed and had asked if she might still work at the big house.

"That is until I start a family," she'd added shyly. "But Michael's mam says she'll look after any little ones if I want to work."

"You'd be more than welcome," said Jessie. "What would I do without you? Maggie is getting frailer, and thank goodness your sister Hettie is here to help."

Hettie was the youngest of Lizzie's clan. She was barely out of school but hadn't wanted to go into the mill. She was small for her age but a good worker. Though she was often cheeky to Maggie and the cook, they treated her with amused good humour. Lizzie scolded her but she took little notice.

CHAPTER 55: SECRETS

Life was becoming a routine for Jessie. It was nearly a month before Robert decided that he should sort out his father's belongings.

"Do you want to move into your parents' bedroom?" asked Jessie. "It is larger than ours."

"I'm happy where we are, if you are?" he said. "The front of the house is draughty, and we have a nice view over the hills from our window."

They decided to tackle the clothes first. Helen came to help her mother sort out Melissa's clothes. Though she had been dead for a few years, Matthias had not had the heart to get rid of her personal things.

"Look at these!" said Helen, hauling out dresses and petticoats from a large trunk. Among them were dresses much too small for her grandmother.

"Some of these are from when she was a girl," said Jessie, holding up a dress trimmed with lilac lace. "She doesn't seem to have thrown anything away. Would you like to take them and see if you can alter them? Or perhaps you could just use the fabric."

"It's like a treasure trove," said Helen, hugging a blue sprigged muslin dress to her waist. "I'm sure I could do so much with all this material."

They found a bundle of letters tied with blue ribbon. Jessie glanced at them.

"I do believe they're love letters from Matthias. It looks like they're in his writing. Better give them to your father to decide what to do with them."

"Can we read them?" asked Helen.

Jessie shook her head. "Your grandmother kept them private, so they should remain that way."

They put the letters aside and delved once again into the trunk. Once they had taken out all the clothes, they found a quantity of bedding at the bottom.

"Would you like these for your home?" Jessie asked her daughter, examining a sheet. "These are cotton sheets, and they seem in good condition. Or we could offer them to Eleanor for when she gets married. Lizzie might like some for her bottom drawer."

They came across some sheets that had been repaired by cutting through the worn part in the middle and sewing the sides together.

"These could be cut into cot sheets," said Helen, unfolding one of the sheets out to the light.

Jessie smiled. "And will they be of use anytime soon?" she asked hopefully. She was distressed to see the miserable look on her daughter's face.

"Don't get your hopes up, Mama," said Helen. "I promise you, you'll be the first to know if I'm expecting."

"Is everything all right?" asked Jessie gently.

Helen was immediately defensive. "Yes, of course. Anyway, there's enough bedding here for all three of us girls. I'm sure Lizzie would appreciate some, and you can ask Eleanor too. I'll take the repaired stuff and sew it into cot sheets. Some of it is good quality linen."

They began putting the trunk's contents into piles on the bed. Then they turned to a chest of drawers. No sooner had they pulled the first drawer open than Helen froze in alarm as the chimes from the granddaughter clock in the hall echoed round the house.

"That's twelve o'clock," she gasped. "I'd better get home. I haven't done a thing for Hadrian's dinner."

"Surely he knows you're helping me," said her mother.

"I'd better go," said Helen. Giving her mother a swift kiss on the cheek, she almost ran out of the room and seconds later the front door closed behind her.

Jessie stared at the contents of Melissa's private life and wondered. Something was not quite right with Helen's life. She did not like Hadrian and instinctively knew he was making her daughter unhappy.

The front door sounded again, and Robert came upstairs and into the bedroom. He slipped an arm round Jessie's waist and kissed her cheek. "And how are things going?" he asked. "My goodness, look at all this stuff."

"I don't think your mother ever threw anything away," chuckled Jessie. "I've just noticed your baby shoes in a corner of that drawer."

"I thought Helen was helping you?" said Robert.

"She had to hurry home to feed Hadrian," explained his wife.

"Yes, us husbands need feeding from time to time," he laughed. "Or we grow into ravenous beasts." He growled roguishly and nibbled her ear.

"Give over, you daft 'apporth," she said with a chuckle. "I'm sure we'll find something to stop you turning into a ravenous beast."

In the afternoon, Helen appeared very subdued. Jessie noticed bruises on her wrist that had not been apparent that morning. Tactfully she didn't mention them to her daughter, but she was becoming very worried about Helen's life.

In the chest of drawers they found gloves and fans and lace collars and cuffs and all sorts of trinkets that Melissa had treasured. There were nightdresses that Jessie might use and underwear that was fit only for rags. Helen was pleased with all the stuff she was taking away and already making plans aloud for cushion covers and silky shawls.

"You'll be busy," said her mother.

Helen smiled, no doubt thinking of the money she might make. Though Hadrian might take his share, she still had her secret hoard that he had not discovered.

There was a long slim satin pouch in the bottom drawer, somewhere where Melissa might have kept her gloves. Helen picked it up, and to her surprise it felt heavy. Peeping inside she found a small bottle. She read the label, and it said 'finest tincture of laudanum'. Helen turned towards her mother with her find, but Jessie had left the room for a moment. On some instinct Helen slipped it into her pocket. Her grandmother was not the only person used to keeping secrets.

At the weekend Robert went through his father's wardrobe. Matthias's clothes were old and worn and much too big and old-fashioned for Robert and his sons.

"I might take them to the workhouse," suggested Jessie, lifting a heavy overcoat from the back of the wardrobe. "Somebody might make use of them."

It was as she struggled to haul it to the bed that she heard the chink of metal. Delving into the pocket, her hand emerged with a small fabric bag. She tipped the contents out onto the coverlet. A pile of bright sovereigns twinkled in the sunlight. Carefully she counted them as Robert and Helen looked on.

"There's twenty," she said. "Matthias must have put them aside for an emergency." Jessie rummaged in the other pockets and found a roll of notes. She handed it to Robert and he untied the string around it and unrolled the thin paper. A pile of unfamiliar banknotes was revealed.

"These are Confederate dollars," he said in surprise. "I thought my mother had taken them to Liverpool to be cashed."

"Perhaps he kept some back in the hope the South might win," suggested Jessie.

Robert shrugged. "Who knows? He certainly kept his little hoard of sovereigns a secret."

They gave the children four sovereigns each and kept the remaining eight. Robert gave his father's watch and chain to Matt, as he had a good watch himself. To Jack he gave the gold studs and tie pin. There were only small mementoes for Jessie and Helen. Robert gave his daughter a brooch with a small compartment containing an intricate pattern of woven hair.

"That was my grandmother's," he told her. "That's her dark hair, twisted with a lock of Melissa's fair baby hair, and the brown one is Eli's from when he was a boy. Granny Gorman weaved the pattern with the hair herself. I remember being fascinated by it as a small boy."

"I've only ever known Uncle Eli with grey hair," said Helen.

"I remember his hair was brown when I was a little girl," said her mother with a smile. "He often had a gala day for the children of his workers. We had sandwiches and cakes and games and races."

"I was only ever allowed to watch," said Robert with a sigh. "My father didn't want me to mix with the other children. I longed to join in."

"Eli joined in," remembered Jessie. "He pretended to nearly win the races. Then he began huffing and puffing just before the finish line. He really enjoyed himself. I must invite him over for a meal and remind him."

Melissa's jewellery had long been secretly sold to save the mill. Soon the rooms were empty of the personal belongings of two people who had spent a lifetime collecting them. Within two short days, everything had disappeared.

Lizzie was grateful for the bed linen that Jessie had given her. "Michael and I hope to be married soon, and this will come in very handy," she said shyly. "His mam and dad are glad we're moving in with them, as his dad hasn't been too good."

Jessie knew that Michael had been doing most of his father's work in the stable. He'd taken over the garden and most of the driving, leaving his father to feed the horses and care for the harness and tackle. He ate his meals in the kitchen of Overdale House at Jessie's suggestion to ease the burden on the family budget. Matthias had never offered the men two wages, but Michael had always worked with his father to help him out. That was no problem when he was single, but now he was to marry Lizzie, Jessie knew there would have to be proper provision made. The family lived rent free above the stables, but that didn't provide the price of an extra wage.

"I'm going to have a word with Robert," she told Lizzie. "Matthias thought people could survive on fresh air. He never gave Robert a proper salary either, but things will have to change."

There were many things about to change at Overdale House.

Lizzie and Michael wanted no fuss for their wedding. Jessie offered Overdale House for the wedding breakfast, but Lizzie politely declined.

"With Michael's folk not feeling too well and with so many of my folks that we can't invite them all, we thought it best just to have a quiet wedding," she told Jessie. "But I do hope you'll come for a sup of wine and some bride cake at the stable house."

So one quiet weekday, Jessie and Helen slipped into the church to see Lizzie wed.

The house was quiet when Jessie went home. She slipped down to the kitchen to see if she could be of use.

"We're fine here," said the cook, busy with dinner. "You go and put your feet up."

It was the last thing Jessie was used to doing. She suddenly felt as if she had no purpose in life. The house felt empty once Robert and Matt left for work in the morning. Helen was busy sewing and selling and had branched out into another couple of mills with the help of Lorna. Though Jessie often bobbed down to see Helen, her time with her daughter was necessarily short as she knew Hadrian didn't like to find her in his home when he came back for lunch.

With a sigh she picked up a book and began to read. She hadn't had time to read in an age.

CHAPTER 56: BROTHERS

Jack had been at Sandhurst for nearly two years and was enjoying army life. On his last visit home he had chatted, full of enthusiasm, about the end of his training and his eagerness to begin real army life. Jessie dreaded the thought of her son being sent into danger, but Jack blithely ignored her worries, seeing life as a great adventure.

"He has all the confidence of ignorant youth," Robert told his wife as they lay in bed.

She could not sleep, and her restlessness had disturbed him too.

"How can he know the misery and destruction of war, as we do, when all he hears of is heroism and battle honours? The paintings all around him are of stalwart men of action, and what little blood that is shown is on the enemy."

"But he seems so young," she sighed. "Deep down I'd hoped he would have tired of the army — the discipline especially. But Jack seems to thrive on it."

"We'll just have to pray that he stays safe," said her husband. "Now let's try and sleep, or we'll be like sleepwalkers in the morning."

But Jessie stared at the moon shadows on the ceiling as Robert rolled over and began snoring softly.

Jack came home two weeks before his passing out parade. He was unusually sober.

"I expect you've been busy," said his mother, looking carefully at her son.

He seemed to grow taller every time she saw him. "We've been drilling and drilling 'til my feet hurt," he admitted.

"Are your boots all right?" she asked.

"They're fine. Some of the lads in our platoon just can't seem to get it right, though. We've had to practise and practise until it's perfect."

"We're looking forward to coming to watch you," said Jessie, hugging his arm. "It's a pity your grandfather isn't here to see you. He'd be so proud despite his objections."

"I suppose I saw him off in a way," said Jack.

"Don't say that," protested Jessie. "Hadrian didn't help. But your Grandpapa's time had come. 'Three score year and ten' the Bible says, and he'd passed that. Every day is a bonus after that."

"I forgot you came from a family of bible-bashers," said Jack, laughing. "Grandad Jacob is always quoting it at me. He gave me a bible before I went off to the grammar."

"I didn't know that," said his mother.

"It's not something I was going to boast about," chuckled Jack.

"It would do you a power of good to look in it sometimes," chided Jessie.

Jack became serious. "There is one thing, Mama," he said quietly. "Will our Matt be coming to my passing out parade?"

"Yes, of course," said Jessie.

"Only…" Jack hesitated and could not look her in the face. "I was wondering if you might persuade him otherwise."

"I'm sorry?" she asked in surprise. "How do you mean?"

"It's just… It's just… Well, I don't want my comrades to make fun of him. There's a slow lad at the local pub, the pot boy. They rib him something rotten."

"But James and Godfrey have met Matt when they came to tea. There was no problem then," his mother reminded him. These were Jack's two friends from the grammar school, and one had joined up with him. "And anyway, Matt isn't slow. He's bright as a button, just a bit slow speaking," protested Jessie.

"But that isn't the whole corps," said her son. "And even Godfrey made a few remarks."

"Oh he did, did he? Are you ashamed of your brother?" demanded Jessie angrily.

"No, no! Not really," Jack tried to deny.

"If you are, then it's you I'm ashamed of. If other boys mock him, that's their problem. They aren't as brave and noble as they like to think themselves. But I'm surprised at you," she snapped. "Matt is probably braver than the lot of you. You've seen how he tries his best, even when he's in pain."

Jack looked very ashamed. "I know," he admitted, cowed by his mother's anger. "I just didn't want to hear him made fun of."

"Well, I tell you now, if Matt isn't to go, then neither am I." With that, she left him looking stunned and alone and stormed out of the room. She nearly bowled Matt over as she flew out of the door.

He grabbed her arm, not only to steady himself, but to draw her into the morning room. "I heard most of that," he said with a sad smile.

"Oh no!" Jessie was distressed.

"Maybe he's right. I don't want to spoil his day. You and Papa must go. It's a long way for me anyway, and I'll probably be at work."

"I'm not going," said his mother firmly. "I'm right ashamed of him."

"No need to be," said Matt. "He's only trying to protect me. You know what people are like when they see someone with a disability. You only had to talk to Grandpapa."

"And he was wrong," snapped Jessie.

"You're right," said Matt with a grin. "Tell you what, I'll go anyway. By now I don't care what people think. But I don't want you to miss Jack's big day. We'll all go."

His mother hugged him. "Did you hear me tell our Jack that you're braver that the lot of them?" she laughed.

"And Mother is always right," agreed Matt, laughing too.

They linked arms and went to see Jack. He was sitting in the parlour with his head in his hands.

"We've decided that we'll both be there to see you parading on your big day," said Matt. "I'm hoping to see you all go down like dominoes. Then we'll see who has the last laugh."

Jack looked so relieved. "Are you sure?" he asked anxiously.

"I wouldn't let Mama miss it for the world," said his brother.

Jack came and shook his hand. "You are the bravest," he said solemnly. "And if I hear anyone say anything against you, I'll knock their block off."

The journey down to the military college was long and tiring for both Matt and his father, but they all enjoyed it. Helen made Jessie a new dress for the occasion and her mother drew many admiring looks with its simplicity but fashionable elegance. Jack of course was resplendent in his uniform, and the drilling and marching went entirely to plan, despite Matt's teasing predictions.

"I'm being posted to Ireland," Jack proudly told his parents.

"Not too much danger there," Robert comforted his wife on the train journey home.

"And what about the Fenians?" asked Jessie with alarm.

"You'd have to ask your friend Mary about them," teased Robert. "Wasn't her father an Irish strike breaker?"

"Many, many years ago," she admitted. "Many people in the town never forgave the Irish. I always liked him, though. He was a very gentle and kind man, just looking for work."

"There you are, then," chuckled her husband. "Maybe our Jack will land among gentle and kind people too."

"I hope so, but there's such a lot of unrest in Ireland right now," said Jessie. "The Government has defeated the Home Rule Bill yet again. I'm sure they're sending more soldiers to Ireland to quell any unrest."

Robert smiled at his wife. "I suppose you've been reading the print off the newspapers again. You're as bad as your father for that."

Jacob was well known for burying his nose in newspapers for an age.

"It's the only way to find out what's going on in the world," Jessie reminded him.

"Or joining the army," suggested Matt with a grin.

"I wouldn't back any Fenians against your mother," Robert teased her. "She's a force to be reckoned with."

"Even armed with a rolled up newspaper!" chuckled Matt, and the two men began laughing. They ignored the withering looks from Jessie as they brandished imaginary newspapers. She had to smile at their antics in the end.

"You mustn't worry, Mama. Jack will always land on his feet," said Matt.

"At least he'll have a steadier landing than either of us," joked Robert, and they began to laugh again.

Jack was duly sent to Ireland, and his infrequent but cheerful letters quelled some of her worries. All the same, Jessie could not help but secretly worry about her youngest son.

CHAPTER 57: MATT

The icy hand of winter had the Gorbydale valley in its grip. Matt's pony Bob slipped and struggled on the icy cobbles, and it took him an age to reach the Endurance. He'd slid from the poor creature's back halfway to his work and led him through the snow, clinging to the saddle to steady himself.

Eli met him at the mill gate, followed by Norbert, who took charge of Bob.

"Well, lad, I didn't expect you this morning. You must be perished," he said. "Half the workforce is late, especially those from up the hills. Come on in and get a brew to warm you up. Miss Fitch managed to get here."

Matt was shivering as he sat down at his desk. Charity provided him with a drink of tea in a mug, rather than his usual cup. He grasped it with frozen fingers and savoured the warmth filtering into his hands.

"Keep your coat on for a bit," she urged as she replenished the kettle and knelt to put more coal on the office stove.

"Thank you," said Matt humbly, touched by her concern for him.

Eli came into the office. "This weather doesn't look like breaking anytime soon," he said. "Perhaps you'd better stay with me until it does. We've plenty of space. You can have Honora's bedroom."

Matt hesitated. He had rarely been away from home and the familiar things that made life easier for him. "Yes, it would be sensible," he admitted. "I did struggle this morning, and the end of month accounts need doing."

"I'll send one of the big lads over to your mother with a message, and she can send a few things over for you," said his uncle. "It'll be a nice change to have a bit of company."

Matt smiled up at him with immense gratitude. He had been tempted to turn back, unsure if he would reach the mill. His innate sense of duty had urged him on. Staying with Uncle Eli was a perfect solution. He had some plans he wanted to share with his uncle.

That night, as they sat by the fire after their evening meal, Matt began to outline his ideas to save money for the mill. Eli sat quietly as he listened to his great-nephew.

"So you think I should give Mac Barry the elbow?" he said. "And get somebody in to replace him?"

"Yes, he doesn't pull his weight," said Matt eagerly. "And he's been very impudent to Charity, er, Miss Fitch."

"And to you, I think?" said Eli, who missed nothing.

Matt blushed and stayed guiltily silent.

"I'm sure you're right, lad. But you do know he's the only breadwinner in the house. His grandmother was a grand worker when I first invested in the Endurance with your grandad. She'd worked the new machines before the frame breakers put her out of a job by smashing them up. She showed me and Matthias the ropes. We were hand weavers then. We knew nothing about these new-fangled machines, but she was quick on the uptake. And her daughter was a rare worker too. It would break her heart if I put her son out of work. Mac's a bit mouthy, I grant you. I might have a word with him."

"Oh no, please don't do that," said Matt quickly. "He'd probably blame me for telling tales anyway."

"And there we have it, lad. Do you want to make enemies?" asked Eli, watching Matt intently. "A workforce who is with you is more productive than one who's against you. Look at your Grandad Overdale. His workers resented his methods of bullying overseers and threats of losing jobs. Once they were trained, they went and found work elsewhere if they could. He was always complaining that he couldn't keep his workers. Now your father has no such problems. He was telling me his production's up."

It was true. Matthias had been forever grumbling to Robert, though still he ignored his son's advice. Robert had urged his father to stop the rigid petty rules about docking wages, but Matthias would have none of it.

"Some of 'em would get away with murder just because they can't get their backsides out of bed in time," he'd grumbled.

Matt guessed what resentment would have resulted at the Invincible if wages had been docked because of the hazardous weather conditions. He knew his father would do no such thing. Eli had welcomed his latecomers with hot tea and cocoa, grateful that they had arrived at all. His workers were known for their loyalty.

Next morning, Charity seemed distracted and hardly able to concentrate on her work.

"Is it your mother?" asked Matt gently.

She turned to him with a tired shrug. "How did you guess?" she said. "When is it ever anything different?"

"I'm sorry," said Matt. "I know my Grandpapa could be difficult, but our house was big enough to avoid him. But you're there alone with your mother."

Charity nodded with resigned agreement. "But she said some awful things to me last night." She looked near to tears. "She called me a useless old maid."

"I don't think you're useless," Matt defended her vigorously. "I couldn't do without you. And anyway, that's unfair. You keep your household going with your wages from the mill."

"I know. I have kept our home provided. But just recently one of Mother's cousins died and left her some money. Now Mother has a bit of financial independence, my wages aren't as important to her."

"That's damned unfair," he protested. "I mean… I do apologise for my language."

She smiled at him. "I feel like swearing myself sometimes too," she admitted.

"You can go ahead if you like. I won't object," said Matt with a chuckle.

"Anyway, I suppose I feel miserable because she's right. Who'd want to marry anyone with a mother like that hanging round her neck?" sighed Charity.

Matt's heart began thumping so hard, he was sure she might hear it. He felt hot and tense. Here was a chance for him to speak. But what if she laughed at him? Could he really laugh off a rejected proposal and pretend it was all a joke? How could they continue to work together with such embarrassment? But if he didn't speak, he might live his life without ever knowing how she felt. The situation was torture as it was.

"I'd marry you," he said quietly, though he felt he was about to explode.

She stared at him, looking unsure at what he'd said. "You mean…?" she asked.

He nodded. "Yes, I do," he said boldly.

A slow smile spread over her face. "Oh Mr Overdale!" She didn't answer for a long moment. Matt froze with anxiety, but she was still smiling. "This is a bit of a surprise. But why not?"

decided Charity. "We make a good team. We get on well together, and I think you're ever so brave. I knew you liked me, but I never expected… Well, why not?"

She laid her hands on his shoulders and kissed him gently on the forehead like a child. She looked about to kiss his cheek, but his arm slid round her waist. He drew her to him and kissed her full on the lips with all the pent-up passion he possessed.

Her eyes opened wide with surprise. "Oh Mr Overdale!" she said breathlessly.

"I think you might call me Matt," he said with a slow smile.

With that, she held his face and returned a kiss as passionate as his own.

They were interrupted by a tap on the door, and Uncle Eli strolled in as he usually did at that time of the morning. His eyes widened when he noticed them hurriedly disentangling from their embrace.

"Oh, I'm sorry. I should have knocked louder. I didn't realise anything was er…"

Matt grinned and went to shake Uncle Eli's hand. "You can be the first to congratulate us, Uncle Eli, I mean Mr Gorman," he said, laughing. "Miss Fitch has just consented to be my wife."

"Well, our Matthew! Well, I'll be blowed. I'm real chuffed for you. And you too, Miss Fitch. I'll have to call you 'our Charity' from now on, out of work, mind." He shook her hand vigorously. Then, asking "May I?" he kissed her warmly on both cheeks when she nodded consent. "Who'd have thought it?" he said as he cheerfully went back to work. "I'm right chuffed."

Later, he called Matt into his office. "Have you asked her mother yet?" asked Eli cautiously.

"I've only just asked Charity," confessed Matt.

"Eh, she's a bit of dragon is that one. I wish you luck, son," said his uncle, looking doubtful.

"Charity has hinted as much," said Matt. "But it's got to be done. Anyway, Charity's of age, so she can please herself. But of course I don't want to cause a rift in the family."

"Wise lad," said Eli. "You just be your charming — and tactful — self. That should win her over. You know what I said about making enemies. Avoid it if you can."

"I will, Uncle Eli," said Matt with a grin. "I'd best go and mention my engagement to Grandad." With that, he went to tell Jacob his news, with a warning to keep it quiet until he'd asked Charity's mother and told his own parents.

The meeting with Mrs Fitch went as well as could be expected.

"So you want to deprive me of my only child's support, do you?" said Mrs Fitch with a pathetic attempt at a sob.

"Oh yes, indeed," said Matt with what he hoped was a winning smile. "I'm quite set on it. I believe you've recently come into a sum of money. You could perhaps employ a little maid to keep you company."

"My daughter had no right to discuss my private business with a stranger," she retorted.

"With her fiancé," corrected Matt. "Charity is of course of age, but we wished to have your blessing. That's only right and proper. And family is important," he reminded her.

"Yes, of course," conceded his future mother-in-law. "In the circumstances, I couldn't provide a dowry."

"And I shouldn't expect one. Charity's own lovely person is all the fortune I need," said Matt gallantly, turning to Charity with a wink.

She squeezed his hand. "So you'll give us your blessing, Mother?" she asked.

"I suppose I better had," said her mother. "The lad seems determined, despite his gammy leg and the fact that you're an old spinster."

"Hardly old," protested Matt. "And my gammy leg is no bar to us having a full and fulfilled life together."

He produced a bottle of sherry from his coat, and Charity filled three glasses and her mother's twice again as they toasted the happy couple.

Jessie and Robert were surprised and delighted when Matt arrived home two days later and told them his news.

"Good on you, lad," said Robert, shaking his son's hand vigorously.

"I'm very glad for you, son," said Jessie, kissing her son's cheek. She had met and liked Charity. "Another one leaving the nest," she added dejectedly.

"Er … I was wondering if we could come and live here," said Matt, looking hopeful. "There's plenty of room. It would be easier for us both if I could live where things have been adapted for me."

"Won't you be living with her widowed mother?" asked Jessie in surprise.

"Not with that old dragon, we won't!" said her son. "She treats Charity like a skivvy. But Charity will pull her weight while she's here. If she's not helping me, that is. I couldn't cope without her."

Jessie was overjoyed. At last the rooms of Overdale House would not be empty. There might even be the possibility of other additions to the family to fill the old nursery.

CHAPTER 58: MAGGIE

Maggie was ill. She was not in the kitchen when Lizzie arrived for work.

"Go and get the old bag of bones out of her bed," complained the cook.

Lizzie found Maggie unable to raise herself from her small bed in the eaves.

"I'm … sorry … I … can't…" she gasped, struggling for breath.

"You stay there and don't worry," Lizzie instructed her. "The missis will send for a doctor. You're not well, Maggie. Just lie back and relax. We'll get you help."

Doctor Andrew didn't look reassured once he'd examined her. "I think it's phthisis," he said. "Her right lung is hardly moving."

"We should write to Dolly," Jessie murmured to Lizzie. "She might not get here in time, but at least she should know."

"Aye, please … write … to our … Dolly," whispered Maggie, who had heard the quiet suggestion in the silence of the room.

"We must send a telegram," suggested Jessie.

It took a few days for the telegram to arrive in Louisiana. Although it was minutes passing by cable under the Atlantic, its journey to the remote state took longer. Dolly was immediately anxious when the rider delivered it.

"I should go to her," she said, weeping.

"I'll go," said Albert. "Maybe I'll be in time."

They quickly packed him a bag, and Nathan drove him to the railroad at Monroe to catch the train to New Orleans. It was a long and arduous journey, but eventually a tired and anxious Albert arrived in Doveton.

He had sent a telegram from Liverpool to say when he would arrive, and Michael and Helen met him with the gig at the station. Their gloomy faces told the story.

"We sent another telegram, but you must have missed it," apologised Helen. "Maggie hung on until the day before yesterday when she knew you were coming, but her poor old lungs gave out. I'm so very sorry."

"It's a shame they couldn't send me by cable under the Atlantic," said Albert, close to tears.

Helen put a comforting arm around his shoulder. "She was very peaceful at the end," she said. "We looked after her all we could."

"I knew you would," he told her, his voice broken with grief. "I wanted her to come and live with us at the plantation, but she felt she was too old to travel."

Helen raised her head as they passed Overdale Lodge and saw Hadrian scowling through the window as he noticed her arm, linked with Albert's to comfort him. She immediately slipped it away, biting her lip at her carelessness.

All Albert could do for his grandmother now was make the funeral arrangements.

"Will she be buried with her husband Tommo?" asked Helen, although her mother was behind Albert, silently shaking her head in warning.

"Tommo is in a pauper's grave, like Seth," Albert told her, looking embarrassed. "I didn't think my uncle deserved a proper funeral as he drowned trying to rob me."

"I'm so sorry," muttered Helen.

"No, don't be. But I'll make sure Mam has a proper grave and a proper headstone," he said. "She deserved it."

There was a surprising number of people in the church for Maggie's funeral. All the folk from Overdale House were there of course, but many of her old neighbours came to pay their respects and commiserate with Albert.

"She was such a kind lady," said an old friend. "She might not have had much herself, but she wouldn't see anyone go without. Not that she'd let on to that Tommo, the old b… I shouldn't swear as I've just come out of church, should I?"

Albert smiled. "I know what you mean." He stood chatting to his old neighbours as the family politely waited for him. "I'll walk up to the house," he told Robert and Jessie. "Please go ahead. I won't be long."

"Shall I wait with you?" asked Helen.

He shook his head and smiled sadly. "Thank you, but you go ahead. A quiet walk will do me good after this morning's sad ceremonies."

Helen reluctantly joined her family on the gig. She glanced back at Albert as he received the sympathies of his old neighbours. He was a nice man, a good man despite his upbringing with the violent Tommo and Seth and timid Maggie. Then he'd been hauled off to America with a mother who'd initially abandoned him and a stranger for a father. Hadrian, on the other hand, for all his privileged upbringing, was selfish and unkind.

Albert stayed another few days, arranging for a suitable headstone for his grandmother. He chose a white marble stone adorned with a carved flower resembling a daisy. Helen helped to choose the wording.

"I think 'A beloved grandmother and mother' would be good," decided Albert. "That covers all situations. She was a mother to me for many years."

He looked so sad that Helen wanted to hold him close and comfort him. Knowing her actions might be reported back to Hadrian by his cronies, she curbed her instincts.

Some days later, it was with much sadness that Helen said goodbye to her American friend at the station. "I do hope you don't forget us here in Gorbydale, now that your grandmother is no longer with us," she said.

"I can never forget your kindness," replied Albert with a smile. "I suppose it would not be appropriate to write to a married lady such as yourself, but I will surely write to your father and ask after the family." He had felt Hadrian's hostility in the brief meetings he had had with him.

"Oh, please do," said Helen eagerly.

It was as well he had not promised to write to her. Hadrian had been sulky with Helen since Albert's arrival. He had accused her of flirting with their visitor, despite her protests that she was only comforting the bereaved young man.

"And we all know that one thing leads to another," snapped Hadrian. "I'm not daft. I know what a damned tease you are. Look where it's got me, saddled with a silly bitch without a penny to her name."

She was about to snap that she had more money than him behind her. It was tempting to add that it was mostly through her own efforts, but she knew that would only lead to more trouble. She wished Hadrian could be more like Albert.

CHAPTER 59: A CONFRONTATION

Dolly was relieved when she received Albert's telegram to say he was on his way home. She'd been tearful all the time he was away, remembering her mother and how she'd battled with life. In a way, she felt she'd abandoned Maggie as she'd half-abandoned Albert. Although she'd been living in Gorbydale, she was not always there to protect them from Tommo and Seth. She tried to quash her guilt with routine and caring for her daughter.

Nathan called to Dolly as she was reading to Marguerite. "Can you come out for a moment?" he asked.

Three men were waiting on the porch. They looked nervous, clutching their hats in front of them. Dolly recognised two of them as Barney's grandsons. The third she knew was from the Amiens village.

"These men have come looking for work," explained Nathan. "Barney told them to come and see me, but I've explained the Amiens plantation belongs to Albert now and that you're looking after it for him."

"But Barney and Zeb do all the hiring and firing nowadays," said Dolly. "Why didn't they just ask them for work?"

Nathan sighed. "There's a problem."

The men nodded solemnly.

"Raphael and Gabriel have been sharecropping over near Monroe. And Andy here had some land nearby. They thought they could make a go of it on their own, working for themselves and helping each other out. But they needed some tools and equipment to get started. They've got into debt with a local carpetbagger named Brownlow. According to him, the debt keeps rising. Now they're working his land like slaves just to pay off the debt."

"Oh dear," said Dolly, unsure of what to think. "Can't they just work for us and pay some of the debt off with their wages? We could do with some more workers so we can drain that land to the south and plant it."

"So we could," agreed Nathan. "But this man Brownlow is chasing them for the money, and he's threatening to have them thrown in jail. Then Brownlow pays the jail to send out a chain-gang of prisoners and they end up working for nothing again."

"But that's not fair," protested Dolly, incensed at the injustice of it all. "How much is the debt?"

"Thirty dollars," said Nathan.

"Can we afford to pay it?" asked Dolly, glancing at the downcast faces of the men.

"We'd pay you back, Mrs Dolly," said Raphael. "Sure we would. Work for nothing if we have to. I'd rather slave here than for Brownlow. But the debt keeps growing and growing with this Brownlow, even though we don't borrow no more money from him. We can't see no way out. We wanted to work for ourselves, but this man's got a grip on us and when Brownlow says we owe him, no white man's goin' to believe us otherwise."

"Is that thirty dollars each or thirty between you?" she asked.

"Gabriel and me is thirty dollars," said Raphael, glancing at his brother.

"I's eighteen dollars fifty cents," said Andy. "He and his rowdies are threatenin' us all the time. We make a little money and it all goes on the debt, but the debt don't get no smaller." He hung his head and shook it in despair. "And the store charges us more for anything we buy. It's like they want us to sell ourselves back into slavery and we can't do a thing about it."

"It isn't fair," decided Dolly. "Have we got the money to spare?"

"You have some put by for when Albert comes home," Nathan told her. "It's whether you want to lend Albert's money to the boys."

Dolly didn't hesitate. "Albert would do it in a wink," she said firmly. "How much did you borrow at the start?"

"Fifteen," said Gabriel, "but according to Brownlow, it somehow growed."

"Then Nathan or I will go with you and negotiate a fair return. I'm not shelling out for Brownlow's greed. Is he a bible-reading man?"

"I guess so," said Raphael, looking unsure.

"We'll try the usury angle," decided Dolly. "The Bible forbids it, and I'm going to quote it."

Nathan laughed. "I never saw you opening a bible."

She tapped her forehead. "All that chapel going stuff in Gorbydale is up here somewhere. We'll take Jeremiah with us. He used to be a preacher."

As it happened, they did not have to confront Brownlow at all. The next day a broad, well-dressed man together with a man with a thick black beard rode up to the house.

"My name is Brownlow," he said, puffing out his chest. "I hear you're harbouring fugitives from the law."

"Yes, I've heard about you," said Dolly, standing above him on the porch. "The men you mean have not been arrested for anything. They are not fugitives. And from what I hear they are victims — victims of usury — a law against God and man. It says so in the Bible."

Brownlow looked taken aback to be challenged. The men turned to see Nathan and Jeremiah coming to support her.

"They owe me money, and if I don't get it I'll have the law on them all right," he insisted. "They signed a paper."

"Oh, you shall get your money," said Dolly. "But certainly not the money you are demanding. I shall pay you the original debts, plus the normal interest as demanded by a legitimate bank. You're not practising your *usury* on me. And was the men's signature witnessed, I wonder?"

Brownlow looked wary.

"I'll take our cause to law if I must," Dolly said, fixing him with a steely eye.

"Ain't you the woman, I mean the lady," the whiskery man corrected himself, "that won the court case over that Amiens place?"

"I am indeed," confirmed Dolly proudly. "And that too was a just case and a jury of just, Bible-fearing men agreed with me too." The more she spoke, the more a strong Southern accent emerged.

The bearded man leant over to Brownlow and muttered something. They both stared at Dolly, silent for a moment.

"I'd take what my wife offers if I were you," said Nathan pleasantly. "That way you'll have your money back and you can rent out the land to other sharecroppers. Otherwise you might end up with nothing. I assume you've seen my wife in court?" he asked the man with the beard.

"I was on the jury," he answered with a look of reluctant admiration for Dolly.

Nathan quietly advised Brownlow again.

Brownlow's brow darkened. "All right," he decided. "I'll take what you got."

"And of course you'll destroy the papers?" asked Dolly. "In fact, you can burn them here, when I get you the money. I assume you've got them with you."

The men glanced at one another and reluctantly nodded.

"And I'll write out a receipt saying that the debt is null and void," said Dolly triumphantly. "And a copy just in case it is needed for a jury," she added with a wry glance at the whiskery man. "Perhaps you would care to help me, Jeremiah?"

He willingly followed Dolly into the house.

"Would you gentlemen like a drink while my wife does her paperwork?" asked Nathan politely.

They again glanced at one another.

"I don't mind if I do," said Whiskers.

Though Brownlow frowned, he dismounted his horse and sat on the porch as Nathan invited him to. "I hope you got something strong?" snapped the carpetbagger.

Dolly asked Diana, her housekeeper, to get the men some drinks and went up to her chest in the bedroom. She sighed as she took the repayment money from its hiding place under her clothes. She had wanted the money to give to Albert to show that she'd been looking after his plantation. Raphael and the others had promised to repay their debt and her son would have willingly offered it, but she still felt as if she had failed him.

Dolly and Jeremiah took some time. Nathan was talking pleasantly to the bearded man when they emerged from the house. Brownlow stayed angrily silent, sipping his whisky. He looked annoyed as Dolly offered him the money and the receipts to sign. She asked to look at the papers concerning the debt, raking her eye over the signatures and muttering that there were no witnesses. Then she insisted that he burnt them right there. For a moment, he looked as though he would throw the burning papers into the house. Dolly was instantly alarmed as to what he might do, but the papers flared in an instant and he stamped them out on the porch. Their business concluded, the two men mounted their horses. Brownlow raked Dolly with a wrathful glance before he rode away.

"I hope Brownlow doesn't decide to take any revenge on us," sighed Nathan. "But Finlayson is a decent man. He lost his farm to carpetbaggers after the war. I feel he has some sympathy with our men but daren't admit it. He may look ferocious, but his look is more intimidating than his nature. A decent man down on his luck, I think."

"You always see the best in everyone," said Dolly, smiling. "All the same, I hope I haven't stirred up too much trouble from Brownlow."

"We'll put a watch on the Amiens plantation for a few nights," decided Nathan, "just to be safe."

Raphael, Gabriel and Andy thanked Dolly and Nathan warmly for their help and promised again to repay them. They were more than happy to mount a guard on the plantation for a few nights.

"We left our equipment on the shareholdings," reasoned Andy. "Ole Brownlow can add that to his payment. No doubt he'll sell the picks and shovels to some other poor suckers."

Dolly felt sad for them that their dream of farming their own land had faded. She hoped that Albert would understand when he arrived home.

CHAPTER 60: GOODBYE TO AN OLD FRIEND

Barney was sick. Zeb called over to see Dolly, his face suffused with misery.

"I don't think he's gonna pull through this time," he said, fighting tears. "He said he wants to talk to you. If an' that's all right with you, Mrs Dolly?"

"Of course it is," said Dolly grabbing her shawl.

She called to her housekeeper, Diana, a niece of Aunt Hattie's. Hattie was now living in comfortable retirement after her long years of service. Clemmie often went to keep her company and do little tasks for her protector.

"Diana, will you take care of Marguerite for me? I'm just going with Zeb to see Barney. Will you tell my husband where I've gone?"

"Sure will, ma'am," said Diana. "Don't you worry none."

Dolly climbed aboard Zeb's wagon and they drove at some speed towards the Amiens village.

There was a gaggle of women around Barney's house. It was the largest house in the village, well maintained and painted white. The women parted to let Dolly through, bobbing little curtsies as she passed. She nodded to them with an anxious smile and went into the darkened cottage. Lilian, Barney's wife, led her through to the bedroom, her eyes wide in fear and anxiety. Dolly found Barney in bed, lying in a weary sweat. She gently took his hand.

Zeb slipped a chair behind her, and she leant down to her old and trusted friend.

"How are you, Barney? I should have brought you something to help you, but Zeb was all fired up to get me here. Are you in pain?"

"No, ma'am," he answered with a weak smile. "Just so damned tired. I can hardly keep my eyes open. But I needs to tell you something, Mrs Dolly. Zeb, you go out while I speak to Mrs Dolly." Even this brief speech seemed to tire him. The moment the door behind his son closed, Barney squeezed Dolly's hand. "I seen the master," he wheezed.

"You mean Jesus?" asked Dolly in surprise.

"No. That day at the plantation, I seen Master Clement."

"Oh." Dolly felt sick.

"But you mustn't worry none. He ain't with us no more."

"You killed him," she said in a horrified whisper.

Barney shook his head. "No, ma'am. In a way, he killed his self."

Dolly was mystified as Barney gathered his strength to speak more.

"Zeb's boy was playin' round the old house, and he come runnin' and he was that scared, sayin' as he'd seen the ghost of old Clement. Some of us men went over to investigate. We held back when we saw you talkin' to him, but we could guess what he was sayin'. We saw you push Miss Marguerite behind your skirts."

He paused and tried to clear his throat. Dolly saw a mug of water nearby and helped him to a sip. Barney squeezed her hand to thank her.

"I said, 'we ain't gonna let that devil hurt Mrs Dolly and her girl' and we was about to come and get him. But then we saw he was going to leave. So we followed him along the road. He saw us coming after him and he knew we meant business. He threatened us with a gun. 'Can't shoot us all,' I tells him. 'I reckon some of us is willin' to die for Mrs Dolly.'

"So he begins to run. And then the whisky catches up with him, 'cos he falls on the ground and he can't catch his breath. An' his lips are blue. We couldn't do nothin' for him. He's gone, Mrs Dolly, and we didn't kill him. Seems like he killed himself with the whisky an' all."

"Where is he now?" Dolly asked anxiously.

"We buried him deep in the woods. Ain't nobody goin' to find him."

"Thank God," she said and burst into tears. "Thank God, I'm truly free."

"Been free some time, Mrs Dolly, but we was all sworn to secrecy. Martin and Job are dead now, and they can't tell our secret. Rufus, he's too old to remember. And Zeb's boy, if ever he remembers, he still thinks he saw a ghost. If there was any hint that Master Clement was dead because of us, we'd be blamed and the lynch mobs would be on their way here. We weren't stupid enough to say anything and put a rope round our necks." He closed his eyes, worn by his struggle to breathe. "But I wanted you to know before I died."

"You mustn't die, Barney," urged Dolly through her tears. "What would I do without you?"

"My Zeb's a good boy. You can trust him. He'll see you right."

"I know, but please don't…" she tried.

"All men gotta go sometime. I reckon I'll be goin' to a better place," whispered Barney. "Been singin' about it all my life." He pressed her hand in comfort again, but his hold was fading. "Best get my lady and my boys," he murmured.

She hurried to the door and immediately, without saying a word, Lilian and Barney's sons and family gathered round his bed. Barney blessed them all with a feeble smile and closed his eyes. Then his breathing ceased. They stared at one another for a moment in disbelief.

"He's gone," said his wife with a heart-wrenching sob.

"Looks like he's looking at the Promised Land already," whispered one of the women.

It was true that in death, Barney's old wrinkled face had relaxed into a beatific smile. Free at last.

Dolly stood frozen in a trance in the corner, tears trickling down her face as the word of Barney's death filtered out. Someone began a mournful hymn, and the voices swelled around the house and village.

"What will I do?" she asked pathetically as Zeb approached her.

"Pa said I had to give you something when he passed," said Zeb gently. "You mustn't worry. He's been ailing for some time, and we know the ways he worked. We've been doing his work as he instructed. He didn't want you to know that in case you worried. But you mustn't worry. It'll be fine. Just wait there."

She didn't feel as if she could move. The only stalwart thing in her life since she had arrived in America, besides Aunt Hattie, had been Barney. He had been her mentor and protector, and now she knew he had freed her from the grip of Clement's existence.

Zeb arrived back into the room and handed her a small box. "My Pa said to open it when you arrive home," he cautioned, "and when you are alone. People might ask questions."

Dolly stared down at the box and slipped it into her pocket. Then she remembered her duties.

She went to Lilian, who was still clutching Barney's hand and weeping silently. Dolly took her free hand. "I'm so very sorry for your loss," she said. "He was a great man. We're going to miss him so much. If there's anything at all I can do, anything at all, please let me know."

His wife nodded silently and turned back to her husband. Dolly felt it was time to go and leave the family in peace. She felt she had neglected Barney since her marriage to Nathan and now he was gone.

Zeb drove her home and, though he spoke of all the work they had been doing during Barney's decline, she hardly heard a word. What Barney had told her in his dying moments could hardly sink in. Clement was dead. She was free. But was she legally married to Nathan or not? Should she tell him? He was such an upright man, would he reject her as a bigamist, albeit an innocent one? Her head was bursting with all she had been told. She just gave way to her grief, and even Zeb was alarmed by the animal howl that burst from her in her misery.

"My Pa's at peace now," he told her, trying to stem her copious tears. "He's at peace."

And she heard in his voice an echo of the strength and assurance of his father and began to feel calmer.

"One day at a time," Barney had told her, chuckling at her impatience for the cotton to grow. "Everything happens in God's good time."

Nathan met her when she arrived home. He immediately gave his condolences to Zeb when he heard their news.

"I'll call over to see your mother," he told him. "In due time, we can all talk about the Amiens place."

He gently helped Dolly down from the wagon and held her in his arms as she sobbed into his shoulder. Then he released her for a moment as they paused to say goodbye to Zeb.

"Come along in and tell me all about it," said Nathan.

Dolly knew she could never tell him all that had passed. She was reminded again as she felt a hard corner of the little box as she pressed against her husband.

"One of the boys told me Barney was taken bad, but I didn't think it was so serious. I'm sorry he's gone. I know you'll miss him. We all will."

Diana made her a reviving drink, and even Marguerite seemed to understand that her mother was grieving.

"Don't be sad, Mamma," she said, snuggling beside Dolly on the settle.

"I'm sad because Barney's gone to heaven, love," said her mother, tears welling again in her eyes.

"But it's nice in heaven," said Marguerite. "Aunt Hattie told me so. He'll like it there."

"I'm sure he will," murmured Dolly.

It wasn't until later that she remembered the box. Slipping up to her bedroom, she sat at the dressing table and felt in her pocket. The small rough box lay before her and she hesitated to open it. She lifted the lid and saw a gleam of gold. Barney had wrapped the watch in a piece of old felt. She drew it out and stared at it, remembering how she had once sold it and provoked Clement's rage. She opened its cover but didn't hear the sweet tinkle of a tune as she expected. The watch had run down. She read the inscription — *Cher fils*: beloved son. She thought of Albert and wondered how she could pass the watch on to him without causing suspicion.

Once again, Dolly was caught in a mesh of lies. She had thought that with her marriage to Nathan and a clean start, she was done with all deception. Her youth had been lived pretending Albert was her brother; her marriage to Clement had been a sham. She was so weighed down by the burden of her dilemma that she did not hear the door open behind her.

"What's this?" asked Nathan, staring at the watch lying limply in her hand.

She stared up with sad reddened eyes and burst into tears. She was done with lying, and every one of her secrets tumbled out as she told him everything. "He wasn't dead. The lying bastard wasn't dead," she sobbed.

Nathan listened, saying nothing. He was quiet for some time, and Dolly's heart sank.

He's going to reject me, she thought and felt her heart about to burst.

"Well, this is a strange how-de-do and no mistake," he said eventually. He sat down on the bed beside her and took her hand. "But we can just go and get married quietly somewhere, maybe Baton Rouge, and that should make it right."

Dolly threw herself into his arms, and the watch tumbled to the floor with an unexpected tinkle. Everything was going to be all right. She was free, free from lies and free from Clement at long last.

CHAPTER 61: AN ACCIDENT

It was almost midnight, and Jessie was slipping on her nightdress to go to bed when she heard urgent banging on the French windows below her bedroom window. The window overlooked the patio and, in the warmth of the night, was open. Whoever was calling must have seen the light from her parlour. Robert was below, taking the opportunity of the quiet house to look at some of the mill's accounts. Listening intently, she heard the creak of the patio door as her husband opened it. Then, to her surprise, she heard the frantic voice of her daughter. Slipping on her dressing gown, Jessie hurried downstairs. Her husband had an arm round Helen and glanced up at Jessie in bewildered appeal. Helen was in tears, her words garbled and incoherent.

"What on earth is the matter?" asked Jessie.

Helen looked up, her eyes wide with terror. "I've killed him," she gulped, through her tears. "I didn't mean to," she added in an appalled whisper.

Jessie couldn't believe that she'd understood her daughter correctly, but a feeling of dread crept slowly over her. "Sit down and tell me what's happened," she insisted, leading Helen to the settle. "Who have you killed? What are you talking about?"

"Hadrian. I've killed Hadrian," said Helen, her sobs becoming calmer now. "I didn't mean to. I just wanted him to go to sleep; to leave me alone. He's … he's … a beast."

"What do you mean you've killed him?" asked Jessie insistently, bewildered by her daughter's confession.

"I found a bottle of Grandmama's laudanum," sobbed Helen. "I only gave him a few drops. I didn't think…" Then she began sobbing loudly again.

"Shush, shush," cautioned Jessie, patting her daughter's back to calm her. "You'll wake the house."

"Are you sure he's dead?" asked Robert. "Your grandmamma slept like the dead when she'd taken that stuff. Are you sure?"

"His eyes are open and staring," said Helen. "Staring, staring at me. I did it, Mama. I know I did it. Will they hang me?"

"What do we do?" Jessie appealed to Robert.

"I have no idea," said Robert, looking stunned. "We'd better go over and make sure she's right."

"You must send for Doctor Braddock," said a quiet voice behind them. They turned to find Matt in his nightshirt. "Tell the old fool that Hadrian had some sort of seizure. Had he been drinking?"

"He's always drinking," said Helen bitterly. "He found my savings and stormed out. He'd been at the Bridge Inn all evening. I argued with him when he came home, and he got into a temper and turned on me."

"Then Braddock should put it down to an accidental overdose," said Matt. "He's an old idiot, and he won't notice what's happened. Don't on any account send for Doctor Andrew. In fact, I'll go myself. You and Mama and Papa go back to your house. I'll be there shortly."

Jessie looked at her son. How did he have such wisdom is his young head? "Matt's right. The sensible thing is to make this look natural," she decided, taking wholeheartedly to her son's suggestion.

Not for one moment did she think to condemn her daughter for murdering her husband. She had never liked Hadrian

Lightfoot. She knew he was a bully and that Helen was unhappy with him. Now she was determined to protect her daughter by all means possible, whatever she had done.

They hastily dressed, and Matt hurried away to the stable. They heard his pony's hoofbeats as he rode away to the doctor's house. Then they hurried back to Helen's house. The door was wide open and, as their daughter had said, Hadrian lay inert on the bedroom carpet, his eyes staring at nothing. Jessie clenched her teeth and firmly closed the stare for good. She was tempted to place a towel from the washstand over his face, but that would mean admitting that they knew he was dead. She noticed the spilled bottle of brandy and a broken glass.

"He was going to make me drink it," whispered Helen, trembling. "He said I was a cold bitch and a shot of brandy would warm me up. Then he just crumpled. I didn't mean to kill him, honestly I didn't." She burst into tears again.

"Don't touch anything. Now let's go downstairs and wait for the doctor," suggested Jessie, putting her arm around her trembling daughter.

Robert looked stunned. "She must have given him enough to stun an elephant," he mouthed to Jessie, knowing she would be able to lip-read.

After years of working at the mill before she married, it was a useful skill, especially when the children were younger. Jessie took a final glance at the scene and shook her head in bewildered despair. How could they have found themselves in this nightmare? Only time would tell if they would survive it.

"Should we tell the Lightfoots?" she asked Robert.

"Not until we've seen the doctor," he advised. "We don't officially know if he's dead yet."

But they both knew it was a certainty. It seemed an age until they heard hoofprints and the wheels of a carriage.

Doctor Braddock blundered in, followed by a pale and anxious Matt. "Where's the patient?" he said grumpily. It was obvious that he'd just pulled on a pair of trousers over his nightshirt.

"I'll take you upstairs," said Robert. "You stay and comfort Helen," he told his wife.

Up in the disordered bedroom, the doctor bent over Hadrian. "Couldn't we get him on the bed?" he complained. "My damn knees aren't up to kneeling."

Robert looked round at Matt, who had followed them upstairs. His son nodded and with distaste helped his father to manhandle Hadrian onto the bed.

Doctor Braddock's feet crunched on the broken glass, and the smell of brandy permeated the room. "Been drinking, eh?" he snorted. "That'll be what's wrong with him. No doubt his wife panicked when he passed out. He'll have a sore head in the morning."

Robert glanced at Matt and said nothing.

The doctor cursorily examined Hadrian, then leant in closer. "I can't feel his heart," he said, looking puzzled. He felt for a pulse with no result and then asked for a mirror. Holding Helen's hand mirror against Hadrian's face, he searched in vain for some sign of breath. "You know, I think he's dead. I think the damn fool's drunk himself to death."

A wave of relief passed over the faces of Robert and Matt.

"Are you sure? My daughter will be devastated," said Robert.

"Oh, I'm sure all right," said Braddock, lifting an eyelid and seeing Hadrian's staring eye. "Dead as a doornail." It was then he noticed the bottle of laudanum on the nightstand. "Don't tell me the fool's been taking that stuff as well?"

"I don't know," stammered Robert. "Perhaps if he was drunk, he took too much by mistake."

"Aye, that's likely," sighed the doctor. "I see too much of it these days. Doesn't usually kill, though, just knocks 'em out. It's the combination that's done it."

"I'd better tell my daughter," said Robert. "You stay with the doctor, Matthew, and perhaps clear some of that glass out of the way." He handed his son a handkerchief. "Watch your fingers. Leave the glass on the washstand," he suggested with a nod towards the basin. "We'll clear it up later."

Matt nodded agreement, quickly grasping his father's purpose. If the Lightfoots were to be summoned, they should see the evidence of their son's drinking.

Jessie and Helen stared up with anxious eyes as Robert came downstairs.

"Alcohol poisoning made worse by the laudanum," he murmured. "The doctor says he drank himself to death. We should send for the Lightfoots."

"Will you go?" asked Jessie. "We shouldn't send Matt on such an awful errand."

"I'll ride over on Bob," decided her husband. "It will be better coming from me. Will you be all right?"

Jessie nodded. "We have to be brave, don't we, Helen? The doctor says that Hadrian drank himself to death. The doctor knows what happened, doesn't he?" she insisted.

Helen nodded dumbly and began to cry again.

It seemed an age until the doctor came downstairs. He was still there when Mr Lightfoot arrived.

"What's all this nonsense?" Hadrian's father demanded. "Surely my son can't be…?" He stared at Helen's red and weeping eyes.

She just nodded.

"Where is he?" he asked, becoming subdued.

"Your son is upstairs," said the doctor abruptly. "I cleaned him up the best I could. He still smells strongly of drink, though."

Hadrian's father looked affronted. "How dare you?" he protested.

"This poor young woman has just been widowed by her husband's overindulgence in drink. Don't you take the high horse with me, sir," said Doctor Braddock.

Mr Lightfoot scowled at him and hurried upstairs.

"I'll be away to my bed. I'll call in the morning," said the doctor wearily. "I'm very sorry for your loss, my dear. Try and get some sleep."

"I think my daughter will be staying with me for the rest of the night," said Jessie. She looked to Helen, who nodded dumbly. "I can't leave her here with a dead body in the house."

Sometime later, Mr Lightfoot came wearily downstairs, followed by Matt. "The young fool," he said, manfully fighting tears. "The young fool. What will I tell his mother? She will be devastated."

"I'm very sorry you've lost your son," said Jessie sincerely. "It's such a shock for us all. It's been such a terrible accident. It doesn't seem possible. Helen is just in pieces. I must take her home to rest."

"I would like to stay awhile with my son's body," said his father. "Then I must get home and tell this tragic news to his mother and sister."

"Helen, do you have your door key handy?" asked Jessie. "Give it to your father-in-law. I have a key at home that we can use in the morning." She turned to Mr Lightfoot. "Please stay as long as you like. And give your wife my sincere condolences.

We will have to arrange a funeral, but we can talk about that again."

With that, the Overdales left the house.

"I pointed out the broken glass and the empty brandy bottle," muttered Matt. "He spotted the laudanum himself and mumbled something about his wife using it."

So they wearily trudged home, though there was little sleep to be had that fateful night.

CHAPTER 62: AN INQUEST

Helen was reluctant to return home next morning, but Jessie persuaded her that she must.

"His parents will be there, no doubt. Just remember that it was an accident," she insisted quietly. "You didn't mean to kill Hadrian. Just don't say anything. If he was at the Bridge Inn all evening, there'll be plenty of witnesses to say he'd been drinking. They'll probably conclude that he'd put too much laudanum in his drink by accident."

They found Mr Lightfoot in the hall waiting for them. "My wife is upstairs with my son's body," he told them.

There was no need to explain, as they could hear her howls of misery.

"Dora is with her," he said as they accompanied him upstairs.

Helen hesitated on the stairs, afraid to see her husband's body, but her mother encouraged her gently upwards. She was trembling and crying when she reached the bedroom.

Mrs Lightfoot was prostrate over her son's body. Dora stood by, looking anxious and afraid.

Hadrian's mother turned to Helen. The searing hate in her eyes sent both Helen and her mother a step backwards. "You poisoned him, you bitch," snarled Mrs Lightfoot. "I know you poisoned him."

"Mother!" protested Dora.

"Mrs Lightfoot," said Jessie sternly, stepping in front of Helen for protection. "My daughter has just lost her husband. I suggest you curb your wild and wicked accusations and respect her bereavement. I'm very sorry your son has died, and I don't want to add to your misery, but Doctor Braddock said that Hadrian's overindulgence in drink has caused all this misery."

Hadrian's mother jumped to her feet and faced them in fury. She was just about to spout yet more accusations when someone entered the bedroom.

"Good morning," said Doctor Braddock.

"Oh Doctor, I am so glad to see you," said Jessie, filled with relief. "Have you come with the death certificate? Then we can arrange poor Hadrian's funeral."

He shook his head. "I'm afraid not," he said wearily. "My nephew Doctor Andrew has this morning reminded me that as Mr Lightfoot's death was sudden, an inquest must be arranged. I should myself have put his demise down to natural causes. I mean, the man was known as a toper."

"How dare you?" shrieked his mother.

"I'm afraid it's the law, madam," said the doctor calmly. He turned to Mr Lightfoot, who had arrived upstairs with Robert. "I think your wife is somewhat overwrought, sir. Granted, she has just lost her son, but such hysteria is not helpful in this situation. His grieving widow, young Mrs Lightfoot, is bearing up with decorum. I suggest your wife tries to do the same."

They all turned to a trembling Helen. Her father stepped forward to support her, and she began to cry and buried her face in his shoulder.

Hadrian's mother looked as if she would attack the doctor. "An inquest, yes, that will bring the truth out into the open. She's poisoned him, I know it," she cried. "An inquest will prove it. She's poisoned him."

Taking her arm, her husband dragged her out of the bedroom. Dora scurried after them, looking apologetic. Harsh words followed Mr Lightfoot back into the room.

"My daughter is taking her home," he told them with a sigh. "I do apologise. Losing our only son so suddenly has been a great strain on her."

"Please don't apologise," said Jessie graciously. "It has been a strain on us all. And after a sleepless night, all our nerves are strained."

"Perhaps we should go downstairs to talk," suggested Robert.

He stepped forward and covered Hadrian's face with a sheet. A strong smell of alcohol wafted into the room, and Jessie glanced at Mr Lightfoot and knew he'd smelt it too.

"I should take this laudanum, I suppose," said the doctor, popping the small bottle into his pocket. "It might throw some light on the matter." He glanced at Helen. "Which side of the bed do you sleep on?" he asked unexpectedly.

She silently pointed to the side opposite the nightstand that had held the opiate. The doctor shrugged and left the room.

They were downstairs drinking tea brewed by Jessie when Doctor Andrew arrived.

"I thought you might like some help," he told to his uncle. "Would you mind if I take a look at where it all happened?"

"Please yourself," said Doctor Braddock, looking annoyed. "Young bloods, they think they know everything," he complained when his nephew disappeared upstairs. "I'd have put it down as natural causes myself, saved all this paperwork. But then no doubt your wife would have objected," he said, scowling at Mr Lightfoot.

The inquest was held at the local magistrate's court. The coroner, who arrived from Manchester, looked bored to be dragged out to the insignificant little town of Gorbydale. Doctor Braddock gave a brief account of what he'd found that fateful night. He produced the laudanum bottle as evidence.

"There's not much in it," he said, holding it up to the light.

Doctor Andrew filled in more details and spoke of the broken glass and the empty bottle on the washstand. "The body smelt strongly of drink," he added, ignoring the protest from Mrs Lightfoot in the gallery.

The landlord of the Bridge Inn gave evidence that Hadrian had spent the evening drinking. "He must have had plenty of money on him, because he was buying drinks all night." Then he made a remark that made all the court sit up and take notice. "He was complaining about his wife," he said with an embarrassed glance at Helen.

All eyes turned to her.

"Yes, and…?" enquired the coroner.

"He was complaining that she was er … pardon me for saying, your honour … saying she was frigid, 'ice cold' he said. Then he said he was going to 'warm her up' that night all right and some other very rude remarks that I couldn't repeat in mixed company. Then he bought a bottle of brandy."

"Presumably the bottle that was found by the body," decided the coroner. "What brand?"

The landlord told him. Braddock didn't have a clue, but Doctor Andrew confirmed that that was indeed the bottle he'd seen.

"I think we'd better have a word with Mrs Lightfoot," decided the coroner.

"Yes, I want to tell you what has really happened to my son," cried Hadrian's mother, struggling to her feet.

"I am of course referring to young Mrs Lightfoot," snapped the coroner. "The deceased's widow."

Helen looked shocked.

"You'll be all right," murmured her mother. "Just answer the questions and you'll be all right."

Helen was visibly trembling as she stood before everyone. She began to cry in fear.

"Get a chair for the young lady," commanded the coroner. "Don't be afraid, my dear."

"I'll try my best," she murmured through her nervous tears.

"So was your husband drunk when he came home?" he asked.

Helen nodded.

"You must answer," the coroner instructed.

"Yes, sir," sniffed Helen. "He was very drunk."

"And did he try to give you a glass of brandy?" asked the coroner, obviously in view of the landlord's testimony.

"He poured a glass of brandy," admitted Helen, staring at him in appeal. "I … I … don't know if it was for me. He took a big drink out of it himself."

"I see. And did he put some laudanum in the glass?"

"I don't know," she said, biting her lip. "I was getting dressed for bed."

"But the laudanum bottle was present, and Doctor Braddock has shown there was not much left in the bottle. So we might conclude that the drink was laced with laudanum," decided the coroner. "Would laudanum in brandy make the drinker, should we say 'warmer'?" he asked, turning to Doctor Andrew.

"In small quantities it could probably make the drinker more er … relaxed," answered the doctor tactfully.

The coroner nodded. "And in his drunken state, would the deceased know what quantities to put in the brandy to achieve the desired effect?" he questioned.

"Probably not," admitted the doctor. "If Mrs Lightfoot had taken a large dose, it might have made her unconscious. As the deceased himself took a large swig, together with the amount of alcohol he had already consumed that evening, it seems to have ended in this tragedy."

"Hoist by his own petard," muttered someone in the courtroom and earned the coroner's disapproving glance.

"She poisoned him," howled Mrs Lightfoot from the balcony.

"He seems to have poisoned himself," retorted the coroner. "In his attempt to 'warm up' his wife, in his own words, he has brought about his own tragedy. I would say this is an accidental death. That is my verdict, 'accidental death by alcohol poisoning'."

"No!" howled Hadrian's mother.

Her husband led her away, still protesting. He was looking grim. Dora scurried after him, looking nervous. Helen swayed as she stood up. Robert and Jessie bundled her out of the court and helped her onto the gig. They were surrounded by sympathisers.

"I'll bring the death certificate to the house," called Doctor Andrew as they left.

"Poor girl," declared someone in the crowd. "Fancy one of the Overdales getting mixed up with that drunkard."

Helen felt wretched, wretched and guilty. They had mistaken her nervous tears for grief. She was free of Hadrian, but the guilt would live with her forever.

CHAPTER 63: AN ORDEAL

Hadrian's funeral was yet another ordeal. The vicar didn't help by basing his sermon on the evils of drink. The church was packed with people, attracted by the notoriety of Hadrian's death. Mrs Lightfoot glared at them, her eyes hard with hatred. This didn't encourage any sympathy for her, even when she broke down in tears and repeatedly wailed in grief. All the sympathy was for Helen, and deep down she knew she did not deserve it.

Jessie politely invited the Lightfoots back to Overdale House.

"Thank you, Mrs Overdale, but my wife is feeling unwell," said the lawyer with a polite bow. "In the circumstances, I'm afraid we will be going home."

Mrs Lightfoot was about to spit out some venom, but her husband hissed something in her ear and he and her daughter managed to bundle her into their carriage and take her away.

Although the funeral cortege had left from the lodge, Helen had been staying with her parents. So unwilling to go back to the lodge and the memory of her husband's staring dead eyes, she had gratefully accepted Jessie's suggestion that she should move back home.

The evening before, Honora had arrived from London to support the family, and they were all pleased when Arden arrived on the morning of the funeral with Jacob. No one knew what had really happened except Helen, Jessie and Robert, and of course Matt. They had all pledged the utmost secrecy. So Helen had to endure the sympathy of Honora and her uncle, all the while feeling unworthy of their kindness and anxious that she would blurt out the truth.

"You look very peaky, my dear," said Honora. "Why don't you come and stay with me for a while? You look as though you need a change."

"I should really sort out the lodge," said Helen with a sigh. "But I should love to visit soon, if I may?"

Jessie interrupted. "Why don't you go back to London with your Aunt Honora now?" she suggested. "It will save you all the unwanted attention from the town. I can sort out the lodge, and I'm sure Lizzie will give me a hand. It will be easier for me to ask Hadrian's father to collect his belongings if you're not there. I can bring your things back to Overdale House."

"If you're sure, Mama," said Helen, anxious to escape but not to burden her mother.

"I'll have plenty of time," decided Jessie. "I like to be busy, and it will take my mind off all that's happened."

"I'll be staying with Uncle Eli for a couple more days," Honora told her. "It will give you time to put some things together."

Helen still seemed undecided. Jessie quietly took her to one side.

"This has been a terrible strain on you," she told her daughter, gently stroking her hair.

"I feel so guilty," whispered Helen and began to cry.

Jessie could understand why, and her own conscience was niggling her too. She knew deep down that what they had done was wrong, but she would not let Helen suffer for a silly mistake. She was determined to protect and support her daughter.

"Just remember you didn't mean to do it. Both Doctor Andrew and Doctor Braddock said if he hadn't been drinking so much, it wouldn't have happened. Please go with Honora and take a break from all this misery," she pleaded with her daughter. "The change will do you good. I'll go and see Lorna Napier at the Dove Mill and explain the situation. When you come back, we'll set up a little sewing room in the attic and you can start up your business again. You might even get some new ideas when you're in London. I'll bet the lasses in Doveton will be delighted if they know you're selling the latest London fashions."

For the first time in days, Helen's eyes lit up with this prospect before her. Jessie knew with relief that her daughter would go with Honora.

"I'll go," decided Helen.

They both went to give the news to Honora. She had been talking with Arden by the French windows. They both turned, and Jessie was struck by how close and friendly they seemed. How she wished that her brother and her friend had married and completed the family.

Honora gave Helen a hug. "You'll be most welcome," she said.

Jessie was relieved that Helen would be leaving town for a while. She went to Robert to tell him. He was sitting alongside Matt on the sofa. Her son looked weary.

"We've been having a little chat," Robert told her, when she mentioned Helen's trip. "Matt and Charity have decided to postpone their wedding until next year in view of all the upset."

"I'm so sorry, Mattie," said Jessie. "I wish it could be different, but I'm sure you're right."

He nodded and looked miserable. "We were hoping to get wed in the autumn. Just a quiet 'do', you understand. All the same, we feel we should wait a bit until all the fuss has died down."

"You haven't told Charity about…?" asked Jessie in alarm.

Matt shook his head, though it seemed to wobble in a way it hadn't done for a long time. "Why get anyone else involved?" he sighed. "But she'd have understood anyway."

"It will all be over soon," Jessie reassured him.

Though in her heart she wondered if they would ever be free of the guilt. Mrs Lightfoot would forever accuse Helen of murdering her son but, because of her own hostile and hysterical nature, no one would believe her. Jessie was apprehensive that one day someone might take her seriously.

So some days later, she and Robert helped their daughter into the gig and, with many tears and much advice, waved her goodbye. Helen was going to pick up Honora from Eli's house to go to the station at Doveton. Arden too was going to meet them there, to travel as far as Manchester with them.

The train was late.

"Please go and sit in the ladies' waiting room," said Arden. "You don't have to keep me company on the platform."

"No, I'll wait with you here," decided Honora.

"You don't mind if I go, do you?" said Helen. "I hardly slept last night."

"Poor girl," said Honora as they watched her go. "She has had such an ordeal. But to be honest, I'm sure she's well rid of him, especially if he was anything like his mother."

"She was much too young to get wed," agreed Arden.

"I don't know if that makes any difference," said Honora with a chuckle. "You can have old fools as well as young ones."

"And would you think me an old fool, if I made a suggestion?" he asked.

Honora was intrigued.

"I haven't stopped thinking about you," Arden confessed. "I know I once said 'our ship has passed', but I'm wondering if it was just lost in a storm. Surely we could begin again? Would you even want to?" He looked so forlorn as he asked, as if expecting her to reject him. His face lit up as she said:

"I would love to. But you do know I'm probably too old to have children?"

Arden laughed as he took her hand. "That will be the least of our worries. I should dearly love to kiss you, but I would hate to offend the morality of Doveton station."

"And traumatise Helen," said Honora, laughing.

"Yes, should we tell her that her foolish old uncle has lost his heart once again to the same woman?" asked Arden, kissing her gloved hand.

"Perhaps in a while," suggested his beloved. "She has enough going on in her young life at the moment. Will you write to me as soon as you can and tell me where I can contact you? I'll write my address for you when we get on the train."

Helen looked bemused as she left the waiting room when the train trundled into the station. Her Uncle Arden and Honora were deep in a very intimate conversation, and she immediately noticed they were holding hands. They didn't even notice her approach until she was almost beside them. Then they discreetly dropped hands as if she wouldn't notice. All the way to Manchester they were smiling at each other. Just before they left the train, Honora scribbled down her address on an old envelope and passed it to Arden. Helen wondered if she should mention all this when she wrote to her mother.

CHAPTER 64: A LETTER FROM ENGLAND

Dolly eagerly opened the letter bearing the familiar face of Queen Victoria on the stamp. For all her years in America, she still missed her home. Though she had lived a poor and sometimes precarious life there, in the humid heat of a Louisiana summer, she remembered the cool green hills wreathing Gorbydale and the soft summer rain.

She quickly skimmed the letter and then reread it again. "Well I never," she said, her eyes wide in surprise. "Helen Overdale's husband has croaked."

"Croaked?" asked Nathan with a chuckle. "Is he a frog or somethin'?"

"No, no. He's dead. Jessie just says, 'We have had a sad bereavement in the family earlier this year'. Hadrian — what sort of name is Hadrian? Anyway, he's died. Oh, and Mam's headstone has been erected and 'it looks splendid', she says. She's going to have a photograph taken and sent to us. That's good of her. She says how much they miss Maggie."

"Let me see that?" demanded Albert, reaching out for the letter. Dolly was surprised by his urgency. He read the letter swiftly and then stared into the air. "What's the date of the postmark?" he then asked.

Dolly picked up the envelope and tried to decipher the mark. "Here, you'd better read it yourself. It's a bit hard 'cos it's smudged," she said.

Albert scrutinised the postmark as his mother watched his odd behaviour. Was his intense interest in Maggie's headstone?

Then a peculiar thought popped into her mind. Surely her son's interest could not be in the Overdale girl?

"This could have happened at least a year ago. The mason said they needed the ground to settle on the grave before they could erect the headstone," said Albert thoughtfully. "Perhaps I'd better go over and see the stone for myself."

Albert had been working on the plantation for a while now since he'd left the college, but Dolly knew he was restless. Privately she wondered if her son had inherited his father's hankering to travel. Though Clement had inherited the Amiens Plantation, he was no farmer. Or was Albert's yearning of a different nature? She remembered when she'd visited Gorbydale with Nathan when Albert was young and how Helen had taken him under her wing, defending him from her brothers' teasing. Dolly's suspicions seemed to be coming to fruition.

"I hope you'll delay your visit 'til after the harvest," suggested Nathan. "We've more cotton planted this year, and we'll need all the help we can get. That headstone won't be going anywhere."

"Er, yes," stammered Albert. "Of course."

His gaze again wandered off into the distance, leaving Dolly to wonder about her son.

Albert reread Jessie's letter. He wondered when Hadrian had died. Then he decided to write and send his sympathy to Helen. Surely there would be no harm in that? He didn't know if she would be grieving. He'd met Hadrian and didn't like him. The man's sneering attitude had altered abruptly to charming in an instant. Albert instinctively knew he wouldn't trust him and then knew his own judgement was clouded with jealousy. Then he remembered the shipbuilder's son. Full of his own admiration for Helen, he'd recognised it in Charles Kearsley too. And Kearsley was in England and well placed to comfort the grieving widow. Albert was desperate to travel to Lancashire. Yet he had to comply with his stepfather's wishes to stay until the cotton harvest. The Amiens Plantation was his responsibility, and he couldn't expect Nathan and Dolly to work it for him. They had done their duty by him while he was at college and, although there was no grand mansion now, the plantation was thriving.

Albert worked the fields in a dream. Dolly watched him and knew that his heart was elsewhere. She just hoped that he wasn't about to journey to Gorbydale and offer his heart to the Overdale girl, only for it to be rejected.

CHAPTER 65: A CURSE

As Albert had guessed, it was almost a year since the unfortunate event at Overdale Lodge. Matt and Charity were planning their quiet wedding. She was a frequent visitor at Overdale House. Jessie liked Charity with her straightforward and practical manner, and the girl was resolute in her protection of Matt.

"You know I promise to be a good wife to Matt, Mrs Overdale," she told Jessie earnestly.

His mother smiled. "Oh, I can see that! If anything, you spoil him," chuckled Jessie. "And please don't call me Mrs Overdale. It's so formal. Even Mrs Jessie is a bit much. Just call me Jessie, or even Mama like Matt if you want to."

Charity nodded.

She had few relatives on her side of the church on her wedding day. Her mother and an aunt and uncle and her mother's great friend Mrs Broadhurst were her only supporters. Her uncle gave her away and her bridesmaid was an old school friend.

The Davenport clan were out in force. Jessie's father Jacob and Alice, together with John and his family were there. Jessie smiled to see Honora sitting beside Arden, as Helen predicted they would. She felt sad to see Helen wearing deep purple, sitting on her own beside Robert. Her daughter would surely be remembering her own wedding to Hadrian. Jack, who was serving in Ireland with the Lancashire Fusiliers, had been unable to get leave for the wedding.

The ceremony was simple but full of meaning. The Reverend Tyldesley, who had taught Matt and Jack, was now the vicar.

His sermon was full of praise for his old pupil and his courage in his adversity. The young couple left the church wreathed with good wishes and full of hope for the future. Only the loud Mrs Broadhurst commented on Matt's awkward walk down the aisle with a dubious compliment.

"I must say, he walks quite well for a cripple," she remarked in an audible whisper.

Robert touched Jessie's arm and gently shook his head.

She gave him a wry smile. "Don't worry. I won't attack her today!" she murmured.

Helen was quiet at the wedding breakfast at Overdale House. She hung beside Honora and Arden. She and Honora had grown close during her stay in London. Leaving Gorbydale for a while had been good for her. She had scoured the London stores when Honora was at the hospital. Now she had arrived home with plenty of new ideas and determined to make some progress with her sewing enterprise. Jessie now had to warn Helen that she was working too hard. She frequently found her daughter hunched over her sewing machine in the attic with the light fading. It was as if Helen's passion for Hadrian was now channelled into her work. She had made her own dress and her mother's for the wedding.

"I suppose you'll give up working at that dreadful mill now?" Mrs Broadhurst asked Charity.

"Charity won't have to do that, if she doesn't want to," Uncle Eli defended his protégé. "She's a valuable member of our workforce."

"Oh, I won't leave unless Matt doesn't need me," said Charity firmly.

"Oh, I'll always need you," said her new husband with a chuckle. "You're my right hand — and my left one too, if it comes to that."

"Speak up, I can't hear you," demanded Mrs Broadhurst.

"Can I hit her now?" Jessie asked Robert with a wicked grin.

They were all glad when the woman went home, taking with her an enormous slice of bride cake.

The young couple were going to stay at a hotel in Manchester for a few nights before going back to work.

"You know I'm sorry I had to sell Primrose Cottage," sighed Uncle Eli. "There's many a young couple from our family spent their honeymoon there. It were a lovely place. My old home, you know?"

Jessie linked his arm. "I know, Uncle Eli. Robert and I spent our honeymoon there too. And Jack and Elsie. Perhaps if trade picks up, we might be able to buy it back."

"Aye, trade," said Eli with a sigh. "The papers are saying there's trouble in South Africa. The Boers are at it again."

Jessie felt a cold shiver brush her shoulder and slither down her spine. A memory of a wedding long ago and the rumour of war in America came back to worry her. Jack was serving with his regiment in Ireland, but who knew what his country might ask of him?

The following day being Sunday, the family went to church in the morning. Melissa had always maintained that it showed a good example to the workforce, and Jessie had grown into the habit. Her younger days had been spent as a Sunday school teacher at the chapel. Robert and Helen often accompanied her to church. They were seated in their normal pew when she felt Helen uneasy beside her.

"The Lightfoots are here," she whispered.

To the Overdales' relief, since Hadrian's death the Lightfoot family hadn't bothered to come to church. Now, there across the aisle was Mrs Lightfoot glaring at them.

"You'll be all right," Jessie murmured, taking Helen's hand to comfort her.

The Reverend Tyldesley had based his sermon on forgiveness that morning. Though it seemed that forgiveness was the last thing in Mrs Lightfoot's heart.

The congregation filed out into cold sunshine, politely shaking the vicar's hand and murmuring polite greetings. Then Mrs Lightfoot burst through the door, ignoring the vicar and followed by her anxious husband.

"A curse on you hypocrites!" she cried, pointing an accusing finger at the Overdales. "You murdering hypocrites."

"Come, my dear. Do not distress yourself," said her husband, grabbing her arm and dragging her away towards their carriage.

She tried to struggle free, but he held her in a firm grip.

"Do you want me to lose my clients?" Jessie read his lips as he manhandled his wife into the carriage.

"How distressing," said a woman churchgoer, touching Jessie's arm in sympathy. "I think the loss of her son has turned her mind. Everyone knows he drank himself to death. I'm so sorry, dear," she said, turning to Helen. "I meant no harm. But I don't think his mother can accept it."

"No," said Jessie. "Poor woman. I don't know how I'd feel if I lost one of my sons. Or my daughter," she added, turning to Helen and putting a protective arm around her.

"Let's go home," suggested Robert, appalled and looking drawn by what had happened.

The vicar approached them, shaking his head. "I'm so sorry that should have happened outside the church," he commiserated. "It doesn't look as though she listened to my sermon, then," he added.

The family were shaken as they climbed aboard the gig and arrived home with relief.

Helen began to cry. "What have I brought on the family?" she sobbed. "I wish I'd never seen him; never fallen for his lies. He never loved me anyway, only the thought that I might have money. I was such a fool."

"You were young and inexperienced. Oh, Hadrian could be charming when he wanted to be," said Jessie, trying to comfort her daughter. "I might have fallen for him myself when I was your age. You'll find someone with a genuine heart one day."

"I never want to let a man come near me again," said Helen with fervent determination.

Jessie smiled sadly at her daughter. "We'll see," she said. "Who knows what the future holds?"

The Lightfoot curse was forgotten until the day that Jack wrote to his parents.

I will shortly be posted to Egypt, he wrote. *I am so looking forward to this land of opportunity and adventure.*

"I do hope Jack comes home before he goes all the way out there," said Jessie, staring in misery at his letter.

"He'll be fine," Robert tried to reassure her.

"Oh, you mean like Taylor Walmsley was fine in hot foreign climes," sighed Jessie. "I'm sure I'll be worried all the time our son is away."

"But Crispin Pettigrew is fine in India, and Amisha has two healthy babies now," reasoned her husband.

The photograph of her old friend Amisha, sitting rigidly with her botanist husband Crispin was in pride of place on their mantelpiece. On their knees was a plump little girl called Jessica and a baby boy named after his father. Jessie glanced at their confidently smiling faces and was comforted a little.

CHAPTER 66: A NEW LIFE

Life had been miserable for Helen. She hardly left the house except to go to Doveton to see Lorna with her wares. She hadn't been to church since Mrs Lightfoot's outburst. As she stood nervously at the bus stop, she felt as if everyone was staring at her, judging her for a murderer. Albert's visit was a welcome change to her monotonous existence. He had at last managed to travel the Atlantic to see her.

He came down to breakfast in a cheerful mood. The previous day he'd visited the headstone for Maggie, clutching a huge bunch of flowers.

"*Margaret Tate (Maggie), Beloved Mother and Grandmother*," he read aloud.

"I think the *Rest in Peace* is apt," said Helen, who had accompanied him. "It's a fitting epitaph for her after all her hard work."

"She was the first mother I knew," he said quietly. "Her life was hard, and mine would have been too if I'd stayed here."

There was a bare patch of earth over a grave some yards away. It had a wreath of wax flowers covered by a dome and several wilted sprays of flowers. Helen glanced at it and bowed her head.

"That's Hadrian's grave," she said, pointing it out to Albert. "I never visit it. Those flowers will be from his mother. His father came to discuss the headstone last week. He asked if I wanted to have 'beloved husband' inscribed on it."

"What did you say?" asked Albert, anxious to know.

"I said in the circumstances it might be best just to have his dates. His mother wants 'beloved son'." She hesitated and began to speak slowly and thoughtfully. "The coroner at the inquest decided that Hadrian might have put the laudanum in the brandy to … to 'liven me up' someone had heard him say. The coroner said Hadrian had made the mistake of drinking it himself and that's why he died. The verdict was 'accidental death'. Let's go home," she said suddenly. "Graveyards are such miserable places."

Albert paused to take one last look at his grandmother's grave and Helen was immediately sorry.

"Oh no … I'm sorry. I didn't mean… You stay and … and…"

"Look at a grave," said Albert with a wry smile. "I know it's only her mortal remains, but I want to do them honour. I'll stay a moment, if you don't mind."

Helen nodded and hurried away.

When she'd left, Albert casually walked over to Hadrian's grave. He read the card on the flowers.

To a beloved son, cruelly slain, from his grieving Mother it read. He ripped it from the flowers and shoved it in his pocket. Later, in a quiet moment he had a word with Robert and showed him the card.

"She's just a foolish woman, grieving for her son," said Robert. "Take no notice of it."

"It isn't that," said Albert. "This is slander. It would hurt Helen if she saw it."

He was surprised by Robert's reaction. "Please forget it and just don't mention it to my daughter," Helen's father insisted.

Albert was astounded that Robert's first instinct wasn't to protect his daughter from local gossip. He decided to take matters into his own hands. That afternoon, he strolled into the town. He soon found the solicitor's office and walked in.

"May I speak with Mr Lightfoot?" he asked the clerk behind the desk.

"May I enquire about your business?" the man asked officiously.

"It is a personal matter," said Albert firmly.

"But..."

"Concerning his wife."

The man nodded and knocked on an office door. He slipped in on being summoned, then he beckoned Albert in.

"This concerns my wife?" asked the solicitor.

Albert placed the card on the desk. Lightfoot read it with a grim expression on his face.

"So you've come from the Overdales'?" he decided.

"No," said Albert. "Mr Overdale and his family, in their kindness, are reluctant to prosecute a grieving mother. But I am here, sir, as a friend of the family, to tell you that this is gross slander. I believe the court decided that your son brought about his own demise. And furthermore, he could easily have injured his wife in the process. You, sir, should tell your wife to desist these foul accusations or you will find all this scandal brought up again in court. She may find herself in very deep trouble. It will do your firm's reputation no good."

Lightfoot was taken aback by Albert's anger. "I will speak to my wife, of course," he said hurriedly.

He picked up the card, but Albert held out his hand for it. "You understand, sir, that this is evidence," he said firmly.

The man nodded. "I will speak to her," he repeated humbly.

"Thank you," said Albert. "That is all I require. I am confident we will have no more of these accusations."

With that, he left the office. Later that evening, he had a quiet word with Robert.

Helen's father sighed with relief. "Thank you," he said. "I didn't want to be seen harassing a woman who had lost her son."

They agreed to say nothing to Helen.

The next morning, Albert found Helen in the breakfast room. "Good morning. It's a lovely day," he said cheerfully. "Do you fancy a walk in the sunshine after breakfast? I miss the fresh greenery when I'm in Louisiana. It always feels so hot and humid."

"Yes, the fresh air will do you good," Jessie told her daughter. "You can show Albert all the changes in the town since he was last here."

"I wouldn't want to go out into..." began Helen in panic.

"Perhaps we can walk around the grounds. I'd surely like to walk up to that little white building on the slope. I'll bet there's a fine view over the town."

Helen hesitated. Overdale's Folly had been the scene of her own great folly and where she had been discovered in the compromising situation with Hadrian. All her troubles seemed to have stemmed from that moment. She looked thoughtfully at Albert and his kind smiling face. He didn't seem the type to force himself upon her.

"Yes, that would be nice," she admitted. Why be afraid of returning to the scene of her downfall in the bright daylight? "I could do with a breath of fresh air."

They strolled at a leisurely pace up the broken path towards the Folly. Where the path was wider, they walked together and chatted comfortably. Since they were children, they had always been easy with each other. Even though she had teased him herself for his funny accent, she had saved him from the worst of her brothers' teasing. When the path narrowed as it rose up, he went ahead and turned with an outstretched hand to help her over a rough patch of ground. Helen took his hand and smiled up at him.

They reached the Folly, and Helen found it had deteriorated since her last embarrassing visit. Thick chunks of plaster carpeted the flag floor.

"Perhaps it would be safer outside," suggested Albert. "But this surely is a fine view. It's a good place to see your father's mill."

Helen was silent as she gazed over the town. Though the horizon was wide and expanding, she felt trapped by the small building behind her.

Albert turned towards her with a quizzical look on his face. "I believe, according to my mother, that this is the very place I was conceived," he said with a chuckle. "Clement Duplege took advantage of her at this very spot."

Helen glanced back at the crumbling folly. "I can well believe it," she said bitterly. "Hadrian almost persuaded me to go the same way."

He then asked her a surprising question. "Did you love your husband?"

Helen was silent for a moment, remembering the heady days when she could hardly wait to catch a glimpse of Hadrian's face. "I thought I did," she admitted quietly. "But I hardly knew him. I was young and bedazzled. He was very handsome and charming, and he thought my family had money. He wasn't happy when he found out it was all an illusion."

"You aren't happy now, are you?" he asked gently.

Helen shook her head. "Hadrian's mother openly accused me of murdering him. I feel as if everyone is staring at me and wondering, though they support me to my face." She bit her lip.

"We get on well together, right?" asked Albert.

She smiled at him. "We always have done, somehow. Remember when you visited as a little boy? You were so shy, but we were always friends. And when you came again to see Maggie, Hadrian was very jealous of our friendship."

They stood in silent thought, remembering those days.

"Why don't you come away with me now?" asked Albert quietly.

Helen stared at him.

"I mean it," he insisted. "I've thought about you a lot. I haven't stopped thinking of you since my last visit. We're friends and we get on well together. You may not love me now, but I'll take care of you. I pray that in time you will grow to love me."

"Oh Albert," said Helen, close to tears. "Oh, thank you so much for saying those lovely things. It means so much to me." She hesitated, her conscience heavy with guilt. Her father was bewildered by what she had done. Her mother understood but was anxious that Helen's actions would come back to haunt them all. Helen wanted to be honest with Albert but could destroy her family with her confession. "But you don't know what…"

She could never have dreamed that he was so perceptive. He took her hand and stared earnestly into her eyes.

"When I was a little boy, I was determined to put rat poison in my Uncle Seth's beer. He was a brute and a bully, and I wanted to do away with him. He terrified Mam and me when he was drunk. Mam had put the poison on a high shelf out of my way. We often had rats in the house down there by the river. One day I even climbed on a high chair and tried to knock the bottle off with a stick, but I was only a skinny little wretch and I couldn't reach. But I would have done it if I could."

She stared at him. "You know," she said.

He nodded. "I guessed," he admitted.

"I didn't mean to kill him — just knock him out for the night, so that I didn't have to endure…" She began to sob, and he put a comforting arm round her shoulder. "It was the combination of the laudanum and the drink that killed him. I honestly didn't mean to…"

"I know," Albert said. "It was an accident. And if I'd managed to poison Seth, probably Maggie would have got the blame. She could even have been hanged. We've both had a very, very lucky escape."

Helen dried her eyes. "You won't tell anyone, will you?"

"Never," he told her vehemently. Then he grinned mischievously. "You could always make sure by marrying me. Isn't there some rule about a husband not testifying against his wife?"

"I'm not sure," Helen admitted with a smile. "I think it's a wife testifying against her husband."

"But you'll think about it?" he asked. "It could be the solution to everything. I'm lonely; I love you. You feel trapped; I could be your escape."

"Oh Albert, you're so much more to me than that," said Helen, giving him a hug. "You're so kind and thoughtful. I saw the way you were with Maggie, and I was most impressed. But it's a big, big step. Can I think about it?"

"Take all the time you like," he said. "If you can't decide now, you can write me back in Louisiana and I'll come right over and get you."

"It's a very tempting offer," said Helen, laughing. "I feel you know me through and through, though we've spent so little time together."

"I know what you mean. Soulmates, they say. Are we soulmates, do you think? Would you want a big wedding in England?" asked Albert. "I mean... That's if you...? I wouldn't want to presume."

Helen shook her head. "I've done that once, and it wasn't a great success, was it? Soulmates?" she echoed. "I think perhaps we are." She hugged his arm as they headed back to the house. They had never even kissed, but they were both happy.

Jessie raised an eyebrow as Helen and Albert entered the house, laughing and chatting as if they had known each other all their lives, which in a way they had.

"The fresh air has done you good," she said, smiling.

"It certainly has," said Helen as she ran up to her mother and hugged her. "And so has Albert."

That evening, Helen's family were pleased to see her so animated and more like her old self.

First thing next morning, she dragged Albert outside. "I'll come with you," she decided. "I needed to sleep on it, and when I woke this morning I knew I wanted to be with you."

Robert looked surprised when Albert asked if he could have a word with him before he left for the mill. He looked stunned when Albert asked his permission to marry his daughter.

"Are you sure?" asked Robert.

"I know everything that happened," said Albert firmly. "Helen didn't tell me, but I knew she was troubled and I guessed. And it doesn't make a scrap of difference. I want to marry Helen and I want your permission. I promise to try and make her happy."

"You've done well enough in the few short days you've been here," said Robert with a chuckle. "I haven't seen her so happy in a long time. But you hardly seem to know one another."

"I know it might seem strange to you, but I've thought about your daughter for a long time. I want to look after Helen and make her happy, and I think I can."

"If Helen is sure, then you have my blessing, son. It will be a great pleasure for me to see my daughter married to Nathan's boy," Robert told him.

Jessie was equally stunned when Helen told her Albert's purpose. "Does he know?" she murmured.

"I confessed everything, and he understands," said her daughter solemnly. "Oh Mama, I'm sure I'm doing the right thing." She hugged her mother, looking anxious. "But my only worry is that I'll be so far away from you and Papa and the boys. Will you mind?"

"Of course I'll mind. I'll miss you, but I only want you to be happy," Jessie told her. "Albert seems a nice boy. I've always liked him. But I do hope it's not a case of 'marry in haste, repent at leisure'."

"Who knows that better than me?" said Helen bitterly. "If I hadn't been so besotted with Hadrian, I might have realised what he was like before I married him. I was always sorry I didn't take your advice to go and stay with Honora until the scandal died down."

Albert wrote to his mother with his news. He stayed another month. As Helen came to appreciate his kindness, mixed with a quiet confidence, she knew that she'd made the right decision. Albert and Helen got married quietly in Manchester by special licence with only her close family present. Later, the young couple met to celebrate with the wider family at Overdale House. This was also their chance to say goodbye before they set sail for their new life together.

Jessie quietly wept as she waved her handkerchief at the ship sailing out into the busy waters of the Mersey.

"Only Matt at home now," she said with a stifled sob. "Thank goodness he and Charity decided to live with us, or our home would feel empty."

"Jack will come home on leave too, don't forget. And he'll be finished with the army one day," Robert told her confidently.

It was a confidence that was soon to be cruelly crushed.

CHAPTER 67: SCARLET JACKETS

Jessie stared in bewilderment as the unfamiliar carriage drove towards Overdale House. She'd noticed at once the bright scarlet of an officer's jacket but, however hard she stared, from a distance the passenger didn't look like her son. She grabbed Robert's arm and dragged him to the window.

"Jack never wrote to say he was coming home, did he?" she questioned. "Perhaps the letter is late. But that doesn't look like our Jack." She turned to Robert, but he clutched her arm and turned a ghastly white.

"We have to be brave," he told her with a catch in his voice.

"What do you mean?" she demanded, staring anxiously into his pallid face.

"That man is from the army. Something might have happened," he said in a desperate whisper.

"He can't have…?" she said as an unthinkable thought was fuelled by her husband's behaviour. But in her heart she knew that something was desperately wrong. She suddenly felt faint and sick.

"He might just be injured," Robert told her. "Let's find out."

They hurried to the front door and flung it open. Matt was coming down the stairs and joined them as the carriage stopped by the open door.

"What is it? What's happened?" cried Jessie as she hurried to the officer and hampered him as he climbed down.

The driver stood to attention, holding open the carriage door. He stared with something like pity at her anxious face.

"Perhaps we should go inside, madam?" the officer suggested. "Perhaps your wife may be better seated while she listens to what I have to say," he told Robert.

Robert nodded. "Come on, love," he coaxed Jessie, slipping an arm round her waist as he led her into the house.

Her fear made her heavy against him, reluctant to enter their home and discover the reason for the visit.

"We have to be brave," he coaxed.

"I'll get some brandy and hot water," said Charity, assessing the situation and wanting to be helpful.

Robert nodded as he helped his wife onto the sofa and sat beside her. It was left to Matt to offer a chair to the officer.

The man introduced himself but, in their anxiety, neither Jessie nor Robert registered his name. "I was Jacob's commanding officer in Ireland," he said. "It would be hard to meet a nicer chap, keen, competent, full of ideas, but a bit of devilment too," he added with a smile.

Matt nodded and smiled in agreement, knowing his brother well.

Then the officer's face turned immediately serious. "I'm so sorry to have to tell you…" He hesitated, and Jessie could not hold her patience any longer.

"Is he alive?" she cried.

The officer shook his head. "There was an accident, a foolish accident on board the ship just before we arrived in Liverpool. The sea was rough. Many of our men were seasick. The metal stairs were wet and slippery. Your son slipped and fell down them. He banged his head on a metal rail. I'm afraid he never recovered consciousness. I'm so terribly sorry."

"No! Oh no!" howled Jessie. "Not Jack gone! I can't believe it!"

Her husband tried to comfort her as she buried her head in his shoulder and shook with sobbing emotion. The officer looked uncomfortable. Charity hovered with the brandy and a flask of hot water. She offered some to the officer, who gratefully accepted a glass. Robert accepted some too and tried to persuade Jessie to have a sip.

"You've had a shock," he advised. "A terrible, terrible shock."

"So you offer me the demon drink!" she sobbed, shaking her head. "Nothing will ever quench my heartbreak — nothing." With that, she buried her head in her husband's shoulder again and became frozen in her grief.

"I need to speak to you about the arrangements," tried the officer. "When the formalities are done, there will of course be a full military funeral. No doubt you would wish for it to take place in your own hometown?"

"Yes," agreed Robert. "We would want him buried here at home, wouldn't we, love?"

Jessie just nodded into his shoulder with another heartrending sob. He was immobile, supporting his wife, but the soldier opened a document case and looked at him expectantly.

"Perhaps you can take over here?" Robert asked Matt.

He gently eased his wife into his son's waiting arms and took the officer to a table nearby.

"You'd better tell me what wants doing," he said wearily. He struggled to contain his grief, but then his tears could not be constrained. "He was our youngest. Always a bright spark. Full of life. I can hardly believe it. At least he wasn't slaughtered on some foreign field. We can have him home. It's a poor thing to be grateful for, but it will have to do in the circumstances."

The news spread swiftly around the town. The Overdales had lost their son. Jessie lived for days in a trance. The army arrived and arranged everything. The Fusiliers were on leave before they embarked for Egypt. Red uniforms were everywhere. Once her heart had lifted whenever she spotted the familiar crimson coats. Now she could not bear them. They should have been Jack, laughing and carefree, proud of his achievements, excited by his opportunities in life. Now she had seen his lifeless body, a cold shell of her bright boy.

The funeral was a spectacle for the town, the smart parade of soldiers, the coffin draped in the regimental flag, the fine eulogy by his commanding officer, the rifle shots over the grave. Jacob Overdale was buried in style, but his grieving mother hardly noticed. There was one thing she noticed, though. As she left the graveyard beside the church, clinging hard to Robert's arm, a figure stood beside the gate.

"Well, now you know how it feels," said the one scathing voice in the crowd.

Jessie looked up to see Mrs Lightfoot, her face a mask of bitter triumph.

"How ironic! A fatal accident. Well I never. Now you know how it feels," she repeated with a harsh laugh.

The crowd mumbled angrily against her as she turned and walked disdainfully away.

Jessie felt sick. The woman was right. How could she bear so much misery and not realise what Hadrian's mother had suffered too?

"At least we had a son to be proud of," whispered Robert, squeezing her arm. "We must bear up and do him proud."

Jessie took a deep breath and tried to straighten her back. "Thank you for coming," she murmured quietly to the mourners in the churchyard. "It is much appreciated."

"The audacity of that woman," sniffed Charity's mother, who now counted herself as one of the family. "I'll be taking my business away from that husband of hers."

Jessie doubted Mrs Fitch had much in the way of business anyway, but she thanked her all the same. "But I have to feel sorry for her in a way," she admitted. "At least I have one son left, and now he's happy with your lovely daughter."

Mrs Fitch preened herself, happy to be associated with the lofty Overdales.

Months later, the Lightfoot office was closed. Many of the townsfolk had been outraged with the conduct of the solicitor's wife and removed their business. There was now a frequent bus service to Doveton and access to solicitors there. Mrs Lightfoot had become increasingly erratic and arrogant in her grief, and Jessie and her family later heard she had been sent away to the country. Still Jessie could not help but feel guilty for her part in her daughter's deception. It almost felt like poetic justice that she too had lost her son.

CHAPTER 68: NEW SHOOTS

A pall of gloom hung over the Overdale home. Although Jack had not been living at home for some time, still the anticipation of his visits had died with him. Jessie felt lethargic, her usual vigour drained, and though she tried hard to hide it, tears often sprang unbidden to her eyes whenever she caught sight of something that reminded her of her son.

Robert threw himself into his work, and the mill was booming. He and Matt seemed to talk of nothing else in the evening. Uncle Eli had arranged for some of his frames to go to the Invincible while he bought more suitable looms for his business. He had a ready supply of customers, and the Endurance was thriving too. Matt had craftily arranged for Mac Berry to go with the looms to his father's mill, and his antagonist had found the presence of the younger female spinners more to his liking and stayed.

One ray of hope for Jessie was that Arden was home. While he was back in Gorbydale between ships, Eli had persuaded him that he was needed to supervise the transfer of the machines between the mills. After some thought, Arden abandoned his life at sea to oversee the business. Though at first he was rusty at his old job as an engineer at the Invincible, his old skills came rushing back and he was soon familiar with his new task. Once the machines had been installed, Robert asked him if he would take on the job as chief engineer.

"We've always got on well," Robert told him. "I need someone I can trust."

Arden tactfully did not mention their ancient argument about slaves. He knew well that Robert had been enlightened by his stay in America. "You know it was always my ambition to be chief engineer at the Invincible," he said with a chuckle. "The American Civil war put a stop to all that. But I think I've had enough of the sea right now, and it's time I settled down. I'll be very happy to accept your offer."

Jessie beamed as her husband and brother shook hands.

There was more redeeming hope for Jessie as the days went on. Matt and Charity had been on a visit to her mother. There was an air of exhilaration around them as they entered the dining room.

"We've got something to tell you," said Matt with a grin. He smiled at his wife and she nodded. "We're having a baby."

Jessie was overjoyed. She knew that Robert had given his son some fatherly advice before his wedding but didn't like to think deeper about Matt and Charity's private life. Now she had proof of their loving relationship.

"I'm so pleased for you," she said warmly. "Oh, it will be lovely to have a baby in the house again."

She had hoped that one day she'd hold Helen's child in her arms, but that was a faint hope for the future.

"We went to tell Charity's mother first," explained Matt.

"That's only right," his mother told him. "Oh, I'm so thrilled for you."

"Congratulations, son," said Robert, vigorously shaking Matt's hand and kissing Charity on the cheek. "Just think, I'm to be a grandfather. Oh, but I'll be married to an old granny," he teased Jessie.

"Less of your cheek," she scolded him.

She immediately began making plans with Charity. When was the baby due? How would they refresh the nursery? Now that Lizzie was beginning a family of her own, who could they find to help with the baby?

"How will Matt cope on his own at the Endurance?" asked Jessie with a sudden thought.

Charity laughed. "Oh, I'll work for as long as I can," she said. "And during that time, I'll train up a young lad to help Matt."

"A lad?" questioned her husband.

"I'm not having a pretty young thing helping you," said Charity with a grin. "Look what happened to me!"

New life was coming to Overdale House. It would never replace Jack, but it would continue life's circle within the family.

There was more curious news in the days ahead. One Saturday, just before noon when the mills closed, Lizzie came up to the bedroom where Jessie was sorting out some old baby clothes from a chest. Some of the pretty layette had been stitched by her mother for her youngest brother Eddie. As Jessie had always loved sewing, she had even made one little gown herself as a young girl. Babies grew so quickly they soon outgrew the tiny clothes, though Charity might like new stuff for her child. Memories flooded back as Jessie folded the tiny garments back into place.

"There's a girl and her father in the kitchen," said Lizzie, looking anxious. "They've come from Ireland. They say they've come about Jack."

"About Jack?" asked Jessie, feeling very puzzled. "I'd better come." She followed Lizzie downstairs. "Didn't you bring them into the parlour?" she asked.

"They wouldn't budge from the kitchen," said Lizzie with a shrug.

In the kitchen Jessie found a weather-beaten man, nervously clutching his battered hat in front of him. Beside him was a pretty dark-haired girl in a rough woollen skirt, nervously clutching a plaid shawl around her. Her wide blue eyes were anxious and wary.

"What can I do for you?" asked Jessie.

"Good day to you, ma'am. It's like this, ma'am. The girl here, she and your boy, 'twas Jack, they've… I don't like to say, ma'am. But they've been up to things they shouldn't, ma'am. I warned her, ma'am, not to get mixed up with them soldiers, ma'am, but you can't tell the young anything." He paused for breath and scowled at his daughter. His accent was strong and his speech rapid in his agitation, but Jessie got the gist of what had happened.

"So you knew my son Jack?" she asked the girl gently.

The girl nodded vigorously and began to cry. "I didn't know he'd passed until I went to the sergeant," she sobbed. "He told me to go away and he said some awful, terrible things. But Jack … well, he was lovely to me. He said that if I needed help, 'tis to his Mam I must go. My father here… He's that ashamed of me, he won't have me near the house. I'm with an aunt at present, but she's an auld one, and I can't stay there 'cos there's only one bed. And he said to go to his Mam if I needed help, and my father brought me here…" She trailed off, and her tears flowed like a silver stream down her pale face.

Jessie stared at the shawl. There was definitely a bulge concealed in its woollen folds. "You're having a baby?" she asked in surprise.

The girl nodded. "We didn't mean to, ma'am. I'm a good girl, honestly I am, and he was so lovely to me and we just…"

"Not so good as you think," snapped her father.

"He said we'd get married when he came back from that place with the big statue things," sniffed the girl.

"Egypt," suggested Jessie.

"That's the one," said the girl. "He said he'd write, though I can't read, but I know a girl as does. But he didn't write, and I waited and I waited, only I didn't know he'd passed." She began to cry again.

"What's your name?" asked Jessie.

"Mairaid," said the girl simply. "Mairaid O'Connor. He called me his sweet Marie. He said 'I'll marry sweet Marie' and made it into a song for me."

Jessie wasn't sure what to do. She glanced at Lizzie, who shrugged. The girl seemed genuine; her tears could not be disguised. Jessie resorted to practical matters. "Have you had anything to eat?" she asked.

"No, ma'am," said the father, glancing hopefully to where delicious smells were drifting from the pot on the hob.

"I was dreadful sick on the boat," said the girl. "But I'd be very grateful for a bit of bread and some broth."

The cook was already dishing some stew into a bowl. She skimmed some of the juices into another bowl for the girl and cut two large chunks of bread. "Tell me if you want more," she told the visitors with a sympathetic smile towards Jessie.

"I will need to speak to my husband," decided Jessie. She hoped the girl was genuine. It would be wonderful if Jack could live again through his child.

Jessie warned herself to be cautious. Would Robert reject the girl for immorality as Mairaid's own father had done? Jessie herself was just anxious not to condemn the mother of her dead son's child.

"What would you like to happen?" she asked Mairaid's father.

"I'll not have her home," said the man firmly. "She's a bad example to her sisters, and anyway, we can't afford another mouth to feed. Your son is responsible, and perhaps you can find a little place for her and help to bring up the child. She can make herself useful about the house."

The girl nodded. "I'm used to hard work on the farm. I need just enough to keep me and the baby," she begged. "I don't want my baby to starve alongside me. I'll go away when the child is weaned if that's what you would want. But I beg you to help my baby for Jack's sake."

"Yes, we'll help if we can," confirmed Jessie. "But I must speak to my husband first."

She went into her parlour to await Robert, leaving the father devouring the stew and the girl sipping nervously from her bowl.

Robert was as shocked as Jessie was when he arrived home. Matt and Charity went down to the kitchen too to see the girl and her father. Matt began gently talking to her about his brother. In his quiet way he teased out some answers and seemed satisfied with the result of his subtle questioning.

"I think she's genuine," he murmured to his father. "She and Jack were drawn together by chance. She was delivering milk with her father to the barracks. He was lonely away from home. He told her all about Gorbydale and the mill and his brother with the wobbly legs!"

"Very well," said Robert.

He had a quiet word with Jessie, who was determined to help the mother of Jack's child. He agreed Mairaid was to be welcomed into the family. She bid a tearful farewell to her father, who seemed anxious to be rid of his errant daughter and relieved to abandon her to the care of strangers. She sat at the kitchen table looking anxious and afraid as Charity and Matt did their best to reassure her. Jessie immediately made herself busy with practicalities and went to arrange Jack's old bedroom for their new resident. Robert followed her up to the room.

"Well, this is a turn up for the books," he said, glancing round his son's old bedroom. "Who could have seen this coming? The young scamp."

"The poor girl!" said Jessie.

"He must have been lonely away from home, and she seems a nice enough girl. She obviously fell for his charms," decided Robert, shaking his head in disbelief. "I'd have thought he'd have more sense."

"Sense was never one of his attributes. He always was a harum-scarum," remembered Jessie with a tearful sigh. "He was too charming for his own good."

In the kitchen, Matt and Charity were trying to make their visitor welcome.

"So our baby's about to get a new cousin," said Matt kindly to Mairaid.

"You're to have a baby too?" she asked Charity with wide eyes. "I'm told it's terrible painful."

"We'll be fine," Charity reassured. "Matt's mother has helped with babies before. She almost delivered Matt herself."

Mairaid looked amazed.

Over the next few days, they fell into a routine as the girl settled in. She was quiet at first but anxious to be of help in the kitchen. She was soon found chatting away with the cook.

"I like her," Lizzie told Jessie. "She's very willing. She'll be all right."

Mairaid was still very timid with Jessie and Robert and nervous when she ate at the table with them, spilling things and tearful. Jessie reluctantly asked her if she would prefer to eat in kitchen, and she immediately said yes with a look of relief. Jessie recognised that the girl was anxious about her strange situation. Mairaid was not a wife or a relative, but she carried Jack's child. Jessie was determined to protect her and the baby she carried from the likes of Mrs Fitch. Charity's mother was appalled and disapproving of an unmarried mother in the Overdale household, but Jessie ignored her. She hoped that in time Mairaid would become less anxious and join the family upstairs. That choice was for the girl herself to make.

Jessie sat with Robert in the evening sun. Their bench overlooked the valley and the mill. Down below they could just see the chimneys of Overdale Lodge, empty at present, but it had been offered to Arden. He wasn't afraid of any ghosts that might linger there and would be moving in within the next few days. Jessie knew he was writing to Honora in London and hoped that they would soon get together. She had great hopes that her friend would be able to practise medicine in Gorbydale soon. Honora might even be willing to help deliver Charity's baby and Mairaid's too. The thought gave Jessie great comfort. So many of the family had left the earth, Melissa and Matthias and, worst of all, her beloved son Jack. She could not mourn Hadrian with all the trouble he had left in his wake, though she felt some kindred sympathy for his distraught mother. Helen was far away in America, but hopefully she would see her again one day.

"These are strange days," said Robert thoughtfully. "I never thought to see our Matt as a father. And Jack … well, that's another kettle of fish. But the mill's doing well, so we can cope with all that. I miss Helen, though."

"I'm sure she'll come home to visit," Jessie reassured him. "At least the house is coming alive again."

He took her hand and smiled. "I know the house felt empty for you with my parents gone and the children growing up and away. I suspect you felt underused. You'll soon have your hands full when our grandchildren arrive."

"I can hardly believe I'm going to be a grandmother," admitted Jessie.

Her eyes drifted over to the Invincible, the mill that had dominated all their lives. She remembered when she was a spinner, working as relentlessly as a cog in the machines. In all her dreams she had never expected to be the mistress of Overdale House with all the problems that had fallen at her feet.

Now Jessie's life was like a spring flower. It had lain dark and dormant since her son had died, and now it was opening fresh leaves to the warmth of the sun. Many years before she had climbed the hill behind her home on Weavers Row and watched rare blooms brought in with the cotton seed from America. They had flowered and died within a couple of seasons. Jessie was like the native heather, tough and enduring from season to season, weathering the storms. Now new shoots were growing in the family, and she hoped that she would survive many years to see them thrive too. She remembered her old friend Kezia, anxious to go back to her own home in America and help nurture a new generation.

"Home is where your heart feels right and easy," she had said.

Though Jack was always in her thoughts, Jessie felt a quiet acceptance flow over her. With hope for the future in sight, she felt right and easy in her own home and at the heart of her family.

A NOTE TO THE READER

Dear Reader,

Thank you for taking the time to read this book. This book submitted for review when Christine sadly and unexpectedly passed away in January 2020.

Christine always had a love of writing and, after attending creative writing classes, a tutor encouraged her to write short stories for magazines. To have her work in print in magazines (over 200 in various publications) was wonderful but to have a book, and be a published author, was a dream come true for her.

Christine's dedicated research into the cotton industry, American Civil War and the plight of all the people involved led to her first novel, *Song of the Shuttle.* This was initially a standalone story however, the characters had other ideas, and insisted on being part of a trilogy. Indeed, the Davenports and Overdales have been a part of our own family life for such a long time. It is a pleasure, and a great comfort, to be able to see this book completed and the saga completed.

We would love to hear your thoughts on this story so please take a moment to post a review on **Amazon** or **Goodreads**.

The Evans Family would like to give a special thanks to Sapere Books for their continued support in making Christine's dream a reality.

Rest in Peace Christine.

SAPERE
BOOKS

Printed in Great Britain
by Amazon